ON THE ROAD TO CUASTECOMATE

JOHN OSBORN

authorHOUSE®

AuthorHouse™
1663 Liberty Drive
Bloomington, IN 47403
www.authorhouse.com
Phone: 1-800-839-8640

First published by AuthorHouse 8/3/2011

ISBN: 978-1-4567-6945-1 (e)
ISBN: 978-1-4567-6267-4 (dj)
ISBN: 978-1-4567-6268-1 (sc)

Library of Congress Control Number: 2011906966

Printed in the United States of America

DISCLAIMER

I have included in this book a series of real experiences and imaginative stories. In the fictional tales the geography is mostly factual but the characters and their actions are primarily figments of the author's creative mind. Any resemblance to present or past actual individuals and their lives is purely coincidental.

INDEX OF CONTENTS

1 ON THE ROAD TO CUASTECOMATE

Unlike Saul or Paul there was no flash of light, no seeing a need for a change in my life, but some revelations did appear to me on the road to Cuastecomate. It is a quiet road, a little dead-end backwater on the Costalegre in the State of Jalisco in Mexico. The total distance from the junction with the main coastal highway 80 to the ocean is only two and a half kilometres, but it is a useful road. For me it was the place where I thought through some real revelations.

I suppose I have written on and off most of my life. At first I concocted two page essays for school, and then I always wrote up special trips when I was a kid. Coming from the flatlands of London England I had this unlikely interest in mountains and climbing. I put it down to my Scottish heritage thing that developed as a passion when I became a teenager. This passion led to a thirty-six hour trip on a coastal steamer from London docks to Aberdeen and a bus ride across to Braemar. From the youth hostel at the Linn of Dee I walked solo the twelve hours through the Lairig Ghru in the heart of the Cairngorms to an Outward Bound style two week course at Glenmore Lodge beside Loch Morlich. I came home to write-up this escapade of sailing, canoeing, bird-watching, hiking and rock climbing in the laborious words of a middle teenager. When I reread it I find that what I wrote was simple reporting, with little reflection on emotions and how I felt. The only excited part of the essay was a description of the thrill of actually doing roped together rock-climbing and my first ever lead. I suppose we often remember the first time we ever did anything about which we feel passionate.

Two years later I managed to get to Finland for two months with the British Schools Exploring Society expedition, and that led to another diary-like description although this time the passion was over forestry and building a corduroy road to get the vehicles out of the swamps. There were also some very descriptive and memorable parts of this tale about the various tactics to handle mosquitoes. Again the trip described another first where the Finnish border guard introduced us to saunas and flagellation with birch branches. Kinky communal cleansing while camping could be the headline.

University life and requirements caused my writing to change style and content. True I still managed to write about mountaineering trips to the French and Swiss Alps. There were also a few epic mountaineering tales of winter heroics on Ben Nevis, freezing digits in the Lake District, and mistakes not to be repeated in North Wales, but for the most part University writing tended to be passive, in the third person and technical. Well there were courses to complete and examinations to pass. It was not until I went to Australia that I started to dabble in tales of fiction again. Unfortunately these early scribbles were snuffed out when I launched into another three years of education, and for post-graduate courses the words had to be very scientific and quite thoughtful. Universities have this idea that PhDs must embrace original thought and new perceptions. This thought process put a damper on creative and imaginative writing for a while but never extinguished the flame.

In my professional life I had to write a lot. People wanted to know about things and one learnt to be complete yet concise. Occasionally one could get carried away and slip in on page twenty a comment that "if you have read this far I will buy you lunch". Over thirty years in government service I didn't have to buy many lunches and so I learnt that brevity was rewarded with merit marks. Scientific reporting doesn't lend itself to verbose scenic descriptions and an over-abundance of adjectives tended to be skipped. Cryptic comment over-ruled literary style. Writing in the first person in an active voice wasn't government-speak.

As the years passed and children grew up and waltzed away I found more time to write, and I let my imagination wander away from the rigours of professional forestry and people management. There were still the occasional special sports activities that caused the pen to quiver excitedly over climbs that were near the edge or sailing races that had moments that were potentially life-threatening. I used to crew for a friend who raced on Lake Ontario and I worked the foredeck handling the jibs and spinnaker. The last two races in the beginning of October were called Frostbite races for good reason. It is at the end of September and start of October that a series of cold fronts come chasing across Lake Ontario, and as the front comes through the wind will veer at least ninety degrees and the attendant gusts will knock the boat flat if you are not paying attention. I was standing on the foredeck looking aft when all I could see was the lee rail deep underwater and we were close to capsizing. Now twelve miles out in Lake Ontario in October is not a place to test the temperature of the water and it looked very likely that was about to happen. Hypothermia doesn't really care whether you are wearing a life jacket or not when the water is close to freezing. All I could do was slacken off the jib sheets and hope the skipper was awake! As we were racing I really hoped the skipper was awake. Several yachts lost their masts in that race and one crew did drown. I certainly didn't write-up that experience in the passive voice!

Eventually, for most of us that is, there comes a time when we hang up our boots and retire from professional life. The office no longer commands our attention. Mark you, this day and age the office is often your home, your car, or wherever there is an internet connection, but for us old-timers it usually means a real old-fashioned office. The routine changes and suddenly I had no need for the three million people all around me so my wife and I brought our retirement discussions to a conclusion. Now I had been lucky because for the last three years of my professional life I had been on assignment in Zimbabwe, working towards the conclusion of a ten-year project. We had written up the final reports: we have transferred technology and expertise to our hosts: we had enjoyed the experience but it was time to go. As the project wound down there was free time to think about what to do next. I sat down with my computer and let my mind wander over options. Selecting some forty potentially desirable locations in the world I laid out a list of over four hundred questions in several categories including climate, topography, culture, health, finance, food, political stability and so on. For each question and each location I tried to score from one to ten my rating of the answer. It's true I didn't know enough to answer all the questions accurately but with a little research I made a best guess. Fascinating I thought, because the overall conclusion with the highest score was to stay where I presently lived, along with the three million people in Toronto. I took the analysis back home from Zimbabwe to Ontario Canada and laid it on the table for discussion.

Like most husbands I thought I had some idea how the wife thought. Wrong! I had obviously missed several relevant questions that were not included in my four hundred. My wife also had some very different ideas about scoring. The net result was a fact-finding trip to the west coast. If you look carefully you will have noticed that old-timers have created several centres of frenzied activity within Canada. The geriatric crowd knows what it likes and you'll find an assortment of crustie's colonies scattered across the country. There is a strong contingent up the east side of Vancouver Island. When I looked on the map and did a little measuring I found that British Columbia is further from Mexico than Ontario. I pointed this out to the wife, as going south for the winter was becoming a desirable routine on retirement, but all she said was that we needn't go via Mexico City any more. Now I'll say this with no disrespect to the people of Mexico City, but their airport was built for fit people. First of all it sits up at five thousand feet or more. Secondly, most international flights come in at one end, gate forty something and your connection is down at gate one – about a kilometre away. In between, apart from a lengthy lung-stretching corridor, is gate nineteen where you discuss civil liberties with Mexican Immigration. When the Canadian Federal government built Terminal Two at Toronto airport they decided to put into practice another Federal government policy – keep fit. So Terminal Two at Toronto is similar – long, thin, and your gates are always miles apart. Obviously the Mexicans consulted the Canadians although they didn't explain about the altitude. Last time I was through Mexico City I was pushing a friend in a wheel-chair and I wasn't in training for anything special at the time!

As I read through my emotional tale of the trip out west I recall some observations. You have to realise that my wife and I both climb mountains and so by the time we had reached Calgary my wife thought they could zipper together the western border of Ontario and the eastern border of Alberta. I gently pointed out that we might run out of food, fertiliser, and friends that way but she had a point. By the time you hit the British Columbia border my storybook reminds me that there really are only six maybe seven overland ways into this Province, and every winter all of them get closed by mudslides, avalanches and other "acts of nature". The provincial brochures told us we were entering "God's Country" and I was never sure whether God was keeping the heretics out or keeping

British Columbians in to ensure their conversion to the true faith. When I learnt more about the province I came to realise that there were several "true faiths" in BC.

The eastern side of Vancouver Island is home to killer whales, porpoises, several shoals of wandering salmon all watched over by a dedicated population of retirees. Now it is true that there are some people in Parksville and Qualicum Beach who are not Old Age Pensioners but they are thin on the ground. The same could be said for many of the communities up and down the east side of Vancouver Island and why not? The scenery is dramatic with a variable coastline, great views across the strait to the coastal mountains, a mild climate and despite many unbelievers a dry summer season. Most people are convinced or perhaps just deliberately misled by BCers that it always rains on the west coast. True, November tends to be grey and it has been known to rain every day of that month. Mudslides, canyon washouts, and floods do occur but then you shouldn't build on outwash plains and alongside scenic rivers. As a student at the forestry school of the University of British Columbia I learnt that Douglas fir is a fire climax species on the east side of Vancouver Island. Translated into non-techie terms that means Douglas fir would eventually become the dominant or prevalent kind of tree along the east side of the island. This is because it is so dry that fire comes and changes the forest that frequently. In any forest succession there on the eastern side of the island you never get beyond Douglas fir, unlike other parts of the island and much of the west coast which tend to go beyond Douglas fir and climax into spruce and cedar. Now it is quite difficult to get a good forest fire going when it rains every day, like in the cedar and spruce forest. However, where we get Douglas fir and fires it obviously doesn't rain that often. So, without any rain gauge or weather records, that tells me the east side of the island is typically sunny, warm and trending to hot! Just what many old crusties like.

Despite my waxing enthusiastic about all these forestry indicators my wife didn't find anything up and down the east coast of Vancouver Island that caught her eye. We toured in and out of new developments, old developments, gated golf-course communities, ultra-modern designer houses, on the coast, in the forest, you name it but no satisfaction. Of course some of this discomfort may have come from the fact that I had decided to be frugal on this trip and camp. For us this means sleeping on the ground in tents and although I might have enjoyed this all my life, including my recent living in Africa, my wife hadn't laid her fair hips on solid mother earth for some time. Even shopping didn't change her mind! There was a glimmer of hope when we visited Victoria. I made a point of revisiting all of the many pubs I had frequented when out there as both a student and a consultant but my wife was more interested in the ambiance of the downtown core. True enough, just outside the city Butchart Gardens will gladden anyone's eyes as will the gardens at Royal Roads but those pleasures were essentially those of a tourist. Given my wife's passionate patriotism for being a Canadian I thought she would find Victoria too English. However, she said she found it quaint. I pondered on this and wondered if this characteristic was why she married me because I too am English. Well, you never know now do you? Still, at this point in my life I wasn't going to ask. We left the island on one of BC's famous ferries. I can remember smiling to myself as we twisted and turned through the islands from Swartz Bay heading for Tsawwassen with a good clear view of Mount Baker lording it over the Lower Fraser Valley. Still thinking about the ferries I remembered that W.A.C. Bennett was the Premier when I was a student at UBC in Vancouver. At that time people had estimated that if he put guns on all the ferries BC would have a bigger navy than Canada itself. Since then the ferry service has gone through some rough patches with super-fast catamarans that were so fast and disturbing that they became white elephants: accidents that shouldn't have happened and fares that seem to have no ceiling. If we lived on the island my wife explained no one would come to visit. It is either too expensive or impossible to get a passage on the holiday weekends. Obviously my wife was grasping for reasons not to live on the island and so we ventured inland.

The other major colony of retirees in British Columbia is in the Okanagan. Once again climate and weather have a lot to do with it but then so does the grape! When you don't have to get up at six every morning to make that two hour commute to the office it is possible to imbibe a little the night before and not feel like shit as you sit fuming in stalled bumper to bumper traffic on some stretch of highway in the early morning predawn. You remember the feeling? You're still doing it. I sympathise. Come to think of it why do Canadians drive on the Parkway and park on the driveway? Why do Freeways have tolls? Funny language eh?

For me the Okanagan offered something better than the grapevine, two things actually. There are many well-maintained and challenging golf courses conveniently located up and down the valley. From my early years, starting at age seven, I have always found this game both a challenge and a relaxation. As a kid I used to play sufficiently seriously on the junior team that I concentrated, and that drove all other thoughts and worries out of my head. Apart from being an enjoyable walk in pleasant surroundings I found it a great game, and as a youngster I always played really hard before any school examinations. That cleared my brain of any last-minute unconnected fragments of data. I have always believed in learning as you go and not trying to cram everything into the brain in that last week before the exams. That is the time I go golfing, climbing, sailing, or anything else to take my brain right out of intellectual exercises and into challenging or life-threatening situations. These keep me focussed.

In addition to the multitude of golf courses the Okanagan valley and its surrounding topography offers a wide array of hiking opportunities, and although my rock climbing slippers are gathering dust along with the slings and karabiners, I can still put one foot in front of the other in rough terrain. With open ponderosa pine hillsides low down and denser Douglas fir, white spruce and ultimately lodgepole pine higher up the forests are sufficiently open to walk almost anywhere. My friends from coastal BC are amazed for two reasons. Firstly, you can see things, other than the green tunnels that contain you on the coast, unless of course you clamber for three hours or more into the alpine. Secondly, the terrain and the trees do not constrain you to the well-trodden path. There are opportunities to wander and explore without feeling you are reaching the point of needing to be rescued from some one-way only gully.

Now if this was to be "home" I needed to be subtle on this trip with my wife. I did have one big advantage. My wife is city born and bred and had never lived in a community smaller than one hundred thousand people. Rolling countryside, forested hills, sparkling lakes, terraced vineyards didn't have the same appeal as box stores, shopping malls and some of the other trappings of civilisation. Small communities somehow were not going to cut it. We rolled down the hill past the "painted lakes" with their mineral content through the dry brown hills embracing Highway 3 into the border town of Osoyoos. This is desert country. In fact they claim this is the northern end of the Sonora desert that dominates the countryside around Tucson Arizona. Osoyoos is frequently the hottest community in Canada on any summer's day. It challenges Lytton in the Fraser River canyon. Osoyoos is a summer holiday community for thousands of visitors and contains two golf courses, a very productive and successful First Nations Band offering products and services to the public, and an attractive lake that is neatly cut in two by an imaginary but well-guarded border with our cousins to the south; the good old US of A. Osoyoos hosts four thousand resident souls and was decidedly too small for the wife.

With this example serving as a benchmark I cunningly turned north and we spent time in Penticton. This is another charming Okanagan town neatly placed on a kilometre or so of dry land between Lake Okanagan and Lake Skaha. Obviously in times past, some time in the last Ice Age probably, the town site was definitely underwater, but today it offers two beautiful sunny sandy beaches, several golf courses (we mustn't forget the golf courses), a rock climbing mecca on nearby Skaha Bluffs (but now we're too old) and a larger array of shops. It also hosts close to fifty thousand souls. My wife started to pay attention and make comparisons.

By the time we ventured north again and reached the big-time in Kelowna I was almost home free. When we first came to this part of the Okanagan the recent wave of new box stores in Westbank didn't exist but just after we drove over the old floating bridge (a unique structure in itself) we hit pay dirt. Shops, stores, familiar names and a multitude of shopping malls adorned both sides of Highway 97.

'Yes dear, this has possibilities,' said my travelling companion. We stayed a few days and harangued several Real Estate Agents. I quietly pointed out that Kelowna boasted a population of one hundred thousand people and that didn't include those folks over on Westbank. We had reached a civilisation threshold number. True enough we did drive north again to Vernon and then on again through Armstrong, Enderby, Sicamous and the TransCanada Highway One and ways east back to Ontario but the seeds had been sown. We both liked Kelowna.

Six months later we were in Mexico and while we were there we sold the house in Mississauga Ontario. Everything was efficiently expedited through emails, faxes and other electronic wizardry of the twenty-first century. We returned home to Mississauga about to be homeless for the first time in thirty or more years. So we did what most parents do in that situation. We went and stayed with our kids. At this point in our lives both our boys were living in a crowded house in Jasper and working on trail maintenance on the ski hill. We crashed there for a week, gently moving one of our sons onto the floor while his parents commandeered his bed. I mean to say, what are kids for? You've already spent many hours and numerous dollars looking after them to this stage so why not a little payback? We only stayed a week.

About two months earlier I had wisely waved the wife goodbye as she boarded a plane from Toronto to Kelowna on a house-hunting mission. You have to realise that I could live in a cardboard box, well as long as it was close to a golf course and hiking trails, but my wife is a little choosy. Find us a good place to live love I said as I kissed her au revoir. Well I hoped it was au revoir and not adieu. Given we like going to Mexico perhaps I should have said hasta luego rather than adios. Sufficient to say my wife found a house quite quickly and it turned out to be close to a golf course. Just visualise, our driving range is only fifty yards away so how close can you get? It has a view – a vital criterion because we didn't want to live in subdivision like we had done for most of our working lives and so this was different. If I turn to face away from the driving range I can hike in the adjacent forest fifty yards the other way. Now it's true Kelowna doesn't have enough shops to satisfy a city-girl but we're working on that. The location also provided one other very valuable feature and that will eventually bring us back to the road to Cuastecomate. You thought I had forgotten about that didn't you? If you're old enough you might remember the song about Alice's Restaurant as sung by Arlo Guthrie in the sixties. He in turn spins a long tale about the garbage and twenty-seven eight by ten glossy pictures with arrows and a paragraph on the back of each one etc. before gently reminding you that the song is about Alice and the Restaurant. Like Arlo says, bear with me and we'll get you there.

Travel to and from Mexico is easy from Kelowna, well easier than flying out of Toronto because Mexico City airport no longer features on the itinerary. One airline and three hops bring us from Kelowna down to Manzanillo. Goodbye overcast, cold, snow, slippery driving and winter clothes. It's time to organise some house-sitting, mail collection and other insurance-driven chores before we pack and fly away. Make sure we've got enough tea bags. Don't forget the sharp knife this year. Did we leave the beach towels down there in our boxes? Do you think the airport will be open after all this snow? Check the internet. Success, we're off, we're out of here and en route to the sunny south.

You have to realise that the village of Melaque on the west coast of Mexico is quite a cultural difference from Canada. I can still remember the first time we ever saw it. In 2003 my wife and I had toured a little of Australia so I could revisit my old home and worksite. While we were in Australia a large and damaging earthquake had rocked the west coast of Mexico and destroyed the home of our friends. After many anxious emails we made contact and found that they were safe and happily settled in Melaque. It appeared that this was a beneficial discovery and move and they enthusiastically recommended we come there in 2004. 'Come down you'll love it' they said. How many times have you done something, gone somewhere, tasted something because someone said, 'Try it, you'll like it'? We get on well with our friends. We enjoy their company, do things together, share common interests and so we made reservations for Melaque. It's all about trust you know.

In the beginning of time the settlement may have started off as just Melaque, a little fishing village on the sheltered end of a bay beside a rather sluggish river. Over time it expanded and/or embraced next door San Patricio. This village is named after Saint Patrick as recognition for some Irish military gent who fought in one of Mexico's internal wars along with a few of the boyos. There are many San Patricios in Mexico. With no discernible break you suddenly find yourself in Villa Obregon, the next village or perhaps suburb.

Our friends picked us up from the Manzanillo airport and instead of turning east towards Santiago and Manzanillo seaport we headed west up the infamous coastal highway 80/200 and through the town of Cihuatlan. We left the state of Colima and entered the home of tequila and mariachi in the state of Jalisco. I suppose when I think back we should have been more alert. However, it had been a long and tiring day flying down the west coast of North America bouncing out of Seattle and Los Angeles, and so it came as rather a shock when we turned off the topes-laden highway into little Venice. Well that's what it looked like, that first impression. Somewhat unusually for this part of the world it had been raining for three days and the sky was still a leaden grey and pouring buckets down on the ground. Small somewhat squalid houses stood as islands in streets of water. I assumed they were streets as our friend calmly turned off the highway and drove down between rows of houses. He made several twists and turns and I later learnt this was because some of the streets were impassable because of the depth of water. Despite his efforts we still managed to rock and roll because hidden under the water were some ill-defined potholes. When I was in Zimbabwe they claimed you could hide rabbits in some of their potholes, but then they smiled and said you could hide a giraffe in the ones to the north in Zambia! I quickly assessed that these potholes were only rabbit size as there was no need to try and hide giraffes in Mexico. They don't have any.

I looked at my wife. We had trusted our friends. Where were we going? As I lurched across the back seat when the car suddenly dropped its right front wheel in a particularly deep hole I thought this is different.

This is not quite the same as the civilised golf-course oriented country club atmosphere of gated Club Santiago where we stayed for the last three years in Mexico. There we had paved streets, sidewalks with palm trees, white painted houses with driveways, garages and swimming pools. Here we had --- well something different.

And Melaque is different. It's close to Cuastecomate for one. I haven't seen much of Mexico but Melaque is certainly an interesting example of that country. Here the sounds, the smells, the sights and even the walking are different. Just imagine the array of sounds. We have the overall hustle and bustle of people out on the street walking, talking, shopping, praying, and riding bicycles. Lots of people. Vendors are out with carts or trucks crying out advertising cheap vegetables, fruit, fish, ice cream, bread, cakes, water, and even cooking gas. The cry of 'Egaz' rumbles around the streets. Instead of a newspaper, radio, or internet the local news and forthcoming events are broadcast from a loud speaker mounted on top of a slow-moving van touring the streets. Hear ye, hear ye! Being a catholic country there are churches in every village. Each church rings bells to summon the faithful to prayer. Affluent churches ring bells to tell you the time, on the hour, on the half-hour and in Melaque on the quarter hour as well if the whole edifice is not broken, as it often is.

They make good use of the schools here with two set of classes using the same buildings. One set of kids attends from eight to two and a second set attend from three until who knows when. School starts with the national anthem: loud, patriotic and usually somewhat off-key and certainly not chorally coordinated. Once a week the school band plays along as well. The kids try, and this is the state of mariachi, but 'don't give up your day job'. Actually, one shouldn't be so critical as the kids are young and they are better than the local army camp's efforts at music.

But it is not just the humans that create noise. There are the dogs.

There are dogs in the street that spend most of the day lying in the dust in the way. Then there are the dogs that run up and down on the first floor verandas yelping as you pass by only to arouse their relatives who run all over the flat roof above adding their voices to the chorus. Most exciting are the big dogs that people keep on the property behind the fence as guard dogs. They have a special routine. They run quietly to the fence and just as you pass by they bark loudly. Now this is not directly aimed at you but is a message to the neighbour so that their dog can run down to the fence and as you pass by their house he too will bark. I don't speak the language but you can guess the translation goes something like this.

'See if you can make him jump higher. I got both feet off the ground.'

'Woof, woof. See I made him leap and turn round at the same time. Nearly fell over. Hey, look, here comes another human. Your turn again.'

Not to be outdone there are the roosters. Everyone in the village keeps chickens. Now its true, we all like *pollo asado* once in a while with roasted potatoes or rice, a little hot sauce and a couple of tortillas. Roast chicken is a meal fit for a king but does everyone have to be involved in the pre-production end of the meal? Roosters keep the flock in line, keep the hens from straying. Unfortunately in Mexico it seems that the roosters have this inferiority complex and they have to keep shouting at the hens. It's either that or they like to hear the sound of their own voice crowing all the time. They certainly don't know anything about dawn.

Being by the sea some of the other birds get vocal, especially when the fish are running. Up and down the beach there are flocks of very noisy pelicans and less noisy cormorants. Gulls squawk as always but fortunately the boobies and the frigate birds are silent swoopers. Just to fill in the gaps we have parrots and there are several pet macaws in the village that delight in singing along with the roosters and the dogs.

Once you've managed to live with the different levels of noise there are the differences in smell. Out in the evening you can wander along the ill-lit streets and the wonderful smell of jasmine wafts through the air. Very enthusiastically you decide to come out the next day in the daylight and see where the bush really is. By morning you have forgotten the idea or you have forgotten where you were last night. One of the reasons you have forgotten is the overwhelming reek of the authorities burning the dump. Unfortunately plastic bags are a curse of third world countries. Of course they aren't so pretty lining the ditches and hedgerows of first world countries either. Burning plastic is noxious and nauseating as the odour wafts over the village. In between these two extremes are other tropical flowers, diesel fumes, cooking pork fat, fresh fish and the smell of corn tortillas. On the outskirts of Melaque, just as the road to Cuastecomate rises from the river valley up into the hills, any walker must hold their breath. One can only assume it is some form of primitive sewerage treatment process but I have never been brave enough to venture close and find out. It's another one of the mysteries of Melaque.

I would expect that the sights in Melaque are not unique, and can be found in other parts of the world, but they are very different from our home in Canada. The sunrises and sunsets here tend to be dramatic and that is primarily because of the dust in the air and believe me there is lots of dust in the air. Most shop owners and householders spend thirty minutes or more each morning spraying and sprinkling water over the road in front of their premises. Within a week of arrival from the chill of Canada the gringos are asking,

'Have you got a sore throat?'

'Perhaps it was someone on the plane with a cough and cold?'

'I feel a dry hacking cough coming on.'

'Yes, I've got that and itchy eyes too.'

'Do you sneeze a lot?'

So is it gringo gripe in this land of paradise or just the dust?

One other interesting sight is watching people walk in Melaque. Now you have to know how the roads are built here to understand this. This is earthquake country and although Mexico is the land of reinforced concrete the road builders here had a lot of common sense. When they eventually changed from dust and dirt roads they decided to surface the road with river rocks. The individual rocks are eight to sixteen centimetres across and coming from a river bed they are nice and smooth. They are also fairly round or oval shaped. Moulded together with packed dirt they produce a firm, durable, easily maintainable surface but they are a challenge to walk on. Riding a bicycle isn't so exciting either but lets stick with pedestrians for a moment. When an earthquakes moves the surface up and down it is relatively easy to pick up the rocks and repack them. If the road was concrete you would have broken tilted unwieldy slabs of concrete to break up, remove and then replace. With the boulders it is easy. So why walk on the road anyway? Why not walk on the sidewalk?

Yes Dorothy, there is a Santa Claus and there are sidewalks in Melaque. However, sidewalks appear to be a householder's responsibility. Now Juan at number twenty six has made his sidewalk some ten centimetres above street level but Carlos in number twenty eight decided that four centimetres was quite adequate. However, this didn't sit well with Angelica in number thirty who made sure it was a good step up to sixteen centimetres. In daylight this isn't a problem, it's just a series of steps. Mark you, over time some of the sidewalks do develop cracks, lists and an air of uncertainty. At night-time it is something different because street lights are few and far between. Because of the street cobbles and the sidewalks gringos learn to walk with a curious raised foot. It resembles high-stepping and it is hard to get a good rhythm going. Just to add to the high-stepping excitement there is rebar, or reinforced steel rods. I have never found out the details but it is rumoured that house taxes are a lot lower if the house is unfinished in Mexico. Mark you, I have never found out whether anyone pays house taxes anyway but every house sports a floral array of rebar sprouts. Every house looks like it is about to have another storey added on, another extension. So rebar tends to be a way of life and of course several pieces end up embedded in the surplus concrete on the ground, on the sidewalk and even in the road. These add to the adventure of walking in Melaque, especially at night time. Hence high-stepping.

As it is hot and humid in this part of Mexico I favour walking in the cool of the day and that means walking at night. I want to stay fit and I hike regularly at home so how to maintain some stamina when in the subtropics? Without being absolutely ridiculous it is cool enough to hike so you get home just after the sun rises over the horizon and that is soon after seven down here. The walk there and back takes one hundred minutes and that means leaving the bed before six. Six o'clock in the morning you say? And you are on holiday? Are you crazy? That is absolutely ridiculous!

Yes, no and no again respectively. At six o'clock it is wonderfully cool most mornings. Humidity may vary but importantly it is relatively cool at six. And no we are not on holiday. When you move every year to stay somewhere for two months that is not really on holiday. We go and live in Mexico for two months every year. It is another home. We have the same neighbours; the same crowd around the pool and the same local shops. Yes it is different but it is another home. Crazy? Now that is a more difficult question. Let's just say that although I personally hike alone on the road I do meet several other regulars coming and going. As it is dark you get to recognise voices and silhouettes. You get to know their dogs and their gait. Perhaps we are all crazy?

The hike starts with the first fifteen minutes of civilisation. Streets are empty and quiet and I might see a solitary policeman walking the neighbourhood. We exchange good mornings and both carry on on our separate ways. Soon though we leave the bright lights and uneven sidewalks and looking carefully we cross the main road and enter into the dark world of the countryside. The Army barracks are silent, although within thirty minutes or so reveille will trumpet discordantly across the dawn sky. The dogs at the corner grocery store wake and run out. Needless to say it is the smaller mass of fur that barks and yaps whereas the larger dog just looks, lifts its leg and pees.

Looking up there in the predawn towards the coastal hills when the air is cool the sky is clear with a blaze of stars as we leave the loom of the village. Constellations taught to you as a child stand out. There is the plough, or the saucepan, or Ursa Major depending on the background of your teacher. The two back stars point to the pole star which is hidden behind the dark grey silhouette of the hills but you know it is there. Your mother told you so all those years ago. Orion twirls around with his sword and you search for the W of Cassiopeia. Having held your breath for one hundred metres as you pass the sewerage treatment facility the road decides to curve and take your breath away. Now it isn't the view that is breath-taking, or the sewerage plant, but the gradient. In a car you have to change gear. On a bicycle you have reached that decision point of grinding away in a very low gear or getting off and walking. On foot you think of something to occupy the mind so you can't feel the ache in the knees. Here, on the road to Cuastecomate you imagine. Here, as you slowly grind up the kilometre to the top of the hill you let the mind concentrate on words, on stories, and sometimes on memories. I suppose there are six bends to the top of the hill but the trick is not to see them as you let the mind put the story together.

Just over the crest of the hill you can hear the water running in the pipe between Melaque and Cuastecomate. The little cottage in the woods is quiet but the rooster calls. Some years a dog comes hurtling out of the darkness and a quick flash of light and a shout from your voice halts the charge. The bark turns into a growl and flashing your light across its face leads to it slinking back to the safety of the chickens. Your heart rate had just slowed down on reaching the crest of the hill and now the black thing from the swamp has wound it up again. How about some peaceful vision and a story about lazy afternoons rowing on a placid river but then the imagination jumps to canoes and whitewater? Just slow it down you say. You lengthen your stride as you make the long descent towards the ocean. Already you can hear the soft pounding of the waves on the shore.

This is where you had that confrontation with the cows a couple of years back. Black cows on a dark night walking quietly on a bitumen road are hard to see. They don't have headlights and you certainly need to keep away from the rear end, lights or no lights. Your first indication that there is something down the road in front of you is a gentle clip of a hoof and your foot finding something soft, squishy and smelly. Cattle you infer. That particular night I didn't have a torch for some reason and the moon had decided it needn't make a showing. The little Mexican quietly moving his stock at this peaceful hour was clad in dark clothing and it was only a clear 'buenos dias' that alerted me to the situation. It's true there were only six cows but they were all black, large and determined to fertilise the road. I skirted the hazards and vowed to be more attentive on the return trip. Onwards and downwards we strode and I let my mind go back to creative thoughts.

Depending on the phase of the moon this walk can be completely dark or bathed in surreal moonlight. This morning I had a nearly full moon and no cloud cover so the road is bathed in light and the shadows sharp. You can almost see the source of that low menacing guttural sound coming from the roadside bushes and the torch adds a face and head. It's only a Chihuahua-sized dog and although the sound is attention-grabbing you realise the size of the possible attacker is small. But then the mind flashes to that scene in Monty Python's movie of the search for the Holy Grail, where the wee white rabbit in that Scottish cave beheads people by tearing out their throats, and you realise that size isn't everything but strategy and tactics are important. Discreetly you move to the centre of the road and avoid any of those dangling tarantula spiders that might be hanging from the roadside trees, and you look carefully with the torch to see whether any of the scorpions have decided to cross the road in your path: small things with strategies. Carelessly you almost trip over the cats-eyes that line the centre of this narrow road and just as quickly the mind flashes to the rotten suspension bridge, the awesome canyon and the voice from on high in that other part of the Python movie where the merry troop of knights searching for the Grail have to answer three questions to pass across the bridge. You remember the first asked what was your name, and the second what was your favourite colour, but you can't for the life of you remember the third, which was something about a blue bird mating every fifth year when flying south and you trip over the cats-eyes while concentrating. As you stumble you smile and remember the conversation with the wife where she explains she has difficulty with how your mind jumps from subject to subject.

'I just can't keep up,' she says. 'We were talking about Mike and Mavis and suddenly you mention meringues. You've gone A, B, C, and suddenly K instead of D my love. I've lost you.'

You mutter 'Yes dear', 'of course dear', 'you're right dear' and all the other phrases necessary to keep the marriage happy and fulfilled and then you realise that your wife is happily sleeping back in the apartment in Melaque, and you hope she is sleeping peacefully now that you've ventured out on the open road. As you trip on the cats-eye for the third time you suddenly become aware that you are another thirty yards up the hill and you grin

21

within yourself as once again you've achieved mind over matter. See, that bit of the climb was easy wasn't it? Just let the mind wander a bit more. Overall this road is a simple climb up a hill and then down again to the ocean and the safe-swimming bay at Cuastecomate. The hotel by the ocean is typically empty and half the houses are owned by Americans. This means they are occupied when the economy and safety of Americans is good and empty otherwise. At seven o'clock in the morning the seafront restaurants are closed. I'm usually there around six so that is not really relevant dear reader but I thought you should know. Like any self-respecting Mexican village you enter on the road with a well-defined and pronounced topes. Topes, or speed bumps, sleeping policemen, whatever you call them are used effectively in Mexico to slow you down. I had noticed the same in Zimbabwe where they didn't use school crossings or crossing guards but sharp, high speed bumps either side of the school zone. Taken at speed you would lose your undercarriage and redesign the suspension on coming down to earth. Slow baby slow. Slow works in Mexico too.

There are a few street lights as you come into the village, which is good as the road surface deteriorates rapidly with several judiciously placed potholes. The village dogs come out to greet you. Each year it is a new challenge to see whether they bark, they growl, they cower or they show their teeth. Fortunately I was a boy scout and so I am always prepared. Well, not for the cows on a dark night I wasn't but there are always exceptions to every rule!

The street light by the alleyway down to the beach is my turning point. Check the watch. More or less normal speed. Feeling good? Sure, why not? It's a cool morning and peaceful to boot, smelly too! Turn and contemplate the return.

Each early morning hike is in itself a little adventure. I do this solo and so I am aware of the surrounding dark forest. Bushes rustle. There are lizards here, goannas, coatamundis, javelinas or wild pigs and so the forest is alive with things going rustle rustle in the dark. Owls hoot and occasionally you see them swoop across the pale sky. Something larger crashes through the scrub and you wonder what. Walking in the middle of the road, well away from the ditch on the edge you catch your foot in the cat's eyes and tell yourself to pay attention. You've let the mind wander again. But then isn't that what you want? Here is the best time imaginable to let the mind wander and conjure up all those words.

Thinking back, all of my more recent writing has started on this road. Initial thoughts, refined character descriptions, detailed dialogue have all started life on this road. To take my mind away from the uphill trudge I have conjured up visions, story lines, situations and what might come next. Yes, I know, I suppose I could have done all that sitting in a deck-chair soaking up the sunshine but the rhythm on the road has proved a better stimulant. The atmosphere of the cool morning, the gradual lightening of the sky and the cresting of the hill on the return trip to see the silhouetted eastern horizon have proved helpful to managing Michael through his machinations. That last grunting grind up to the final top of the hill let me feel Samantha dance her way up her hard climbs. The gradual dawning of the day as the forest comes alive helped me think of Daniel as he managed the family estate. Harder in many ways have been the thought-through conversations. There have been times on the village to village walk when I have conjured up some incredibly real and provocative dialogue. Every year I tell myself I should take down a voice recorder and speak the lines, say the words. Capture the dialogue on sight so to speak but then again shouldn't I remember the good parts? If it was that good surely I can recapture it when I sit down at my computer? Do I walk to keep fit, to help write or just for the experience?

Mexico has also helped the writing part as well as the visualisations. Predawn I walk. In the morning I swim and read so what can one do in the afternoon when it is hot? My wife is off playing Mah Jong and so I could just take a siesta. No, we need to stimulate the little grey cells. When would be a better time to write? Sit in front of the computer and put that Railroad Tycoon simulation game away and be creative. Remember those imaginative thoughts and visions of this morning. Remember and write that stimulating dialogue, those lurid descriptions, and recapture the emotions of sorrow or fury you had created this morning on the road. And so we write. What I had started as a youth, let lapse as an adult, has seen a new birth as a senior. I have always been a morning person. I think best before midday and afternoons are going through the motions on automatic pilot. So take the inventions of the dawn and just transcribe in an organised fashion in the heavy heat of the afternoon. Reread it the following morning to liven up the ponderous text. It's bound to need a jolt of reality or a new infusion of creativity but do the robotic work of typing in the torpid afternoons.

Coming down the hill this morning, and just before I reached the zone of holding my breath, I was thinking about how to end this tale. This particular morning I had been remembering a very special adventure I had with my two sons climbing Mount Edith Cavell just south of Jasper in Alberta. The mountain dominates the western skyline on the early part of the south-bound Columbia Icefields Parkway from Jasper and stands over eleven thousand feet high. Ever since my two sons had worked on the ski hill of Marmot Basin outside Jasper and just north of Mt. Cavell I had a longing to climb this mountain. Walking up and down to Cuastecomate this morning I had recalled those adventurous twenty four hours. We had all enjoyed the walking and scrambling with patches of snow thrown in. Never serious enough to need a rope yet exposed enough to pay attention. The final ridge has the precipitous north face dropping away beneath you on your left as you climb carefully but easily to the summit. It had been a great day with a clear sky and extensive views. All three of us stopped often to take photographs and we shared a rest and a snack by the summit cairn. I hadn't climbed with both sons together for a few years and this was a memorable day. As I walked resolutely through the darkness in Mexico I recalled our step by step endeavour. In my mind the three of us were just walking slowly and very tiredly on the return from the climb up that last slope to the car park below Cavell Meadows, and in reality I crested my little hill on the return morning hike. The lights of civilisation lay before me, as did an orange and brown pall of murky air. From the memory of the clear mountain air around Edith Cavell I descended into the reality of smog and a strident early morning cry of 'Egaz, Egaz'. It was almost like the muezzin's call to prayers from the minaret.

Another little trip on life's highway I thought. That led me into how did I know this? In fact how did I know anything? I had just finished reading a book which amongst other things told me about the Big Bang theory and how everything exploded. However, the author pointed out that I wouldn't have seen this explosion. Not only was there no one there to see it but for the first two hundred million years or so there was no light to see anything. So, I thought, how do they know it ever happened? Here was knowledge that didn't come from sight, sound, touch, smell, taste but from mathematical reasoning. Someone's mathematically-based reasoning said it was so. I was quietly mulling over this, with the occasional 'buenos dias' as there were now more people ascending my hill, when I reached the zone of 'hold your breath'. At the end of the zone I realised that such reasoning was far beyond my limited knowledge and I eased into the final ten minutes through the village. People were on their way to work: dropped off from cars, from buses, riding bicycles or just walking. Diesel fumes enveloped me. I held my breath. I passed the street cleaner filling the barrel marked 'basura' as he redistributed the dust to another part of the road. I strode heartily over the last little dirt road section before the new interlocking tiles still wet with the early morning hosing. Past the bungalows where my sleeping friends dreamed of seeing rare birds and crocodiles in the lagoon. Past the office and good morning to our friendly manager before we go into ten minutes of stretching and contortions called exercise. Another day begins. I finished another walk along the road to Cuastecomate.

GRANDPARENTS AND GRAND PARENTS

I came into the world born lucky. What else could I have been because I joined the human race in a school? However, before you get the wrong idea, my mother was there when the school had become a hospital, just as war broke out in thirty nine. To avoid any imminent danger my mother had moved to Ipswich so I can't claim any cockney background like my sister. Why Ipswich I never knew, and didn't think to ask when my parents were still alive. How many things do we think about when it's too late?

After six days, when it became apparent that I hadn't got the talent to play for Ipswich Town Football Club, we moved back into the embrace of the East End of London. I told you I was born lucky and I make this statement because all four of my grandparents were there to greet me when I returned back to the city from the country. My father's parents lived in Manor Park, which sounds very posh but wasn't. My mother's parents were then living in East Ham, which is Anglo Saxon for East hamlet and that wasn't true either. Both pairs of grandparents lived in two-storey terraced houses in streets of terraced houses surrounded by other streets of terraced houses. Welcome to the East End. Actually that isn't quite true either as my father's home backed onto the green and white orderly expanse of the City of London cemetery. My mother's home backed onto the main line from Fenchurch Street station in London to Tilbury docks and Southend. This wasn't green and white but the view did offer a chance to collect engine numbers and watch powerful 2-6-4 tank engines haul eight or more packed carriages of commuters to and from the city. Not quite the peace and quiet of the cemetery though.

I wasn't just lucky when I was born, but then again six months later. By then the phoney war was in full swing and everyone in England waited with baited breath for the next move. I didn't have baited breath as I was trying to die from double pneumonia. It's sort of related I'm told. As luck would have it my mother's mother, a dear little Scottish lass called Annie, did a lot of mothering and I survived – obviously you say or you wouldn't be reading this. At the same time my own mother was trying hard to survive in hospital from something unrelated to pneumonia, double or otherwise, but we both saw 1941.

If you have never had the good fortune to have grandparents I should tell you that you missed something in life. You missed an opportunity to learn all sorts of things that your own parents never did have the time to teach you. It's a bonus in life. You also learn things that only grandparents know, like what were your parents really like when they were young and did they really get up to that much mischief? How come they won't let me do that then? Fascinating stuff.

The other good piece of fortune that came my way when I was born was location. My father had made his way in the world and the Civil Service paid him a reasonable and reliable wage. Initially my parents lived in a flat in Ilford, but when I threatened to arrive they decided that the flat wouldn't be big enough for three of us and so we moved down the street so to speak to a house, which my father rented from an unknown and unresponsive Mr. Robinson. Looking back I suppose there was no reason why I should have known Mr. Robinson. He didn't come weekly knocking on the door looking for the rent and neither did he send one of his heavies. Obviously my father organised this financial transaction in some civilised way. Unresponsive though, well there I did have a beef with Mr. Robinson and it happened not long after we arrived in his rented house.

They say there are three key words in Real Estate and they are "location, location, location". True, it's an oft-repeated cliché but here again life was kind. I spent most of my early life in Mr. Robinson's rental house, which like those of my grandparents was a two-storey terrace house in a street of terraced houses but this time we backed onto something wonderful – a golf course.

On my father's side of the family all the members are said to be born with a ball in one hand and a pack of cards in the other. My father's father spent hours with me with both a ball and a pack of cards. Under his careful tutelage I developed hand and eye coordination until I was allowed to play darts in the house, a real step up and acceptance in the family. Being English I learnt to play cricket, and although grandfather didn't change the arm I threw with, which was my left, he did teach me to bat right-handed. We also went out along with my father to Wanstead Flats, which were probably part of the Manor's Park in days gone by, and kicked a ball about. As a result the golf course at the end of our garden immediately and for several years following became our local cricket pitch and football ground. Now the Golf Course maintenance staff and some of the local caddies, yes the Club had caddies in the early days, did try and persuade us that the course was private and not for such low-life sports like football and cricket. It wasn't until I was nearly eight before I realised that the golf game itself could be so challenging and so fascinating. My father had played a little and he encouraged me. My mother, bless her heart, would come out almost predawn so she couldn't be seen and play with me as I learnt the subtleties of that wondrous game. Again, the hand and eye came from my grandfather and his strict adherence to watch the ball. My father's father had been a police constable all of his life and in those days one didn't argue with policemen. He was strict and I thank him for it.

Did you ever think back to when you first learnt to throw or to kick? Which arm, which foot? Somewhere inside each body cell there is this chromosome chappie, well more than one really but there is one and somewhere along its length there is this even smaller gene thing and within that there is this infinitesimally small notice board. Pinned to it there is this note that says "brain right side dominant". Well, that's what mine might have said, and I learnt that in zoology classes, although much later. Dominant right side of the brain - so I threw left-handed because some things get all crossed over between the brain and body they tell me. The trouble came early on because my father is right-handed, and so are both his parents and his sister. Oddly enough his older brother was left-handed. So much for the logic of genetics. Father told me to place the left hand up high near the end of the handle and the right hand up tight beneath it.

'Watch the ball son. Square the bat against the ball. Stick that left elbow out in front and step forward, well left if you think of it that way and square the bat onto the ball. Good lad. Now again. Move the feet depending where the ball bounces and square on. That's right,' and it was right, right-handed to play cricket, but I bowl with my left-hand and that made it hard to learn to bowl googlies from my dad.

I went to school when we still had pen and ink. Most of you won't remember such things but they followed the quill pen era so we had metal nibs that slotted onto wooden pen handles and little ink wells recessed into school desks. These were neat and when she wasn't watching you could splash ink over the tidy writing of the little girl next to you in class. This gave rise to that important diagnostic tool in murder inquiries called splatter analysis and a howl from the little girl. Wet ink smudges, and when writing left-handed the hand quickly catches up with the recently-applied letters and you get an inky hand. You also get illegible writing.

'No Johnie. With the right hand please. I know you're left-handed but the school says right-handed for writing.' I liked my teacher. She was warm, beautiful and spoke with a clear singing voice. I wanted to please her but we never had any apples so I wrote right-handed. I still do and wonder whether she remembers me.

So I have this right-handed, left-handed thing where the little notice on the gene chappie says the right-hand side of your brain is in charge. Fortunately this is not completely true that the hemispheres of the brain influence one's right-handedness. It's the left side of the brain that's the logical analytical scientific side rather than the artistic, imaginative, lateral-thinking right brain side. I might be left-handed but I am not right brain dominant. As a result my singing went off key when my voice changed. I can paint, quite well by numbers, but the artistic flair and visualisation is lacking. It's funny really because for the very small detailed areas on the board, you know the numbers 57, 58 and 59, I use my right-hand with the school-inflicted fine motor skills, but for the large swaths of numbers 6, 7 and even 9 with the broad expanses of brown and ochre for the extensive sand dunes I use a brush in my left hand. Perhaps I should try Japanese writing and get my body stuck in neutral trying to decide which hand to hold the brush?

The dominant right lobe, or perhaps just part of this right lobe in my brain influenced this power in my left side. I wield a table-tennis bat, or paddle for some folk who perhaps have this Canadian canoe thing as part of their background, with my left hand even though it was my parents who taught me the game. Actually, in our house we played "ping-pong-ricochet-watch the glass" but I'd better explain. Both my grandparents had this magnificent fortress structure in their back gardens. These structures had curved corrugated iron walls that joined at the top as a roof and this was camouflaged with earth and grass. Neat steps led down into the bowels of the earth with beds on each wall. In contrast our family air-raid shelter was indoors, which was not so exciting but far more practical, and that is where I learnt to spin a ping-pong ball. My father had this fast topspin service and my mother had a deft backhand slice. I needed to be quick and alert as I stood at the other end of the air-raid shelter and returned the ball back over the net. Our indoor shelter, a Morrison shelter I believe, was a metal frame in which I sensibly slept for most of the war. We would listen to the engines on the V1s and keep whispering 'keep going keep going' because when the engine quit the movement of the bomb would change from forwards to downwards. On arrival at terra firma there would usually be an explosion and several bits would go flying. For some five seconds it was not so firma on the ground and the bits would include houses, gardens, arms and legs. I slept in the shelter.

The top was a metal sheet about eight feet by four feet. I know this is not your regulation table-tennis size and so my game is oriented in the middle and short. I'm kind of missing a foot all round but I can catch those edge shots. Let me explain. The metal top was fine and the ball bounced nicely with a resounding ping. Unfortunately there were a few bolt heads where the top was fixed to the frame below. These gave rise to the one in ten ball ricochet and a flight which followed an erratic Brownian movement. Quick reflexes were the order of the day and the left hand had the power for the quick flick and successful return.

This air-raid shelter lived in the lounge in our house, which was Mr. Robinson's house really remember. The lounge, which was a word used by people struggling to get into the middle class, and was a step up from the front room which in turn was a step up from the front parlour, was a room containing an upright piano, another necessary prop for the aspiring middle class and several over-stuffed pieces of furniture. The sofa of this inevitable three-piece suite served as my trampoline and the somersaults were certainly self-taught. Practice came to an untidy end however when I managed to bounce clean through the front bay window and cut my knees to shreds. This necessitated a mad rush to the hospital where I was dutifully bandaged and dismissed as a low priority patient. Considering they were dealing with lots of people who had been close to V1 and V2 rockets when they landed I suppose I should have understood this attitude. Also in the lounge was a costly piece of furniture called a bookcase. Now this was no ordinary bookcase. First of all it had cost my father his life. Not directly of course. The tobacco companies had this competition and if you smoked two or three boatloads of their cigarettes you won a bookcase, which my father dutifully did, sometime before the war. He died, much later after the war, from some complications of emphysema and lung disorders and so the bookcase came at a price. It was a splendid piece of furniture with solid wood buffed to a high gloss and made up of four shelves which could be taken apart for easy moving. Each shelf stacked cleverly onto the one below and the lowest fitted a solid base. The contents were protected from the ravages of dust and little boy's sticky fingers by panes of glass that lifted up and over to allow access to the precious tomes. Both my parents were avid readers and they passed that trait on to me too for which I am truly grateful. The glass panes were a useful feature as dusting was not one of mother's strong points but the glass was a hazard in the game of ping-pong-ricochet-mind the glass. Although a table tennis ball doesn't pack much punch a hastily swung bat searching for that erratic ricochet does – hence the name of the game.

The dominant left foot meant I played inside left, outside left, left half and ultimately left back on the football pitch. I could never understand the move to left back as I was not tall and strong but the coach insisted that I was now too slow to play anywhere else. He noted that although I was not big and strong he knew that I played rugby and reckoned I could discreetly take the opposing forwards legs away. My parents never taught me skiing, which was a shame because I could have done better if I had learnt to use the right leg as well as the left leg when turning. On cross-country ski courses I favour those loops which keep turning right as my strong left leg can curve me that way whereas the left hand turn requires much mental preparation and complete elimination of the left foot! Perhaps the greatest blessing with regards to left-hand and right-hand is my learning about golf. As you place two hands on the club I naturally picked it up right-handed, just like a cricket bat. Thank you father. Your ashes scattered on the eighteenth green of your home course can rest happily in the knowledge that we got that right. My strong left arm pulls the club down hard through the ball and I have no strong right hand trying to take over and beat the hell out of the grinning white ball. For a while we tried left hand low when putting. You know the theory, where the lower left hand pulls the club and the ball towards the hole and because it is my stronger hand there should be no yipping and yawing. Keep it square just like the cricket bat in my youth. The trouble is the right hand gets upset because it feels it is being ignored and so it surges into action and there go the fingers again and another three-putt green. Now I'm in awe of people who can play golf one-handed. The game's hard enough without that challenge but father's early cricket lessons proved very helpful.

Even in golf though there comes a time when neither hand is very useful out on the course. You're standing on the tee in the pouring rain and the wind suddenly decides to move the rain more horizontal than vertical. Already you are three down and your opponent is grinning and cheerfully embracing the typical golfing weather. Placing the hands on the club you make sure the thumbs are properly aligned and the right hand is not too low and trying to get into a power position, and you swing smoothly even though the feet squelch a little, and coming through the ball you feel wonderful, and wet, and the ball takes off as does the club. Slipping through your wet hands the club sails majestically on a perfect take-off angle some fifty yards down the fairway and a good twenty yards further than the ball. Looking at your opponent you cheerfully concede the hole, the match, and maybe the whole bloody game so let's go and be sensible and have a drink in the Club House? Trudging back from the fourth tee-box, realising you were only three down at that stage, it is a long walk as you are on the far side of the course when both hands let you down. But you forget all about that as you drip at the bar and lift the glass, with the left hand of course. Right side or left side? It's an interesting mix of genetics and environment.

Think back, really far back and where did you learn to count? My father's parents played whist, played cribbage and they played dominoes. They also played darts onto a board hung up on the living room door and protectively surrounded by an old piece of scrounged plywood. All these games involve numbers, counting, adding, subtracting. Okay so they don't include multiplication and division but I wasn't at school yet so be patient. Hours spent with grandmother playing cribbage, making up fifteen two, fifteen four, fifteen six and a pair makes eight. Playing dominoes where we played threes and fives as well as matching tiles: learning at my grandmother's knee.

Living in Mr. Robinson's rented house in Ilford meant we weren't far from either pair of grandparents. Virtually every Sunday morning my father would cycle over to his parent's house and check how they were and see whether anything needed doing. Another lesson I thought. When I was little I would sit on a special small seat bolted to his crossbar and look forwards where we were going. That started me on my geographical learning of remembering roads, turnings, directions and where things were. Before long I had graduated to a small bicycle and would carefully ride inside my father on these weekly visits. For me these were extra special. It was just at the end of the war and my grandfather had retired from the police force and worked as a night watchman at the local sweet factory. Sweets were still rationed. For those of you who weren't there at the time everything had been rationed and there were two things you did not lose. One was your personal gas mask and the other was the ration books. My grandfather would bring home small packets of sweets and the sherbet lemons were my favourites. Nibble away at the end and suck the powdered sherbet out of the middle. Treats with my lessons.

Mark you, as I told you, my father's father was strict. I can remember not wanting to have my hair cut around age five and being walked there firmly with a grip on my ear that had practised on seasoned criminals. 'Short back and sides barber.' Firmly, no arguments. My father's parent's house didn't contain many books as it was a house of games. Alternatively it was a house of jobs and I learnt to polish shoes under the firm guidance of my grandfather. His life as a policeman had meant a disciplined regime of pressed uniforms, clean whistle and brilliantly shining boots. First I learnt to fit the shoe on the right part of the four-sided boot last. Then apply the polish with a rag and prepare to brush your arms off. 'Spit a lot son, spit on it and polish until you can see your face.' 'Yes granddad.' and my arms wore out. Both arms. Right and left.

Outside my father's parent's house I celebrated along with everyone else in the street on VE day. There were bonfires at intervals down the street and we all dressed up to shout and sing and dance. For me the war had been an adventure with excitement and humorous incidents. As I said before I was born lucky. Houses either side of us were bombed out of existence. We would rush to the air-raid shelter clutching gas masks and whatever else but be lucky. Next morning there would be new holes in the rows of terraced houses but our family lived through all of this.

Grandparents, parents, aunts, uncles all survived and we all lived in different parts of London.

Although the house was never directly on terra infirma we did have some close calls. The unresponsive Mr. Robinson didn't react very fast when we lost our roof, our windows, our doors and parts of the internal walls. Over time things got patched up but the house was rather draughty for a while. In the last year of the war I was going to school and that was always an adventure. In the classroom we would hear the siren and we would all rush downstairs to the basement until the all-clear sounded. Fortunately the lessons were not very intellectual at this stage of my educational career and so the interruptions were not too damaging on the learning process but I will never forget the sound of the siren.

Perhaps it was the siren, or the bombing, or the destruction which jerked the patriotic heart strings because I grew up as a young child wanting to go in the navy. This was surprising as none of my parents or grandparents had been in the armed forces. Not only had I wanted to go in the navy but I also wanted to go in submarines. Looking through various books as I explain below I had seen and imagined the stupidity of standing in a line at point blank range and firing at someone firing at you. It wouldn't matter whether you were right-handed or left-handed, although being left-handed in a Roman Legion's battle order might have been like trying to write left-handed with pen and ink. Whatever, the up front, in your face, Company will advance, British Army way seemed suicidal. Yours truly, with the logical left-side dominant brain thought that was dumb. If you're going to fight for King and Country then fight to win and be smart about it. If you are not big and strong then be sneaky about it, hence submarines.

Now I can explain that this approach is certainly genetically based. As a sweeping generalisation people from the north of England are plain, straightforward, clear simple-speaking in your face folk. It's eyes front, forward march, straight ahead stuff. In contrast, and in another sweeping generalisation, us folk from the south, especially those of us from the city like London, are more devious. We feint and dodge. We're people who speak with a forked tongue. Think about it. London is full of immigrants. They all come in from wherever and struggle to get a toe-hold, get accepted, get established, find a place, an occupation and get ahead. I came from London. Okay, so I missed out on the first six days when I ran away but all my folks came from the south. Your northerner knocks on your door and when you ask who is there he replies, 'It's Mr. Middlethorpe from York. I've come to marry your daughter Betsy. Open the door please.' When you open the door the said northern gent walks forward, over your foot, your leg and the rest of you as he comes in to find Betsy. Not so the southerner. Imagine you hear a knock knock on the door. 'Who's there?' you ask and the southerner replies 'Who do you want it to be?' and so you say 'Sally Anne from next door, 'cos the wife's out playing cards down the community centre and won't be back until ten.' Your southerner now changes voice and replies in a pseudo high-pitched falsetto which is thin but sexy 'Let me in then please and I'll talk with Betsy later.' Keen and eager you open the door and the southerner leans forward so you can see the cleavage and is careful not to knock the blond wig askew and you stand there transfixed by this image. After a good minute you manage a question, 'Won't you come in?' and the southerner goes coy, wriggles a bit and twirls around on your doorstep but listens carefully. When he is sure his partner has successfully walked Betsy through the kitchen door out back he pouts and just says 'Not tonight dearie' and leaves you standing there unmolested, untrampled and missing Betsy. It's just the approach is different, and so going into submarines and their sneaky cut and run tactics appealed. Genetics however deemed otherwise.

At sixteen, still planning to follow a naval deck officer career, I applied to the Royal Naval College at Dartmouth, the training ground for British Naval Officers. We passed the three days of written tests, right-handed, which included general knowledge and intelligence tests. Following these examinations I attended a naval training establishment for three days of physical assessment. Much of the time the eight applicants worked in a gymnasium demonstrating how to move planks, ropes, barrels from A to B without dropping them in the shark-infested floor space between A and B. Under the critical eyes of three or four gold-ringed naval officers we showed we could take command, give orders, follow orders, work as a team and be quick and efficient about it. Good clean fun whichever side your brain works but it was the medical that was my downfall and that was genetically determined. However, before we come to that career-stopping day let's add the story of the intelligent talking. My grandparents and parents had fostered my ability to talk. 'Stand up and recite that poem you learnt. Tell grandmother what you did yesterday. Tell us about bomb shelters.' I was lucky because my school too fostered the skill in talking. We had debates and oral presentations at age nine and ten and so by the age of sixteen I felt confident about my oral skills. I could yap as well as the best of them and then we had this interesting experiment with the navy. The eight applicants sat around a large well-polished table and the four assessors distributed themselves out of sight around the walls of a large and well proportioned room. With us at the table sat a naval medical chappie, and this one was a psychologist, and he was chasing and assessing mental capabilities. Relaxed and carefree this officer threw subjects onto the table, figuratively that is, and told us to discuss them. This was not the place to get tongue-tied but it was also not the place to put your foot in your mouth either. How about think before you speak? Back in the gym we should have thought before we acted, or instructed. Now we had to think again, but think quickly, think succinctly, and speak with clarity yet authority. Support not contradict:

add not detract: elaborate rather than dismiss but don't be led by the nose into dead ends as our naval friend tried to do with us. Here was a chance to let the neurones in both sides of the brain fire. Both barrels. Then there was the subtle question of accent. Some of the other applicants came from schools like Oundle, like Harrow and spoke accordingly. Some of us spoke like we came from the East End of London where the letter "h" occasionally gets lost. But all for nought as the next naval medical chappie had a different kind of assessment to make and that proved fatal, well career-changing rather than fatal.

Medically I felt fine. Young, fit, good weight for my height and build, ten toes, two hands and the usual accessories that go with a young man. I had passed all my medicals to date, including the struggle at six months with double pneumonia. At this point in time in England the medical profession assessed colour blindness with a book containing simple figures, letters and diagrams. The images in this book had been carefully and cleverly constructed by some medical science type to be made up of many solid circles each of certain colours. Depending how the cones on the retina in your eyes worked you could correctly see number four, number seven, letter B, letter Q and a house shape rather than others numbers, letters and shapes if the cones weren't distinguishing red, green, brown, blue or whatever. Simple but clever stuff. I wasn't colour blind. The navy had a different approach. I was sitting alone in my singlet and shorts in a room along with this naval medical chappie who I had never met before and he is sitting close because he is going to assess my eyes. I noticed that he didn't have any book. Different I think. In his hand he holds a switch. Flicking the switch the room goes pitch black and you realise that this is really different and you wonder about this naval medical chappie you have only just met. You can hear him breathing because he is that close and then he asks 'What colour are the lights?' My mind recognises it is a calm, well-modulated voice and definitely upper-class and as you register this you ask 'What lights?' Here I had to pause because if this had not been a Royal Naval College Entrance Examination I would have asked, 'What fucking lights? I can't see any bloody lights,' but then I remembered why I was here and spoke accordingly. Very politely and calmly the voice in the dark elaborated by saying 'The lights at the end of the room.' Just as politely and a lot less calmly I replied that I couldn't see any lights and immediately the switch was pressed again and we were both somewhat blinded by the overhead fluorescent glare.

Not surprisingly the navy wanted to test whether any future deck officer could see navigation lights. You know, those red and green lights that tell you whether the ship in front of you is steaming away from you or about to run you over. They also give you an indication, depending how high up in the sky they appear, whether the ship is five tons or fifty thousand tons, and this is also important to recognise quickly. If the latter then you advise the crew that there is likely to be some rock and roll in five seconds which might upset their breakfast of liver and onions and if you have time you add that this is not some special requested music over the tannoy for dancing! Now I could see red and I could see green. I could also see all the other colours of the rainbow but I couldn't see those bloody little lights down the end of that darkened room. Genetically, physiologically, I was short-sighted. Now I knew this and up until that point in time I had successfully bypassed this handicap. I told you I was from the south and therefore devious, sneaky. At any doctor's medical assessment I would memorise the bottom two lines of the normal eye-test chart as I walked into his office and when asked to read the lowest line I could see I would faithfully run them off from memory. Simple. I was vain and I didn't want to wear glasses. Only nerds wore glasses and I was a jock right? Never was quite sure where this particular trait came from because both my parents and all my grandparents were good honest folk. Obviously an aberrant gene somewhere. But, let's come back to the younger more innocent days.

My mother would walk me to her parent's house in East Ham. This was a couple of kilometres through the back streets but it involved an exciting dash across the main Romford Road. From an English point of view this was a broad road of about six lanes wide although there were no lines painted on it. Moreover there was no centre median either and it was a busy road. We had a choice of crossing places and none of them had traffic lights, zebra crossings or any other aids to pedestrians. It was look, guess, take a chance and run like hell. My mother always thought this was a lark. She was like that. 'Take a chance son and go for it.'

My mother was of the school of "nothing ventured nothing gained". Watching her ride a bicycle I was always glad in retrospect that she never learnt to drive a car, but I did learn when to be bold. Coming back of an evening when there were no street lights in the blackout, vehicles had hooded headlights, and my mother was holding my hand and guiding the pram containing my sister, it really was a strategic decision of when to go for it.

Education at my mother's parent's house was a little different. My grandfather was an engineer for starters and he had worked at the factory just down the road as a tool-and-die-maker. When he retired he brought some of his skills home with him and built a workshop at the end of the garden which rattled a lot when the heavy trains went past. There I had my first lessons in hand tools. I learnt when and when not to use a hammer, screwdriver, chisel, hand-drill and ultimately the unwieldy brace and bit. As I became stronger I used a plane, 'Although watch the blade son 'cos it is real sharp', and it was. I progressed to jigs, to clamps and to joints (the woodworking kind at this stage for although my grandfather was a rebel and had been fired from many jobs he was straight as an arrow). Then we had to learn about rasps, files, gouges, spoke shaves, mallets, squares, straight edges and the fine art of sandpapers. My grandfather's rough and gnarled hands held mine and showed me how to use all these things. Magic. He made toys for the family, big and small. Model forts with a moat for real water complete with a tap to drain it, all over my mother's carpets! Doll's houses for my sisters, complete with working lights, furniture, staircases and a front that opened. I had a sledge that doubled as a wheeled wagon. It worked fine as a wheeled wagon but it was so heavy that I would have needed a precipitous mountainside to turn it into a working sledge but thanks all the same grandfather. Try as he might though my grandfather could never interest me in his passion for growing sweet peas. Gardens were for cricket and football but not in this garden please. Sport here was rowing and so off we would go on our bicycles and find a park with a lake and rented row boats. 'Lean forwards son and let your back do the work. Easy now and don't force it. Feather the blades by rolling the wrists. Make a rhythm and move nice and steadily.' Back on the bikes and off home. 'Race you!!'

Indoors at my mother's parents house was a learning centre of a different kind. I don't know how many hours I spent as a child flat on my stomach on the floor of the living room kicking my feet up behind me and pouring over one of the ten volumes of the Children's Encyclopaedias by A.J. Mee. For me this became one of my escapes. I could travel the world and I probably learnt much of my geography from the maps and pictures of the various countries in those books. There was literature of prose and poetry, riddles and puzzles, transport with detailed diagrams of marine engines and the colours of railway companies, mythological tales of Greece and how the heavens look in the night sky. When I was older I could practice my French, learn the Morse code and puzzle over geometry questions but when I was very young I would just look at the pictures. Fascinating photographs of places far away full of mystery and excitement. Foreign lands full of different looking people and animals and plants not seen in England. I'm quite sure part of those hours spent silently turning the pages imbued in me my love of travel, of railways and feats of exploration. My mother would talk quietly with her mother about cooking, dress-making and children while I was learning how to do faggot stitch.

You say you don't know anything about faggot stitch? Well it has nothing to do with any derogatory term, or any gay individual with a pain in their side. It is a knitting expression, or activity. My grandmother taught me plain and purl although she never allowed me to knit socks. This was just as well as I would have taken years to produce one pair but I did manage a long long scarf without too many dropped stitches. Faggot stitch, once mastered, was quickly forgotten although it became an inside joke between my mother and me. My mother's mother also taught me embroidery and this ended up with several rather lopsided green plants around the edges of tablecloths and a badge later in Wolf Cubs. It also resulted in some fine motor skills which I could then apply to delicate chisel work in grandfather's workshop.

At my mother's parents house I learnt other board games. We played Halma, which is a similar game to draughts (translate into checkers). From draughts I eventually graduated to chess with my grandfather. Mind games, strategy games, positional games and a need to think. We also played cribbage and dominos but grandmother taught me a rather old-fashioned but fascinating card game called Bezique. I still play. Here was a game where you had to know your numbers: how to make decisions between this scoring array versus another, and know when it might be best to change tactics. Maybe even cut your losses. Think about it. These are life skills.

At Christmas time our family alternated between parents on Christmas Day and Boxing Day. As our family got older it was easier to bring the grandparents to us. My mother was the youngest of four and the focal family gatherer in her family. Everyone came to our house and I grew up knowing several cousins as well as aunts and uncles. This inevitably led to another set of learning because my mother would party with charades, treasure hunts and loud and vocal card games like Pitt. These activities would involve teams and I learnt how to move quickly with either grandmother around the house in the treasure hunt, and how to have grandfather improvise in charades. When we were quite young the treasure hunts were based upon pictures of animals and plants that needed to be posted in certain labelled boxes scattered around the house. Later, as we grew older, the clues were rhymes which you had to decipher to know what you were looking for before chasing round the house to find it. Teamwork. Dialogue. Understanding. All human interpersonal skills and I never realised that I was learning.

My luck stayed with me for many years. I moved into being a teenager and still I had all my grandparents. The visits changed and still I learnt new things. We would talk and I could listen and understand. What was life like fifty years before? My grandfather had walked the beat as a police constable when Barley Lane in Ilford literally was a country lane. I could relate to this as I watched the fields where my father and I cycled to pick wild blackberries become a new housing estate. Grandfather's engineering factory down his street closed as the area became gentrified. People put real fitted baths in their houses and toilets were indoors. We still played cards. We still threw darts. Television came, although it was covered with a crocheted cloth over the screen for much of the time, like some ornament. I rarely heard the wireless in my grandparent's houses. We talked. We listened. Eventually I grew up, went to University, got married and left for Australia. I stayed lucky as all four grandparents were still alive when I left. They were a learning experience I never can forget. Grand times. Grandparents. Grand parents.

3 FORGET GRANDDAD

THE BUCKET OF THE BACKHOE dipped firmly into the edge of the pit and tore at the soil as the hydraulics forced the toothed edge into the hard ground. Dry up on the top but already starting to get moist and slippery under the tracks of the machine as they deepened the pit. Typical London clay and further down beneath them it would be oozing with water.

'Keep that edge straight there Marty or we'll have old Tom on our backs about quality,' shouted Harry as he leant on his shovel watching his partner manipulate the hoe's controls.

'Who's in charge of this team Harry?' asked Marty as he pulled the edge of the pit forwards. 'It's you leaning on the shovel mate and I'm doing the quality work. You just make sure there's nothing amiss.'

'Okay kid. You're the one with the driver's ticket,' and Harry shrugged inside his donkey jacket and made a couple of useless passes with his shovel. Marty settled back in his seat on the hoe and lined up for the next bite.

'Hey. Hold up. Back off Marty. Pull out mate 'cos you've found something new.'

Sure enough Marty noticed that the bucket wasn't cutting into the gravel and clay but into what looked like ashes or old clinker.

'Shit. Now you've done it,' cried Harry.

'What?'

'That's an arm. Well it looks like an arm with them bones. Hold on there Marty.'

'A what?' and Marty leant out of the cab to hear Harry and look a little better at the cut face.

'An arm you young tosser, a bleedin' arm, although it looks so white it ain't really bleedin'. We'd better call Tom. This'll hold everything up. Look what happened when they found all those old bones at St. Pancras. Held up the work there for weeks so there goes our overtime bonus. Trust you to find something Marty.'

'Give over whining Harry and call up Tom. Don't you go and bugger anything up with your shovel either. That special team needs to get here and check it out – archaeological or something.'

Tom, the site foreman came over and called Marty and Harry all sorts of names for finding a way to stop work but he knew that nothing would happen here until the special team came over and discovered what or maybe who's arm Marty had unearthed.

The men were working on the new line that would take the high speed trains from the Chunnel into London. At the moment these trains travelled at 300 kph in France and Belgium and raced under the channel only to slow down to a 100 kph crawl in England. It had been over one hundred years since the English had last built a railway line in England. Using today's technologies, with several Tunnel Building Machines (TBMs), the new line carved its way from Dover through the chalk of the Downs and under Bluebell Hill. Then it raced across the Medway, under the new QE II Bridge and over the M25 in Kent before tunnelling the two kilometres under the Thames. Finally, from Dagenham, it tunnelled its way into Stratford and on again tunnelling through north London to appear in the restored and rejuvenated majestic Victorian station of St. Pancras. Some ten thousand workers constructed just over one hundred kilometres of new revolutionary railway line. They moved and replanted over one million trees, found Roman relics, and even older elephant tusks. The line terminated at St. Pancras station with its revolutionary single span glass-covered arch over the platforms. It was while the crews were working on the extension to St. Pancras to accommodate the new lengthy high-speed trains that they found the mass grave. When the Victorians first built St. Pancras station for the Great Central Railway in 1868 they had to move parts of the cemetery. Alongside the parish church of St. Pancras had been an extensive burial ground and navvies at that time moved the bodies to rebury many of the souls in a mass grave. The opening of the mass grave gave rise to a long delay while bodies were identified, catalogued and moved reverently elsewhere. The project manager Allie MacAdam said she had expected to find a few bodies but seven thousand was a bit much.

At Stratford, using part of the site of the old Great Eastern Railway headquarters, the construction company decided to build a large pit to serve as the maintenance and storage yards for the high-speed trains. Rather appropriately they called this the Stratford Box. It was fifty five metres wide and a kilometre long. Harry and his young oppo Marty were part of the crew creating this pit, although finding the arm certainly slowed down the creation. Delicately, the special archaeological team picked apart the soil debris entombing the arm, a leg, another leg, torso, head and ultimately a second arm. A dirty white, somewhat unappealing set of body parts lay unearthed on the table and as the special team couldn't find anyone else inhabiting the immediately surrounding area they decided it was a one of and let Marty carry on. Tom was relieved and

Harry bullied young Marty to catch up on production to earn them the necessary bonus. The construction crew lost interest in the body.

After all the routine tests the archaeologists decided that the body was some fifty to sixty years old and not very interesting. The body appeared to be intact with no broken bones and thought to be that of a man in his fifties or sixties. The forensic pathologist couldn't see any obvious cause of death. At first she thought the victim might have died in a bomb blast in the war, and as there were no broken bones he could have been asphyxiated by the blast, but then again he was definitely buried and not just lying on the surface of the ground. With more than enough work and with the construction engineers breathing down their necks the archaeological team was only too keen to turn the discovery over to the local police force and forget about the body they had labelled "Granddad".

'Well PCDickson, who is he then?'

'Sarge how the hell should I know. There's no clothes. There's no teeth. All we've got is a wired together set of old bones. The bugger looks white, old and definitely past his sell-by date. He's supposed to be in his sixties or thereabouts and I know I'm not related.'

'That's a fact Dickson. I don't see 'im singing reggae songs either so he definitely ain't one of yours.'

'That's racist Sarge.'

'Sergeant to you young Dickson. So son, if there's no teeth where are you going to look next?'

'Fingerprints Sergeant. See if he's got a record. Missing persons. War-time records of victims. Could have been in the war Sergeant. My old gran said there was lots of bombing here in the East End what with the docks and the railway yards. Doodlebugs and all sorts gran said.

'Course Bethnall Green next door got it worse than us she said. She was telling me about her sister who lives up by........'

'Dickson put a sock in it and leave off about your old gran. It's granddad here we're supposed to listen to and he don't have no fingers you may have noticed. Well, none with skin on for you to go looking at whorls. What else does he tell us?'

'Sweet FA Sergeant. Sweet FA. Anyway, how come we've inherited the old bugger?'

'The powers that be constable, and in this case that means Detective Inspector Cecil Lester for you and I, decided that granddad here didn't die of old age, disease or any other natural causes. D.I. Lester, my boss and your ultimate and important superior has decided someone murdered granddad, and as we are C.I.D. sunshine we have to find out who. It is sometimes easier son to find the murderer if we know who is the murderee. Do I make myself clear? And you constable have been selected to find out who granddad really is, or perhaps was. Inspector Lester heard that you were supposed to be some history nut about this area. He heard that you were some groupie to do with the old Great Eastern Railway? When he heard this, and when he remembered that his previously forgotten-about father, who he disowned very early in his life as apparently the gentleman was not actually his father according to his mother, and therefore had no real blood relationship, had been some important person in the old Great Eastern Railway and its successor the LNER, and so he thought of you. He'd heard you spent hours, maybe days chasing old records and looking for the glory days of steam.'

'Yes Sergeant, and one of those glory engines was named "West Ham United". B17 Class she was and that Class all had names of footie teams but number 1672 was special as far as I am concerned. You should be too Sergeant 'cos you're a Hammer's fan like me. Over a 'undred years ago now Sergeant the 'ammers started. It was in 1895 there was this

Thames Iron Works football team who played their first game. That Company built over a thousand ships and all sorts of bridges. You know, like Blackfriars and Hammersmith. Then their football team became West Ham United in 1900.'

'Son, I don't need a history of West Ham, the railway, or its engines, I just want you to find out who granddad is or was. And although I might be a Hammers fan, and truly excited about locomotive number 1672 or whatever, given where that backhoe operator found granddad he might have been a railway employee as well as a Hammer's fan. In fact that is such a good thought you should check with the railway and see whether anyone went missing in the forties and fifties.'

'Christ Sarge. With the war on there could have been thousands of buggers went missing. They tell me people got blown to pieces in the blitz. My old gran' was telling me........'

'Dickson, enough of your old gran. Do it for the glory of the old Great Eastern Railway son and stop griping.'

'It was the LNER by that time Sergeant. The Great Eastern Railway got amalgamated in 1923 into the LNER. Back in time you know.'

Sergeant Pettit looked at PC Dickson and the young constable thought about going back in time, quickly, to 1940, to 1923, to anywhere given the look on his sergeant's face.

'Well now it's 2007 constable, and D.I. Lester wants to know now, as in today or this week at the latest. Do I make myself clear?'

'Yes Sergeant.'

True enough, there was some glory in the story of the Great Eastern Railway. In 1839 the Eastern Counties Railway (ECR) built and operated a line from Mile End to Stratford with a five foot gauge. This line extended into London (Bishopsgate) and further out fifty miles into Essex to Colchester. The line converted to standard gauge in 1844 and became the driving force to create the Great Eastern Railway in 1862 through the amalgamation of ECR with all the small railways servicing Essex, Suffolk, Norfolk and Cambridge.

George Hudson built New Town, or Hudson's town really in 1847 as the site of the locomotive works, carriage sheds, goods yard and the central offices of this proud but typically East Ender cheap little railway. Over the years the lines expanded to include much of the East coast of England south of Boston and north of the Thames. Main lines ran to the longest pier in the world at Southend, to cross the North Sea by ferry from Harwich, to the fish markets of Great Yarmouth and Lowestoft, to the agricultural cities of Norwich and Cambridge, and all the hinterlands in between. In the great amalgamation of 1923 the Great Eastern Railway, along with several other famous Companies became the London Northeastern Railway, the L.N.E.R. with its record-setting Mallard out of Kings Cross and its equally revolutionary Claud Hamilton 4-4-0s in their special blue livery out of Liverpool Street. The London terminus for the old G.E.R. moved from Bishopsgate to Liverpool Street Station and the primary main line ran out to Stratford and on eastwards through the countryside-sounding names of Forest Gate, Manor Park, over the Roding at Ilford and on through Chadwell Heath. These were stations serving areas that all became suburbs of eastern London and the commuter housing developments of south-western Essex. Servicing most of this main line and continuing this role into the nineteen thirties and forties Stratford was a focal centre for this railway. Most of the people who lived in the Newtown part of Stratford, up against the boroughs of Leyton and Manor Park, were railway employees and proud of it. Stephen White was just one of those employees as had been his father and grandfather before him.

Stephen entered the world in his parent's house in Alma Street in early 1900 and visited St. Paul's Church in Maryland Road soon afterwards where the Reverend William Ferguson presided over his christening. Although the railway built the town and its infrastructure it was the workers who contributed their small donations to build the magnificent St. Paul's Church in Maryland Road. By 1865 this large church housed over one thousand ever-sinning souls. Well it did until the Luftwaffe destroyed it in WWII and its modest replacement held a measly three hundred worshippers. Back in the early nineteen hundreds Stephen's devout parents had reserved pews in the Church as they were regular churchgoers. As good devout sinners they were also regular patrons of the Engineers Arms in Alma Street. Right after the christening Mr. and Mrs. White celebrated Stephen's arrival with a few friends. John Saunders, the publican arranged for a good spread as he saw an opportunity to foster local community spirit. New Town was like a little village with most of the folk associated with the railway.

Soon after the building of New Town there had been a school for the sons of railway workers in Angel Lane. Then in 1865 St. Pauls had opened a Hudson's Town National School but this was replaced by Colegrave Primary School on Henniker Road in 1882. Like his father before him Stephen attended Colegrave but he left school early and went into apprenticeship for the Great Eastern. Because of his work Stephen's father was exempt military service when conscription came into force on March 2, 1916, but Stephen ended up in France in 1918. The horrors and stupidity of this experience strongly influenced his opinion of officers and people in charge and this stayed with him all of his life. However, Stephen also learnt from his father to keep his head down and his mouth shut. Gradually Stephen progressed in the railway work force and he was an experienced and reliable fireman when he turned thirty nine. In the summer of that historic year of 1939 Stephen qualified as an engine driver and this let him avoid enlistment. After the memories of the First World War Stephen certainly wasn't going to volunteer.

Just before this move from fireman to engine driver Stephen met Josephine and the first time was really a chance encounter. Coming home from an overnight run Stephen had popped into the tobacconists on Windmill Lane for a packet of Woodbines. As he turned round from the counter he accidentally bumped into a pretty young lady who had just asked Mr. Charters behind the counter for two boxes of Swan Vestas and a small packet of Saint Bruno for her dad. Both of them ended up dropping things on the floor and they gently bumped heads as they stooped down together.

'Hey I'm sorry luv. Didn't 'urt I 'ope?'

Josephine giggled. 'It's not your 'ead that's the problem it's them 'ands. Never mind, the stains will come out with a little turps.'

'I'm right sorry there miss.' Stephen looked at his hands. He had washed them after his shift coming off the engine but he always had hands looking like this. Sort of went with the job he thought; coal grime, grease, and oil outlined the lines in his hands. 'Can I 'elp with the cleaning?' and Stephen offered his hands towards the young lady.

Josephine backed up. 'No no,' she said, 'I think you've done enough already. Please keep yer 'ands to yourself.'

'You look out there Stephen,' said Mr. Charters. 'That's Danny Paisley's daughter you're trying to manhandle.'

'Well at least I can be polite enough to walk you 'ome and get yer coat cleaned for you,' offered Stephen.

'You're a brave one,' said Josephine with a laugh in her voice. 'Perhaps you don't know my dad?'

'I know him alright love. I work for the railway, same as your dad, although I don't have the following he has.'

Dan Paisley said yes to Stephen White cleaning his daughter's coat, and walking out with his daughter provided he could count on Stephen's support in any Union activity led by Dan. Stephen thought it was a small price to pay and a year later he sat anxiously in the front pew of St. Paul's Church waiting for Josephine on the arm of her father. In that eerie quiet of the phoney war Stephen and Josephine got married and settled down renting the upstairs of number fifty two on Waddington Road. This was above the shop of James Fryer and right next door to the Waddington Arms. At that time Josephine had been working in one of the sweat shops in Whitechapel but Stephen managed to pull some strings so Josephine could work cleaning in the railway head office.

'Let's keep it all in the family luv shall we?' suggested Stephen. 'We're all part of the railway family,' he added, and that is exactly how it turned out. Son John was born in February 1942, around the time that Hitler gave up on bombing airfields and decided to bomb civilians instead, as well as certain strategic sites like railway yards. As the war progressed the number of skilled men diminished and maintenance in the railway fell off. Locomotives and trains got bombed, derailed and working parts wore out. The quality of the coal was poor and train operations became more and more difficult and dangerous. The regular routine of railway operations was disrupted and whereas Josephine had started married life with Stephen living on scheduled times this now became more and more haphazard. She never knew when to expect Stephen now and communications were often severed with air raids and the subsequent fire and explosive damage.

Josephine's work day usually started at noon and she cleaned an array of meeting rooms and spare offices. By five o'clock most of the office staff had left for the day and she moved into their offices. Her routines included emptying wastepaper baskets, dusting, polishing, vacuuming, cleaning windows and even re-arranging furniture for some rooms. At least I don't have to clean out the fireplaces and black the grates she thought. That's too much like Stephen's job and she laughed within herself at the idea of both of them doing the same thing for the Company.

'Mrs. White, you'll have to stay late tonight,' said Mr. Lester. 'We've an important meeting in the boardroom this evening but I need it cleaned for another meeting early tomorrow morning. I'll expect a really good job mind you. These are important people. Very important people,' he added.

'Yes Mr. Lester sir. Can I pop home on my break to tell my mum I'll be late? She'll be worried otherwise.'

'If you must but be quick about it,' retorted Mr. Lester and he scowled at Josephine. 'This is important and the boardroom must look sparkling. Not your usual lick and a promise mark you.'

'Yes sir.'

Back at her mum's house Josephine explained that she would be late tonight and would it be alright for young John to sleep over as she didn't want to wake him when she came home.

'I think Stephen's away until tomorrow mum. Well, that's what he told me but then again the schedules are all over the place now and so I never really know when to expect him. John should sleep okay mum. I'll just pop in to see he's okay now and then I must dash. That Mr. Lester was quite sharp about wanting a good job done this evening. I've got a key mum in case I come back here but if I'm really late I'll just go home and be back here tomorrow morning for John.'

'John's fine luv. We'll see to him. You get back to your job darlin'. Got your gas mask? Never know in all these air raids what's coming next. Those doodlebugs are a right fright.'

Josephine did a little more of her regular routine and then did a last check on the boardroom. Everything there was neat and tidy. Leaving the room Josephine walked back up the corridor to Mr. Lester's office. She knocked.

'Enter.'

She turned the handle and poked her head around the door. 'The boardroom's fine Mr. Lester. I'll carry on with my other rooms and then wait until you have finished in the boardroom.'

Mr. Lester sat at his desk holding a glass in his hand. He seemed to be looking into space thought Josephine. She coughed.

'What's that, what's that?' asked Mr. Lester as he suddenly noticed Josephine.

'The boardroom sir,' answered Josephine. 'It's all set sir.'

'Yes, fine, right, good, and remember to stay to clean up afterwards. Important meeting. Important people. Yes, good, you get on now,' and he supped from his glass.

Reginald Lester sat moodily looking round the now empty and untidy boardroom. Cigarette and pipe tobacco smoke still swirled around above the paper-strewn table. Despite the war, rationing, and hardships for most folk the black market whisky left its own aroma in the atmosphere. Son and grandson of Directors in the old Great Eastern Railway Reginald had jump started his career in the Railway Company. However, his lack of talent and apparent inability to manage people had left him sitting in this one position for a long time. He was a frustrated man – frustrated with his job, his non-existent career, the deprivations of war-time and the fact that his society wife had just told him that neither of their two children was his. The bitch, the jumped-up bitch and him with the established family line, and now his two sons, his heirs to the family name weren't even his. He looked around the room and the emotions boiled up inside him. The important meeting, this past meeting with important people had got him nowhere. Overlooked again, rejected, patted on the head and re-assured that he was doing a good job despite the lack of machinery, spare parts and reliable manpower. He pulled the bottle towards him and generously splashed amber fluid more or less into his glass. I'll get even with you you sorry bitch he muttered to himself as he recalled his wife's sneering face. Just as he was getting morose and really down on himself Josephine knocked at the door and opened it.

'You've finished sir?' she asked looking around the room. 'You said you wanted it cleaned for early tomorrow morning sir so I stayed as you asked.'

'Yes yes,' said Mr. Lester. 'Put all the papers in the box by the table and do whatever else you've got to do.'

Josephine put down her dustpan and brush, the duster and the polish, and started collecting up and emptying the ash-trays off the table.

'Your husband's a driver now isn't he? Away tonight is he?'

'Yes sir. He's on the run to Harwich I think. Something special but he can't tell me what with all the security sir.'

'Deferred was he? 'Cos of his job?'

'Yes sir.'

Mr. Lester drank heavily from the glass in his hand and refilled the tumbler.

'Good man is he? Good husband? Serves you well?'

'He's a good man sir. Been with the railway all his life, since he was a kid. Like his dad before him.'

Josephine lent over the table to gather the various papers together and Mr. Lester swallowed his new drink. He stood up appearing to get out of Josephine's way as she collected the various papers around the table.

'Think I could serve you well do you? Think I'm a good man do you?'

Josephine continued with her collection of papers trying to gather them together. She bent over to pick up the box off the floor to put the papers away when she suddenly felt herself seized from behind and thrust forward over the arm of one of the large club chairs around the table. Before she had a chance to turn she realised Mr. Lester had his hands lifting her dress and thrusting his body up against hers.

'Bitch,' he said. 'I'll serve you well. I'll show you who is a good man here. I'll be the driver.'

It was over almost before it started. Mr. Lester stood up and adjusted his clothing. He looked at Josephine and sneered.

'Remember, the Railway recommends who is and who is not deferred. At Stratford I'm the Railway remember. Don't make me change my mind over any drivers will you? You can carry on now and make sure you put all those papers in the box. You've missed a few.'

Mr. Lester walked unsteadily out of the room and left Josephine in shock.

Although she never said a word Josephine's mother noticed something had happened but she kept her own counsel until she could talk with her husband Dan. The parents decided to keep quiet until Josephine said something, but she never did. And, as chance would have it, Reginald Lester did get recognised and he left Stratford in late 1942, but by then Josephine knew it was too late to think of mentioning anything to Stephen. Alan White came into the world in March 1943 and all the family were delighted with a brother for John. When people were being killed all around them it was re-assuring and positive to have new ones born. Alice and Dan Paisley did both notice that Alan had fair hair, unlike his father or his brother. However, no-one else did and the family grew up happily surviving the bombing, the V-1s and the V-2s with the indiscriminate destruction of London.

The family and the people all around them were even happier in 1945 with VE Day when the street got decorated with flags and bunting, and folk had food, dancing and bonfires in the street. Stratford Works had over two thousand happy people that day. Stephen graduated to being a senior engine driver and moved into handling the partly refurbished mainline locomotives. Soon after the war ended he was promoted to the driver for the "Hook of Holland" boat-train leaving Liverpool Street Station for Parkeston Quay in Harwich and the North Sea ferry across to Holland. His B17 locomotive hauled the eight to ten sleek teak-paneled coaches. With the regulator wide open for part of the run across the undulating Essex countryside this express made good time. But Stephen's skill and reputation also precipitated his downfall. Because he could handle difficult situations he was asked to drive an old J17 goods locomotive pulling a load of fish wagons to Lowestoft. This engine was built in 1903 as a Holden Class F48 and incorporated much of the design and elegance of the famous D14 Claud Hamilton passenger locomotives. However, by 1947 this old locomotive had seen better days. With its wooden roof on the cab and an old Belpaire firebox it was a working relic, but in the years right after the war the four old companies were struggling hard to keep any rolling stock going. After minimal maintenance and war-time restrictions on repairs most locomotives had one or more problems. With a faulty and unreliable pressure gauge for the leaky boiler even Stephen's expertise couldn't foresee the steady drop in the level of the water over the Crown Sheet of the firebox. The inquiry called it a BLEVE (Boiling liquid expanding vapour explosion) where the boiler literally explodes when there is no water over the top of the firebox and the metal buckles. When the firebox roof collapses the entire boiler is subject to intense heat and any water vapourizes in a flash. With a boiler pressure of 180 pounds per square inch and two thousand gallons of superheated water an explosion converts this to three million gallons of steam. Stephen and his fireman were killed instantly and the subsequent derailment held up the mainline for three days.

Dan Paisley and his Union members went looking for someone responsible – someone who forced members to operate dangerous and unreliable equipment but management hid behind excuses of expenses, war-time activities and the knowledge that within the year the four companies would be folded into a great catchall called British Railways. Josephine got a pension from Stephen's service but little else. Being her father's daughter Josephine had been brought up believing in the rights of workers and having fair working conditions. Moreover, the strong communist beliefs of her father had also given her thoughts of revolution but she was canny enough to wait for the right moment. She filed away her grievances. Her parents shared with her the knowledge they had supposed about Alan and the tale of Mr. Lester became a tightly guarded secret of Josephine, Dan, Alice and Dan's dad Jack. Father and son, Jack and Dan Paisley were both great believers in bringing everyone to a common level. They all waited for the moment.

Gradually, Stratford, England and the rest of the world moved into the fifties and times changed a little. Josephine watched the two boys laughing and playing down the street. She tilted her head to one side and smiled as her two sons came home from school. They were playing marbles down the gutter. Alan's fair hair shone in the bright sunshine and he turned to make some comment to his brother. John stopped and shouted something back but it was said in jest and the game continued gradually moving the precious marbles back home.

'What's for tea mum?' asked John as he picked his favourite jet-black nigger special up out of the dust.

'We haven't finished,' complained Alan as he too picked up his marble, but just as quickly he switched thoughts and looked up at his mum to hear the answer to John's question.

'Mr. Heinz "57" special,' said Josephine, 'but only for boys with clean hands.'

'On toast mum? We've gotta 'ave toast. Maybe with jam for afters. On the second slice eh John? Sweet and savoury mum, with cups of tea so all the food groups. Fruit too mum. We ought to 'ave fruit.'

Josephine laughed and tousled Alan's hair. 'All this learning is doing my head in son. We'll see what we've got but a quick scrub of hands, face, neck and knees comes first. Indoors the pair of you and let's get some of the street grime off.'

'Mum did we get any post about the eleven plus? Some of the kids at school have got their results, but not everyone. Have you heard?'

'No luv, I 'aven't 'eard anything. There's been no post John.' Josephine set about slicing the bread for toast. Having done that she looked in her small pantry and picked out the blue can. Wish I could do something better for the boys she muttered to herself but there was precious little money coming in from her pitiful pay-packet and Stephen's pension.

Robert Hitchcock, the current manager at the Stratford offices, was a dynamic young man and quite personable. Qualified as both an engineer and an accountant, Mr. Hitchcock was in charge of an inquiry as to some of the practices, and especially some of the financial affairs that took place in the early 1940s. It was ironical, at least it was for Mr. Hitchcock that the man he was investigating in some detail was Reginald Lester. The irony, and this was completely unknown to Mr. Lester, was that he was Robert Hitchcock's father. A short encounter with a family maid, a rapid dismissal, and an unknown birth had left Mr. Lester unscathed and unknowing but Robert Hitchcock never forgot the stories his mother told him. Rather than have this inquiry confrontational, and having learnt the weaknesses of his quarry Mr. Lester, Robert Hitchcock decided to investigate past events in a friendly and sociable atmosphere. A lengthy afternoon led into an early evening and a very drunk Mr. Lester. Claiming an important evening engagement Mr. Hitchcock decided not to pursue the matter that evening but told Mr. Lester they would continue their discussion on the next day. Mr. Lester was very grateful because he too had an important engagement that evening although he didn't explain that his engagement was a sure-cert visit to the Romford dog track where he intended to recoup some heavy losses from earlier in the month. He mentioned to Mr. Hitchcock that he had arranged for his driver to come and collect him around seven, and he would stay supping this fine whisky until that time if his host didn't mind. Robert Hitchcock had decided to execute his final damming remarks in the cold morning of the following day and so he said that he didn't mind at all. He left Mr. Lester in the boardroom.

Fate spins, weaves, evolves, circles and swoops around to embrace us all in the mysteries of life and for all of us there comes a time when it is our time. When it is the right time. Josephine was still cleaning offices at the railway and she eventually came to Mr. Hitchcock's office. Although he had got older and put on weight Josephine recognised the slumbering man – the man who had raped her. In her mind, and remembering the words he had said about him being "the Railway" she held him responsible for the death of her husband Stephen. It wasn't hard for Josephine to press the pillow over the mottled drunken face of Mr. Lester as he sat sprawled back in the chair of that same boardroom. A life for a life thought Josephine. Having finished her work and tidied up the boardroom Josephine stopped off at her dad's house on the way home. Dan's father, Jack, who had been an engine driver back at the turn of the century, said he knew just what to do. Dan took charge though and told Josephine, 'You just go home love like normal. You've done your bit and we'll take care of the rest. What you don't know you can't tell about. Come on dad.'

For the first fifty to sixty years the Stratford sheds had constructed locomotives. They still had the record for the fastest ever time to build a locomotive when the crew constructed a tender locomotive from scratch in just nine hours and forty seven minutes. Proud men who believed in themselves would work hard when there was respect, respect from management. Back in that time Stratford was still constructing locomotives and there had been a series of maintenance pits and ash pits in an old part of the works. Now that Stratford was no longer building locomotives this part of the huge yards was quiet and empty. Jack and Dan walked over to the office block where Josephine had been working. Silently, and without being seen by old Nigel the night-watchman, they entered the basement and secured a porter's trolley and a tea-chest. Lots of foodstuffs for the canteen were stored in the basement and so there were lots of suitable materials. The freight lift ran from the basement up to the top floor. Nigel never noticed the hum and the whine as the lift rose carrying Dan and his dad. It didn't take the two men long to strip Reginald Lester, discovering a useful wad of cash for the dog track in his pockets, and bundle his body into the tea-chests. With the body folded into two tea chests and another one holding the clothes they descended in the lift. An uneventful trundling of the trolley led to the old quiet area of the yard. No-one saw them. Mr. Lester became part of "the Railway" as he had said. They returned the trolley to the office basement, again without checking with Nigel. Because they knew where everything was, and who would be around, it wasn't hard for the two men to conveniently find a place to incinerate the clothes and the tea-chests. Dan had even been smart enough to remove Reginald Lester's rings and precious false teeth.

'That should give someone a bit of a poser if they ever find him dad.'

'Aye son.'

Mrs. Lester, now Mrs. Simmonds, had not seen or heard from her divorced husband for ten years or more. She and her two sons had severed all contacts and she had re-married a stockbroker in the City. When questioned by the police regarding the apparent complete and mysterious disappearance of Mr. Lester she had no ideas and had no desire to be bothered any more about it thank you officer. Her two sons were both boarding pupils at Harrow and knew nothing about their departed father. Both boys, although still named Lester, thought of Mr. Simmonds as their father and they had no knowledge or interest in Mr. Lester. So, no family concerns but Mr. Lester's driver had reported the failure of his employer to show for collection at the railway offices at seven-thirty that evening so someone was missing him. The police interviewed Nigel, the night-watchman and he had seen Josephine leave around six but not seen anybody else. Away the police went to talk with Josephine but she said she had left him sitting in the boardroom. She had no idea where he might have gone.

'He was fine when I left him officer. I suppose he was rather drunk and red-faced but I think he had been in a meeting all day with the Manager, Mr. Hitchcock. I cleaned up like I always do and then did other offices. Suppose I left around six officer. Old Nigel would have seen me go and I clocked off normal like. Just sitting in a chair he was. Mr. Lester that is.'

When the police talked with Robert Hitchcock they discovered the reasons for the meetings. The fact that Mr. Lester was under some suspicion led to the idea of suicide but where? Where was the body? Yes, Mr. Lester had been the manager here many years previously, and yes he did know the area but an extensive search didn't find any body. Further questioning of Mr. Hitchcock revealed his past and his parentage and that led to an intensive search for how, when and where Mr. Hitchcock could have killed his supposed father as revenge for his mother. Then again there was no body, no weapons, and no opportunity really, although the police did recognise that Nigel wasn't the most attentive of night-watchmen. Mr. Lester was a big man and no single person could have made him vanish. After some days, and then weeks, the missing person, about whom no-one really seemed to care became a statistic, a file of interviews and reports, and ultimately a cold case. Out in the railway yards the body gradually disintegrated as did the railway yards themselves. By 1991 the Stratford Railway Yards finally closed and the area became a derelict and deserted piece of industrial history.

The finding of a body in 2007 started as a poser for keen railway groupie Napoleon Dickson. The constable methodically trolled through records, reports from all sorts of authorities but because of re-organisations, fires, burst water-pipes, poor record-keeping and just plain bad luck the old file of the missing Mr. Lester didn't find its way into Dickson's search in that first week. Computerisation had helped with the cataloguing and filing of old records but when a file is lost, misplaced and never entered into the database even computer searches don't help. Other more recent, more urgent, and politically more significant events happened all around the C.I.D. Section and Detective Inspector Lester was looking forward to retirement at the end of the year when he turned sixty. D.I. Lester was walking down to the Section's work area to talk with his sergeant about stopping PC Dickson when the Station's PA system squawked into life. All hands were needed as a riot had broken out at Upton Park following a match between West Ham and Arsenal. As this was a typical London grudge match tempers were flying, fans were fanatical and the uniformed squad there had been submerged in the numerous battles taking place on the streets. Before D.I. Lester reached the squad room the Sergeant had turned to PC Dickson and said, 'Right son. Sounds like our uniformed boys need some help as usual. Leave granddad.'

While the force was out trying to keep the peace at Upton Park a new young WPC brought a stack of files into the C.I.D. offices. With no-one there she dropped them casually on the first desk she could find. Sooner or later they will find their way to the right desk she thought. She had forgotten it was Napoleon Dickson who had asked for them. As fate would have it Cecil Lester came that close to discovering the fate of his forgotten and dis-avowed parent. The Paisley family that knew anything about it were all dead. Josephine never knew what happened to Mr. Lester and she too had died in 1990 before the discovery. John White grew up from playing marbles in the street but kept his hand and eye coordination as a professional darts player. Despite strong urging from his mother's parents John never joined the railway. Alan White, still fair-haired and blue-eyed, continued as the driver of the new diesels on the main-line to Harwich just like his presumed father Stephen. After the lengthy fracas at Upton Park, when all the fighting bodies were booked and the paperwork cleared away, PC Dickson returned to the office and his investigations only to have his Sergeant walk into the room and firmly assert on orders from D.I. Lester 'Forget granddad', and so he did.

ONE FOR ALL OR ALL FOR ONE

I SUPPOSE IT WAS CLOSE to being a palindrome. True it wasn't as pure as "Able was I ere I saw Elba" but then the phrase "One for all or all for one" had a little more real life connotation. Apart from Napoleon, who was really concerned about seeing Elba, able or otherwise? I suppose my other phrase could be asked of a lot of things. The fact that the words had symmetry appealed to me, although posed as a question the phrase puzzled me. When you are sixteen there is the feeling that your whole life is ahead of you. It is a time when you start to realise that you are adult, well nearly, and that you can think for yourself. The revelation is both wonderful and worrying. There is an entire world out there and it could be all yours. There is also the nagging realisation that despite the advances of *Homo sapiens* it is still dog eat dog out there. But to come back to the initial words: I could translate the phrase into rugby or tennis as far as I was concerned.

One for all meant playing as part of a team: playing for and with the fourteen other blokes that made up our rugby team. In contrast, when I played tennis, everything and everyone was all for me, all for one. And so as I lay in bed that night, and thought back over the events of my sixteenth birthday and the cumulative events of my sixteen years, I took stock.

There was me: Andrew Mills, a callow youth with pimples, just starting to shave and the oldest son in the family with a younger brother and sister who don't really figure in this story. My father, Richard Mills, worked up in the city as part of the banking machine that kindly looked after our money and handed it back to us during restrictive hours for a fee. Sometimes I had this vision of mice turning wheels turning cogs turning drums which contained narrow slots that would release bank notes at intervals. These notes in turn would be counted and recounted by other mice before being re-introduced into a new set of wheels, cogs, drums and finally being released back into my mother's hand as she spoke respectfully to the teller, the first mouse in the chain. My father went to work every day at the same time, wearing one of the three suits he owned, and dutifully returned on the same train at the same time every evening, wearing the same suit and a perpetual frown.

'Good day at the office dear? Just sit down and read your paper with this cup of tea while I get your supper. The children have already had theirs so you'll have peace and quiet.'

What a life! Was it a life? Did I have this to look forward to? How did my mother manage? Wendy Rogers had been pretty, vivacious and even adventurous in her youth. She passed eight subjects in GCSE at 'O' level and spent two years in the sixth form studying history and English literature.

'That was a good start Mum so what happened? Why didn't you go to University? Why didn't you marry someone exciting? Why did you stay at home?'

'Well dear, there was my mum and dad to look after you know. Your grandfather had fallen and injured himself at work on the factory floor and my mum was already suffering from lung cancer. They had no one else in the family to earn any money and no one to look after them. My younger brother Ronnie was born with a hole in his heart as you know dear and so he couldn't do any work. What else could we do?'

'So after all that schooling, all that effort you went out to work in an office?'

'Yes Andrew, I really didn't have any choice. I had responsibilities. That's what happens as you grow up love. Suddenly you find that life catches up with you and things don't go as you planned them. But, I was lucky. I found your dad and that made a big difference.'

'Don't see how you think you were lucky. You still look after your parents and now you have our family to look after as well. Didn't you want to do something different? Didn't you want to get out and enjoy yourself? Come to think of it where did you meet dad? I can't really see him down at the local pub or at any dance hall.'

'No love, we met in Sainsburys. I was pushing my cart and just as I turned the corner of the aisle your dad came round the corner and we bumped into each other. He was trying to carry his groceries around in his arms and when I knocked against him they all cascaded down onto the floor. I apologised, he apologised and we ended up going to the pictures.'

My mother sighed as she looked at me. 'He was good looking Andrew. He didn't have his bald patch at that time. He was friendly and could tell funny stories. Already he was doing well in the bank with a responsible position. It looked like an improvement in my life. Suddenly I had someone to help with money and support. I had someone to share things with. Someone to talk with and listen about my life.'

'But didn't you have any friends Mum? Didn't you have any old friends from school or even the office where you worked? Did you ever go out when you were working at that office? Didn't you go to dances, the pictures, even out on shopping trips up in the West End with some girl friends?'

Somehow I couldn't imagine not having friends to do things with. At school I had lots of friends, and every week, at least on Friday and Saturday nights we were out somewhere.

On weekends if we weren't playing matches three or four of us would go out to the local parks and kick a football around or just race round on our bikes.

As I lay in bed I cast my mind back to the times out with the chaps at school. We had hiked a few times in the countryside, although most of those trips weren't the best. In the local parks we had played tennis, gone rowing, even gone sailing a couple of times but after Peter fell in the water and nearly drowned we stopped that. Of course we had always gone out down to the shops and ogled the girls. Going to an all-boys school it was important to be seen as a girl chaser. None of my closest group had girl friends so there was always a lot of banter and hopes, not that any of us really knew what we would do if we did meet any girls.

My mum had asked me whether I wanted any girls to my party. When she asked, my younger sister Susan giggled and told mum that I didn't know any girls so who could I ask?

'But you must know some girls Andrew? Doesn't your school have dances or matches against girls' teams or something? I realise they don't play rugby but aren't some of your tennis matches against mixed doubles?'

'Mum, you may remember that I don't play doubles, and I'm not old enough to go to school dances. The school doesn't let pupils in until they are in the sixth form. Even then, listening to the chaps in the sixth, it doesn't sound like a huge success. Most of the lads don't have much idea about dancing.'

'Maybe I should teach you Andrew. You really ought to know a little bit about how to hold a partner, where to move your feet. I could find some of my old records and I could teach you to dance.'

'You'd probably need to wear boots Mummy to protect your feet,' giggled Susan. 'Although perhaps Andrew is quick on his feet from playing his sports. Are you light-footed brother dear? I think I'll watch if you're giving lessons Mummy.'

Girls I thought, the great unknown. Still, not really relevant to the primary question. I still had two years to go at school and the academic part is fairly straightforward but the question is still tennis or rugby? I suppose that decision may affect what I should take in the sixth. If I played either of the two sports there is a time limit or an age limit when the body can't cope with top level ability. Do I want to be a coach, or a trainer? I know I don't want to go up to the city every day on the same train and see the same people like dad. As I closed my eyes my brain flashed pictures of sweeping passing movements along the line of three-quarters and the winger going over for a try in the corner. The crowd at Twickenham roared approval. Then my brain jumped to a sequence of three aces in a row to win the first set six-four on Centre Court. The balls slowed down, the brain quietened and I slept my way into my sixteenth year.

The next day was Saturday, and although my dad didn't have to go to work I had to go to school. In the morning I attended the usual five lessons. Being in the fifth form with serious exams at the end of the year meant the workload was high. We had French followed by History and then Geography. After the mid-morning break we had two periods of Mathematics with trigonometry. I day-dreamed a little trying to apply forces, angles, distances into directions and parabolas of tennis balls but got side-tracked into memories of a recent match and didn't hear the question.

'Mr. Mills, are you with us today? Does your busy schedule allow you time to join us for some mathematics? Would you like to explain the last example I was describing?'

'Yes sir, no sir, I didn't catch all of the question sir.'

'True Mills, but let's hope that your concentration improves this afternoon and you manage to catch the football.'

Laughter ran around the room at my discomfort.

'Homework will encompass pages forty nine to sixty two and that includes the exercises on page fifty three. There will be a test next Tuesday. And Mills, I expect a try this afternoon in lieu of your apparent absenteeism this morning. Dismiss.'

The room echoed with the closing of books, banging of desks, shuffling of feet and released chatter of boys' voices. We all filed out and dropping our books off in our lockers we hung about before lunch.

'Has Dampier posted the team for this afternoon yet?'

'I haven't seen it. It wasn't on the board at break.'

'Was the First XV team posted?'

'No, there was nothing on the Sports Board.'

'Hell, how am I going to know what to eat if I don't know whether I'm on the team?'

'Barker you gluttonous pig, you eat everything and anything so it doesn't matter whether you're on the team or not.'

'Suppose John Harkness is still captain for us?'

'Makes sense. Playing fly-half lets him see both the scrum and where we are on the pitch. He's a good head anyway.'

Seeing that it was the middle of December it was wet, and a cool wind blew the grey overhead clag about in the sky. The opposing School Teams had arrived with both their First XV and a Colts team to play us. Kick-off was at two in the afternoon and it would be almost dark by the final whistle.

One for all I thought as fifteen rowdy boys undressed and put on their rugby gear for an afternoon of excitement. Jockstrap, black shorts, black and blue hoops on the shirt, same for the socks and then the boots. Check the cleats were all there and screwed in tight. Tighten the laces and flex the foot inside. Ready for action.

'Right chaps. They don't look very big but I remember from last year they had two really fast wingers. So, the scrums we should win as we're really good there. Harry, you're the key man in the line-outs. Freddie, as the lock and with our extra power we may let you keep the ball in the scrum and dribble it several times. We'll just see how that goes. Now, out in the backs,' and here John looked at Tim, Lance, Ken and me. 'We'll keep it tight and safe to start with and see how strong they are. I seem to remember their full-back being slow and not too good with his hands so I may kick a few up and unders. I'll pass the word. Otherwise, just play hard. Should be our game to win. Let's get out there.'

The pitch was wet and muddy with all the rain and as the opening whistle blew a gentle drizzle started. My mum and dad don't come to our matches, unlike many of the other parents. I suppose dad likes to relax after a hard week's work turning the cogs in the bank machine and mum just has so many other things to do. Every weekend she's over at her parent's house helping them with groceries, cleaning, and cooking a few meals for the week. Her younger brother Ronnie is on a disability pension but he does do things around the house and he has learnt to cook which does help mum. Still, I wish dad would come out the odd time just to see me play. Even when I got selected to play for the County dad didn't come to the game.

Still, I suppose I was lucky. With a weight of thirteen stone and standing six feet tall in stockinged feet I was a force to be reckoned with on the rugby pitch. The other good news was that I could run. Sure, I wasn't a sprinter for the Athletics Team but for thirty or forty yards I could really run. With my weight and speed I played as a three-quarter on the team. Tim was outside me on the left as the winger and on my right I had Lance and then Ken as the right winger. Patrolling behind us with his two good kicking feet was Rory MacKenzie. As a full-back Rory was amazing. He could make the ball curve really well to gain distance along the touch lines and he was fearless as a tackler. With a mop of unruly red hair he was the personification of a wild highlander. Friends, team-mates, one for all. The whistle blew and we were off.

As the game started the rain decided to pelt down more seriously, and soon the field became super slippery and the ball harder to hold. We had the superior scrum and we won all our put-ins and we kept the back line close together for shorter safer passes. Their tackling was good and with the soft conditions you could do flying tackles with impunity. The match was tight and at half-time we led by seventeen to ten. After we had taken the plate of lemons over to the opposing fifteen John got us all huddled together on the touch line for a quick couple of comments.

'Fine chaps, we're in charge of the game and we just need to keep the pressure on. Scrum, you're doing really well given the conditions. We're winning all of our balls and upsetting them a lot in their line-outs. Now the wind's behind us in the second half and so I will probably try a few high kicks. The ball is really slippery and that will make it tricky for their full-back to catch. Andrew, Lance, I'll keep the ball high and down the middle, away from their fast wingers. Your power and speed should result in some turnovers. I'll try not to kick it too far down the pitch to give the scrum time to reach any loose ball. We'll just punch a big hole down the middle.'

We huddled in the rain and darkening gloom. Steam rose from our sweating bodies. The team felt together. The all was doing well. I looked around me and I felt good: great game, great time and good to be alive. The referee blew his whistle and away we went for the second half.

John kicked the ball high in the air down the middle of the pitch. Lance and I had both seen John's signal and with Tim and Ken on the wings we had swept down the field encircling the ball. Their full-back was in the right position but not prepared as I jumped as high as I could to catch the ball. My forward momentum thumped me against his body with my hips bouncing off his chest. As he fell backwards I struggled to find a firm landing for my feet in my forward rush. I managed to avoid planting my left foot in his face but my right foot caught his arm and I half stumbled. As I was about to pitch forward I caught sight of Lance just ten feet off to my right. A quick flick and I moved the ball laterally into his safe hands as I ploughed my nose and forehead into the muddy turf. My momentum turned my head into a ploughshare for a brief moment and I could hear the pounding of boots going past my body as my ears were pressed against the sodden ground. Within seconds though I heard the cheers, and I slowly picked myself up to see Lance had successfully scored a try between the posts. Teamwork: great scrum, good protection from the flankers, steady hands from Doug our scrum-half, spot-on kick from John and just as he suggested – drive a big hole down the middle. Result, five points and two more for the conversion; way to go.

We kept our shape and our dominance for another five minutes before the final whistle blew and we ran over to the touch-line to line up. John organised us in the two lines and we clapped and cheered as our opponents filed off between us and we all agreed it had been a great game. The rain poured down and it was hard to see across to the far touch line in the gloom. Five minutes later we were all shouting and splashing about in the large concrete bath trying to get the mud out of our toes, our finger nails, our ears and for me out of my nose! The team celebrated its win, its togetherness and how well we all did. When we heard that the First

XV had been beaten and we had won we felt even more successful and bragged of more wins to come. A great time was had by all.

Back home mum had returned from her parent's house and was sitting quietly watching television. My sister Susan was contentedly playing with her doll's house and my little brother Norman was colouring. Dad snoozed in his armchair by the fire.

'Good game love?' my mother asked in a whisper. 'Quietly Andrew as your dad's asleep.'

I walked over to my mother and sat down at her feet. 'Yes Mum, it was good. We won. Wish dad would come out to some of our games though. Most of the other chaps' parents are out there Mum. He should see me play, especially after I got selected for the County team for kids my age. I'm good Mum, really I am.'

'Sure you are Andrew. Of course you are good love. You wouldn't have got selected otherwise. You said that there were people at that County game looking for young players like you for the National team didn't you?'

'Yes Mum. A couple of them spoke to me after the match and asked what I wanted to do with my life. You know, they wondered whether I was going to play rugby seriously. Whether I wanted to play as a career?'

'I don't know about that Andrew. Wouldn't that cost a lot dear, and what about schooling and a job? Would you want to do that?'

'Dunno' Mum. Suppose I'm not really sure. What do you and dad think?'

'Daft I think,' said dad as he stirred in his armchair. 'What's the point, running around in the rain for a couple of hours chasing a ball? And after that, after you've got injured or just can't cut it, then what?

What sort of career is that? After all the time and money we have put into your schooling you going to throw it all away on playing football?'

'Rugby Dad, rugby not football.'

'What's the difference? If you do that all you'll have as you get older is an ability to drink. What sort of education is that then? No, go into the sixth Andrew and then get a good steady job. Take some responsibility son. Map out a career for yourself like I did. School, College, working at the same time of course, and then into a safe steady job. That's how it is done. Look at my dad as an example. He worked his way through school and then into apprenticeship. His family couldn't afford College and anyway it wouldn't have made sense with him going into the insurance business. He did well and that helped me get a good education. Same with you and your brother. I do well and so you both go to good schools with real opportunities in front of you. Support this family I do Andrew. My salary pays for everything: the house, food and your schooling young man so don't you forget it. You'll have to think pretty soon what you're going to take in the sixth so you can get your life channelled into the right College. Important to meet the right people. Make the right contacts. What do they call it today, networking isn't it?'

'Yes Dad. The Careers Officer at School came and told us all about that. He thought I had an aptitude for sports though. When he heard that I had been selected for the County in rugby, and won those junior tennis tournaments with a chance of Wimbledon next year, he was quite excited. He thought I should seriously think about a career as a professional sportsman. He thought I had potential.'

'Andrew get real son. Only the very best people do that. I mean really the best. That's not us son. I don't do any of those things and your mother never has done. Where do you think you've got any talent from? It doesn't just happen son. All the top people had parents who were good. No, doesn't make sense Andrew. Stick with the things you know like I did. Work hard and take responsibility for your life. Don't you agree Wendy?'

'I don't know Richard. Maybe Andrew here needs to expand his horizons. Think outside the usual careers. I used to play tennis as a girl and was quite good at it if I remember right. I even won a few junior junior tournaments.'

'I never knew you played tennis Wendy. You've never said before.'

'Well I had to drop it didn't I Richard, when dad had his accident? I had to drop everything: school, play, everything and look after my parents and young Ronnie. There wasn't time for things like tennis but I was good when I was young. Maybe, just maybe Andrew has some of his talent from me.'

My father snorted and picked up the newspaper on his lap. 'See my bank's shares have gone up again. We're doing well. That will help if Andrew decides to drop out of the work force and not make any contribution to this family. Actually Andrew, isn't it time you started thinking about a part-time job? Most of the sons of my colleagues at the office have jobs now. Paying something in to their mothers; paying their way so to speak. I should ask at the Bank and see whether they have any possible part-time work for you. It could be a good experience and you would get to meet some real working people. Once you're in the sixth you'll have more free time.'

'Dad, I will have to work in the sixth you know. It's serious stuff and I'll still be playing rugby for the school team. Anthony Gooch at the Tennis Club asked me the other day whether I would have more time to practice there. He's the Head Pro and he thinks my game would improve if I practised more.'

'Andrew, you've turned sixteen and it's time to think of the future son, time to think of a paying career. So let's have no more of this sport thing can we? It was fun while it lasted but you've got to grow up and join the real world, the working world just like I did.'

I looked up at my mother but she closed her eyes and leant back in her chair. She adjusted the volume controls on the TV and the programme's sound increased a little in the room.

'Mummy I've finished this one. Make me another one. Do it for me now.'

My brother's demanding voice sounded in my ear as he came over to his mother.

'How about me Mummy? Don't I get any attention now? Won't you play with me Mummy while we dress up little Miss Gloria here? She needs a new dress Mummy. This one's dirty and rather torn. Make me a new one Mummy. Gloria needs a new one.'

'And I need a new colouring drawing Mummy. Look at me first. I asked first. I was first.'

I stood up in the room and looked around me. Dad had gone back to his world again and mum was besieged with demands. I went out into the kitchen to check on my tennis clothes. There was a big match tomorrow and I had asked mum to iron my white shorts. Sure enough my best tennis shirt and clean pressed shorts were neatly laid out on the table, along with white socks. I knew my shoes were clean as I had done those myself. I walked out of the kitchen and finding my sports bag I carried it through to the laundry. Careful not to dump any of the rugby pitch that had attached itself to my dirty shorts and shirt on the floor I unloaded my gear into the washing machine. I put in the soap and set the dials. When that was underway I took my boots outside onto the porchway at the back of the house and scraped off most of the mud. With a brush and a bucket of water I sluiced the boots clean and packed newspaper inside to dry them and keep their shape. Back in the kitchen I collected up my clean tennis gear and took it up to my room. From the cupboard I pulled out my tennis bag and three racquets. I slowly fitted everything inside the bag ready for tomorrow. Tomorrow was all for one I thought. Turning on my transistor I quietly listened to some pop music, easy listening and relaxing. I slowly let the excitement of the rugby match drain away, reliving the odd movement and surge of activity, and then gradually let my mind drift into the sharper, more incisive and urgent activity of tomorrow's matches. Singles, one player, just me and all for one.

Next day, the Sunday morning I was up early. Down in the kitchen I got myself a healthy breakfast in preparation for the big match. Lots of fluids I thought: it's always quite dry in that sports complex. All of the other members of the family had decided that Sunday was a day of rest and so it was quiet and peaceful as I checked over my gear for the match. Fan support wasn't a big item in our house but then it was up to me to make my own way in life. What was it my dad had said last night about joining the real world, the working world? Dad I've got to dream: I've got to work at what I do well and despite your comments I play sport well. Other people earn their living that way. Sure, but my dad would just tell me that might be fine for other people but not for the likes of us, we're ordinary. Christ dad, did you ever have any drive and ambition? Mum told me she did but then she explained about responsibilities. At sixteen do I have responsibilities I asked myself? Sure. Be kind, loving, giving, sharing with family and friends but is there anything else? The clock on the mantelpiece struck eight and startled me out of my reverie. Time to go.

'You off then Andrew love?'

'Yes Mum. My first match is at ten and I need to warm up before that.'

'Take care then son. Do well for us will you? Give it your best shot.'

'Sure Mum. I always try and do my best. You and dad coming to my big match this afternoon? You said you might earlier this week. It's a qualification match for Junior Wimbledon you know and I'm still the favourite to win. Can't you come?'

'Maybe Andrew, we'll see. Your dad wanted to repair the garden shed today love. He half expected you to help him I think. He was talking about it yesterday. I think he thought you should pull your weight with jobs around the house.'

'Mum, you've known about this match for weeks now. I've told you how special it is and an opportunity to get to Wimbledon. We can do the shed any time.'

'We'll see Andrew. Just go carefully love anyway. Come here and give your mother a kiss before you go. I love you son, I really do and wish you well.'

I slung my tennis sports bag securely over my shoulders as I wheeled my bicycle carefully out of our small congested garage. It was a thirty minute ride to the sports complex where our indoor courts were. Yesterday's rain had eased off but the temperature had fallen overnight and there were patches of ice in shady corners. The sports hall was crowded and noisy with lots of people bustling about. I changed quickly and grabbed my gear to find my warm-up court.

'Game to Mills. Mills leads by five games to three in the second set,' intoned the umpire. I picked up three balls and scrutinised the covers. Bouncing one of them I quickly rejected it and slipped the second into my pocket. I looked down the length of the court at my opponent. Reginald Thomas stood six feet six, even at age sixteen, and had long arms to add even more reach to that elongated frame. He was good and quick on his feet. Trouble was he couldn't control his back hand. Trouble for him that is. I threw the ball high in the air and swung the racquet around and up with my left arm to catch the ball in the middle of the face on a slightly descending and sideways action. This put topspin and sidespin on the ball and when it caught the centre line it spun sharply away from lanky Mr. Thomas. Although he had been guarding the centre line and offering more space on his forehand side I thought I could pull him out of balance on his backhand side. True he managed to catch the ball with the frame of his racquet, and as luck would have it the ball came straight back weakly over the net, but it was an easy put away on his forehand side. He was already off balance from his first return and I was fifteen love up.

Okay Andrew, think again mate and now what to do? He will expect a ball angled well out of court on his backhand side again. Look where he is standing? Yours to call Andrew, yours to think through. You and you alone in this game. One more bounce and decide where to aim. I stood with my front right foot nudged up close to the centre mark. I looked towards the side line next to Reginald. Another hard flat serve down the centre line resulted in a convincing ace.

On my third serve my opponent decided to change tactics and he chipped and charged. I had served my first ball into the net and my second was decidedly short. There he stood, this gangly spider hovering over the net awaiting my return. In that split second flash when I looked at him he seemed to be able to cover the entire net so over the top then. My topspin lob was good and sent my opponent scrambling fast to the back of the court. However, the lob wasn't good enough for me to charge the net and avoid a well placed passing shot and so I quickly positioned myself at the centre of the baseline. Just as well really as Reginald got round my lobbed ball and hit a real flat blaster to my forehand. Sure I reached it and used the power of his shot to return the ball but his placement had pulled me out of position and he neatly finessed his drop shot to leave me flat-footed. Thirty fifteen.

I looked around me. The seating area around the court was full and the crowd attentive. They were all watching. They were all watching me.

So play Andrew, play. Concentrate son and win this with brains as well as brawn. They talk about the loneliness of long distance runners; well in many ways I felt just as lonely. It was all up to me. I served hard and flat into the body and Reginald was jammed trying to use his forehand and pulled the ball into the net. Game point. Set point. Match point.

It was somewhat anticlimactic really as I repeated my first serve of the game and Reginald couldn't reach it. A clean ace and a great way to finish I thought as I came up to the net to congratulate my opponent on a fine match. I'd won six four and six three.

The next and final match of the day for me was still two hours away. Well maybe a shower and a cool off would be in order and top up the fluid levels.

'Hi Andrew. Great game. You looked real good out there.'

'Hi Donna. Thanks. Was a good game. Reginald's all arms and legs and they seem to extend on the court.'

'Hey Donna, what you doing with my nemesis?' Reginald walked over and folded his long arms around Donna. 'Did I say you could talk with the opposition?'

'No Reginald love but I thought I would congratulate Andrew as no one else appears to be doing so. Your parents not here Andrew? Thought your young brother might like to see his older brother do so well, sort of hero figure. I always supported my brother Robert when he played tennis.'

'Well done young Mills,' said Mr. Thomas as he came over from a group of his friends. 'I was just saying to my wife how well you play against our Reginald. You use your head as well as your hands and feet. I could almost hear you thinking out there during that last game. It's nice to see someone use their brain in this game. Reginald, you think about that son?'

'Er no Dad. What should I have done?'

Mr. Thomas laughed and put his arm around his gangly son. 'Take a leaf out of young Andrew's book. What's Andrew's weakness?'

'Dunno Dad. Don't think he's got one. Have you Andrew?'

Now it was my turn to laugh, but as I thought about the question there was something. I looked at Reginald standing there with his father's arm around him and his own arm wound around Donna.

'Maybe not a weakness Reginald but you've certainly got something I don't have.'

'Which is Andrew?' asked Mr. Thomas.

'Support before and after the game,' I said. 'Sure I know it's singles, and it's all for one out there on the court, and you have to play your own game, but it must be nice to have the support off the court.'

'Good thought Andrew,' said Mr. Thomas.

'I'll give you a hug,' added Donna and she wriggled out from under Reginald's arm and wrapped her own arms around me. 'Well done Andrew,' she whispered in my ear.

I blushed and stood there probably looking a little foolish. 'Thanks,' I stuttered and turned away to find somewhere less public. I walked back to the changing rooms and took a shower. Sitting on the bench I thought about the morning. There was the anticipation before the game: the sizing up of the opponent and the internal searching of how did I feel today? Was I up for it? Was I hungry enough for it? That had all gone well and I had enjoyed the game. All my shots were there and I managed myself well on the court with good positioning. I had lots of energy and mixed up my game with different tactics. Overall I had concentrated on Reginald's weaker backhand as a match strategy and that had been successful. Yes Andrew I told myself, you did okay kid. Inwardly I laughed.

My opponent in the more important afternoon match was a relatively slender Japanese youth with arms like steel and bullet-like deliveries. He was left-handed like me and this always causes me to rethink how best to attack. When he served his shots were typically flat and fast: there was little if any finesse but his placement was spot on.

I won the first set in a tie-break and felt drained. My opponent bounced down to his end of the court and juggled three balls about on his racquet. He selected a suitable pair and turned his inscrutable face towards me. Game on Andrew. I looked, I saw, I heard, I acted, I ran, and how I ran. He was good and within twenty minutes I was down five two. Think Andrew. What have you seen kiddo? Where are the weaknesses? He's moved from side to side very successfully on that baseline but has he ever come in to the net? Can he volley? Can he run forwards and backwards as well as sideways? Down five two and thirty all. Think dam it.

My two flat aces moved the score to five three. I wiped the handle of my racquet with my towel and decided to change tactics for his serve. There was some interrupting noise in the crowd for a moment and my opponent turned and walked back behind the baseline. Looking up I noticed that Reginald and Donna had come in and were sitting in the area reserved for players. Donna smiled and turned her thumb upwards. Well not quite all for one I thought as there's at least one person cheering for me.

Two chopped backhands cut with backspin crawled over the net and I was leading love thirty in this ninth game. The third time I tried this the ball failed to crawl over the net. Okay Andrew, think about some variety lad. The next serve had less pace on it and I crushed it into the corner and well away from my opponent's backhand as he rushed the net. Unfortunately the following serve traced a line virtually down the centre of the court and I couldn't reach it with my forehand. Now when serving into the ad court a lefthander will typically curve the ball towards the edge of the court and spin it away from a righthander. What would my opponent do against me, a southpaw? The serve came straight at me, trying to jam me but I moved my feet very quickly to my right and I hit a flat forehand into his backhand corner. Five four and me to serve. Breathe again Andrew but keep those brain cells linked boy. We crossed over and I had a chance to smile at Donna as I passed by the net. Even Reginald grinned back at me. However it was lonely by the time I got to the baseline and organised the balls for my serve.

I would sooner forget the next fifteen minutes. Perhaps the emotion of going solo overwhelmed me. I didn't see or hear the crowd. All I heard was the swish of the ball and the flat tones of the umpire. Second set to Yokomura. One set all. Yokomura leads by one game to love; two to love; three to love in the third set. Andrew lad your future's a little on the line here. What did dad say about work, meaningful work, wage-paying work? Are you serious about this said the gremlins in my head or is this just play? You bet I said, I'm bloody serious about this. Well then lad, pull your finger out or it will be a long ride home – a long lonely ride.

Chip and charge; two successful drop-shots, a couple of topspin lobs and one phenomenal cross-court passing shot all helped. Gritting my teeth and setting my mind back into gear I changed the score back to three games all and boosted my confidence in the process. I can do this. I know I can. Still, let's do this one step at a time; one point at a time. Yokomura had a similar game plan. Without it being obvious he took some of the pace off one or two of his serves and I overhit the ball beyond the baseline. Suddenly a very sidespin second serve appeared and I lifted the first two or three of these too high only to see them thunder past me. Match point. My throat was dry. My legs ached. Stop whining Andrew. It's all up to you now, you and you alone. Great return. Deuce.

With no tie-break in the third set we reached seven games all. Then eight-seven. Then match point. My match point this time. Breathe. Look, think, see it and then do it. Yokomura expected my serve to curve away pulling him off the court as his forehand was not as strong as his backhand and he knew that I had seen this. Now if he knows this and he knows that I know this he might think I will serve down the centre to his backhand. And then again…..! Andrew son, this is all set for you to win so go for it and stop pissing about. Look, and see he is standing more to his left expecting the forehand. Think, if you serve down the centre line and go to the net he will not have any angle to pass you easily. See it, see the shot right down the centre line and his possible return straight at you for you to volley away. Fine, so do it. I hit that first serve so well right down the centre line, well out of reach of his backhand, and a full inch over the service line. I smiled inside and took a deep breath. Full of confidence now I hit the same shot for my second serve but this time it was a full inch inside the service line and the game, the set, and the match were mine. Have faith Andrew.

Cycling home that night I smiled inside again as I relived the weekend. There was the anticipation, the excitement of the action and the joy of winning on Saturday when we all shared that great rugby game. Then the Sunday brought the initial first game challenges, which we dealt with, leading to this just passed fantastic afternoon. You thought it all out Andrew. You mate, you, your brain, your body and all your crazy mixed-up teenage emotions. The bus driver however didn't allow for Andrew's unexpected skidding of his bicycle tyres on an icy patch and the back wheels of the bus crushed Andrew and his brain, his body and all his emotions. Any one for all and all for one thoughts drained away on the cold wet street as Andrew's whole life came to an abrupt end.

PLAYING FOR PRINCIPLES

COMPARED TO OTHER PEOPLE I thought I was lucky, gifted really. Just turned sixteen and signed up with a Premier Division Team. Sure I'd been working at the Club for years now. I'd picked up towels and other gear from the changing room: chased balls over the pitch and out of the stands: helped with line painting and fixing the nets. I'd have done anything just to be there, at the Club, on the pitch. Sometimes I would stand on the playing field with a ball at my feet and just imagine. I could hear the crowd; hear the cheers, the shouts and the cries to pass or to shoot. Swinging my leg I sent the ball gently curving into the top corner of the net.

As a really young child I had played in our street with all the other kids. Playing assie we called it: short for playing on the asphalt, the surface of the road. Sometimes we played with an old tennis ball but occasionally one of us would have a real football. Pickup games with coats or woollies for goals and front gardens providing the sidelines. Four kids, six kids, whoever was around and had time on their hands. Sometimes, on the weekends, a few of the older lads would play, and occasionally one or two of the dads. Friendly lively competition it was with lots of shouts and a wide array of skills.

I lived in a working class neighbourhood in our town. All of the dads worked somewhere or other and most of the mums worked too. We all lived in row upon row of terrace houses with non-existent front gardens and a small narrow strip out back that was usually reduced by the outdoor privy. Four streets over, by a bend in the river we had a municipal park. Perhaps the river was a flood plain and too dangerous to build houses. Still, when our houses were built, before the turn of the century, I doubt whether anyone would have cared about flood plains. Anyway, it was good for us because we had this park. Well it would have been good if the park got any attention. No, that's not true because the park did get attention but from the wrong people. Homos hung out around the bogs. Drug dealers lurked in the shadows of a few big old trees and kids skidded their bikes over any grass that challenged the bare gravel.

A few of us had tried to organise some real football matches in the park but the ground was rough and the sharp stones cut knees and legs in hard tackles. There were no lines and no goal posts. It was an uphill challenge, even if the game was on flat ground!

In contrast, just two streets the other way was the Club. Big stadium with stands on both sides. We all stood in those days. Why do you think they are called stands then? But our Club was posh and in the main stadium they had seats. The terraces at both ends behind the goals had crush barriers to make sure no one got hurt in the excitement of seeing a goal scored. The pitch itself was regulation size but there was little spare room before you were over the sideline and into the crowd. But to stand there, to stand in the middle of the pitch and just turn round and round and imagine. Magic, that was magic when I was really young.

'Taylor, Taylor, you quite done just turning round and round out there son? This is a practice sunshine not a bleeding fairground. You going to join us or pretend you're a bloody merry-go-round?'

'Coming coach, coming.'

I ran over and joined the rest of the squad. This was the junior team and I suppose I felt a bit pissed off as I had expected to be training with the senior team. Just a week ago I had come into the Manager's office with my dad and a solicitor friend of his. Dad and I agreed that I really didn't want any poncy agent. What we wanted was real simple. The Club knew how good I was. They'd seen me play for over four years now and most of the players had told me I had potential, good potential. I hadn't hid my ambition about wanting to play for this Club, my Club, and the only Club which held my interests and passions. Sure I wanted to play football professionally but I only wanted to play for my home team. The Club had thought I was good enough to join them. In fact they were quite anxious to sign me up before anyone else heard about me. That Monday afternoon dad had taken time off work. He was a bricklayer, a master craftsman, and his foreman knew all about me, Pete Taylor.

'Harry, go and sort your son out,' the foreman had told dad. 'Young Pete's good mate, real good. He'll be a credit to the Club and we could do with some young talent. The last couple of games they've been playing like a Second Division Team, team of old women. All of us around here support that Club and we'd all like to see it do better. So Harry, get him signed up and make sure he understands we're counting on him. Tell that old fart of a Manager, Mr. take-it-easy Roberts that the kid needs to be on the First Team this season. He's good Harry. So, take the afternoon off and get it sorted mate.'

The three of us walked through the imposing main entrance and up the stairs towards the administration area. Dad had never been in this part of the building and he was impressed with all the fittings and furnishings, especially the big trophy cabinet.

'It's a good Club Dad,' I said rather proudly. 'Been here a long time now. Has a good record over the years. In the top division most of its time.'

'Yes son,' dad had said, 'and it's our Club.'

The Manager's secretary was Rosie Gartner and I'd met her around the Club several times. 'Just sit down Mr. Taylor and you too Peter. And you're Mr. Young sir, is that right? Mr. Roberts will be with you in just a minute. Can I get you anything, a cup of tea perhaps?'

'No thanks Miss Gartner,' dad said. 'We'll just bide our time here thanks.'

The meeting with Mr. Roberts and the Club lawyer went well. They were surprised about how little money I wanted although they tried not to show it. My dad let me explain my future ideas and thoughts.

'Mr. Roberts I want to explain one or two things that are perhaps a little different for me. I don't want to appear presumptuous but you know all about me as a player. You've seen me often enough now but over and above playing I want to make sure about a couple of other things. Can I take the time?'

'Sure Peter. It'll be good to get things spoken out right from the start. Go on son.'

'First and foremost Mr. Roberts I want to play and do well, do my best in fact. Not only in any of the matches but also in practice, in the gym, wherever. Second, I only want to play for this Club. I don't want to be traded. I'm not chasing money Mr. Roberts and my passion is this Club. Thirdly, I'd like the chance to get involved and help the local kids of our streets. All around this Club Mr. Roberts are your young fans. They live around this ground and they are passionate. I'd like the chance to get them off the street and into better games on pitches. Our local park Mr. Roberts could be a great place and I think with some help I could get them organised and into local matches. Give them some pride and a chance to practice what they see here most weekends.'

Mr. Roberts laughed. 'Think any of them are any good young Peter?'

'I came from the local streets Mr. Roberts,' I said. 'There'll be others like me. You'll see.'

'Okay son, okay I hear you. Anything else?'

'One more thing Mr. Roberts, just one more. I realise that I can't play football all my life and I would like to work towards that time with improving my education. I want to finish school and try to get to College. I'd like to try and get some professional training in both sports and business.'

'Thinking of becoming a manager then are you?' Mr. Roberts asked.

'Don't know exactly Mr. Roberts but I would like to have a sensible future, an educated future. Whether I become a coach, a trainer or whether I leave the game completely I don't know. I'd like to think my future here is with the Club long-term, and with the local streets, but I'd like to have time to work towards this. I'd like to think that you and the staff here can work with these requests. I'm not costing you any fortune, as well you know, but I would like you to think on these ideas.'

'Peter, you've got it all mapped out son. Things change you know. You're what now, just turned sixteen and you think you know it all? I'll make a note Peter and your dad's friend here can work with Mr. Phillips to come up with some sort of contract. No doubt you've talked all this through with your dad and that's good. Leave it with the lawyers now. You concentrate on the football. Mr. Taylor, thank you for coming in with Peter. He's a good lad and we all think here in the Club that he'll help our future. Good afternoon to you all.'

So there it was. I signed up with the Club and set about becoming the best young football player England had seen for a while.

Two years went by and it all came true. I was good. Not only did I play for the first team all of the time but I also played for my country. My scoring record continued to climb. Mr. Roberts honoured my requests but then he was saving the Club a fortune anyway. I continued to ask for relatively little money and there was lots of speculation in the media why I didn't transfer and play for real money. A couple of the other top teams talked about the offers they would make me but I wasn't interested. My Club was important to me. I also had the chance to work on my other ideas. With some juggling of schedules I managed to finish High School and get good marks. Soon after the start of the new football season I enrolled in University and managed to explain how I would try and fit professional football into my studies. I started off with Physical Education plus some basic Business courses. I also looked at the requirements for kinesiology. Might be helpful if I end up a trainer or a coach I thought.

My real interests though were with the local kids. Although I wasn't claiming a fortune in salary I was well enough paid to have some spare change. I didn't buy a house or drive a flashy car. In fact I never moved out of my mum and dad's house just down the street from the Club. My lifestyle really didn't change and so after we fixed up the bathroom at home I started talking to the local council about the park.

Now you have to realise that I had played football in our local streets all my life. As I became a bit of a star for the local Club nearly everyone recognised me around our neighbourhood. It was easy getting to talk with both the kids and the parents. For an autograph I managed to persuade some of the blokes that if we could offer to do a little bit the council would find a way to improve the park. I told them all I had offered to pay for most of the changes, and we would find a way to reduce the vandalism and look after any improvements. I took several of the dads and a couple of the mothers over to the council office and we all started to understand how this could benefit the neighbourhood. Several of the kids started to get excited about the idea too and over that autumn I managed to pay for a renovated changing room complete with showers and toilets. We also talked with the local builders and put together goal posts and netting that came from the local hardware store. From the Club I found an old line painting machine hidden away in a corner and we salvaged that to fix up some lines.

The hardest part was working out the teams, but then dealing with people is always the tough part. Traditionally we had played one street team against another but I wanted to change that. That had led to street gangs and warfare; turf wars and stupid animosity. If we were going to do this and really help the entire neighbourhood why don't we deliberately mix up the players? After some begrudging arguments we had street teams but each team had to include at least four players from other streets. At first we just had eight teams with all kids up to age sixteen but as the idea became successful we managed to run young teams for kids still in Primary School.

I can still remember that first match. It was a Sunday morning and nearly all the neighbourhood was out in the park that day to watch. Here was Peter Taylor about to score another success or maybe fall on his face. My dad was out there with me and I was the referee. One of the teams was based upon our home street, the Lambton Road Lions, and they were playing against Sheraton Road Rovers. I gathered both the teams together in the middle of the pitch before we started.

'Okay lads. We'll play forty minutes each way with five minutes or so at half time. We've got two touchline blokes waving scarves and what we say goes. This is the first match and we've lots of folks out here watching to see whether this idea works. You all know the rules so let's have some fun but nobody goes mad out here. I don't have any cards but I'll send off anyone who buggers it up for the rest of us. Understood?' They all nodded. I told them we would try and start as we meant to go on and so

I had them line up facing a sideline. Starting from the end one team went down the line shaking hands with the opposition, just like a real game.

Although it was late September it was warm enough for Lambton Road Lions to play stripped to the waist. None of us had any uniforms and the Sheraton Road team players wore a mixture of colours. Actually two of them wore my Club team colours.

'Thought these would help us win Peter,' they told me. 'You always do well in these colours.'

'Today I'm neutral,' I replied, 'but good to see you support the Club.'

The game went well and one or two of them had some good ball skills. None of them knew much about playing as a team but then what would you expect if all you had ever played was street football? The Lambton Lions goalie was the young son of our next door neighbour. Dennis was thirteen and already he had good hands. He was wearing a pair of his dad's work gloves from the factory and these worked really well for him. A couple of times he was severely tested with hard shots from Pauli Conti who was a big Italian lad from Sheraton Road. During the game I watched and it seemed that the "foreign" players all seemed part of their respective teams. They weren't left out and at half time each group huddled together to talk about their progress.

The score at half-time was three two for Lambton Lions. I stood and talked with my two volunteer sideline helpers.

'Well Peter, how's it going?'

'We've still got a crowd watching,' I said. 'The game's interesting enough that nobody's gone for the exits.'

'Not like your game three weeks ago Peter. Christ you lot looked awful that match. The stadium was half empty when they blew the final whistle.'

'You're right there Mr. Dodds. We didn't have our game faces on that day. The coach was out of his mind after that game. He threatened to play the entire reserve team for the next match if we didn't smarten up. Still, the match here looks entertaining enough. The kids seem to be doing okay. There's certainly lots of effort out there.'

'Not a lot of skill though Peter.'

'Maybe, but is that the point? Look, we've got a real pitch for a real match. They all seem to be having fun. We've got eight teams set up from the neighbourhood and everyone is talking about it. I've even had a couple of the dads talk about a senior league or something. Anyway, one step at a time eh? Come on, they've had five minutes and the crowd will want a band next for half-time.'

At the final whistle we still had a good crowd, a score of five-five and twenty two lads panting their way off the pitch. The changing room had hot water so they had obviously got that old boiler fixed I thought. It was crowded in the changing room as we had another match following straight away that morning. I had persuaded a Club team mate of mine to referee this second match. Lenny MacDonald was black, spoke with a singsong voice, had a shiny bald head and came from Kingston Jamaica. He was a riot and a good friend. He also came from an even poorer background than I did. His stories of where and how he grew up made me realise how lucky I was to have been born where I had been. Our family may not have had much in the great scheme of things but we had a house, work, food on the table and no rioting in the streets. When I told him what I had been trying to do he thought the idea was worthwhile and he was willing to help. So he was the referee for a match between Dunstan Road United versus the Tewksbury Thrashers.

When we had discussed this overall idea we had agreed that each Team could choose its own name. True, the original eight teams named themselves after their own street but the second half of the name was up to the players. I wondered about the mindset of the lads from Tewksbury

Crescent. This street was probably the poorest in our neighbourhood with the houses on one side of the street backing onto the canal. The terraced row buildings were damp, old, and a number of the occupants out of work. The Thrashers I thought. Well, we'll have to wait and see.

One reason for asking Lenny to referee was so I could wander through the crowd and listen to the comments and see whether the locals thought this idea could work. It was okay for me to have this bright idea and think I was doing good but what did other people think about it? Was I just pissing in the wind or would this work? Most of the kids I had talked with thought it was great, but was it just a flash in the pan, a one of?

Lenny did the same as I did and had the two teams line up before the start. They went through the hand-shaking routine and then Lenny tossed the coin for the captains to choose ends and kick-off. The pitch itself was flat but there was quite a wind blowing up from the river. The Thrashers kicked off and I started my wander through the crowd. Most people acknowledged me and several of the men stopped me and said well done Peter. A couple of the mothers asked me why the girls couldn't play. I suppose I hadn't thought about that. I didn't have any sisters in my family and I had not even thought about the idea. No reason at all I must have said. Can we see whether the idea works first and then if so we can work out how to include the girls? When I got to think about it I suppose several of the girls did play in the street games. I'd just never noticed.

Behind the goals the nets looked okay. Two or three little kids had gathered there to run and collect the balls kicked over the goal line. 'Hi Peter. How come you're not out there playing? You playing next week? You going to coach the Lambton Lions? They could use some help after that last match. Are we going to play sometime?'

'Hi lads. Good to see you out. Collecting the ball for us are you? Thanks, it all helps. Some of your dads were asking about a junior team. Want to play?'

'Sure, all the time. Want to be good like you.'

I carried on to walk down the other side line.

'The Thrashers are a wild bunch Peter, and they've drafted in a couple of lads who work in the brewery, tough lads.'

'As long as they play by the rules Mr. Truscott there's no problem. Lenny out there will keep it all proper. He won't take any lip from any of them.'

'Who gets to play Peter? Can the teams draft anybody?'

'No, not anybody. With a few of the dads we drew a line on the map around our neighbourhood. It's more of less half-way between us and the next tube station on either side. The river bounds us down here and the High Street was the other boundary. We've tried to keep it local to start with. I really wanted our kids to get a chance to play on a pitch rather than just the streets. We had this park and it was sitting here getting vandalised. Seemed a waste. Just thought we could all make a neighbourhood effort.'

'Great shot. See that Peter? That's young Phil Larkin. His dad said he was good. Kid's got a strong boot there. Is this all to get some talent for your Club Peter? You looking for local youngsters?'

I laughed and looked at Mr. Truscott. 'Maybe Mr. Truscott. I started on the streets here. Wish I'd played for the Lambton Lions.'

The group all laughed. 'No Peter, we think you jumped over the Lambton Lions son.'

'No reason we can't find another Peter Taylor though. Enjoy the game. Thanks for coming down and supporting the lads.'

I wandered on and stopped to watch the game. Lenny was good I thought. He was only twenty but he was so fit and fast. He could run backwards faster than most of the lads on the pitch ran forwards. The whistle blew and one of the Thrashers glared at Lenny.

'You fouled him son. You know it and I know it. Free kick for the shirts.'

The half-naked Thrasher player glared again but back-pedalled after Lenny's firm look.

Uniforms I thought. Playing stripped to the waist is okay in September but it'll be a little parky in January. January, wonder whether this idea will last until Christmas even? Perhaps I should talk with our coach. We changed uniforms last season and the season before. What happened to all the old shirts?

Listening to the crowd most of the folk sounded positive. Then again, it was a fine sunny September morning and our neighbourhood wasn't strong on church going. Apart from reading the Sunday papers and the titbits out of the News of the World what else were they going to do? The pubs weren't open yet. Lenny blew the final whistle and I walked across the pitch to say thanks.

'Bit rough in places Peter.'

'They're only street kids Lenny. What do you expect?'

'No mon, I was talking about the pitch not the players. Still some gravel about. You may have to make sure the referee has got a first-aid kit handy. You're going to get some cut up knees and legs out here.'

'The odd cut isn't going to stop any of this lot Lenny. We're street kids and the odd knock or two won't hurt. No disrespect man but we don't have AIDS down here and so a little blood won't hurt. Still, I'll take your comment back to the council and we'll see whether we can tidy up the pitch. Otherwise how did it go?'

'They all had fun Peter. There was a hell of a lot of running mon and the exercise did me good too. Teams are a bit uneven but then you've got kids from sixteen down to what, eleven, twelve? Still, we kept all the rough stuff out of it and even the smaller kids got into the game.'

'It's a challenge Lenny. I've had kids asking me about a junior league.

I've had mums asking me about games for the girls. I've even had some of the dads asking whether we can have a senior league. This is only the first couple of games ever. I was walking around trying to hear what people think and they want grand expansion.'

Lenny laughed and put his arm around my shoulders. 'You don't know what you've started Peter. It's a great idea mon but you've just learnt that once you start something everyone comes asking for another bit of the action.'

'Somehow Lenny, if this does work, I'll need to get the neighbours to help run it. It can become a real neighbourhood project. I know I live here, I'm part of the neighbourhood but they need to get involved too. I suppose like everyone else I've other things to do.'

'You sure have mon and that includes training. You remember training Peter? Round and round, up and down, over and under?'

I laughed at Lenny's comment. 'Sure Lenny, training, and school too for me. I suppose I asked for it back when I first signed up with Mr. Roberts. I told him I had some special requests, unusual requests and one of those was education.'

'You're lucky Peter. I never had the chance for much of that schooling. Not that I had the brains to learn anything if I had gone for very long. But you mon, you keep at it. All the blokes in the Club know you're a little different. Sure we all respect your ability to play football. We know you're good playing up front on the team, and you have the magic boots with your ability to score, but you also think about other things Peter. You've got ambition and you've got principles. I've heard you talking in the Club about players and the good idea about mixing us all together, people from all over. I heard you've done the same thing here.'

'How do you mean Lenny?'

'Well the eight teams you've started all play for different streets around here don't they? Even the names of the teams are the names of the streets.'

'Yes. I thought that made sense to start with. All of the kids here play football in the street. It's how I started.'

'Me too Peter, me too. That's all we had but you went one step further I heard. You wanted to mix the kids up so they got to play with as well as against the next street. You wanted to make sure the whole neighbourhood got involved with each other. To me that's the same as hearing you want to play in the Club with people from all over. What is it you were saying last week, something about United Nations? I didn't hear all your comment but you were arguing for people to help each other not fight each other. Anyway, whatever mate, today was great and I'm glad you asked me to come and help.'

'Thanks Lenny, you did help. I just hope that the next couple of games go as well.'

It was the next year, when I was nineteen, that my ideas came round to smack me in the face. My football for the Club was going well. We were second in the division and playing well as a team. I still managed to score most games and had developed my skills in passing so that the opposition were now less certain whether I would shoot or not. All was fine on that front. At Uni my first year had gone well and I felt confident that I could manage these two activities. The local street league had survived that first experimental year and we had the eight teams all going strong. In the late summer we had started four junior under eleven teams. After some discussions with the council and the parks staff we had organised to play the junior matches across one half of the regular pitch. The parks staff had dug some holes on the sidelines and we could easily put up goal posts for these junior matches. Thirty minutes each way, a shorter pitch and a size three ball made for a good game for the youngsters. Three of the dads took over this junior league and we decided to have the teams coed up to age eleven. That at least pleased some of the mums. So, what was the trouble?

'What's up Peter? You don't look 'appy son?'

'Hi Guido. You're right mate. I've got a problem.'

'Can I 'elp? You know me. 'appy face that's me.'

I laughed and lightly punched Guido on the shoulder. 'That's you all right. You run around the pitch with that permanent grin on your face. Drives the opposition mad that does. You're a cheeky sod to be sure. But no Guido, this letter here asks me to go to the national selection camp.'

'No problem there Peter. You've played for the national team for what two years now? You're a cert. You've always been a problem for my "blue" national team, the Azuri. So what's the sweat?'

'This year is the Olympics Guido, and so this will end up being the selection for the Olympics team too. Why did FIFA want to get itself into the Olympic circus? We've got our own World Cup and a whole host of regional competitions like UEFA. The beautiful game doesn't need the Olympics. It's all about money and I think that stinks.'

'But playing for your country Peter is magnificent, and getting a gold medal at the Olympics is the tops. Best in the world Peter, best nation. We Italians are filled with national pride. Remember when we won the World Cup? We all went wild.'

I sat on the bench in the changing room with the letter in my hands. Now what do I do I thought. Well first of all I'd better talk with the coach, and then see whether I can see Mr. Roberts before any talk gets out. What's the fuss you ask? I had better explain.

Growing up I had been interested in both history and geography. The more I read and looked at maps the more I thought how un-natural and how disruptive country boundaries were. They were often completely ludicrous, like straight lines across large areas. Africa had been carved up by Europeans with absolutely no thought to tribes or races that lived there. Rivers that were often the road for transport of people and goods became national boundaries instead of the thread binding together the peoples on each bank. And then there was immigration or invasion. New Zealand might be logical except the Maoris never came from there originally, and neither did the people of Iceland, Greenland and so on. Interesting historically you might think but then these people after one or two generations become fierce patriots for their "country". It was all so artificial but that wasn't my real concern. All of this might be acceptable up through the nineteenth century but now the world had become crowded and it was time to unite nations not have them fight against each other. National pride might have been fine with all the jingoism of the last century but surely now we needed to join not divide.

But what about competition you say, and what has this got to do with the Olympics? Competition is fine. The earliest Olympics were competitions between individuals and some athletic teams. Good for mankind I say but now they had become Nation against Nation. The media extorted how many medals each country had won. Because of the rules some athletes became "citizens" of other countries for convenience so they could compete. And to top it off it was the winner on the day that got recognized. Money, money, money, sponsorship and whatever yet surely the winners were the athletes who had competed and done better than their previous personal best. Were they recognised? No, the media extolled the fastest, highest and then waved the national flag of the country in your face. Okay okay you say but it was a person who won, an individual and they were the winner, not the country they came from, but what of team sports like football?

If you want to see the best as a spectator then watch a team of the top players irrespective of what "country" they came from. Even as a player

I far preferred to play with a mix of people. Think about it. Don't you see and play in a more diversified environment? I have always thought that diversification and variety are important, especially as we animals on earth get packed tighter and tighter. If you look at nature the species that survive are those that diversify. As I got older and read a little more I learnt a bit about genetics and the need to keep the gene pool diverse. If the strain was too pure you were susceptible to the catastrophic random events that suddenly swept through and you couldn't adapt. No I thought. Diversification is important. Mix us all up.

So what about the Olympics then? Personally I wanted nothing to do with it. I thought the concept had been strangled in the world of politics, intrigue, doping and greed. No way I thought. So if this trial is for a national team for the forthcoming Olympics I want no part of it. Okay coach, I'm going to drop all this on your head just when you thought the team was doing well. I folded the letter and looked up at Guido.

'You got it sorted Peter? You look like you've made your mind up about something?'

I smiled and tapped the folded letter on my knee.

'Sure Guido. I'm about to commit suicide mate so wish me well.'

'I'll never understand you English,' said Guido. 'You keep too much bottled up inside. You are not passionate enough. You're cold like your bloody weather.'

The coach heard me.

'Peter son, I don't understand you that's for sure. You've always been a bit of a mystery lad although you're a champion player. Personally I'm glad if you don't want to play for any national team. It keeps you fit and available for the Club without any other distractions. Still, with you I suppose you've always got those other distractions that keep me guessing what with your schooling and street leagues. Look lad, I'll talk with the Manager and we'll send a letter back to the authorities.'

'Thanks coach. That's a relief. It's like my street leagues coach. We deliberately mixed them up to minimise street gangs and fights.'

'Sure sure son, I hear you. Off to practice now and help me keep my hair black. I've got too many of them turning white.'

I laughed and said, 'Coach you're bald but we'll do our best for you. We'll win this weekend.'

'Get out you cheeky whelp. You'd better win or else.'

Two weeks later someone slapped a newspaper across my face. 'You've got a bloody nerve. You arrogant bastard, after all we've done for you. Going to thumb your nose at your own mother country are you young Taylor?'

The antagonist walked away and left me wondering what that was all about. I didn't have to wonder very long. The dressing room was abuzz with conversation until I walked in and a quiet fell on the room.

'Well Peter, you've sure stirred things up boyo,' said Liam. 'There'll be people out there today wanting your scalp son. You'd better expect a lot of stick and not only from the crowd. The opposition's got a couple of your countrymen on their team and I expect they'll want to put the boot in too.'

'Sure Liam,' I said, 'but I play this game with certain principles. I stand by my principles and I'll fight for them if necessary. I'll stand up and be counted for the things in which I believe.'

'More power to you Peter,' said Nelson. 'Look at me Liam. I've a Nigerian mother who had parents from Ghana and the Ivory Coast, and my dad came from Liverpool. Coming from Liverpool you can bet that half of him was Irish at least. I'm an example of Peter's principles.'

'You're right there Nelson,' said Liam. 'I've never met a more mixed up bastard in my life.'

We all laughed and this eased the tension in the room. The coach came bustling in.

'All right then lads. Just get your heads around the game this afternoon. You know who you're playing against and what they can do. Nothing else matters now for the next ninety minutes or so. Borrowing one of Peter's ideas just play united. You all know what you've got to do, so as the advert says, just do it.'

The game itself went well as we were two teams in the top five of the division and we all played like professionals. As a football match it was good to play and good to watch. My dad was sitting in the stands and afterwards he told me that the crowd enjoyed the game. What was unusual for me however, were the boos whenever I got the ball. With Liam's comments I suppose I should have expected them. I passed. I dribbled. I even scored a goal but there was a lot of static if I got the ball. Okay I told myself, this is your decision Peter so fight the good fight lad. Stand tall and fight for what you believe in.

At the end of the game I shook hands with the referee. He held my hand for a moment. 'A man of principle Taylor - good for you. I may not agree with you son but it's good to see someone use their head for more than just nodding the ball about.'

Walking off the pitch Tom Braithwaite pulled up alongside me. 'You wanna' mix with all those darkies and towheads? Christ, ain't you proud to be who you are? Shit man, we invented this fucking game and you want to play with the savages. What's wrong with going for gold, going for glory?'

'Nothing Tom, nothing at all but I don't want to wave the Union Jack over my head. I want to play for a team that represents Earth and I want to play against another team that represents Earth.'

'Fucking nutter you are Taylor. You've got your head buried in all those books or more likely buried up your arse.'

In the dressing room I got a message that Mr. Roberts wanted to see me.

'Taylor, there you are. Good game son, good game. Always like a win I do and that last goal was a cracker. Well done. Now Peter what are we going to do about all this national team fracas? The Board of Governors discussed this the other day and they weren't happy with all the negative publicity. It doesn't do the share values any good with this sort of comment from our players. You know they want you to play. You've played for the country before. Why won't you play for us now?'

I stood there and thought how I could explain this. Was I really sure about this?

'Mr. Roberts, you just asked me how I could play for you. Well sir, who are you? What I mean to say is you are Welsh, and coach is Scottish. Lionel our trainer is French. I could go on. If I understand correctly much of the money invested in the Club and a couple of the Board of Governors are American. So, play for us now. Who is the "us"? This Club is a mixture, a mini United Nations. The Club is a prime example of my principles. You get the best if you add variety or flavour to the mix.'

Mr. Roberts sat in his chair and looked at me. 'You've thought a lot about this Peter?'

'Yes Mr. Roberts,' I answered. 'Look, I know I'm only nineteen and still wet behind the ears but this is one thing I suppose I have thought about for a long time. It started partly outside our front door, or through our front room window if truth be told. When I was very young we had street fights, lots of street fights. Fortunately the weapon of choice was a catapult and not a gun or a knife like today. Bruises and broken windows were the usual casualties until one day one of the lads lost his eye. That started me thinking and then I suppose I found the library down in the High Street.'

'The library?' asked Mr. Roberts.

'I started to read about countries, fights, wars, boundary lines and all sorts of things. Do you know that two countries even went to war over a football match Mr. Roberts? So much for the beautiful game don't you think, but it was a country versus country match. Then FIFA started to change the rules and we had teams here in England that were real mixtures of peoples. The league improved. Attendance went up. Good players and good coaches wanted to come here. I noticed all this. There was still good competition and the game started to bring people together. You met blokes in the dressing room you would never have met otherwise. You played with lads who had come from many many different places and backgrounds. We all started to understand a little more about each other. Personally Mr. Roberts I thought this was good, was positive. So, when we started out street football league three years ago I thought why don't we do the same thing? Not street against street but lets mix people up and get to know each other. That way we might stop or at least cut down on the street gangs. My mum wouldn't get her windows broke anymore.'

Mr. Roberts laughed and stood up from his chair. 'Peter Taylor, you're different lad. When you first came in this room with your dad and that solicitor bloke you told me you were a little different. I didn't realise at the time what you meant. I'm still not sure you won't surprise me in another couple of years with something else that is a little different. However Peter, I admire you for playing for your principles.'

RATTLESNAKE POINT

'PHEW, IT STINKS IN HERE. It's hot and stuffy. Let's go climbing?'

I looked at him sitting in his cubicle, his fingers flexing and his cerebral controller whirling kaleidoscope images across his desk-top screen.

'Why not? It beats the atmosphere in here,' I replied. 'The fresh air out on the cliff will be a pleasant change.'

I snatched off my controller helmet and swiveled the chair away from my workstation. One or two students glanced up as we threaded our way out of the library.

'Too much thinking can damage you,' said Mike philosophically.

'Watching your screen I thought you were in free-fall,' I replied. 'Looked like you'd become a free-lance artist rather than a nuclear physicist.'

'Nah, just doodling in technicolour fractals.'

Outside the library a gentle breeze stirred the dome-controlled air. In a world where industrial wastes had soured over ninety-five percent of the planet the only habitable places left were all under climate-controlled domes. Outside the domes the environment was a mix of pollutants, acids, and vegetation mutated beyond belief.

'Rattlesnake Point?'

'Yes, that's a good enough place to go.'

'There's a new route been done there last month I want to try.'

'Called?'

'Phew.'

'Any good?'

'Roger Livesey put it up while tripping out. Says he can't remember much of it. His second had to do the description.'

'What's the grade?'

'As a free climb it's 5.14. Roger used finger suction pads for a couple of moves at force 3. His second had to use force 5 for even more moves.'

In the old days climbers graded routes in a progressive decimal system. For roped climbing this started at 5.0 and moved through 5.9 and into 5.10, 5.11, and upwards, becoming progressively harder. Mathematicians argued that a decimal system couldn't go beyond 5.9 before you reached 6.0. Climbers had other things to worry about. Still, this was before the war; before the world needed domes. Nowadays, to climb outside the domes, you need protective clothing and usually helmets for breathable atmosphere. You could buy special suits that came with clusters of suction pads, mostly on the fingers and hands, but also on the feet. The climber could adjust the degree of suction to keep him or her on the cliff. This is a form of artificial climbing, again like the old days but there is no damage done to the cliff with the suction pads. We all thought it was an improvement on the old method of pounding pitons into cracks in the rock.

'I'll go and get my gear,' said Mike.

'Meet me at the theatre,' I said. 'About twenty minutes?'

'Sure, get ready for a gripper.'

The cliff at Rattlesnake Point isn't high. At the most it is only sixty metres. A limestone escarpment gazes out over a desolate valley that used to be green grazing ground for livestock. The animals are all gone now and the trees have been replaced with a spiky shrubby bush that covers much of the ground. These bushes eke out a primitive existence around the green scummy pools scattered across the gravel valley.

'Not like it used to be,' said Mike. 'Remember the turkey vultures and red-tailed hawks?'

'Yea. They were always gliding easily around with no effort riding the updrafts.'

'Looking for climber's sandwiches.'

'More likely the mice that were eating the sandwiches,' I joked.

They've all gone. Very little lives outside the domes. Few people venture outside into the wilds.

Mike and I walked easily although carefully along the top of the cliff. The industrial pollutants had eroded parts of the limestone and there were several fissures in the ground hidden under the degraded soils. We clambered down to the bottom of the escarpment and walked to the foot of our selected climb. In our space suits with breathing helmets this was a sweaty hike. You could turn up the conditioning on the suits to prevent the visor fogging up but it was still hard to see your toes.

We dropped our climbing sacks at the foot of the climb and hauled out the necessary gear including harnesses, climbing rope, slings, karabiners, nuts, shoes and fingerless gloves. In many ways the sport hadn't changed. It was still a leader climbing up protecting themselves as they climbed and trailing a "rope". The material of the ropes had improved with technology but the purpose was unchanged. The leader protected themselves with nuts inserted into natural fissures in the rock and clipped the rope through snaplinks (karabiners) so that in a fall they didn't go too far. The second climber held the rope to protect the leader should there be a fall. The only difference was suction pads. A climber put on special shoes and gloves and both these were equipped with suction pads and integrated with a powerpack on the climber's space suit.

In the old days, before the war, climbers put chalk and tape on their fingers. This helped them grip the rock better. It made a real difference on those hot sweaty days when there was a naked sun. It also helped in the damp fissures when trying to jam the fingers. Nowadays, climbing in a space suit makes for some restricted movements. Suction pads have become another aid for climbers. Exposed skin would suffer immediately from the UV radiation and so gloves and boots are essential.

'Toss for the lead,' I said.

'Naw, this is too hard for you dad,' said Mike.

'Hell junior. I'm all of five years older than you.' I was pissed off.

'Yes, but climbers peak when they're eighteen and you're definitely over the hill. No pun intended.'

I grunted in acceptance. It had been Mike's idea to go climbing in the first place. He started to untangle the rope. Whatever they had done with the technology of fibres they still hadn't overcome the built-in tendency for ropes to tangle themselves, given the slightest chance you know. Very carefully Mike went from one end of the rope to the other. This also was another old fashioned safety procedure that was now irrelevant with the composition of the ropes but old habits die hard.

We put on our climbing harnesses and Mike tied into the sharp end. He was leading. Slowly he carefully sorted out his rack of climbing accessories; slings, nuts, krabs. I found a safe anchor at the foot of the cliff: out of the direct line in case Mike decided to "clean" off parts of the route. With long established practice we sorted ourselves out without having to say much. I tied myself into the trailing end of the rope and arranged my anchor.

'On belay. Climb when ready.'

Simple phrases that hadn't changed.

Mike looked up the cliff trying to see the line. He turned to me and I could imagine the grin on his face as he said 'Climbing.'

Off he went. Left foot moved up onto a small ledge. Right hand up and pulling sideways to the left to stay in balance. Move up to reach a good crack shaped to accept the left fingers. Slide the right foot up to the sloping ramp to ease the strain on the right hand. Simple rhythmic movements. Man against gravity, or something like that.

I watched carefully and paid out the rope so that it didn't pull, didn't get under Mike's feet and yet wasn't too slack. A runner would help about now I thought but didn't say anything. Mike was leading. It was his mind game.

A tapering groove up left proved to be ideal for a #5 hex. Techie talk for Mike being able to slide one of his hexagonal shaped nuts into the cliff and attach the rope through a karabiner.

'Runner on.'

'On belay. Climb away.'

Mike pondered the next section. Eyes skimmed over the surface looking for what Dr. de Bono calls patterns. According to de Bono the brain operates by recognizing patterns. Then it knows what to do. Climbers look for footholds, handholds, and occasionally holds for other more exotic parts of the body! Mike's brain was clearly having difficulties as there were no patterns emerging from the cliff face.

'Miss this bit out and do the next bit.'

I offered this hackneyed climbing suggestion. Often it tends to stir a leader into action, usually vocal and rude.

Mike continued to search. A tentative hand moved upwards and fingertips flexed over a ripple in the limestone. The arm bent and the fingers slid down again. A shallow groove off to the right accepted Mike's boot and the rubber-like compound folded itself around the limestone. A possibility. The left foot found a rounded nubbin about knee-height. A quick combination of these three possibilities let Mike move up another couple of feet and his left hand could reach a flat ledge. Without hanging around too long Mike pulled hard on his left hand and moved his feet up level with his hands to a delicate mantleshelf move.

'Neat.'

'Needs working out.'

'Looked good.'

The simple vocal exchange said it all. The vibrations ran up and down the climbing rope. You could feel the tension, the capabilities, the mind at work, the body responding, the success, the elation. The climbing rope serves a multitude of purposes.

Mike secured another nut in a horizontal crack and checked that the rope ran freely behind him. A series of ledges allowed him to ascend fairly easily another fifteen metres. Some thirty metres above me he rested on what proved to be a comfortable and hard to leave ledge. A vertical crack led upwards off this ledge and Mike managed to insert another nut firmly in the back of this crack.

'This runner is bomb-proof,' Mike said.

'Well, don't test it,' I said. I had no desire to catch a falling leader. I should have kept my mouth shut.

The wind picked up and blasted the polluted dust over us. Mike shivered on the ledge.

'You okay?' I shouted up.

'Sure, just a ghost walked over my grave.'

'Don't even think it,' I said.

'Ever upwards,' called Mike and turned to scan the face above him. It did not look very easy. In fact it looked bloody difficult. From my viewpoint, at the foot of the cliff, there didn't seem to be dam all for another ten metres. The vertical crack appeared to close up. A rounded rib ran up beside it to lose itself in an overhang. The view from Mike's location didn't seem any better. I watched Mike scan to both the left and the right. Apart from that there was a distinct lack of action at Mike's end of the rope.

I made a quick check that my anchor was secure. The rope ran safely through the belay device. Mike was okay. We were in control.

'Dan, this looks hard.'

'And that sounds like an understatement,' I replied.

'What's the description say?' asked Mike.

'Straight up,' I shouted back. 'It says the crux is getting over the overhang.'

'Hell, I can't even see how to reach the bloody overhang let alone get over it,' said Mike.

As Mike was going to be a while I let my mind wander. While doing one sport you often think of situations in others. In golf they say "never up, never in". In climbing the route won't come to you; you have to make the moves. I brought myself back into the present and paid attention to Mike's moves. There weren't any.

Suddenly Mike stepped up on nothing. This is a climbing expression meaning that his foot stayed put by faith and friction. It needed a lot of both. He slid his left hand up the shallow crack. I heard his suction pack come into play as he reached his right hand up high over the smooth face. He let his right foot come up and scrabble listlessly on the bulges. After a brief moment he retreated back to his ledge. I could hear his breathing and imagine his mind waves. Confusion. Challenge. Opportunities? Suggestions?

'What about solution pockets?' I asked as the ever-helpful and supportive second.

'Yeah, throw me up a couple,' said Mike facetiously while he carefully changed feet on the narrow ledge.

Once again the tremors rippled down the length of the rope. My partner was getting gripped up. Again I checked and prepared for fielding an air-borne leader.

'Climbing,' said Mike through gritted teeth. 'Anything Livesey can do I can do.'

'But he was spaced out -- flying they say,' I reminded Mike.

'Well the bugger can't fly upwards,' Mike retorted.

Once again the left hand slotted up the crack and the suction pads whispered into life. The left foot went higher and its pads were in action. Braced on his left side Mike made a quick movement upwards and shot his right hand to the limit and a finger curled into a solution pocket.

'Got you you bugger,' he extorted. The right foot continued to find a friction purchase on the smooth face and Mike pulled hard on his right hand. The left hand he left in the crack and braced itself against the rounded rib as Mike lent his weight to the right to use this left hold effectively. To help this sideways pull he swung his left leg up high to a sideways hold to push. I didn't speak. Concentrate now.

The left toes slipped a little and the suction pads were ramped up. Pressing on his left hand and left foot Mike balanced precariously. The vibrations shivered down the rope.

'Up, up, you little darling,' Mike whispered. He pressed hard on the left hand gripping the rib and spectacularly swung his right fingers up under the overhang. 'Heaven,' screamed Mike as his fingers slotted frantically into a horizontal crack under the roof. He quickly brought his right foot up underneath him and used the suction pads to brace it. The left hand moved rapidly off the rib and joined its partner in the heaven-sent crack under the overhang.

'Looks good,' I said supportively. Mike now had both hands in the crack under the overhang and both feet braced up high underneath him -- crouching on the cliff like a spring under pressure or a primitive ape of prehistoric times. I suppose it all depended on how you looked at it. I just looked upwards and paid attention to my fearless leader. The recorder on the powerpack registered the level of suction applied so Mike knew how he was doing.

'Only at level two,' he gasped competitively. 'Livesey had to have his at level three.' I watched and memorized the moves for when I had to follow. Mike rested with his arms straight to conserve energy.

'The description talks about an acrobatic heel hook to get over the overhang,' I shouted up.

'Got to get a runner in here somewhere,' grunted Mike. 'The next bit looks hairy.'

Actually I thought it looked bloody unreal and remarkably bald rather than hairy. But then I'm an old man and the youngsters of today have no idea about limitations.

Mike tentatively reached a hand over the overhang to try and find a ledge or crack. If there was a heel hook there had to be something to lock the heel over. His fingers chased sideways over the lip searching for the precious hold. At full arm stretch his right hand found an edge.

'Check there isn't one the other way,' I suggested. 'Before you commit yourself.'

'No,' said Mike. 'I'm sure this must be the one. Livesey is left-handed and this will be a left-arm pull. It must be the one.'

'Just look for a moment Mike,' I urged. 'That appears like a gymnasium move. Make sure there isn't a hold off to the left.'

'Dan, shut up! I'm leading this little beauty. Livesey can't pull up on his right arm. It must be this way.'

You're leading I thought. You make the calls. Mike engineered a couple of stoppers in the horizontal crack under the overhang and clipped the rope through the karabiner.

'Runner on,' he whispered, almost to himself. He was into his own head now. I paid attention to the rope and made sure it would run freely when Mike made his upwards moves. He would do them quickly or not at all.

With both hands locked into the horizontal crack Mike swung his right foot up high and tried to hook his heel onto the ledge over the overhang. The heel caught for a moment and Mike turned up the suction pads. With his foot now higher than his head Mike had to push downwards with that heel and pull hard on his left hand to lever himself up over the overhang. There had to be a right hand hold over the roof to reach and pull on. The left leg became a spare wheel at this stage. No, not if there was any edges to brace the left foot on and help lever over the edge. Mike grunted audibly and the sinews on his right calf stood out clearly as he pressed his heel. The right hand came out over the roof and searched frantically for anything? Nothing!

The right hand slid rapidly right and left.

'There's got to be something,' Mike gasped. With his left hand leveraging wildly in the crack beneath the roof and his right heel pressed aggressively over the lip Mike was pushing hard. The right hand continued its exasperated search for a hold. Nothing!

Rapidly Mike shot his right hand back into the crack under the roof. He jerked his heel off the ledge and swung both feet back on the wall under the overhang. For a moment he was hanging on his arms alone before he got his feet organized. Back to square one.

'Phew.'

'That's its name,' I muttered softly. I could see why.

Mike's breathing panted down the cliff. The limestone wall didn't say a word. Still air all around us held the tension. Even my own adrenaline raced for a moment. My hands flexed on the rope and I licked my lips.

I wondered whether you could mantleshelf onto the right edge hold. There is a climb in the Shawangunks of old New York State that has a similar move, although a lot easier. Shockley's Ceiling also goes over a roof to a ledge off right but that has a vertical crack beside it. The ledge and the crack help a combination of pulling, laybacking and mantleshelfing all in an energetic move. I kept quiet. Mike wasn't looking for outside help. He was looking for inner strength. Still, patterns are patterns.

Once again Mike pulled up under the roof with his arms. He moved his right foot up over the lip and braced the heel. Pulling hard with his left arm he walked his left foot up underneath him as high as he could. Cranking hard on the left hand he let his right arm slide over the roof and scurry upwards for help. Again the desperate search for a hold. The strain showed clearly on the calf muscles. By pushing up on the left foot and jamming his left knee up against the roof Mike could almost edge out into space. He braced himself on the edge of all things. The right fingers continued their dance for a hold. I could hear the suction powerpack whine as the forces increased.

Mike was muttering to himself. 'Where, where?' Relying now on the pressure between his left foot on the face and the left knee jambed under the roof Mike let his left hand slide out of the crack. He reversed his hand and used the edge of the roof as an undercut hold. He balanced with much of his body now out over the overhang. The left hand under the roof kept him upright while the right hand stretched and stretched upwards.

'I've got it. I've got you,' he shrieked. The scream of his voice overwhelmed the silence of the suction powerpack. The power had gone. Mike's left foot started to slide. The pressure between the left foot and left knee disappeared. His right fingers smeared down the wall.

'Dan, I'm coming off. I'm coming off.' This was a different shriek.

'Turn up the suction force,' I yelled.

'It's at maximum. I'm off. Falling!'

The lights went up in the theatre. Mike and I undid ourselves from the seats, shoes, gloves, armrests and headsets of our individual virtual reality machines.

'A feelie can sure let you experience the real thing,' Mike said.

'I know,' I replied. 'Phew, it sure stinks in here.'

Mike blushed.

'Yes. I'll have to go and change my pants. That was too real.'

DIVERSITY CAN SAVE US

I'm writing this as I orbit my doomed world in this alien starship, although writing is not the correct verb as I can not write nor can I speak, well not with my mouth and vocal cords. I suppose it is accurate to say that I am communicating with a machine and the machine is transposing my thoughts and words into vocal speech and text so that the humans can understand. This is a struggle, and it has taken me the best part of five of our months to reach this state of ability. You see I think in a base twelve number system and the machines on this starship work in base thirty two, or even base sixty four, so there is a lot of recalculation or translation going on.

Let me introduce myself and you might start to understand the difficulties I am having in producing this story. My name is Melanidopatoq, and this describes my age or life stage, my fertility capability, plus a unique suffix. I once lived on the planet below us with many other of my peoples that are somewhat different from the humans who had arrived from the stars. They came about five months ago and slowly we have learnt to communicate. My world is obviously somewhat different from that of you humans. To start with we "count", or perform all our numerical analysis, in base twelve arithmetic whereas you humans use base ten for simple things but base thirty two or sixty four for most of your boxes or machines. Everything on our world relates around the human number twelve. Our bodies have twelve fingers and twelve toes. Our days are twenty four hours made up of twelve hours day and twelve hours night and we have twenty four days in our lunar month and twelve months in our year.

The biggest difference between us is what you humans call gender. When I first saw the humans from the starship I couldn't believe my eyes. I had never seen old males and several of my friends and I had to check as I will explain later because it caused some embarrassment and subsequent humour amongst the humans.

Our people have several stages in their life. We all start as babies, or Belani, and this stage lasts from year zero to age twelve. We are all born as males to use the human word. From age twelve to twenty four we are Yelani, and we stay male throughout this stage. Here some of the males can produce the sap which we use later. At age twenty four we change quite quickly and dramatically. Within a year somehow our body changes and we morph into Melani. This stage lasts from age twenty four to forty eight or four twelves. Here our form has changed to human females if I understand the concept. I and my friends on this starship are all Melani. Here we can receive the sap when we are chosen, and here we may or may not produce Belani. By age forty eight we change to our last stage which usually lasts until around seventy two. A few of us may live a little longer but it is not a good thing to do. In this stage we are Wilani, and our form is female but we are no longer capable of receiving the sap. Along with these physical and physiological changes other things happen through the stages and these are fundamental to our people and totally alien to humans.

As Belani and Yelani we develop vocal cords and can make sounds although speech per se is primitive. Both the Belani and the Yelani receive intense education during these stages which is mentally transmitted by Wilani teachers who are specially gifted. Not all Belani and Yelani learn well enough and they are burnt before they reach the Melani stage. Yes burnt, and I will talk about that later as I understand it is a difficult or alien thought for humans. Melani lose their power of speech although we can still hear sounds. All of our communication from this stage onwards is what you humans call mental telepathy. We literally talk to each other by thought transfer. This skill is developed more and more powerfully as we move into the Wilani stage and our oldest people are truly awesome in their knowledge and capabilities. For us, information, knowledge and understanding are paramount but there again it is a different world. We become mutes in human terms yet we can "talk" and "listen" to each other over vast distances. This transfer capability is the only real way I can tell you this story as I can hardly understand human speech and I certainly can not talk. There is one young male human here who I call Dosten, or numbers in our speech. I think he is called Todd on your ship and he can think in numbers quite well, and he is capable in a very simple way of thinking in numbers in different bases. At times I can read his mind and we play very simple numerical puzzle games. He can pose a question in base eight or base sixteen, a numerical question, and we can play with the answers but it is very simple even compared to some of our young Yelani. With the other humans I can read a little of their minds but it is very tiring as I have to keep translating from base ten to my base twelve.

There are six of my fellow people in this starship. We are all Melani and I suppose that is not surprising given what happened over the past year. We are a people where the ruling power is mental rather than physical. What is important is not big, massive, awesome, overwhelming in size and might but in knowing, understanding and ruling emotions mentally. Power is wielded through information. The elders can mind read, can foresee, can message through telepathy, and can see vast distances. It is a world of "strong" people in their minds and not their bodies. Physically we are weak-limbed with low physical stamina. Slowly I think we are losing the power to walk. Most of our older Wilani have younger people fetch whatever they want like food or herbal medicines. Our games are mental – crosswords, memory retention, numerical puzzles, numerical sequences, abilities to see in four dimensions.

Ours is a world where there is no art, no music, no dance, no acting, no creative physical reproductions but numerical puzzles. And if I understand the human concept properly there is no god, no worship, no priests, no ceremony or puzzlement over the unknown, although we do return the dead to our world in a reverent way. There is no search for who we are or where we came from or why we are here. It is all a numerical equation being implemented in loops, in strings, in patterns. Life is fate and like with numbers one can predict probabilities but there are also random numbers and fractals where patterns are sharp and angular. We have no army, no physical battles, no weapons, no strongholds but schools where all toil communally for the benefit of everyone. In a social sense we have no families and new-born Belani go to communal nurseries. We do not know our own offspring but that is of no consequence because we are all one people.

There is science in the growing of vegetation including the numerics of genetics but there is no understanding of the process or any desire to know how it works. From our understanding of your world we have no animals higher than insects. We have no fish, no birds and no vertebrates like mammals. In our waters are arthropods. In fact the whole concept of what you call evolution is unknown to us. However, our plant life, which is diverse and valuable, is of great interest to you as you have never seen plants that actually move, or emit sound or only produce smells at night.

Our people are short, slender and support a larger than Homo sapiens head which I have learnt has an enlarged cerebrum which you tell me is the seat of numerical knowledge.

There is one aspect of our life which seems to interest you considerably and that is our reproduction. It also interests me as I will explain below. I told you the Yelani are all like your males. They do not wear any clothes and they spend most of their life in school being mentally trained. We also use them to fetch and carry and collect plants if they can understand the descriptions. However, periodically, some of the Melani will take them to the Life house where they are beaten. Usually we do not touch each other. It is considered bad etiquette to touch physically in any way and we do not use physical force amongst the Melani or Wilani, but the Yelani we beat to produce the sap from their bodies. This is difficult because some Yelani can not produce sap, what you call sperm I think. Yes, sure they spray waste from their yoss, or what you call a penis, but it takes skill to make a Yelani swell and produce sap. The sap is precious. The Melani collect it and give it to the special Wilani for the gift. Once in her life time as a Melani, a person will be taken by the special Wilani to the Life house. The Wilani decide who and when and for one month this person is treated with the sap. It is smeared inside the body of the Melani by the Wilani using a special rubbery plant stem which has been chewed to be shaped like our concept of twelve. For twenty four days the sap is smeared inside us. We never go back to the Life house after the one month as the sap is precious. Some of us are gifted and obviously fate ordains that our knowledge is important because we bear Belani. During this period of bearing the Belani inside us we are subject to intensive mental instruction from special older Wilani. You would call them teachers or professors. This is to help both the Melani and the growing Belani. After twelve months the baby is born and taken away for training. If a Melani fails to respond to the sap she never goes again.

I told you my name is Melanidopatoq and this tells people I am Melani, I have been to the Life house for sap and born a Belani, which is what dopa means. Toq is my personal name if you like. During the time we are bearing the Belani inside us the Wilani will feed us several plants which have juices to help stimulate the mind. There are also smoke houses where we will sit for several days inhaling the smoke from other plants to add to the brains stimulus. For a Melani it is a very special time and it takes one year or twelve months from the time of the sap to the birth. It was this time when some of us got to think about other things. And it was these other things that caused problems, and the subsequent actions that brought me and my five friends here.

There were six of us, six Melani, and we were all carrying Belani. Inside the smoke house we got to "talk" amongst ourselves but we guarded the talk so any of the Wilani couldn't hear what we were communicating amongst ourselves. Over my past few years, ever since I had been a young Melani I suppose, I had looked at the vegetation and I had looked at us, our people. There were several things we did that bothered me. Some of the Belani were still-born. Several of the Yelani couldn't produce sap and died from beatings, or were burnt if they didn't mentally achieve a satisfactory level of communication. Yelani and Melani all had accidents and we had no knowledge of what I now know to be surgery. Our people died. There were few of us and I could visualise some catastrophe that would destroy all of us. Because of our aversion to salt after we reformed into Melani we never ventured into the sea and none of our group ever explored very far on land either. The few who have tried never returned. It was deemed wise not to travel far and we were weak in the legs. True, a few Yelani did go out to sea on mats of vegetation but they never returned and a few did go up the mountain behind our lands. This exploration ended when they became Melani. So, it appeared to me we were a small group that wasn't going anywhere and there was very little variation in our peoples. We were all trained as we got older into better communicators with better knowledge and understanding of the world around us as measured in numbers. So we knew what you humans call astronomy, and everything about the heavens, but of our own world we knew little except the vegetation all around us.

It was this vegetation that really forced me to think about the one subject that caused all the trouble. The subject of diversification was an area of study, and we Melani all received more and more information about the incredibly diverse array of plants around us. You humans are amazed at some of the plants we have here as there are several things that you have never seen before. Also you have learnt a little that the Wilani know well, and that is the plants we have here have changed over time. Not in any one person's lifetime but the body of knowledge has passed down and several plants have changed. It was this change and diversification that made me think because our people hadn't. We were all the same. We have stayed all the same for a long time. The same light brown colour skin, same build, same colour eyes and the unchanging rigid life-style. Your doctor human, who horrified everybody when he first came and started touching us, was amazed because we had virtually identical genetic structure he said. But before you came I had already thought along similar lines and it worried me.

The six of us talked. When we all agreed that the situation was potentially dangerous we started to talk about what we could do about it. At first we let the ideas be far-ranging and without criticisms or questions. We considered what was the widest conceivable range of options and some of these were suicidal, crazy, physically challenging, mentally extreme, socially unacceptable and just dreams. We realised that we just didn't know enough about ourselves.

I have told you that from being Melani and onwards we never physically touch each other. It is considered indecent, anti-social, and unintelligent. Perhaps primitive is your word. Belani touch. Yelani touch but not after that. When we are hurt, bones broken, insides damaged we treat with herbal medicines. When we die we are burnt. What I'm trying to say is that we don't know what we are like inside. Not only do we not know anatomy but we have no knowledge of how physiology works within the body, and absolutely no idea about what you call cell and chromosome research. We might prize the brain, and we know that a person can lose many parts of the body but still think and communicate, so we realise that the head and what is inside it is precious but we have no idea how this all works. We only know how to improve its capabilities and we prize people with the greatest capacity of knowledge and ability to communicate over long distances. What you call telepathy I think.

The six of us wanted to start with the Belani because we thought there should be male and female Belani. We wanted to let the Yelani grow older and not change into Melani. We thought this may be affected by the way we Melani received the sap. We also questioned why only the one month in our lives. Why not again and again if the first month didn't produce new Belani? Some things that we did and that we had always done needed to be changed.

Quite secretly the six of us started with a small group of Yelani. We had persuaded the Wilani that we needed to change the methods of improving the minds of the Yelani so that more of them would "graduate" successfully. We said that too many of them were being burnt before they had a chance to learn and we were losing people. We started with some of the older Yelani and we found that physical touch caused them to rethink some things.

Toq sat back in the chair looking at the machine in front of her. It couldn't think. It didn't challenge her or stimulate her but it could effectively communicate and Toq thought that was important with these humans. They knew different things, strange things about inside us and how we developed. From them Toq had learnt about the knowledge stored in the machines, well beyond the knowledge in the brains of any of the single humans, and as she could see their pictures she and her friends had examined this information. They had learnt that the humans did have male and female Belani. They learnt that humans reproduced in a similar way with sap from males to females but done in a different way, and apparently more reliable looking at the numbers.

She remembered the times when she and her friends had tried to change a few of the Yelani. Her Melani friends had tried touching and found they could produce sap from the males far more easily than by beating. The trouble was this led to the Yelani getting aggressive, abusive and trying to overpower the physically weaker Melani. When the Yelani tried to take other Melani, not those of Toq's group the Wilani quickly put a stop to that and the Yelani went mad. The six members of Toq's group were taken away and put in a special area where a powerful group of Wilani bound us mentally. Then, within three or four months, we all realised that we were with Belani again. What had we done? The Wilani were worried, scared and put strong mental bounds on us. The six of us talked when we could without the Wilani knowing. Perhaps we had made a discovery.

Despite our revolt, or unconventional behaviour, our Belani were born in the usual way and they were all male, but our six now had more than one Belani in our lives. We had made one change. We had increased the numbers. Who knows what else we could do? It was about this time that the human's starship arrived on our land. I can still remember that first morning because the six of us had been allowed to attend the big annual funeral for the most respected of the Wilani. Perhaps I should explain about our thoughts and practices with regards to death. Many many years ago now we had discovered fire. The story was that it came from a storm through lightening and eventually someone found a way to retain this force and perpetuate it. Over time we improved our use of this force, and we did cook some plants and we did use the force to clear away vegetation including cutting down trees. As we had no cutting tools, or even the concept of cutting, we used fire to cut large trees and we used the wood for shelter as well as cooking. Most of our people lived in caves before that and many still do.

In the very early days we used to lay the dead down on the upper parts of the hillside with the head, the highest part, up the hill. We revered the head and we were in awe of the mountain. The seas frightened and poisoned us. After we had found fire we started to burn the dead but would keep the burnt head and place that up the hillside. Belani and certainly any Yelani who didn't learn enough were also burnt but there we burnt the whole body and the head was of no consequence. After more years passed the custom changed again and it became the practice to eat the cooked brains of the Melani and Wilani as the Wilani thought that was the seat of knowledge. We really revered the whole body and so there was never any dissection, dismemberment and we burnt it to let the elements return to the earth. After it was burnt we observed that the parts gradually returned to the earth. We also noticed that places where the burning had been done grew luxuriant vegetation and the best fruits. The goodness had been passed on and that reasoning led to the eating of the brains. Pass on the knowledge.

The human starship landed when we were burning the Wilani and it caused chaos because you emitted fire as you came down from the sky. The mind messages were rampant across the entire community and the noise was overwhelming. The six of us renegades managed to slip away and we were amongst the first to see you humans emerge from your starship. It was strange because you all looked like silvery fat animals with round shiny heads yet you walked on two legs like we did. The mental noise amongst us when you took off your heads and then your skins was deafening and many of the Wilani were researching desperately trying to recall anything similar in their minds. Then one of you opened your mouth and moved your arms and hands. We could hear but not understand and then the observation went round and we were all amazed. Two comments immediately raced throughout our minds. You all had five fingers on each hand and three of you had white hair. The three looked old. Saq, one of our group ran forwards. We all read her thoughts. We six knew what she had to know but how was she going to find out. We had only recently learnt to touch. We still had to fight the concept that it was forbidden, rude, disrespectful and just not done. I should explain that although the Yelani went about naked we Melani all wore a covering that you humans call a shift or a dress. It is easy to lift up and see the rest of the body but you wore something quite different.

Saq stopped and we all heard her ask you who you were. You ignored her. I later learnt that you couldn't hear her telepathic question. She had no vocal speech and you couldn't read her mind. We listened as Saq thought how she could ask. She boldly and tentatively lifted one of your crew's hands and we heard her count the digits. At five we all gasped. Then she had a positive thought and she lifted her hand in front of one of your crew. When she had lifted her hand she counted. We all heard her counting from one to six and you looked puzzled, amazed and we could hear a little bit of your mind processing. It was only much later we realised we had to translate from base ten to base twelve to hear you but it was slow and difficult. At that first meeting none of this was possible.

We could hear Saq thinking how to find out whether you were all male. You wore some clothing we could see so you might be Melani but Saq couldn't see how she could find out. Then Saq had another thought and we all thought it was another way of communicating. We couldn't speak to you and you couldn't hear us but we both had eyes. Saq lifted her shift. In fact, to make it very simple, she took her shift off and turned completely around. We all thought she was being very clever and we all told her so. The Wilani were unsure and some said we should all walk away. Nothing happened. You didn't understand Saq's question and she put her shift back on not knowing what else to do. We all walked away and went back to the burning. You were alien, unable to communicate and definitely a weaker animal with smaller heads and you all looked like Yelani, undeveloped animals.

Over the next two weeks we seemed to go our separate ways but on a very small scale we did interact. Saq went into the starship on day three and came back with the knowledge that you were like the Yelani and knew all about touching and the sap. She was excited. I had met the young human I called Dosten because he could think in numbers. He had a machine and he was asking our earth what it was and analysing the content. I had never seen anything like this before but I could understand the machine. Once I realised that the machine communicated in base thirty two I quickly did the interpretations. I must have distorted the machine with my thoughts because Dosten suddenly became upset and I could hear his brain churning but couldn't understand. Suddenly I wondered whether he thought like the machine and listened to him in base thirty two but it was still chaos. Experimentally I flipped through the numbers in other bases and suddenly I clicked. Slowly, very slowly and with some difficulty I could understand some of Dosten's mind. After a few minutes making sure I could really understand I decided to talk to him through his machine. I found I could tell the machine certain things and have the machine visually show Dosten some numbers on a screen part of the machine that he kept looking at. I posed an elementary numerical question on his screen. He looked puzzled. He looked at me and I mentally nodded. He didn't understand. I cleared it off his screen and tried again and this time I looked straight at him. His face changed and he did something with his fingers and I saw what he had done on the screen and could hear what the machine was doing. He was right. He had answered my puzzle. Slowly, so very slowly we gradually built up an ability to communicate through his machine. That night I shared my knowledge with my friends.

It appeared that Dosten had also communicated with his other crew members because the next morning four of you came to see us. This was the beginning of an exchange of who we were and what we did. Over the following week we six all went into the starship and we saw and heard many many strange things, exciting things and some of these helped the six of us decide what we had to do.

Although you were all male, and therefore undeveloped, you did know and do some things we knew nothing about. Two of our Yelani had tried to put some logs together on the sea and move off the land. Their bodies washed up on the shore and three of your crew found them first. We didn't know this until Lata and Byell, two of our six told us that evening and what they told us both horrified and fascinated us. We all had to go and look the next day. Two of your crew had laid the bodies out on a ledge, or what I now know to be a table. They hadn't burnt them; they had opened them. This was sacrilege, or what you would call sacrilege but we six had let our minds be open as we struggled to learn new things. We all wanted to diversify and expand our knowledge base. We all felt we had become too specialised, too bound up in only one form and one way of life. You had opened the bodies of these two Yelani. One of you slowly explained the different parts inside and over the next two days we learnt about structure and function. Once this barrier had been partially overcome we six spent all of our time with one or more of your crew. With your machines we could communicate in a way and we six gradually saw an opportunity to evolve. Your crew understood that some of our people didn't want us to do this but they physically kept any Wilani away and our six could mentally keep them at bay. We tried to tell the Wilani that this was for the best. This was for the betterment of our people but they thought we had lost our minds: we had gone mad and they cast us out. Now we really needed the humans for protection.

Together we went with the humans over a wider area of our world. You went high up into the mountains but we couldn't follow too far because we were weak. Then you went out onto the ocean but we didn't go there either because of the salt. You were amazed at the plants, at the lack of animals, at the stages of development of what you called insects. We had difficulty understanding that you had to use machines to detect the subtleties in some of the plant smells as you obviously had a poor sense of smell. We in turn were amazed at machines that cut things, bound things together but most of all by machines that made things bigger. At first this terrified us as though the object was suddenly on top of us or jumping in front of our faces. Our eyesight was good but with some of these machines we could see almost as far as we could communicate. For me it was the machines that made little things larger that were the biggest fascination. Dosten showed me little parts of the plants and then with the machine he made them slowly bigger and bigger and I could see things I had never seen before. This in turn led to flowers, pollen, stamens, pollination, and down further into cells and cell splitting in mitosis and meiosis and then combinations. I slowly learnt about fertilisation and new growth and one of my original questions, back before the humans came was answered. I knew about the sap, the Melani and the Belani. I knew how we were created, reproduced.

Over time the six of us exchanged our findings and came to an agreed-upon conclusion. To diversify we needed to mate with the humans and see whether we could produce female Belani the way the humans said they could. By now the humans had visited much of the area around where we lived and we understood they were going to leave and visit other parts of the planet. We were still thinking of the implications of this when the humans suddenly became very agitated and we listened to their machines. There was a cosmic event about to happen. None of our knowledge or predictions forecast such an event but we six knew enough mathematics to know about random events and catastrophic happenings. The humans thought the storm would be severe and they wanted to leave as fast as they could. We decided to go with them. We all thought it was our only chance. We had to diversify and our people did not want that. They were doomed the humans said and we blasted off into space. On the starship there was a lot of activity and you insisted we put on special clothes to protect against radiation. We had told the humans about our desire to diversify and how we wanted to do it. They in turn tried to protect us to make sure this would be possible.

The storm passed and for a brief time the humans landed again with our people. We could hear the anguish before we landed. The sound of the Wilani could be heard from far away. They were frightened because they did not know what damage if any had been done but it was an event like none before. The humans asked whether they could test some of the people and explained why. We in turn asked the Wilani and they couldn't accept the question or allow the tests. We flew away. One of the humans came to us and explained what he thought would have happened. He showed us knowledge that was inside the machines on the starship and we all understood that all our people could never reproduce because the radiation had sterilised them. It was the end. Only the six of us were left and we wanted to change our world. We wanted, no we needed to diversify. All six of us thought we would always be in control because we had the developed brains but together with the humans we would evolve into a better animal, a more complete animal, a more resilient animal.

'Peter, that's a really fascinating story. You say you wrote it as an idea for a lesson plan for the Education Centre?'[1]

'Yes Mum. I talked with Auntie Stephanie, and with Enrico about some of the technical things but I wanted to have a story that the teacher could read to the class and then walk in the forest and see the different concepts in the story.'

'So what were the ideas you were trying to explain?'

'Well there are several Mum. I had to check with Auntie Stephanie about the genes and reproduction things as I wasn't too sure of the details but she showed me baby boy lambs and baby girl lambs and she explained how they were produced. Then Enrico showed me trees that have only male flowers and some only female flowers and other trees that have both on the same tree. Enrico also pointed out that the bigger animals, the mammals have males and females whereas the lower animals, like earthworms, are both male and female on one body. So, all of that made me think about our forest and I wanted tell about four different things.'

'And you tell the story to talk about these things?'

'Yes Mum. I'll explain. First, we should realise that if there are other worlds they may look like ours, or be slightly different or be very different. We evolved on this earth in a certain way through circumstances or design. I don't know which but other places could evolve differently and that might make some big differences because of little things. For example, Toq's people have six digits on each hand and foot and perhaps because of this they count in twelves not tens. Auntie Stephanie told me that five digits happened in this world a really long time ago but what would have happened if we had evolved with six? Similarly, Toq's people developed the brain and mental capacity as the dominant sense or capability. So, they were far superior to humans in that capability and

---

1   See Peter's Education Centre in 'Daniel' and 'Gloria' by John Osborn

more precise because it was number driven, whereas humans had less developed brains, communicated mostly in words, and language is less precise than numbers but they had better physical bodies. The humans also had a greater interest in finding out about why things happen, hence their knowledge of physiology, genetics, and the overall search for places and answers. Toq's people had lost their ability to physically speak, might be losing their ability to move very far but retained a sense of smell. The third item I've already mentioned is about the ability to reproduce or perpetuate the animal. In some ways plants have evolved further than animals and are more versatile although animal's ability to move provides other opportunities. Toq was concerned about the unreliability, the lack of success with their method of reproduction, so her people learnt that humans had another method. As the story ends they try this other method as a means to diversify. The last idea is to combine the best parts of both sets of people, a little like Auntie Stephanie does with her sheep breeding, but I was thinking of developing and retaining all of our senses. Humans see, hear, feel or touch, smell and taste but our capability varies. Enrico thought we should have a series of tests where we are blindfolded and just feel or smell different tree barks and try and identify them. Auntie Stephanie thought we could smell and feel different wools from sheep, goats, alpacas and llamas. Uncle Daniel's wildlife helper, Arnold Church can identify birds by their call. After hearing the story the teacher could take us out into the forest and let us experience these things.'

'So Peter, we need to publish this story. Maybe I should talk with my cousin Giselle. She works in Bristol and she may know somebody. Your grandfather may know too. Giselle could translate the story though and we could send it to other countries.'

'Mum, I just wrote a little story to help with our Education Centre. I wanted to personally do something to make it a success. After that weird preacher, you know the Reverend Gabriel Godschild, I felt we needed something more real, more in keeping with our forest. I don't think we humans suddenly appeared as God's messengers. I think humans evolved and our forest lets us see that. I also think we humans might be a better animal if we continue to learn and improve ourselves.'

'Bravo Peter bravo,' said Enrico. 'You have done well. You have taken some ideas you have observed in our forests and enfolded them neatly into an exciting and different story.'

'And Toq and her friends are still trying to learn Enrico. They think they can progress and be a more comprehensive animal.'

'And perhaps that is the most important message Peter. We are all never too old to learn.'

MEET THE NEIGHBOURS

'HAVE YOU NOTICED HOW THE news always tends to be negative mum?' I asked as I scanned the paper. 'I deliver newspapers every morning and the headline is always some disaster, scandal, or derogatory statement about someone. Can't people ever find anything nice to say about things, or about each other for that matter? Don't people ever do nice things in this world mum? Why can't we help each other?'

'People do son, people do, but that isn't news now is it? Good news never sold newspapers Roger but lots of folk do positive things, helpful things. Think about your own life.'

I sat at the table and thought over my mum's question.

'That's a bit of a challenge when I think about it.'

'What are the mottos in the Scout movement? You've been a Beaver, a Cub and now a Scout. You used to come home chanting them all the time.'

'That was so I could remember them. But you're right I suppose. There was "sharing, sharing, sharing" for Beavers and then "do your best" for Cubs and "be prepared" for Scouts. Funnily enough it is the youngest boys who got the best advice for helping people.'

'But then there was "bob-a-job" week and that meant helping people.'

'True mum, I suppose that particular week we did all go out and find people to help.'

'Doesn't just have to be that week Roger.'

'That's right mum, but then I help you with going down the shops. In fact you get both my sister and I to help around the house. Want me to recite all the things we do?'

My mother laughed and tousled my hair. 'No Roger, I know all the things you and your sister do very well, and your dad and I thank you for them. Still, in a way that is part of being a family. We all do our share. Think about outside though Roger. What about the neighbours?'

'Next door, the Parsons don't need any help mum. They both work. They have no kids and Mrs. Parson gets people to come in. Think, they have a gardener in once a week in the summer, and don't they have a char come in three times a week for the house? Then they have most things delivered from the supermarket. Don't think they're short of a bob or two either mum.'

'Okay Roger,' mum laughed. 'You've made your point son. You're right, although I wasn't thinking of the Parsons but what about Miss Abbott on the other side?'

'I never see her mum. For days I often wonder whether she is still alive. The only time I see her is in the summertime when I go and get my ball from her garden and she catches me. It seems that every time I play with Vanessa in the garden she manages to get the ball over the fence, and of course she expects me to go and get it. She looks at me as if it is my fault and points out that it is my ball.'

'And just when you have carefully climbed over the fence and stepped judiciously around Miss Abbott's vegetables she appears and scolds you,' mum laughed. 'Can't win in this life Roger can you?'

'Too true mum. But if I waited for her to ever come out into her garden I would have a dozen balls over there.'

'Nevertheless Roger you might want to think about offering to help. I suppose she must be in her seventies and she doesn't walk too fast. I see her out shopping down the local shops occasionally and I've carried her bags for her back home.'

'You ever been in her house mum?'

'No Roger I haven't. She keeps to herself does Miss Abbott. She has a sharp tongue when she is in the shops and speaks her mind. Knows exactly what she wants and doesn't tolerant fools. I believe she was a school-teacher but she is long retired now. Still, you could offer to shop for her, tidy the garden, or even go down to the library. I know that going to the library is a long way for her yet she is an avid reader. She must have told me that once when we were walking home with the shopping.'

'I suppose I could mum. I'll write her a short note explaining that I'm trying to help people. You know, do something positive. I'll tell her I'll come round next Saturday morning and that way she can give me a list of things to do. She'll be prepared. That'll be better than just knocking on the door.'

'That's a good idea Roger. That way she can think about your suggestion. Just realise son that she may be a little proud and not want to think of getting any charity. People have their pride Roger so be aware son.'

'Sure mum. I'll be, what do you say, diplomatic?'

'Off with you. Talking of help though can you fill up the coal scuttle before your father comes home? Thanks.'

Sitting up in my bedroom I thought about my mother's conversation. Do humans really help each other? Other animals do. Just the other day we had learnt about elephants trying to prop up a weak youngster between two adults, and don't they grieve over their dead? What about whales too? There had been that TV show which had scenes of half-carrying sick members to keep them from drowning. Is that just survival or is that help? Still, Miss Abbott isn't in need of survival now is she? How should I word this letter?

My father came in from work and a quiet fell over the household until dad had fed, sat down in his armchair and lit his pipe. Mum asked whether he had had a good day, as she usually did, and somewhat unusually dad said yes with a smile on his face.

'We had a visit from the General Manager down from Head Office. Usually this results in our boss later giving us all a lecture about the need to smarten up, improve customer service and work harder but today was different.'

'How so Jonathan? What did your General Manager do or say?'

I pricked up my ears. Usually what dad does at work is okay but nothing earth-shattering ever happens. He works in an office that handles investments for people and it always sounds like a boring but necessary part of the great industrial machine. Rarely does he sound this enthusiastic.

'He came round the office as usual and chatted briefly with each of us. Mr. Dawson likes to think he is a people person and in general he does talk and listen.'

'But nothing special dear? No mention of a bonus?' mum said with a chuckle in her voice.

'No, nothing that special, but after he had talked to each of us he had us gather together in the tea-room out back and said he wanted to tell all of us something.'

'What dad, what did he tell you?'

'Hush Roger, your father's telling us. Be patient.'

Dad looked at me and there was a twinkle in his eye. 'He said he had visited other Branches and other Companies and he had seen something here that really pleased him. So much so he said he wanted to offer something to us employees.'

'And?'

'Roger!'

'Sorry dad. I was expecting something revolutionary.'

'Not from an Investment House Roger. Still, although it wasn't revolutionary it was definitely unexpected. He had observed that in our office we all helped one another, more so than any other place he had seen. He thought our Branch worked as a team. Because of that he observed two things that were good. Firstly, we all seemed happy. Now this might seem a funny thing for him to say but he said he enjoyed coming to see us because he always left feeling cheerful. Secondly, and perhaps because we operated as a team, or perhaps because we enjoyed what we did, we were a very productive Branch.'

I watched my mother think about this. She smiled and she turned to me. 'Seems helping people can bring a little happiness and productivity into the world Roger. Just what we were talking about this afternoon.'

'He said one more thing too Joyce,' dad said. 'He thought we should benefit from this ethic and attitude. He said the Company was prepared to sit down with each employee and ask what further training we would like. The Company would pay and cover the cost of any extra people needed to do our work. It might be one half-day per week, or a week's course or maybe longer.'

'Sure Jonathan, but you do the work and the Company gets more experienced or skilled employees. They benefit.'

'Maybe Joyce, but he also said that we could choose which subjects we wanted to study and that they needn't necessarily be related to the job. He felt that helping any of us to better ourselves overall would lead to happier employees and even better results for the Company. Think of it as morale boosting.'

'But what about people who don't want to study, to learn anything new?'

'He mentioned this. To start with he asked us to think about his offer and he'd listen to suggestions within the next fortnight. If there was nothing really positive for any of us he did have another offer and he would explain that if the need arose. Overall he wanted us to think on his first idea for help.'

Lying in bed that night I let my mind wander over the kids in my class. Who did well and how did they do well? Were they the happy ones? Did anyone in the class help each other, other than on the football field that is? Did any of our teachers have us work in groups? We did that in Cubs, and in Scouts. We did several things as a team and had to work together and help each other: or the tent would fall down I thought and laughed.

Next morning I slipped my brief note into Miss Abbott's letterbox on my way to school. With two tests, a tough lesson in History about the First and Second Reform Acts, and then a brutal football match in the afternoon I came home having completely forgotten about Miss Abbott.

'Letter for you Roger,' mum said as I sat down to tea. 'Hungry?'

'Starving mum. Who's it from?'

'What dear? One kipper or two?'

'The letter? Two please.'

'Bread and butter?'

'I'll fix it mum thanks. The letter mum, who's it from?'

'Seeing as there is no stamp Roger I'll guess it is from next door.'

Munching on my kippers I opened the envelope and pulled out the letter. On a single stiff sheet of paper was a brief note in copper-plate handwriting.

'She wants me to go round there this Saturday morning.'

'Well, that's what you offered Roger. Good for you.'

'But I arranged to go out this Saturday morning with Chris and Alan down to the new record shop. They've got an audio studio where you can listen to the records before you buy them. It's great mum. I said I'd go.'

'Roger, think son. You now have an obligation to go and see Miss Abbott. Offering help comes with responsibilities Roger. People don't necessarily want help at your convenience.'

I pushed my kipper around the plate and thought about this.

'She may not want any help,' I said. 'Then I could go out with Chris and Alan.'

'Start on the right foot Roger. Start as you mean to go on. Be prepared to help come what may. Help often requires sacrifice.'

'Sure mum, you're right. I'll tell Chris tomorrow at school.'

'Any thoughts about the Parsons?'

'Mum, I thought we agreed that they wouldn't have any needs. They've got everything they want.'

'Maybe Roger, maybe, but you'll never know until you ask. You may have something they don't have or can't get. If you're going to offer to one neighbour you should offer to both. Do the whole job Roger, even if that offer seems redundant.'

I penned a second letter and slipped that into the Parson's letterbox next morning. When I came home from school I was surprised to see Mrs. Parson sitting in the kitchen with my mother. She held my letter in her hands.

'Roger this is a delightful offer. I know we haven't seen a lot of each other but this letter might be a chance to get to know you better. Let me explain. You know Vincent my husband is a lawyer, and he works all hours. One of his clients is the clinic where I work. I am a special needs psychologist. All of my patients, or clients perhaps, are children. They are children with handicaps of one sort or another.'

Seeing the expression on my face Mrs. Parson held out her hand and held mine. 'Roger,' she said, 'you know we don't have any children?'

'Yes Mrs. Parson,' I said, wondering what she was going to say next.

'I might be a psychologist,' she said, 'but I don't think, act and sound like a child. Many of my patients may relate to another young person. When I watch them in groups they interact very differently from when they are with me. I know several of them love to hear stories.'

'Mrs. Parson thinks you could read for them Roger. Perhaps a couple of hours a week just to sit with some of them and read, and maybe listen too. It is good therapy and helps them deal with some of their other problems.'

'When mum? What about school? How would I get to Mrs. Parson's clinic?'

'Good questions Roger, good thoughts. When I got your letter I took the liberty of telephoning your school. I spoke with Dr. Shaw, your headmaster. He was delighted to hear about your letter and said he would look at your schedule. Anyway, he phoned me back this afternoon and explained that Tuesday afternoon would work if you were at all interested. It seems you have some spares then. I would come and collect you from school and run you home after we have finished.'

'New challenge Roger,' my mum said.

Handicapped I thought; psychologist? Wonder how they are handicapped – bunch of nutters? Working in the loonie bin?

'Frightening Roger or just different?'

'I'm not sure Mrs. Parson. Suppose I don't know what to expect. I'm prepared to give it a try though. I read okay. Trying out for the school play actually. What do you think mum?'

'Not what you expected Roger is it? When we talked about helping we didn't expect this.'

My mother explained how we had talked about help and doing

things for people: about asking both the neighbours and thinking we would hear from Miss Abbott.

'But not from the Parsons?' Mrs. Parson said laughing. 'Thought we had everything I'll bet. Well, you're right Joyce. Vincent and I are lucky. We do have most things. But,' and here she paused and looked at me, 'you have one thing we have always wanted and never had.'

My mother laughed. 'There are days when you could have both of them,' she said.

Next day was Friday and I wondered about some of the changes in my life. Not what I expected from my short note that's for sure mum. Wonder what surprise I'll get tomorrow?

I was up early that Saturday morning and even before breakfast I had taken care of a couple of household chores. Mum as usual made sure I had washed and looked tidy before she would let me out of the house. Round to next door and through the front garden gate. Miss Abbott's front garden was very neat and civilised. Gravel pathways led between raised beds with tiled edges. Rhododendron bushes filled one bed and she had some hydrangeas up beside our garden hedge. Walking up the tiled path I stopped at the door and looked about me. All was quiet. It was just nine o'clock. Hesitantly I tapped on the door using an old brass lion's head shaped knocker.

'Good morning Master Highstead. You are punctual. That's good. I like that. Well come in boy. Come in. I don't bite.'

I stepped over the front door step and into a hallway that smelled strongly of floor polish. At the foot of the stairs was a solid-looking hall-stand with hooks for hats and scarves. Next to that was a large pot-shaped object with funny splayed things coming out of the bottom. Several walking sticks rested in the pot and a furled umbrella. Suddenly I realised it was an elephant's foot.

'In the kitchen Highstead. Come on come on.'

Miss Abbott clickety clacked her way sharply down the hall and into her kitchen.

'Sit then. There on the chair.'

I sat as instructed. She picked my letter up off her scrubbed kitchen table and fixing her spectacles firmly on her nose she reread it.

'Offering to help you say. Think you can help this old lady do you Mister?'

'I hope so Miss Abbott,' I said earnestly. 'I was telling my…..'

'Yes yes,' she said abruptly. 'How?'

Again the question came out short and sharp. Miss Abbott might have been elderly, old even but she exuded briskness and no nonsense.

'Moving heavy things perhaps. Scrubbing, mowing the lawn, going shopping or even changing books at the library 'cos I know that's a long way for you to walk. I go on my bike.'

'Make change can you? Know your arithmetic? Read my writing?'

She thrust a slip of paper at me.

I read the clear copper-plate writing listing the items she wanted from the greengrocers, plus some other goods that I could get at the grocers. A loaf and two Eccles cakes completed the list and I knew they had those at the bakers.

'Nothing from the butchers Miss Abbott?' I asked.

'Observant you are. No thank you. Any questions? Fine. Here's two pounds and a pencil. Write the costs for each item. Don't dawdle. I've two string bags for you.'

I could almost hear her say "dismiss" but she merely handed me the list, the pencil, the two one pound notes and the string bags. She was half-way down the hall before I had collected everything up and gathered my wits about me. Miss Abbott opened the front door and before I could say "gee whillikins" I was out on the street and off to the shops.

So started that Saturday helping Miss Abbott. Nothing special happened on that first expedition and I was soon back knocking at her door with the two string bags banging around my knees.

'Come in. Wipe your feet. Food in the kitchen,' and she had the door closed behind me and clickety clacking down the hall before I could say a word.

'Sit. Show me the list and the change.'

I placed the two bulging string bags on the table, making sure nothing rolled out onto the floor. The apples tried but I caught them before they got too far. I laid the list, the pencil and the change on the table so Miss Abbott could see. I sat.

'Good. You've done well Highstead. Would you like your Eccles cake now with your hot chocolate or would you like to take it home for later?'

I sat there somewhat dazed.

'I didn't expect anything Miss Abbott. I was just offering to help.'

'And you did Highstead, and now I'm offering to sit with you and share a hot chocolate and an Eccles cake. Maybe we'll talk.'

'Yes Miss Abbott. Yes I'd like a hot chocolate, and I've never had an Ecccles cake before so I'm not sure what they are like.'

'Good. Honest answer. I like that.' She smiled and turned back to her stove and the boiling kettle.

Most Saturday mornings we repeated this ritual. Not every Saturday to be sure for Miss Abbott slowly learnt about my life and the things I did. She respected my other interests and activities. Once a month she would write the names of five books and I was told to find two of them if I could and exchange her previous reading. I got to know the hallway with its elephant foot and the kitchen with its warm smells and spartan appearance. Compared to our house it was like a tomb in there with the quiet but Miss Abbott liked to talk. Actually Miss Abbott liked to ask questions as she rarely said anything about herself or her house. She knew a little about our family and slowly she discovered who we were, where we had come from and as much as I knew about mum and dad.

On one of the more demanding expeditions I had to go further into town and look for something in the new supermarket. This shop was a recent introduction in our town and I was quite amazed at the row upon row of shelves stocked with items from the floor to up beyond my reach. This was quite different from the local shops. You even got to collect things for yourself rather than have to ask or order. Different I thought.

'What you doing in here Roger? You don't eat that muck. How come you're shopping on Saturday? Don't you usually hang out with Chris and Alan at Tony's Record shop? They've got that new "Top of the Pops" record in. Heard it?'

'I'm helping my neighbour,' I said somewhat lamely. 'She has special needs.'

'Think you're a Saint Bernard now do you Roger? You should wear a barrel so we can recognise you. Look cute wouldn't he Deidre?'

Deidre tossed her long hair and glimpsed at herself reflected off any shiny surface she could find. 'Dunno 'bout that Roz. Where's that lip gloss you were rabbiting on about?'

'Gotta go Roger. Don't bother to bark. Woof!' Roz laughed and walked away with her arm through Deidre's.

I walked over to the frozen food section to cool off. I was sure I was blushing a bright shiny pink. Roz was a laugh but that Deidre was gorgeous I thought.

'Took your time young Highstead you did this morning.'

'Sorry Miss Abbott. There were a couple of things I couldn't find. I had to ask one of the assistants and he said it would be in next Tuesday, when the deliveries come.'

'Find my special spices? They have those?'

'Yes Miss Abbott. One of the Pakistani girls who works there knew what they were. None of the other assistants could help.'

'Ignorant people,' snorted Miss Abbott. 'What do they teach in schools these days I wonder?'

'I'd heard of it Miss Abbott but I wasn't sure what it was or how you used it.'

'Well that's honest at least. Time for chocolate have you? Time for a chat?'

As I sat at the clean kitchen table with my hot chocolate Miss Abbott looked at me. 'Hear you are helping Mrs. Parson at her clinic?'

'Yes Miss Abbott.'

'Didn't expect that now did you?'

'How do you mean Miss Abbott?'

'When you offered to help both your neighbours you didn't expect Mrs. Parson to need any help now did you? She and her husband both appear to have everything. I'll bet you were surprised when she said yes to your offer?'

'Yes Miss Abbott. Yes I was. You're right. I did think that Mr. and Mrs. Parson had everything but she told me there were two things missing.'

'Two things?' asked Miss Abbott. 'What two things? I heard you were going to her clinic to listen and read to some of her patients. That's good of you. That's not easy.'

'She surprised me too Miss Abbott. She did agree that she and her husband had everything they could want, and that they had all the help around the house that they needed, but she told my mother she had wanted children. She said my mother had something she had always wanted but never had. Mum offered my sister and me to Mrs. Parson straight away and they both laughed. Miss Abbott are you okay? You look very pale.'

Miss Abbott straightened up sharply in her high-backed kitchen chair and looked fiercely at me but I noticed she blinked back a tear.

'Miss Abbott I'm sorry if I said something wrong. I was just trying to tell you about the two things. You are right about the reading though. Sometimes it is not easy seeing whether the kids are listening or not. I'm not sure whether I'm doing anything useful but Mrs. Parson is always very pleased when I have finished. She tells me they listen to me much more than anyone else she has tried. She says they are far more alive after I have left but that makes me sad. Many of them seem to live in other worlds.'

Miss Abbott sniffed and leant forward to sip her chocolate. I noticed her hand shook a little and the spoon clattered in the saucer.

'Mrs. Parson has a difficult job Miss Abbott. It must be very frustrating working with her children. Many of them don't seem to respond to anything. What did you do Miss Abbott?'

'Me Highstead, me? That was a long time ago now, long time.'

'Maybe Miss Abbott, but what did you do? I'm not trying to be impertinent but you've asked all about my family and I just wondered what you did. I know you have an elephant's foot in the hall. Did you live in India, or in Africa perhaps?'

Quite suddenly Miss Abbott laughed and she leant across the table and held my arm with her rather thin arthritic hand.

'No Roger Highstead, you are not being impertinent. You are a very well mannered young man and I enjoy your company. Have you finished your hot chocolate?'

'Yes Miss Abbott. I'll be off then. I'll come next Saturday morning shall I?'

'Please Roger. I've one small item to collect next Saturday but I'd like to show you something after that. Can you spare me a little time after the shopping?'

'Certainly Miss Abbott. I'll make sure to keep the morning free. Goodbye.'

The following Tuesday afternoon as usual Mrs. Parson came to my school and drove me back to the clinic.

'Roger do you know that I watch when you read to some of my children?'

'How Mrs. Parson? You're never in the room when I am reading. You've always said you had other children to work with.'

'The mirror in your room Roger is really a one-way window. I can see in but you and the children can't see out. That's how I can see what happens to the children when you read and listen to them. Without them knowing I am watching I can see whether they are happy, sad, lively, lonely even and whether your presence and words help them. That's how I know they are livelier and happier when you are there. Not just after you leave but actually while you are there. You are helping them Roger. Many of them have improved how they speak over these past few weeks. Many of them are speaking for almost the first time. You have been really helpful.'

'I didn't know Mrs. Parson. I'm glad I could help. I sometimes wondered sitting there and just reading whether I was wasting your time. I like to read you know, and it helps for my acting on stage, but I didn't know whether it was doing anything for you.'

'Roger, I've had a colleague with me for the last three sessions. He was most interested in watching the process. He had interviewed and observed some of the children a few months ago and he's absolutely amazed how they have changed. Not all of them to be sure Roger, but then we are all individual human beings and what works for one doesn't necessarily work for others.'

'Little Janice is more awake now Mrs. Parson. At first she didn't say a word and just sat there sucking her thumb. Now she walks about and sometimes wants to sit on my lap when I read. She has taken the thumb out and helps turn the pages for me. If I read from a book with pictures she becomes quite excited and points and speaks. She doesn't know the right words but she does make noises.'

'Yes Roger, and Janice is not the only one who has changed. You've done far more than you realise Roger. I've mentioned this to both your parents and to your headmaster. They both thought you should know how helpful you have been.'

'Is it the interaction Mrs. Parson? I try to be quiet and peaceful when I read. I also try to make eye contact but in a non-threatening way. You told me not to reach out and touch but several of the children have come closer and sat by me. As I said, Janice likes to sit on my lap.'

'You're quite observant Roger. You're right. You do present a peaceful but interested interaction. When someone speaks I can see you actively listen. To them you seem to want to listen, to want to help. I think that re-assures some of them. Gives them confidence to take the next step which may be talking or touching.'

'Miss Abbott listens,' I said suddenly. 'She also asks questions, quite sharply.'

Mrs. Parson laughed as she looked forwards and concentrated on her driving through the crowded traffic. Still looking forwards she said, 'Miss Abbott is not suffering from any form of depression Roger, although she may be suffering from some sort of withdrawal. I believe she still has her wits about her but I also think she is very sad or repentant about something. I don't know her very well but I think something happened a long time ago that caused her pain. Now that she has time on her hands to think about it I believe it is starting to overwhelm her and consume her. I imagine you going into her house and doing things for her is another good thing Roger. I think she needs to talk to someone as well as listen. Maybe she'll talk to you like my children at the clinic? You appear to be non-threatening and probably non-judgemental at your age. Let her talk Roger if you can.'

Later that night, as I lay in bed looking up at the images on the ceiling projected from my brain, I thought about the comments from Mrs. Parson. Two-way mirror. Sneaky that. Still, I suppose it really helps her trying to understand how to help her patients. Help them help themselves really I thought. Give them an environment where they can develop for themselves. I suppose that applies to all of us. Just look at dad's boss letting all his employees find a place or an activity to move themselves forwards: providing them with an opportunity, an environment to be better people, more helpful people. Strange old world I thought as sleep overwhelmed me.

The week passed by and Saturday rolled around again. Punctually at nine I walked up to next door and knocked.

'Come in Highstead. On time as usual I see. That's good. I've one special request from the drapers. You know where Juliana's is?'

'Yes Miss Abbott, that's next to Thompson's butchers shop. Usually has fabric and ribbons in the window.'

'Right. I've ordered something, a roll of curtaining material. I want you to collect it for me. Miss Lacey in the shop knows me and my order. It's paid for. You just need to pick it up please.'

'Fine Miss Abbott. Anything else?'

'No, that's all this morning and then maybe I'll show you something here.'

The errand was easy enough and Miss Lacey knew about the order, which was a large roll of fabric all wrapped up in brown paper tied off with string. I balanced it on my shoulder and started home.

'You carrying dead bodies about now Rog?'

'Who's in there?'

'Hello Alan, Chris. No, it's an order for Miss Abbott.'

'Let's have a look then? Alan here is sure it's a body. Looks heavy enough. Grab that end Alan.'

'Chris leave off. It's all wrapped up neatly.'

'Here Alan, you pull that end and I'll look in this end. Caw, crappy colour. How about your end Alan.'

'Naw Chris, same pukey colour. No body. Our Rog ain't no body-snatcher. Let's go Chris. Let's leave miss cash and carry here and go down to the record shop. Miss goodie-goodie don't need our help. We'll kiss and say goodbye Rog,' and they both laughed.

Alan and Chris took off down the street and left me with my messed up parcel. Friends I thought: jealous, guilty, teasing, or perhaps just young and full of life? I suppose I am old enough to start thinking about people and their attitudes, people and their intentions. Mrs. Parson was hinting about that last week. Her work must be all about that: trying to understand what makes people tick and what can be done when they don't tick in sync with the rest of us.

While jumbling these thoughts about in my head I had gradually repackaged my parcel. It didn't look quite as neat as when it left the shop but at least it was in one piece.

'Sorry Miss Abbott,' I said as I handed her the parcel. 'A couple of friends got too inquisitive and wanted to snoop at the body I was carrying. Well, that's what they said.'

'Body-snatcher eh Highstead? Accused of body-snatching were you? But I see you fought them off and brought home the corpse in one piece?'

'Yes,' I said.

'Just bring it through to the kitchen and put the parcel on the table.' Away she went clattering down the polished hardwood floor to the peace and quiet of the kitchen.

'Hot chocolate and a digestive biscuit?'

'Yes please Miss Abbott.'

'How did this week go Highstead?'

I sat holding the cup of hot chocolate with my hands and thought on this question. Miss Abbott had never asked about my week's activities before and I wasn't quite sure what she expected.

'You know that I help Mrs. Parson, at her clinic?' I ventured.

'Yes Roger, and I've heard that you are a big help there.'

'Mrs. Parson explained to me this week that she had been watching. She has a two-way mirror into the room where I read and listen to her children and she observes us. That way she can learn what interests the children. She says she can see when they become more alive, when they speak more or move about. It was only this past Tuesday that I learnt about the mirror but she also said that the children are more active and personable when I am there. I think she was happy with this experience. She told me it helped her with her work.'

'And what about you Highstead? Is it helping you?'

I nibbled on my biscuit while I thought about this question. Was I there to help me? Originally this had been an idea with my mother to help others: to try and bring some good news to the week; something positive for a change.

'I think so Miss Abbott. I've done something new. Met some new people. That's broadened my knowledge of people and their situations. I've never seen children like those at Mrs. Parson's clinic or had to think about their challenges with life. And,' and here I paused while I gathered my thoughts more clearly in my head, 'I've never done anything before that really has helped a group of people like that. Mrs. Parson told me I had really helped and when I heard this I had a warm positive feeling. So yes Miss Abbott, I believe it has helped me too. I've become a bigger person. No, not bigger but a more empathetic person and perhaps a better person.'

We both sat silently at the scrubbed plain deal table and sipped on hot chocolate and nibbled our biscuits.

'What about me Highstead? Are you helping me?'

'You Miss? Well I come round a few days and try and do some things for you. I suppose that is helping and again I've learnt a little more responsibility in doing that.'

'Anything else?'

'Maybe someone to talk to Miss Abbott. I've never noticed whether you see many people but then again you seem very content being who you are. Do you have anyone come Miss Abbott, when I'm at school for instance? Do you have any family, brothers or sisters?'

Miss Abbott sat in her chair and looked at me. It wasn't a demanding inquisitive look and it wasn't a retrospective internal look but a simple meeting of the eyes. She pushed her chair back from the table and took her cup and saucer to the sink.

'Time for some answers I think. Come with me.'

I too rose from my chair and followed her back down the hall. She opened the door to what we called the lounge. Mum said that was a better word than front-room and certainly better than parlour, which was what her parents would have called it. I had never known my grandparents as they had all died before I was old enough to know them.

We walked into a clean room that looked quite like ours next door except the furniture was large, dark and white anti-macassar covers lay on the head-rests. I almost expected an aspidistra plant as the room looked that old-fashioned. Ebony-coloured bookcases with glass fronts filled the alcoves beside the fireplace and these were stacked with volumes of hardback books. Somewhat surprisingly there was a black polished upright piano against the wall and the top of this was covered with framed photographs. On the wall between this room and the living room were three other picture frames. I walked over to look. The centre frame contained a picture showing just one person. Wearing a scholastic gown and a mortar board the young lady was smiling at the camera. Peering closer at the picture I noticed the lady looked quite like my mother, or my mother when she was a little younger. I didn't know enough about University colours to recognise what College or University in the gown.

Miss Abbott stood in the centre of the room and watched me. She didn't say anything but just stood there. I moved to look at the other two pictures on this wall. One showed the pupils and staff at Leyton High School in 1960. I thought this looked familiar but I didn't say anything. The second picture was similar but obviously at a different school. It too showed pupils and staff posed for a typical school photo. Written on the border below the picture were the words St. Mary's Girls College 1960. That was twenty five years ago now. I turned from these three pictures and walked over to the array clustered across the top of the piano. They showed a sequence, a progression from baby pictures through youngster to teenager to young lady. I gasped. The young lady was my mother. I turned to look at Miss Abbott. She still stood there in the centre of the room silently looking at me.

'Who?' I asked. 'Why?'

'Look at the big picture on the other wall again Roger and who do you see?'

I walked over to look again at the photo of the lady in the University gown.

'It's a graduation picture surely?' I asked. 'But I don't know where and I'm not sure who.'

'But you think you know who?'

'When I first looked I thought it looked like my mother but now when I look again I can see that it's not, although it is like her.' I hesitated before I asked my next question. 'Is the graduation picture yours Miss Abbott? Is that a picture of you?'

'Let's sit on the sofa Roger and I'll tell you a story.'

We sat side by side on the deep sofa and Miss Abbott turned to face me.

'Over the past few weeks, when you have been round to help me, I have asked you all about you and your family. You noticed that?'

'Yes Miss Abbott, but you never said anything about yourself. I've often wondered what you did. I've wondered where you came from and why you are living here. You didn't seem to have any visitors and I couldn't understand why you would want to live in a suburban terrace house rather than say a cottage in the country. You like to garden and everything is always neat and tidy and I would have pictured you in some village.'

'Maybe Roger, maybe you are right, but let's come back to the pictures can we? The centre one on that wall is me when I graduated from Oxford University. I had gone to Somerville College to read English. When you first looked at that picture you stopped as if you knew who it was?'

'Yes Miss Abbott. Like I just said, at first I thought it looked like my mother but when I went back to look the second time I could see that it wasn't. Then I was surprised at one of the school photos because Leyton High School rang some bells but I can't remember why. I don't know anything about St. Mary's Girls College.'

'You gasped when you looked at the sequence on my piano. What did you see?'

'My mother Miss Abbott, but why have you got photos of my mother? Are all of the pictures of my mother, even the baby pictures?'

'You never knew your grandparents did you Roger? They died just about the time that you were born.'

'Right. Mum showed me pictures of them and she showed me the pictures of her when she was young. That's how I knew the last picture you have is of my mum.'

'They were nice people your grandparents Roger. They were caring and loving people.'

'How do you know Miss Abbott? How do you know all this about my mother?'

Miss Abbott turned on the sofa and reached out to hold one of my hands. She slowly turned it over and peered at the palm as if trying to read my future.

'After I graduated from Oxford I went to be a school teacher at St. Mary's College. As the name suggests it was a convent school for girls, a Catholic convent. I stayed and I found that I loved teaching. Over the years I became a better teacher and eventually I was offered the position of Head Mistress. In 1960 I retired and that photo shows my last year as Head Mistress.'

'Where is St. Mary's Miss Abbott? It is not around here. I don't know the name at all.'

'No Roger, it is up in Shropshire and not far from Shrewsbury. You know where that is?'

'Yes Miss Abbott, on the main road up to North Wales. Dad took us up there last year for a holiday near Portmadoc. I think we went round the Shrewsbury by-pass. Yes, that's right, and there were lots of roundabouts because we had to look carefully at the road signs.'

'Right Roger, and St. Mary's was just off the A5 west of Shrewsbury.'

'So why come here? That's beautiful country around there Miss Abbott.'

'I wanted to watch you Roger. I found out where you lived and so I came to live nearby. I didn't plan to be this close necessarily but this house became vacant and so I moved in next door.'

'But why? We don't know you. How did you know me?'

Miss Abbott looked back at my hand

'Do you have a girl friend Roger, someone special?'

'No Miss Abbott, not really. I have several friends from school and some of them are girls but there is no-one special.'

'I was at University Roger and graduated just after the Great War. Most of the men of my generation had died in that war but I had a special friend who had been seriously wounded in 1915. Slowly he recovered, but he was in a wheel-chair when he decided to go to Oxford. He was very intelligent and potentially a splendid poet.'

'Did he die Miss Abbott, this special friend?'

'Yes Roger. Soon after we had become friends the wounds in his amputated legs developed an infection and he died of gangrene poisoning, but he left me with a gift and a burden.'

I must have looked confused because Miss Abbott gripped my hand more firmly and sounded quite emotional when she said, 'He left me with a baby Roger, a baby girl. I had just graduated. This was in 1920 and I was employed to start work as a teacher at St. Mary's College in September of that year.'

As I sat there with Miss Abbott holding my hand I was doing some mental arithmetic. 'But my mother was born in 1942 Miss Abbott so why do you have pictures of my mother? She obviously wasn't your baby girl. What's the connection?'

'My special friend died in August of that year and I couldn't start teaching at a Catholic Convent School being unmarried and pregnant Roger. This was 1920 remember.'

'But if you were Catholic you couldn't have had an abortion,' I stuttered. 'The church thinks that is murder, even if you could have found where to get an abortion.'

Miss Abbott looked quietly around the room and I watched her gaze as she traversed the row of photos on the piano.

'You are very right Roger and I didn't want an abortion irrespective of my beliefs. I wanted to keep alive the memory of my special friend. He died Roger. Gave up his life for his country and I desperately wanted to keep his child alive.'

'So what did you do?'

'I talked to Mother Superior at the convent and she listened. She offered to help. The baby was born around Christmas and I started teaching in January, one term later than planned. I stayed there teaching all my life and I thanked Mother Superior every day she was there.'

'That's a beautiful story Miss Abbott and obviously your Mother Superior was a very gracious and far-thinking lady, really helpful as you say, but that's a long time ago.'

'In those days Roger there was no such thing as single parents, well not for teachers at convent schools.'

'So what happened to your special gift?'

'Mother Superior arranged for an adoption Roger, with a warm and loving couple who desperately wanted a child.'

'But in those days you never knew who they were? I heard about this recently on television. They've just changed the law or something, about adoption that is. In the old days the birth parents never knew who were the adoptive parents and the child never could find out who were their real parents. Isn't that true?'

'All true Roger, and so I talked with Mother Superior and knew that my daughter was adopted. Mother Superior knew who the parents were. As she became older and ultimately quite ill I would sit with Mother Superior and read to her, a little like you do for Mrs. Parson. She became senile, although today I suppose you call it Alzheimer's disease. When she was lucid she liked it when I read. I had studied English and could read in a way that my voice played all the parts in the book. Like your reading Roger my voice animated Mother Superior.'

'And your little girl?' I asked. 'What became of her?'

'Just before she died, which must have been around 1939 or 1940, and just after the Second World War started, Mother Superior told me what had happened to my daughter, my Margaret. She would have been around twenty and very slowly I managed to find out where they all were. I found out where the parents lived and through a variety of old friends I found out more about Margaret.'

'This is still a long time ago Miss Abbott and still a long way away from here. I suppose I am bursting to know how this joins up with those photographs. There are no photos of your daughter are there? There is only one sequence of photos and that sequence ends up with my mother. What happened to your daughter?'

Again Miss Abbott paused and she smiled at me. 'You really have helped me Roger. Before you came I only had memories. With you I have a little more life. Just like you seem to do with the patients of Mrs. Parson you have made me more alive, more talkative. I thank you Roger Highstead, and I will tell you the story about your mother before you burst.'

Here Miss Abbott actually laughed.

'I'll speed up my story you impatient young man. My Margaret and her parents moved to London in 1942, which was partly to do with the father's job. They moved to Poplar in the East End. Margaret married a Donald Munro soon after living in Poplar and they had a baby girl. Unfortunately the baby got double pneumonia when she was one and had to go to hospital in Bow. While the baby was in hospital an air-raid killed everyone in the family living in Poplar. Margaret, Donald and all their parents were killed. It happened like that in those days Roger. It was a strange situation. Living and teaching at St. Mary's we were all so far away from any war whereas in some of the cities it was a living hell.'

'So this little girl was an orphan overnight in Bow hospital?' I said, trying to keep up with the story. 'Your daughter gets killed and her baby lived?'

'Yes Roger and the baby is your mother.'

'My mother?' I gasped. 'But how do you know? What happened after the air-raid and the hospital? She didn't die of double pneumonia then?'

'No Roger, she didn't die and as you know your mother is very much alive bless her heart. Unfortunately with the air-raids this did happen. All the family might be killed with the V1 and V2 rockets during the war in London but sometimes one or more children would be found in the rubble. They had indoor shelters in some houses and parents would put their children in the shelter while they slept in their beds. Dead parents and alive children. Orphan children just like your mother.'

'But my mum had parents. She told me so. I'm sure we've got some photos showing me in their arms or something. I thought they had a house in Leyton or perhaps it was Stratford.'

'Yes Roger, your mother like my Margaret before her was adopted. A family who wanted a daughter adopted your mother right from the hospital when she recovered. You are right, they eventually did live in Leytonstone which is why your mother went to Leyton High School.'

'But you have pictures of my mother but not your daughter?'

'All of the photographs and records of Margaret were destroyed in the air-raid Roger so I never had any memories of my daughter. But I did find out about Joyce and her new parents. Although I was teaching at St. Mary's I also had another part-time job working for the government. It was through some contacts in the government in London that I found out about your mother, my granddaughter and her new family.'

'But how did you get the photographs? You have baby pictures and all through her growing up, right up to her school photo in her last year at Leyton High School.'

'Your mother's adopted father Roger worked up in the city and I got to know him after the war ended. He was a fine man Roger and he really loved your mother. His wife, your grandmother couldn't have any children and they both had really wanted a child and Joyce was their treasure. Your grandfather knew that I taught young ladies and we often talked about the joys and difficulties of educating girls as England recovered from the war. The fifties were a difficult time. We might have won the war Roger but rationing went on for a few years. There was still a lot of damage to buildings and infrastructure and none of us had much money. It was all a bit of a struggle.'

'So you told him who you were?'

Miss Abbott hesitated. Again she looked at my hand as if seeking inspiration or deciding what she would say.

'No Roger, I never told him. I had promised Mother Superior I would follow the life of my child but I would never interfere. I would observe but not interact.'

'So you never told my grandfather who you were?'

'No, but I did ask him for some photographs. He was very proud of his daughter and he happily gave me the ones you see on my piano. As you so rightly observed they show a progression of your mother from being a little girl up to her eighteenth birthday. The Leyton High School photo of 1960 was the last year for your mother at school.'

'But then what happened? You said the other photo of 1960 shows you when you finished at St. Mary's. That is twenty-five years ago. Have you been here since 1960? I think dad told me we moved here when I was five so that's in 1974. Were you here before us? But that wouldn't make sense as you said you moved to be near us. There's a big gap.'

'Your mental arithmetic Roger is quite good although the answer is a little sad. Let me think back. Do you have time for a little more of the story?'

'Yes Miss Abbott. This is interesting. I can stay as long as you like,' and this time I gently squeezed her hand.

She shuddered a little with my gesture and I wondered whether I had done something wrong. She looked a little pale I thought, and the more I looked she appeared more frail than I had remembered.

'Are you all right Miss Abbott?' I asked with concern on my face.

She brightened and held my eyes with her gaze. 'Yes Roger, just feeling my age occasionally. Now where were we? Oh yes, 1960, that rather eventful year. Well it was for me. I planned to retire in 1965 when I turned sixty five but my body had other ideas. In 1960 I became very ill and spent the next two years in a variety of hospitals and convalescence homes. I may have partly lost my mind and there was some memory loss for a period of time. Still, enough of me, but in those years I lost contact with your grandparents and what had happened to your mother. When I came out of hospital I went to live with a good friend of mine who had a cottage in Church Stretton, just south of Shrewsbury. She too had taught at St. Mary's and I lived there while trying to recover my health. After several years I started to remember things and I must have found your mother's photographs. That in turn brought back a whole flood of other memories Roger and I knew that I had to find Joyce again.'

'So you contacted my grandfather, the one in Leytonstone?'

'No Roger. Your grandfather had retired and no longer worked up in the city. Also your grandparents had moved house and no one at their old address knew or would tell me where they had gone.'

'Then how did you find them?' This was becoming more and more like a detective story, or a lost person story, and I was excited to hear the conclusion. 'Who helped Miss Abbott? This is all about help or about people helping people so who helped you?'

'Unfortunately Roger it was the obituary column that helped. My friend was reading the newspaper in her cottage when she suddenly cried out. She asked about the name of your grandparents, which was Reynolds.'

'Yes, that's right. Mum was Joyce Reynolds before she married dad.'

'And the newspaper said they were dead Roger. They had both been killed in a car accident. The newspaper stated that they were the loving parents of Joyce Highstead (nee Reynolds) who lived in Wanstead. By that time I was feeling a lot stronger and my friend and I drove down from Church Stretton to find where you lived.'

'You came down to Wanstead, to Redbridge Lane?'

'Yes Roger I did. We stayed at a hotel, somewhere in Ilford I think, and when I saw where you were living I thought I could move here and be close. That way if I lost my memory again I wouldn't lose my granddaughter.'

'But you never said. You never knocked and said who you were? After all these years you've never said?'

'I came here in 1975 Roger. My friend in Church Stretton died, quite suddenly. She left me a considerable sum of money as she had no relatives and we had been good friends for years. This house came on the market and I had spoken to the Estate Agents when we first visited. They thought I would be interested and I was. You were six when I came and your sister was three.'

'And you've never said all these years. My mum doesn't know. Doesn't know any of this? She doesn't know that her grandmother is living next door, her neighbour so to speak. When she said I should offer to help she never knew who you were? It's amazing, incredible, almost unbelievable.'

'And the photos help you believe Roger? Why else would I have the photos?'

We sat quietly, the pair of us both thinking our own thoughts. My head was going round and round in circles. I didn't know where to start thinking what this all meant. Our neighbour, our Miss Abbott, was my mother's grandmother, my great grandmother I suddenly realised.

'Can I tell Miss Abbott? Can I tell my mum? You said you promised your Mother Superior all those years ago you wouldn't interfere but you haven't. You've sat here very quietly observing. Isn't that what you promised, to observe?'

I suppose I wasn't paying attention with all my excitement and looking around the room with new eyes. My mother, pictures of my mother and all about her life I thought. I got up to look at the photos again. The life of my mother and right next door. It explains why Miss Abbott is living here, all alone, and right next door when she could be living in a cottage in Church Stretton or wherever. I turned to ask Miss Abbott something and realised that she had quietly fallen over and was sprawled across the sofa. I rushed across the room.

'Miss Abbott, Miss Abbott,' I cried out. I tried to sit her upright and held her hand to feel for a pulse. Her head lolled backwards but she had a pulse. If you faint I thought you need to have your head down, between your knees. I folded her downwards. She was so frail I noticed, so thin. I heard her gasp and a thin rattle came out of her throat. She gasped again and her hand gripped mine. 'Ambulance Roger, ambulance boy.'

I made sure she wasn't going to fall off the sofa and rushed out into the hall. In all my visits I had noticed that the telephone was in the hall. I rapidly dialled 999 and requested an ambulance. I gave the address and listened to the reply on timing. Replacing the handset in the cradle I hurried back into the lounge.

She was sitting leaning backwards with a thin pale face framed by her white full head of hair. She looked very serene and peaceful as if she had satisfactorily completed some task and was content with the outcome. As I walked across the carpet she opened her eyes and smiled. 'My helper,' she said.

'The ambulance is coming,' I managed to say. 'They said ten minutes.'

'Lots of time now Roger. Lots of time. I won't be going away just yet. We'll talk again young man.'

There was a knock on the front door and I spun around and went to answer it.

'Fine son, we'll take over. In here you say. Come on Reg and bring the gear.'

Quickly, smoothly, efficiently the ambulance attendants took over and whisked the lightweight body of Miss Abbott onto a stretcher and carefully covered her with a blanket. Making sure she was safely strapped in they wheeled her out of the doorway.

'Look after her,' I cried out. 'Don't lose my great grandmother. I've only just found her.'

9 DON'T MEET THE NEIGHBOURS

I SUPPOSE IT HAS HAPPENED to all of us sometime or other. Okay okay, you are the exception, and you were born in the same house that you have lived in all your life, but you must admit that is rather unusual this day and age. Anyway, listen up. It has been a good day and the kids have been fun for a change. The house is tidy. I had that neighbour, Joyce Buckley, who I really like over for coffee and my husband's tea is simmering on the stove. I hear his key turn in the lock and his cheerful, 'I'm home love. My but it's good to be home and something smells wonderful. You're looking very lovely today. Come and give us a kiss you beautiful thing.' He hands you flowers and you start to wonder.

'Dennis, you're very cheerful. Obviously it was a good day at the office. Ummm, that feels nice. Hug me tighter.'

'What about me daddy, what about me? Don't I get hugs too? We had a smashing day at school. Miss Almond brought a rabbit in to class. We all got to feed it carrots. Rodney tried to make it eat one of his sweets. The rabbit wasn't interested. Hug me now.'

'Me too me too' and Maureen's younger brother Walter came charging into the hall.

'Children let your father get his coat off and sit down and then he'll hug all of us.'

Five minutes later came the bombshell.

'Wendy, I've finally done it.'

'Done what dear?' I asked as I lifted the lid off the casserole to check on the stew.

'I got a letter today.'

'That's good love. Was it good Dennis? Who was it from?'

'Mummy will we have chips today?'

'No darling, you can't have chips every day you know. You'll end up looking like a fish finger always searching for chips.'

'Fish don't have fingers mummy. You should know that. They have fins. Will we have custard?'

'Yes love. I've made it special, just for you to put on your stew.'

'Ugh!'

'So this letter Dennis?'

'Well you know how frustrated and pissed off I've been this past six months at Grangers.'

'Dennis, the children are here.'

'Sorry dear, but you must have realised that I've been really testy some days. I've tried not to bring the office home and you know that.'

'Yes dear.'

'But some days I've been close to walking out of there, and today I did.'

'Did what dear? Maureen love, don't walk under my feet sweetheart. Not when I'm in the kitchen at the stove. I might trip over you and spill something hot. Just go and play for another five minutes and dinner will be ready. Get Walter to wash his hands for me can you?'

'Yes mummy.'

'Today you did what Dennis? Sorry, you were saying something about walking somewhere.'

Crash, bang, boom is about to happen. The bomb is ticking.

'Not walk dear but sail. Sail, all the way to Australia.'

'Who is Dennis? Somehow I'm not following you.'

'But you are Wendy, you are. You and the kids are all going to follow me. Well, not follow but come with me. All of us. We're all going. It's going to be wonderful.'

Just when I was about to put the lid back on the saucepan my husband decides to grab me by the waist and whirl me around the kitchen.

'Dennis Dennis Dennis!'

I pitched my voice higher and higher as Dennis twirled me round faster and faster.

'I've finally done it.'

Slowly the twirling stopped.

'What?' I asked.

'I've quit. I've finally had enough of the stupidity and second-best attitude at Grangers. Today was my last day. Well, not really but today I put in my notice.'

'So now what are we going to do Dennis?'

'The letter darling, the fabulous letter answered your question. It came today and it said yes. It'll be wonderful. New country, new job, new house, new people, sunshine, wonderful I tell you.'

'Dennis my sweet,' I said looking at my husband's excited face and waving arms. 'Dennis there is something you haven't said. Something you haven't told us, yet. In very simple words Dennis what was in your fabulous letter?'

'Sit down Wendy. Sit down and listen.'

The bomb exploded.

'Australia! We can't. What about the kids, school, the house, neighbours, my parents, your parents, the tennis club, my friends, our friends,' and so I went on. Fortunately I was sitting down.

'We make a new start. Everyone does it Wendy. We all get to move sooner or later. Some of the chaps in my office have moved three or four times already in their lives. We've only had to move the once. It'll be an adventure. The kids will love it.'

'Love what daddy? What will us kids love? Walter won't wash his hands mummy. He asked me about the rabbit. He asked whether the rabbit washed his paws before eating carrots. Love what daddy?'

'How would you like to see rabbits every day little Mo'?'

'Could we, could we? Where?'

'In Australia.'

'What's Australia daddy?'

'No Walter, the question is where is Australia son, but you'll see. You'll soon see.'

And so we did. Dennis did leave Grangers and the letter contained a job offer in South Australia. Back here in England Dennis worked as a forester for a large commercial forest operations company. Although he talked about the "office" he was out in the forest half of his days and I suppose that was just as much his office as the buildings. With a forestry degree he was officially classified as a Forest Officer, as opposed to just a Forester, but I never could see any differences in the words or the activities.

'It's just that a Forester has got a Diploma from a Technical College love and I've got a degree from a University.'

'Big deal Dennis. You both work in the forest and I'd probably find you both bring the forest home with you into the house whatever your qualifications.'

I knew Dennis was frustrated at Grangers. He'd sometimes talk about it in bed when the children were asleep. He did try and not bring his "office" home with him but there were days when he was short and sharp with the kids coming home. But Australia I thought.

We packed. We sold the house. We said goodbye to relatives and friends. I went up to Maureen and Walter's school and filled in forms. We got passports. The days rushed by. We repacked because Walter wasn't sure whether he had packed Andy, his favourite teddy bear, and we couldn't find it anywhere in the house. We finally found it stuck down at the foot of his bed. Dennis had finished at Grangers and so he was in the way in the house. I know he was trying to be helpful but I could cope well enough and had everything to do listed and clear in my mind. Looking back I suppose Dennis was like a little boy in the toy store with a chance to explore a new and exciting world. Australia I thought.

Between all the helter-skelter of showing the house, finalising the deal, and organising with the shippers for the household goods I had managed to find some time to go down to the library and look at books on Australia. My parents had been upset because we were going to the other side of the world.

'Wendy, we'll never see the grandchildren. We'll never see them growing up. Maureen's such a lovely little girl and Walter is a real charmer.'

On some days mum I thought. Grandparents only see parts of the grandchildren and when that part isn't so good, well just bundle them off back to their parents. You just get a taste of their happy side mum. No, I suppose they are good kids. Wonder how they'll find Australia?

The books in the library showed pictures of Sydney and Melbourne. One of them said Melbourne was more English than the English. Always sunny in the pictures I noticed. Then there were pictures of enormous expanses of nothing. Brown, grey, dusty-looking pictures of what I later learnt was the GBA (great bugger all). I suppose it looked a bit different from our forested hillsides with hardwoods and conifer trees interspersed around rolling green fields edged with hedges and stone walls. People spoke English though I noticed. There were horses. Perhaps Maureen would like to learn to ride? The books didn't tell me very much about the people or the customs but then most of them were English now weren't they. The people with shackles on their ankles were all long dead. An opportunity Wendy girl I told myself. Of course my friends thought otherwise.

'What will you do with yourself Wendy? You won't have your friends just down the road any more. There won't be the friendly games of bridge on Wednesdays or the tennis on the weekends.'

'I've heard it's so hot.'

'And all those flies: the ones you don't see on the travel posters.'

'My Robin had a friend in his office who went there on a business trip. Poured every day he said. Absolutely torrential downpours – flooded everything.'

'I thought it was all desert.'

'They've got spiders, enormous spiders. Don't kangaroos kick? I'm sure I read somewhere they kick. Disembowel dogs.'

'Will the children play with the Abo kids? They don't wear any clothing do they?'

Maybe it was less stressful just going to the library and reading the books than listening to my friends. Mrs. Evans at the library must have heard from someone what Dennis was planning to do and she caught my arm one day and asked for a quick word.

'Wendy love I hear that you and the family are all going to Australia. Miss Pullman mentioned to me you had been asking for reference books on the country. Can I give you some advice dear?'

'Sure Mrs. Evans. Yes, Dennis has got a new job in South Australia and we are leaving in three weeks time. We are all sailing from Tilbury docks on a P&O boat.'

'That'll be really exciting Wendy. I envy you, I really do. Anyway, what I was going to say was my David went to Australia some ten years ago now. He writes me pretty regular and he's so glad he went. Sure he says he misses me and dad but he reckons it was the best thing he ever did in his life. Says the country is wonderful. Now he's a salesman for a large agricultural parts company and so he travels all over. Different he says, different from home but still exciting and full of surprises. From what he tells me you should have a great time. I thought I should mention it dear as I know a little bit about the life over there.'

'Where does he live Mrs. Evans? We might be able to say hello for you.'

'That's a nice thought my dear but David says it's a big country, a really big country. He drives for miles and miles without a lot of change in the view he says. His company is based in Ballarat in Victoria.'

'That's fine Mrs. Evans. We're just next door in South Australia. We're going to live in Mount Gambier and that's on the State border. We could go and visit I'm sure.'

'I'll give you the address if you like and tell David you might contact him.'

Looking on the map it appears that Mount Gambier is close to Ballarat. It's only an itty-bitty distance. I had a lot to learn about Australia.

We sailed from Tilbury in September with a grey mist curling over the river. Goodbye England I thought. Goodbye home.

'Well love we're off at last. Next stop Adelaide.'

'I thought this ship stopped before that Dennis.'

'Yes it does love but the next place where we really get off will be Adelaide.'

We must have sailed into Adelaide harbour in the early hours because I don't remember the ship slowing and nudging up to the wharf. We were safely moored with warps fore and aft holding us beside the dock when I awoke. The white-painted gang-plank was securely in place and already the officials were walking to and fro. A manager from Dennis's new company came on board and explained the various procedures and arrangements that had been made. He said he would look after all of the crated items and then he would take us from the Immigration officials down to the railway station for the train to Mount Gambier. The time flashed by and soon we were sitting in the train as it moved slowly out of the terminus and climbed up through the hills east of Adelaide. At midday the train stopped so the passengers could get lunch at the station cafeteria.

'Dennis, it's so hot. The children will burn up out here in this sun. Move them into the shade love. Maureen, put your hat on sweetie. Walter, come here to me please. The porter said there were refreshments in the station building Dennis. We should find something to drink at least. It's stifling out here.'

It had been cool when we left the ship and I suppose the car was air-conditioned but I didn't notice. We moved onto the train straight away and that too was air-conditioned and I didn't know this either. Leaving the train in Bordertown was like opening the oven door. It hit you like a blast from a furnace somewhere. Everyone wore shorts and some sort of thin-soled boots which I later learnt were called desert boots. Also everyone wore a hat, and I mean everyone. We must have looked so different. I listened to the conversations going on around me. They speak English here so why can't I understand them. I felt bewildered.

'Here you go love. A nice cup of tea and I've got lemonade for the kids.' Dennis had appeared with some refreshments. 'And I bought some fruit for the kids to munch on Wendy. You want anything to eat?'

'No Dennis, I'm just too hot. It really saps my energy. I'll be glad when we get to Mount Gambier and can finally rest. This journey has exhausted me Dennis.'

One month later it was December and I started to realise that it would soon be Christmas. How could it be Christmas in this heat? The shops had lights, lanterns, paper-chains, tinsel, and Santa Claus in a red suit at the back of a sleigh pulled by reindeer. The temperature outside the shop was over forty degrees and the humidity down to ten percent. The air smelled of dust and smoke and the heat mirages bounced down the street. Christmas?

Dennis came into the house waving a sheet of paper and looking agitated.

'Don't tell me darling. You've found another job and we're moving to Kenya, Japan, Singapore, Argentina?'

'Wendy Wendy Wendy,' he shouted and picking me up he whirled me around the kitchen.

'Love put me down before I knock the saucepans on the floor. So where are we going?'

'We're not going anywhere darling. You want to move already? I thought you liked it here? You seem happy enough and the kids are having a ball. Miss home?'

'No Dennis, no to all of the above. I do like it here and I'm perfectly happy. It's just the last time you came home waving a letter about we moved halfway round the world. I suppose I'm not sure what to expect.'

'Well neither am I love. This letter is confusing.'

'That's not any great change though is it? We've found several things here to be confusing. How is this any different? Can I read it?'

I took the paper from Dennis. 'This is an inter-office memorandum Dennis, although perhaps an edict from Head Office in Adelaide looking at the letter-head. Seems straightforward love. Thou shall not go over the border into Victoria. Someone doesn't want you to visit your neighbours. Weren't you over there the other day?'

'I don't think so Wendy but then again with the maps they have here I'm not really sure.'

'Dennis what are you talking about? Maps are easy to read. Let me have a look? I did Geography at College you know.'

'Well look here Wendy and you tell me what this shows.'

I looked at the map Dennis unfurled.

'Here is the forest station and this is our house with the office and garage buildings. Okay, and this is the road leading towards town. Nothing difficult there Dennis.'

'Look further and go southeast. Follow the road round.'

'Yes, it goes south from here and then bends away to the east with two, no three roads leading south again towards that road we took to go to the coast. You know, where we saw the black swans on the river. You thought that was over the border didn't you?'

'So you see three roads leading south do you?'

'Yes, three roads before that east-going road joins the State border.'

'And the State line runs north to south in a straight line?'

'That's what it shows on the map. What's the problem?'

'Several,' said Dennis scratching his head. 'It's probably more convincing to show you. Yes, let's do that this weekend. Then you'll see.'

I handed back the map still somewhat mystified and went back to getting dinner organised. You can be a bit obtuse at times Dennis I thought. Still, we keep bumping into new things: things we've never done before like the water softener. Here in our forest station the people live on two sources of water. Most of the worker's houses have two large circular water tanks beside their houses and these store rainfall off the roofs.

Although much of the State of South Australia is pretty dry we have over thirty inches of rain down here in the south-east of the State. This falls mostly in one wet season and there are four months in the year when we never see rain at all and all of our lawns turn golden. Virtually all of the farm folk around us get their water this same way from off the roof. Now our house is a little different. Sure we have a large water tank with a feed from the roof gutters but we also have bore water. This comes from one hundred and twenty feet under the house. I can remember asking that first week we moved into the house why we have a water softener.

'Have you seen the water Wendy, before it goes into the softener?'

'No Dennis. I suppose not. What's so special about it?'

Dennis laughed. 'I should let you fill the bath with it and see whether you really want to step in. You'd be pretty grossed out.'

'Why?' I said. 'Does it smell or something?'

'It looks like blood love. It'd be the perfect pool for a vampire. It is full of iron which is why we need to soften it. Those tanks outside leach out the iron and so most of the colour. I'll bet you Maureen would never have a bath again although Walter would probably think it was cool.'

'Is it safe to drink Dennis?'

'Ignorance is bliss love. Going to make me a cuppa?'

The other thing that took some getting used to was the attitude towards us. Dennis told me it had been a challenge at first.

'Dennis Fowler eh? Another pommy bastard I've got to train I suppose? Well good day to yer mate. Got settled in have you? We open shop at seven-thirty with you getting the gang off to work and then close down around four-thirty. This time of year, when it's hot and dry, the gang get smoke-o mid morning but out on the fire breaks you hear. Place is as dry as tinder right now. No smoking in the bush. You'll have old Harold as your foreman. He's a useless sod but he's been here a while. Don't expect him to do any work or get out of the ute but he knows his way around. The young driver you've got is okay though. Truck takes the women into town twice a week now, no more than that. Anything else you need to know just ask Sandy my clerk here. He'll explain everything. Come on dogs. We're off.'

'And then he ambled out of the office and up to his house. I remember asking Sandy where the boss was going and all he said was "breakfast".'

'And was that where he was going?' I asked.

'Seeing as he was still wearing his pyjamas Wendy I'd guess he was going to get dressed first and then have breakfast, but then again, maybe not in that order.'

'He was in the office in his pyjamas?'

'Seems my boss likes to see the gang off in the morning but that doesn't mean he starts work then. Actually, he does most of his management work in the pub in the afternoon.'

'What do you mean Dennis, management work in the pub?'

'Well you know I run this station down here and Mr. Thorpe, Damien Thorpe runs the entire District?'

'Sure, I understand that. He's got two other foresters up at the big forest and he plunked you out here, out of sight and out of mind by all accounts. He seems to have a resentment to immigrants, us bloody pommies.'

'Never mind that Wendy. Damien's okay, and his bark is worse than his bite, but yes he runs the whole show and he usually gives the running orders in the pub of an afternoon. Look, you know we finish here in the bush around four-thirty? Well what happens then?'

'Usually you breeze in around five dragging half the forest with you, plunk yourself down under my feet in the kitchen and demand a cuppa.'

Dennis laughed and then blushed embarrassedly as he realised that's exactly what he did do. 'True love, probably true, but what I meant was what does the gang do?'

'Dennis I don't know. They probably do the same as you and pester their wives with when's dinner ready.'

'Wrong Wendy, so wrong. At four-thirty the local street racing takes place as everyone comes back here to the yard and jumps in their utes and takes off to the pub. They call it the six o'clock swill. The pubs shut at six and so you only have a short window in which to drink as much as you can. At six you stagger home to the wife or whoever for tea.'

'Charming Dennis, really charming. I have this picture of domestic bliss with the husband staggering over the threshold red-eyed and unsteady on his feet asking for sausage and mash.'

'Yes,' said Dennis laughing, 'and hold the veggies 'cos Australians don't eat veggies. Actually I'm not sure they eat sausages either. Didn't you tell me about that incident in the butchers the other day?'

Now it was my turn to laugh when I remembered what had happened in town.

'A pound of mince, those four pork chops and a pound of liver please. Oh, and do you have any kidneys too? If so I'll take four kidneys.'

'For your dog or your cat love?'

'Pardon. No, the chops are for my family's dinner tonight Mr. Dodgeson and the mince for tomorrow. We'll have the liver and kidneys for breakfast.'

'You mean you're going to eat them and they're not for the cat?'

'They're lovely Mr. Dodgeson. They'll fry up really nice,' I said.

'Stone me love, you poms sure eat some funny grub. You wouldn't catch any real Australian eating your tucker Missus. Meat and potatoes us and go easy on the spuds. Beef mind you, only beef and none of that woolly meat.'

'Let me come back to Damien. It's during the six o'clock swill that he makes all the decisions. He sits there apparently and decides what and where the work will be tomorrow.'

'Why don't you go Dennis? Sounds like you should be there and have your say.'

'Wendy you don't tell Damien anything. There would be no point in going. Damien dictates for the entire District, for all of his domain. You know he's got his sheep grazing in my plantations?'

'How can he do that Dennis? Isn't there some conflict of interest? Some incest clause about having his sheep in his District?'

'He has the grazing lease registered in his wife's maiden name and so no conflict.'

A couple of days later I went into town with the other women on the gang truck. This was a five ton lorry with benches in the back that we used to take the wives into town to go shopping. Our nearest shops were twenty miles away and so twice a week the Forest Station provided this service. Sometimes I went into town in our car but this week I went with the other wives. Being the Forest Officer's wife I got to sit up in the front with Bluey the driver. Sitting beside me was Maggie Winters, the foreman's wife. She was English but from a longtime back. She'd come out to Australia as a war bride and settled. On the trip home she was telling me about the men and their attitude to Dennis. It was interesting to learn what my husband had been doing and how the men saw him.

'Always a challenge at first love. They watch and see whether he really knows what he's doing. Of course it was that much harder for your husband, him being a pom and all. Lazy bunch most of them if truth be told. If pushed they'll do just enough to pass muster but don't expect anything extra, except our Bluey here,' she joshed.

Bluey blushed and held on tighter to the steering wheel.

'Don't know about that missus. I do me job and keep me nose

clean. Look after the utes and the gang truck here, and the fire truck of course.'

'As I was saying dear, your Dennis showed them early on he knew what the job was. Actually he quite surprised my Harold. Seems your Dennis knows how to use a shovel, strain wire on the fences and do the surveys for the clearing contractors. He didn't bugger off at seven-thirty for breakfast like old Damien does either. Out with the gang he was, and for the first three or four weeks he was working alongside so that they could see he knew how things should get done.'

Here Maggie stopped and laughed to herself. 'It's funny really love. I'm not sure whether the blokes were impressed or threatened. They saw quick enough that your Dennis knew the work. What worried them was that he would stay working with them for a lot longer and that they couldn't slack off like they usually do. My Harold came home quite worried after that first week. He thought your husband was going to upset the normal routine. Still, knows his stuff does your Dennis Wendy. The blokes will accept him, for a pom that is.'

'Dennis said it was a bit of a challenge Maggie. All of the men in the gang are his parent's age. He said he had to stand up tall when he explained what the job was for the day or for the week. Telling his "parents" what to do in their own country was a little different but he's come home really enthusiastic. He's so much happier than he was working back in England and that is good.'

'Yes dearie, that is good and I'm glad to hear it. But what about you? This must seem all a little different for you surely? Bet you had shops just around the corner if I can remember England? How are your Mo' and Walt making out?'

I sat back on the front bench seat of the bouncing lorry as we created a dust storm down the forest road and thought on Maggie's question.

'Yes Maggie, it is a little different but it's good different. I suppose I'd

189

never had this kind of challenge before – a little like Dennis really. New country, new people, new customs, even a new language in a way and all of that is good yet still a challenge. I look out of my kitchen window and I don't see sparrows any more but I see lorikeets and small parrots. Across the fields, no the paddocks I should say, we see cockatoos and then flocks of galahs. They really are beautiful when they come in big pink and white clouds. Occasionally one of the big male roos will venture out of the forest.'

'And always the sun is shining,' said Maggie with a chuckle in her voice. 'All I can remember about England was the rain. It was always raining where we lived as kids.'

'Here we go ladies, home sweet home,' said Bluey as he swung the lorry round in the yard. 'Step down carefully now. I'll go and open the tailgate.'

'Snakes,' said Maggie suddenly. 'That's the one thing your Dennis didn't know about Wendy. He could do all of the jobs in the bush Harold said but he didn't know anything about snakes.'

'You get many here?' I asked. 'Where?'

'Yes love we do and they can get everywhere. Tiger snakes are common around here. Bite is poisonous of course but it won't kill an adult.'

'What about the children?' I asked starting to feel worried. 'What about the dog?'

'Teach them to look Wendy and not go poking about in corners and under things. Make sure they walk about in the garden with heavy feet. Snakes feel the vibrations in the ground and will try and hide away but yes, teach the children to be careful. No putting your hands up drainpipes or down holes. Actually spiders up drainpipes are just as dangerous.'

'And the dog?'

'I'd get a cat, or more than one cat if I were you. They're really good against snakes. Much better than any dog I know.'

'I'll keep my eyes open Maggie. Thanks. I'll tell the children to be careful.'

Just when I was thinking how different and how pretty the world looked from my kitchen window now I realised that my paradise was full of lurking monsters; snakes and spiders rather than lions and crocodiles. I suppose Dennis could have applied for a job in Africa and then I would have to contend with lions and crocodiles. Which did I prefer?

That Friday night I found out that the monsters didn't just lurk in the garden either. We had a chimney fire. Back in England we used to have the chimneys cleaned once a year and that was always great excitement for the children. All the furniture got covered in dust sheets. We all waited outside in the garden to see who could see the brush first coming out of the chimney pots. Here it was a little different. Suddenly the kitchen was full of smoke and there was a great roaring up the stove pipe. We didn't have the wood stove on because we were cold - seeing as it was over forty degrees - but I had to do some baking. This in itself was already a challenge as the kitchen floor sloped a little and everything in a baking tray tended to slop sideways. Cakes weren't regular anymore, certainly not rectangular but a slanting trapezoid kind of shape. Anyway, that wasn't the problem.

'Dennis, the chimney's on fire.'

'Yes dear.'

'Dennis the chimney's on fire!!' and this time I sounded a little more urgent.

Fortunately at the Forest Station our house was right beside the yard and Dennis quickly got a crew together and put the fire truck into action. The kids thought this was exciting. I just thought it was terrifying. Maggie from next door had told me earlier that the life of a burning house here is thirty minutes. We ended up with some ruined baking, a very wet kitchen floor and a recommendation to get the chimney scrubbed out.

Burning red gum was very efficient, and it gave off good heat, but it also gave off a large quantity of resins and these condensed out onto the stove pipe. Every now and again these deposits decided to have a fire of their own. One learns I thought. As I said, another lurking monster.

We exposed the story of the map and the edict from Head Office that following weekend. I decided that I had seen enough of my kitchen and suggested we have a picnic. Dennis decided to turn it into a treasure hunt for the kids.

'Search for the elusive road. Let's see whether we can find where the world ends, at the edge of South Australia.'

'What happens on the edge daddy?'

'We'll have to be careful Walter when we find the edge or we will fall off into Victoria. My boss sent me a letter saying I mustn't fall off into Victoria.'

'Will we see rabbits?'

'Probably Walter. I've had my trappers out all week but mostly inside a new plantation. My trappers are supposed to clear all of the rabbits out before we plant the new trees. Know why that is Maureen?'

'They eat the young trees daddy.'

'Is she right Walter? Do rabbits eat trees? They're awfully woody. You don't eat trees now do you?'

'They'd taste all sticky daddy. They're full of robbon or something. Isn't that why the chimney caught fire? How will Father Christmas come down our chimney daddy? It's awfully narrow. He'll never get his sack down our chimney and we won't get any presents.'

'Walter, what about my rabbits?'

'They eat grass daddy. Remember Maureen saw them do that back in England.'

'So Maureen, your brother thinks the rabbits eat grass. What do you say to that?'

'I think they eat both daddy. They must eat your trees or you wouldn't have the trappers do all that work inside the fences.'

'If I get a chance I'll show you what those furry little bunnies do. They might look cute but they cost me a lot of money. You know we plant the trees here in neat rows. This is fine says Mr. Flopsy Bunny and he hippity hops down the row and looks at a tree. Just fine he says and he takes one nip and chops off the top of the seedling. He might not even eat it before he has hopped down to the next tree in the row and calmly chops the top off that one too.'

'Does this kill them? It would if he ate them.'

'No Maureen love, our friendly rabbit doesn't kill them but he takes away all of this year's growth, and often they will grow up next year with a forked top and that is not good.'

'Why daddy? Now you'd get two for one. That must be good.'

'Dennis I think the kids are leading you into a bigger and bigger hole. You should take them out soon after you've planted a new compartment. It'll be easier to show them. Now where are we on this road? Maureen, you are old enough to read a map love. Do you know where we are on this map?'

'Why are those men cutting down those little trees daddy? They're not big enough to go to the mill in town. All the logs going there are big. They're huge on those large lorries. What are they going to do with those little ones?'

'Good question Maureen. Hang on Wendy, I'm going to have to stop and find out. This is still part of my Station and I don't know who they are or what they are doing. They are certainly company trees.'

I watched as Dennis walked over to the ute beside the fence and talked with the driver. He was a heavyset man with a torn singlet and a bush hat. He was smoking and when he talked there was a lot of arm waving going on. A couple of the men who were cutting the trees walked out of the plantation and over to the ute.

'Bloke 'ere Larry says these are 'is trees. Can't understand how come we're cutting. Told him we've got a lorry load for the Melbourne market. You tell 'im. Bloody pom can't understand me.'

'What's up chum?'

'Who gave you permission to cut Company trees? Where's your permit?'

'Look sport, we don't need no permit. Christmas trees these are aren't they? Nod and a wink from Damien in the pub the other night. Few quid under the table and no-one's the wiser. His responsibility, his trees, his deal, easy ain't it? Where's the problem mate?'

'Damien who?' asked Dennis.

'Don't come that one sport. If you stopped here and made out they were your trees you must work for the company. You know who Damien is?'

'And he said just come and cut?'

'Just one load like. Looking around you've got lots of trees. Not going to miss a few are you? Christmas time anyway. Good for the kiddies. Look good in the corner covered with tinsel and all. Anyway mate, we've work to do. Talk to old Damien. He'll put you straight.'

Dennis walked back to our car with a disgusted look on his face.

'Everything okay?' I asked. 'They seemed to think what they were doing was legit.'

'Are they Christmas trees daddy? Some of them are a bit straggly. They've not got many needles. Where are they going on that lorry?'

'You're right on Maureen. They will be Christmas trees for all the boys and girls in the city, and you're right, some of them do look a little open and spindly.'

'Where's the treasure daddy?' piped up Walter wriggling about in the back seat. 'I thought you told us we were looking for treasure?'

'So we are young man and your sister has the map with the clues. So where are we Maureen?'

'Here,' she said and plonked her finger down on the map. 'Just down here about a mile I think we should find a fork in the road and we carry straight on if we're going to the border.'

We drove on down the narrow sandy road. The rows of planted conifers stopped and we entered the blue-grey dusty world of Eucalypts. The trees stood tall and bare of branches for fifty or sixty feet up their slender cylindrical pale grey boles. In places it looked like the pillars down the nave of a church. With some of the species there was very little undergrowth and the whole lower level of the forest was just a vista of slender very straight trunks. Occasionally the forest would contain a very old veteran that had escaped the last destructive fire and this would be massive with long hanging strips of bark festooned down from the upper limbs and a now furrowed and heavily buttressed base to its bole. I suppose I had never seen a forest quite like this until last weekend. The previous weekend we had taken the children to camp and hike a little in an area called the Grampians in Victoria. I remember I joked with Dennis that we weren't supposed to go over the border and he said that only applied to company business and this was pleasure. We had camped near a village called Halls Gap, down by a creek. Here again we were surrounded by these tall grey ghosts with their hanging strips of silvery bark and long blue-grey-green leaves. The tall bare trunks didn't look like trees. Thinking back I couldn't remember any forest looking like that in England. We had beech forests which had grey boles, and often no branches for a way, and even some young ash trees before the bark got furrowed but nothing quite like this. Then Maureen saw something that none of us had ever seen before.

'Look mummy look. Up in the tree. Higher, higher up. By the first branch. It's moving. Look it's moving.'

And it was. A square mass of grey fur which unravelled to show four limbs and a large funny head with cute standing up ears slowly, oh so slowly descended the bole of the gum tree.

'Now don't move Walter or you will scare it. Just stand still love. You too Maureen. You can breathe love but just don't rush about.'

'Will it bite us mummy?'

'No darling. It eats leaves. It won't bite you but it has long sharp claws. See how it digs them into the bark to come down the tree. I imagine they might make a mark on you if it dug them in. Let's just watch.'

The koala slowly clambered down and sat looking owlishly about on the forest floor. It picked up a few leaves and just as quickly discarded them. With an elderly paced gait it ambled across the clearing to another gum tree and just as slowly ascended.

'We were lucky to see that Wendy. I'd heard there were some koalas in this area but we were lucky to have one visit the campsite.'

For the children this private viewing of their campsite's koala was a real highlight. The subsequent hike up Sundial Peak and its views were of little consequence. Even when we drove from the Grampians to see the rock climbing on nearby Mount Arapiles the children were not interested. Dennis was interested though and I had to remind him that he was a grown-up married man now and no longer an undergraduate so forget it. Rock-climbing days are over for you sport.

'Mummy there's no road!'

Maureen's indignant retort brought me back to the present.

'What dear? What's no road?'

'It's like I told you Wendy. It shows on the map and looks just like the road we are on but it's not there. It's like now you see it now you don't.'

'Like the Cheshire cat daddy in Alice in Wonderland?'

'Where's the Cheshire cat?' asked Walter. 'I don't see any cat. Will we see koalas again mummy? He was cute. I wish I could have cuddled him. He wouldn't have scratched me. I'd be ever so gentle.'

'Yes Walter, I'm sure you would have love, but he just wanted to find some more breakfast before his nap. You know they sleep over twenty hours of every day. That's even more than you do Walter.'

'Well I'm awake now and I don't see any koalas, or any cats.'

'The road's not there,' said Maureen indignantly for the second time. 'Are you in the right place daddy?'

'As I told your mother little Mo' the map shows one thing and the ground shows another. Look, there are three roads marked on this map that join the road we are on. Why don't we continue and see whether we can find either of the other two. Sixpence to the first person to see the next junction.'

'Really,' said Walter excitedly, 'sixpence?'

We drove on and Maureen worked out how far it was on the map until we should reach the next junction.

'We must have passed it. Daddy we've gone too far. Back up.'

'I didn't see any junction love. Did anyone see any junction? Is my sixpence safe?'

'Dennis I think your map is so much hot air. Perhaps they made it up in Adelaide. Perhaps that's why you got that letter. No-one knows where they are down here. Maybe there is no border and we could drive on for miles and run out of petrol and be stuck there for ever in no-mans land. We'd be found by the aborigines when they go walk-about and be jangling skeletons for their corroborees.'

'Mummy, mummy I'm frightened. I don't want to become a skeleton.'

'It's okay Walter love. I'm just joking. There will be a border and we won't fall over the edge so don't worry darling. Mummy's just saying silly things. Roads Dennis, disappearing roads love? Drive on and let's see whether road number three is any more obvious than roads number one and two?'

Road number three was another figment of the imagination. Only later did we find out that the roads had been surveyed on the ground years and years ago but never been developed. Sure they had been carefully drawn on the maps ready for actual construction but that had never happened. I found this a novelty. Back home we normally built something and only later did it appear on the map. Here it seems you drew the something on the map before you actually built it. Well I thought light-headedly, we were upside down in Australia!

After another half an hour we reached a very distinctive junction. The road ended. Well, that wasn't quite true as it branched north and south into two sandy trails but there was no surfaced road straight on.

'The border Dennis? This the border we mustn't cross? Don't see how we can anyway as there is no road.'

In front of us was a radiata pine plantation about ten years old with the tree tops swaying about sixty feet above us. Looking north the sandy trail ran straight for a ways and then jogged out of sight.

'We're lost daddy,' exclaimed our map reader.

'No love, we've reached the border. We're here' and Dennis placed his finger on the map. He traced the road line we had driven down to the clear north-south big thick black line which represented the State line.

'So if we turn that way daddy we would reach the road. You know the road to the beach and the black swans.'

'Very good Miss Navigator, very good.'

We had already found that our car was quite good on sandy trails, and although this area in south-east South Australia was mostly sand dunes the area we drove was flat as we followed Maureen's suggestion and went south. After about a mile we saw a green Landrover parked by the edge of a plantation.

'Those trees look a little different Dennis. The cones are bigger. They're not radiata?'

'No love. They're loblolly pine I think, from the south-east of the USA. You know, Georgia and Florida.'

Dennis pulled up by the Landrover.

'G'day. You lost mate?'

'No, well I don't think so. I manage the forests on this side of the border. From the sign on your Landrover you do the same thing on your side. Am I right?'

'Right on. I'm Barney, Barney Dodds. I'm just out checking whether my lazy trappers are putting out the right bait for the bleedin' rabbits. Oh, sorry Miss. Sorry about the language. Didn't see the kiddies in the back. Good day to you.'

'Hi Barney Dodds. We're Dennis and Wendy Fowler and this here is Maureen and Walter. My husband is showing us his domain.'

Barney pushed his hat up off his forehead and laughed. 'Domain,' he chuckled, 'ain't heard that word used around here.'

'Bait?' Dennis asked. 'You mentioned bait for the rabbits. We use a 1080 poison mixed up with the oats we scatter about. Doesn't seem to do a lot though.'

Barney smiled. 'Think about it Dennis. It's hot. It's dry and you're a hungry and thirsty rabbit. You see this nice dry dusty sprinkling of oats and you think seriously. Do I really want to eat this? Then you see a neat scattering of orange juicy succulent carrots. Which do I eat?'

'But we were told we couldn't use carrots. We had to use oats.'

'Right on sport. You can't but we can and very effective they are too.'

'I never knew that. Head Office never told us that.'

'And perhaps that's why you can't go over the border Dennis. Perhaps that's why you were told don't go over the border and fraternise with the enemy,' I said.

'Enemy,' laughed Barney. 'Enemy? The only real times we become enemies mate is when there's a fire on. Then we really don't like you.'

'How's that?' I asked.

Barney pulled out a handkerchief and wiped his hot forehead. 'It's like this Missus. The wind usually blows from the west in this part of the world and that's from you to us. You get a fire and you do your best chasing up its backside but you never manage to put it out before it comes bowling all over my forest. Now your company, and your government for that matter has a funny policy. Well funny for you maybe but not for us.'

'Which is?' asked Dennis.

'You've not been here long mate?'

'No,' said Dennis. 'We came about six weeks ago now. We've not been here long. That's why we are out exploring. I haven't been to this edge of the bush before. We were just going south to the Nelson and Portland road.'

'Trail's okay out to the highway Dennis. You'll be fine. There's no hills.'

'You were saying about fire Barney?' I asked. 'When we become the enemy you said.'

'Sure. You've got this fire, and you've done a good job mopping up the tail end and working along the sides, but the head is still going strong and it comes charging into Victoria.'

'And?'

'Well you all stop here at the border and wave it goodbye. Policy says you fight it in South Australia but you don't cross into Victoria.'

'But that's crazy,' said Dennis. 'The fire doesn't know any boundary, any silly line on the map. We've got what, a chain-wide fire break along this State line? Any fire that's not a slow ground fire will jump that like it doesn't exist. So our crews would just continue to beat at the back of it.'

'Don't you ever tell your boss that Dennis. Old Damien would have your guts for garters mate. Once it's over the State line you stop sport. Not your problem. Wave it goodbye. Anyway, I've got traps to check. Straight down the line mate. Bye kids, bye missus. See you around Dennis, neighbour.'

'Neighbour,' I exclaimed. 'No wonder Head Office told you not to visit your neighbours Dennis. You never know what you might learn if you talk to the neighbours.'

BON ECHO

THERE IS THIS CLIFF ABOVE Lake Mazinaw in south central Ontario that forms the eastern border to Bon Echo Provincial Park. It rises four hundred feet above the surface of the lake and people say the fault line goes down another three hundred feet under water. When you see it for the first time it seems to stretch for over a kilometre down to the Narrows and even then it makes an effort for the next four hundred metres but the foreshore there makes it look smaller. As we are now situated on the Canadian Shield the rock is metamorphosed granite with occasional bands of shale, streaks of white quartz, glittering flakes of mica and pale red feldspar. Facing west the pink-tinged cliff embraces the afternoon sun and offers a rock climbing playground with routes of all standards dancing upwards from the water to the irregular crest.

For several years now the Toronto Section of the Alpine Club of Canada has owned a small Club Hut on the eastern shore surrounded by Crown land and fronting an expansive wilderness area as you go further east. But it is the cliff that is the magnet for the members of the Alpine Club, and most weekends, and sometimes for weeks on end there is a steady procession of enthusiasts motoring down the lake from the Hut to some new challenge. True enough there is a lull from March to mid April as the ice goes out and then again a small dedicated band of maniacs spend a cold wet weekend in mid November hauling the dock out of the lake and walking bare-foot in the snow to ensure the ice doesn't turn it into matchwood come the spring. Peace reigns from late November until mid January when the ice appears to be safe.

In my early years, when I used to go up from Toronto on a Friday evening, I found the entire effort of locating the Club Hut a challenge. With a few friends we arrived at the marina on the western shore around ten o'clock and carted the tents, climbing gear, food, beer, mustn't forget the beer, and several other maybe useful items down to the dock for loading. The next challenge was to find the Club boat, along with the key, the gas tank, the emergency paddles, the lifejackets and any message left from last weekend which might explain why the propeller was bent a little and need to be re-aligned!! After gassing up, loading up, and making sure we didn't have too many people for a safe voyage you tried to find the navigation lights. Officially, legally that is, we should have a green light to starboard and a red light to port. That was thought to be important so that other mad people chasing about the lake at night-time in boats far more powerful than the Club's eighteen-footer can see which side of you they are running into. For over fifty percent of the time our lights never worked and so we posted a hero up front, sitting in the bow with an ever-ready flashlight. For any noise on the left he would put his spread-out hand over the flashlight and produce a weak but red glow. Similarly for any noise on the right he would point the light up over his green face and hope that the image would repel any boarders. Most evenings, in the pitch black of a moonless, overcast sky with no stars, and limited memory of where we were going, it was a challenge to spend twenty minutes crossing the lake looking for an indistinct dip in the silhouetted horizon. Was it the first dip or the second dip coming from the cliff direction someone would ask? A needless debate would ensue and you as the coxswain steered where you thought it was and ignored the debate. After twenty minutes your courage faltered and you asked the hero on the sharp end to keep a lookout for land.

The Club Hut was thirty metres up from the lake's edge in a neat little bay with two rocky headlands. Someone had very wisely mounted a flagpole on one of the headlands and someone even wiser had painted it white. Glory be to God you muttered as the hero's flashlight caught the white pole and all hands would be safe. Mark you, on a rough night with a strong northerly wind, this was a dangerous lee shore and landing was still a challenge. Cut the motor, glide alongside the dock, put out the fenders quickly, keep stray hands off the gunwales and at the right moment as the bed the of lake rose quickly lift the prop out of the water before you add to its already bent shape.

'Catch the dock,' you cry authoratatively. 'Hero leap ashore and make fast the painter. Second mate do the stern warp.'

This would be fine if climbers knew anything about boats and their attendant accessories. So, after the not-to-be-repeated-too-often crash of the boat coming alongside, the resultant conversation would go something like this. 'What's a painter? Who's warped?'

Somehow you tied up, unloaded and carried the cargo up to the Hut. Now if you had been here before you had already made plans with your partner to be first out of the boat and bag your favourite flat campsite. Otherwise you might spend the weekend on some uncomfortable side slope. The appointed Hut custodian for the weekend dutifully unlocked the Hut and lit the hurricane lanterns, although this latter task depended on there being fuel in the lanterns and operational mantles. A shortfall in either meant working in the dark for the evening unless you were thoughtful enough to slip a flashlight in your pocket or on your head.

Officially the rendezvous for the Club boat at the marina on the western shore was ten o'clock on the Friday night and ten o'clock on the

Saturday morning. As most of the group came from Toronto one usually knew who would be where at either of these two times. Occasionally one or two people would come down from the Ottawa Section or even from Montreal and there was always the question on the Friday night whether someone should pop over to the marina and check if there were any latecomers. When this question got talked about you busied yourself with your tent, sleeping bag, foamy and other activities fervently pursuing sleep. You'd done your bit for the night and it was usually the Hut custodian who answered the question. He'd stand on the headland by the flagpole and peer myopically back towards the night light of the marina. If he failed to see any frantically waving flashlight he assumed we were all present and correct and retired to bed like the rest of us.

Arriving in winter time, which was anytime after the ice appeared to be safe, it was a completely different experience, especially if you came up on a Friday evening. To start with there was always the debate about whether the ice was thick enough, especially if this was the first visit of the winter season. Then you had to determine whether the ice was clear, whether there was a little snow, or whether it was knee deep and going to be a long slog? Over the years I suppose I tried a variety of techniques to move a weekend's gear and provisions over the kilometre or so of lake to the Hut. In summer-time the boat could carry a lot. Winter-time you carried or towed it across. Walk or ski was a prime question. Bare ice made for easy walking but the surface was so irregular that skiing became a challenge, especially when carrying a heavy rucksack and towing a poorly packed sledge. However, if you walked you had to make sure the skis stayed attached to the sledge and did not end up left forlornly in the middle of the lake. Pressure ridges in the lake provided another winter obstacle. Lake Mazinaw was over ten miles long and oriented straight north to south. Any strong wind would pick up the ice and pull layers of it over an adjacent section. Before long you had a pressure ridge. I've heard they are quite common in the Arctic and cause some delays for North Pole visitors but then they have sled dogs who can handle such minor inconveniences. Townies, with excessive baggage, on foot, after a long week in the office, find them a pain of the highest order. Clambering over them you have to keep reminding yourself not to flip the sledge over and break the beer bottles!

Arriving at the Hut in the dark in winter-time provides additional challenges. Inevitably some useless group will have dragged the dock out of the lake in the preceding November and left it exactly in the path for reaching the Hut. You don't find this out until you fall off the end of it into a snow bank. The group volunteers a heavy member to plough a furrow up the shore to the Hut and you all heartily applaud a job well done. If the group is small you quickly reach a mutual decision to sleep in the Hut, at least for tonight. Larger groups result in tents going up and lots of muttering about "hard men".

When I first started going up to Bon Echo we had some tentative agreement with the Provincial Park's staff about warning flags on the cliff. Mazinaw Lake is a very popular spot in summertime and the Provincial Park campsite is full most of July and all of August. Many people cruise up and down the lake in motor boats, sailboats, canoes, kayaks, and the occasional escaped air mattress or rubber tyre from the Park's beach. Along the foot of the cliff are several Indian pictographs in red ochre depicting voyages in canoes and fishing exploits. The lake was an important meeting place in days past. Above this varied and slow-moving armada climbers struggle to move ever upwards towards the top of the cliff. Inevitably the odd loose rock, unstable handhold or even misplaced nut will fall and at an ever-accelerating velocity make an impressive hole in any craft in the way. Before we started any climb we would dutifully fix coat-hangars adorned with red material at the foot of our route. The intention was to warn boaters of an overhead hazard but over time it merely served as an advertisement to come and watch the monkeys on the cliff. This in itself was not a problem because you could ignore the rather fanciful suggestions from the cheap seats but unfortunately a few drunken souls thought they could climb up after us and this did prove a problem. Eventually one of the ill-prepared followers would get stuck and an impromptu rescue went into effect. Both the local Park's staff and the Ontario Provincial Police (OPP) who patrolled the lake came shod in leather-soled shoes or boots. Within an hour or so the climbing club members were called in to rescue the drunken park visitor, the Provincial Park's keen employee and occasionally an over-enthusiastic but ill-equipped constable. On some days it was like a sketch from Monty Python. Fortunately we concluded all these pseudo rescue activities with no injuries. However, climbers themselves can get hurt and so once a year the Club did have a rescue practice weekend.

We had one climb, called Top Secret, which offered a very safe and convenient place to practice rescues. At the foot of this climb was dry land, as opposed to the lake, and this provided a flat site to unload the victim off the stretcher. About one hundred feet up the cliff, at the top of the first pitch, was a broad ledge about twelve feet long. We had fixed a series of bolts in the wall up above the belay ledge. The "patient", or victim if you like, and the rescue team easily climbed up the first pitch and tied themselves off on the ledge. The basket stretcher was hauled up to the ledge and the leader set about instructing all of us about our respective duties. Normally when rescuing someone off a climb it is easier to lower than to lift them up and that was the plan. We would lower the stretcher with a rope on each end from the ledge. These ropes ran up through a locked set of karabiners clipped into the bolts. The team carefully strapped the patient into the basket. For a straightforward rescue it was easier to employ one other team member and this person was attached to the outside of the stretcher and guided it down the cliff. To ensure a little reality we needed to add more rope lengths before the stretcher actually reached the ground. This required a very careful locking system to enable any knots to bypass the karabiner brakes and was done one rope at a time. With a careful set-up we could repeat this exercise five or six times during the course of a day and this let most of the participants handle all of the various tasks. Doing this on a warm sunny day with no wind, no rain and in broad daylight was easy but helpful for practice. In reality one or more of these ideal conditions was missing and you needed to be able to perform this activity when stressed out. At the end of the day, when the last "body" was lowered, the team on the ledge collected up all the rescue gear and ascended the rest of the route. For over fifteen or more years we luckily never had to put this practice into effect for real, whereas another kind of rescue seemed to be necessary every two or three years and that was far more difficult.

Porcupines shared their part of the forest with us and we gradually accepted each others presence until salt became an issue. With limited wildlife knowledge amongst the group we did not know about a porcupine's passion for salt. They also have a penchant for the glues in plywood but it was salt that caused the downfall of one of our spiny neighbours. Now climbing tends to be a sport that stimulates the senses, heightens the adrenaline rush and very often gives rise to the need for rapid bowel movements. As a result we had a fine outhouse further up the hillside and well away from any source of water. Early pioneers of the Club Hut site had correctly reasoned that over time we would need more than one hole, especially if the standard of climbing got higher and the fear factor rose accordingly. Forethought led to a wooden structure that fitted onto a ground framework that defined the hole. Once close to full the wooden structure could be easily moved to a second or even third hole ad infinitum according to the dictates of mother nature and human's need to lighten the load so to speak. You also have to realise that with any climbing partnership there is often a slight disparity in skill level between the two members. One bloke is keen, eager, bold, and trying to push the limit. His or her partner is keen, eager, less bold and decidedly happy with being second on the rope. The night before our keen and eager leader is avidly reading the guidebook and deciding on tomorrow's great adventure: the chance to up the ante and move into a higher grade. His or her second is quietly sitting in the Hut and supping on a beer reading comic novels or a treatise on psychological treatment of persons thought to be suffering from delusions of grandeur. Obviously our second is not quite sure about the neurological state of his or her leader. Come the next morning the leader is gung ho, full of wheaties and scientifically arranging their climbing gear according to the suggestions in the guidebook. And our second, our second you ask? Well our second is sitting for the second time on the outhouse toilet seat and trying to ease the quivering in the lower bowel. With shorts and underpants around the ankles the second presses his hot sweaty thighs onto the wooden frame suitably cut to offer a well-shaped seat for such activity. On a warm sunny morning with such a fearless leader the second produces an abundance of sweat. Eventually you can not procrastinate any longer and full of false bonhomie our carefree second saunters down the path to find his fearless leader and explain about one beer too many last night. In the excitement to seem keen and eager our second fails to latch the outhouse door and so they initiate an unfortunate accident. No, not on the cliff dear reader because the keen and eager bold leader does fine on the chosen climb and his second overcomes his early morning weaknesses and sails spectacularly up the route like the climber he is. No, it is back at camp that the trouble has started. Now I'm not sure how good is our friendly porcupine's sense of smell, or his eyesight for that matter but he, or maybe she because we never did sex the beast after the great event, is eagerly searching for breakfast, and wandering through the bush comes across the open door. This close to the seat the smell of sweat would be overpowering. 'Breakfast' comes the porcupine cry and when we reconstructed the scene of the accident afterwards for the official report we realised our spiny neighbour had scrambled up onto the seat and started chewing the tasty wood. Unfortunately the excitement was too much and with or without good smell or eyesight the chomping beast over-balanced and dropped into the pit.

He might have gone un-noticed for a while had not one of the feminine camp-followers, whose other half was probably battling up the cliff somewhere, decided to "spend a penny" as that dreadful smelly outdoors loo seemed to be vacant. Somewhat embarrassed and walking quietly up the hillside, turning round now and then to make sure no-one was following or could see her, the young lady stepped inside. Wrinkling her nose she dabbed a tissue around the seat and turned around to squat. Wriggling her shorts and panties around her ankles she delicately lowered her derriere onto the wood. Relieving herself she thought she heard a noise. No, she definitely heard a noise. Someone was here and perhaps they were peeping. Frantically she looks around but it is a small outhouse and there isn't room to hide anyone. The noise persists and by now she is quite agitated. Turning around a second time she realises the noise is below her and holding her nose and trying not to look she peeps down the hole.

The scream cuts through the moment-before's peace and quiet of the forest. She thrusts open the door and as her panties and shorts are still around her ankles she stumbles on the steep path, and when people come running up to see why the scream she is caught violently trying to pull her resistant underwear upwards. 'There, there, there,' she screams again and the rescuers are torn between looking at her outstretched finger and her over-stretched panties. 'In the hole,' she shouts. 'There's something down there.'

Most of the usual group at the campsite are well aware there is something down the hole but we don't tend to get too excited about a best left unspoken topic. 'Something living' she adds and wise heads nod still a little unsure about this new camp-follower. 'Down in the hole there is a living animal,' she finally manages to explain, and as she has now politely re-arranged her panties and shorts in their more ladylike position the group turns its attention to the whatever is down the hole that is living.

Our climbing club included members from diverse walks of life. We had engineers, we had school teachers, we had chemistry students, we had studious men with PhDs and a smattering of intellectual types with Fine Arts degrees. So we didn't appear too snobbish we also had plumbers, house painters and several brilliant climbers who bragged about their recent new climbs and their ability to live on the dole for months on end. Twenty of us assembled at the outhouse for the rescue operation. With such an over-qualified group of experts we spent the first thirty minutes discussing options but we all eventually agreed we should get the porcupine out. Frantic scuffling noises were quite disturbing when all one wanted was a peaceful passing of time or whatever. Still, first things first, and we successfully lifted the wooden house off the frame around the hole only to be stuck with problem number two. Where to put it? The ground around was steep, rocky and well populated with trees. After some more intellectual discussion we found a convenient space and we all returned to gaze down into the offending hole and our unwanted but living victim.

Another elegant and eloquent debate ensued. We all decided not to volunteer to descend into the hole and manually retrieve our now smelly friend. The engineers described a technically efficient hoist system complete with karabiner pulleys and safety brakes while the Fine Arts experts sketched an artistic very modern series of ramps in the dirt around the hole. One of the girls brought up a garbage can lid and suggested we lift the trespasser up on this primitive platform. We all agreed this idea had merit – it was like the basket stretcher on the cliff for more conventional rescues. How to apply the ropes though? Another intensive search of the hut, our tents, and other people's tents produced some rope that was definitely past its safety date. They say you should retire your rope after it has had two falls and the piece of rope we found looked like it had survived several "Falls" up here on the campsite. We carefully tied four pieces somewhat equidistantly around the lid and lowered our stretcher down. Our porcupine friend didn't look impressed. Scurrying around the bottom of the hole he knocked against it, tipped it upside down, bit it and did everything but sit quietly on top of it. Fortunately one of the twenty-man rescue team was a wildlife biologist and he carefully explained some of the characteristics of this species. Following this lecture it became obvious what we had done wrong. It just goes to show you know that you need an expert on hand to direct these rescue operations. With several long, recently cut birch poles we prodded the stupid animal until it sat on the garbage can lid and we were ready to lift. Just needs the right approach we all agreed.

When it came to lifting someone suddenly had another disturbing thought. As the stretcher approached the surface our victim was likely to come back to life and leap energetically to safety. Stressed as he was one or more of us was likely to be in the escape path and none of us wanted to end up covered in.................quills. The engineers promptly suggested a frame over the pit and longer ropes running over pulleys held from much farther away and safe from any escaping shitty porcupine. When asked they thought this might take a day to build and another day to test so we dismissed this scientific answer. The teacher in the group wanted the engineers to slowly repeat the design idea as he hadn't managed to write down all the details for the rescue report he was writing. Four of us grabbed the ropes and pulled. As the Nike ad once said, "Do it". When we had lifted partway and poked the animal a couple of times to convince it to stay on the stretcher like a good victim one of the blokes suddenly gagged with the aroma, dropped his rope, which allowed the stretcher to tilt and upend our victim back down to the bottom again. I promptly had a fit of the giggles as I remembered a funny story I think Peter Ustinov once told to a University crowd at Oxford or Cambridge about a hoist, a pile of bricks, a barrel and a body and the sequence of events trying to hoist the bricks upwards. In the story several things went wrong just like our porcupine rescue. Then I had another flashback and realised that we were probably a little more organised than the three heroes in Jerome K. Jerome's "Three men in a boat", well maybe I thought. At the second attempt, working as a team, we lifted the lid, porcupine and a quantity of aromatic refuse slowly upwards. At the appropriate moment our unwelcome visitor stepped sedately off the stretcher and ambled unconcernedly into the bush.

After congratulating ourselves on a successful rescue someone civically-minded suggested we tidy up. Somewhat light-headedly we carefully bagged the lid and the not-to-be-reused ropes for safe deposit in the garbage dump on the way home. Trooping back down the hill to the Hut for another necessary beer we had another flash of community consciousness. Perhaps, in the spirit of common decency, we should think about putting the outhouse box back on the frame. After another beer someone suggested we actually do this rather than just thinking about it and we all agreed that made sense. Rescue operations were thirsty work. It must have been around mid-afternoon before a slow-moving group of us traipsed back up the little slope to find the horizontal outhouse box. With a lot of suggestions about up your end, and over to you, down a little, watch that stump, your side Jack and up yours Charlie

Brown we managed to slot the box back over the frame. We all slapped each other on the back over a job well done and sang as we trooped back to the Hut.

'Oy, oy, oy!! You stupid gits have got it on backwards!!'

We turned as one man. One of our smaller-bladdered members had consumed so much beer he had needed the outhouse for personal voiding purposes. He pulled the door and it promptly jammed six inches open as the doorway was now facing the uphill side. Tricky we thought, especially if you were in a hurry. There was another concerted team effort and eventually we finished the job as the sun set and a few of the lads came back from the cliff.

'Had a good day? Done any good routes? Do anything hard today did you? Christ you're a lazy lot hanging around the Hut all day just drinking beer. Jesus, but you do smell.'

Well you think, there are rescues and there are rescues. Some are just a little more difficult and unusual than others.

Our rescued porcupine didn't explain the reason for his appearance very well to his relatives and friends because this kind of rescue had to be repeated at two to three year intervals. Try as we may we found it hard to deter the salt-loving beastie. The other animal of seasonal concern was a black bear but this wasn't around the Hut. Along the top of the cliff was an extensive area of blueberry bushes and come August to September it was a pleasant treat to finish a climb and sample a few berries before descending to the lake again. The berry patch was also a favourite dining spot of a local black bear and he didn't always take kindly to intruders in his garden. There were two climbs on the cliff that finished near the middle of this area and one of them was quite hard. The bold leader was sitting comfortably but poorly anchored on top and taking in the slack to his struggling second when he noticed a movement out of the corner of his eye. The bear rested on all four paws and lifted up his head and sniffed. The bold leader froze. The second wondered why the rope wasn't moving.

'Take in,' he yelled.

The leader tried taking in without appearing to move anything. If I don't move he won't see me he reasoned. I'll just be quiet. Again, this logic demonstrated how little we knew about wildlife. Bears don't see too well and their ears are not very useful either. However, they do have an exceptional sense of smell with their wonderfully designed nose. Our frozen-still and silent leader had broken out in a sweat when he realised he had been caught trespassing in the bear's fruit and veg garden. The bear stood up on his hind legs and moved his head about quite actively sniffing. The anchored leader, feeling like a maiden tied to the stake with the dragon looking for lunch, stayed still.

'Tight rope!!' pierced the silence.

The leader was now not so bold and quite beside himself with indecision.

'Shush,' he whispered. 'There's a bear up here.'

The breeze whisked the whisper away into the ether.

The bear looked uncertain and relaxed onto four paws again. The leader breathed a sigh of relief. Quiet fell again on the little tableau.

'Tight rope!!' once again broke the silence. The bear's ears pricked up and his nose caught a new scent. He started walking towards the alien smell.

'Shush' came a louder whisper, 'Shush for God's sake. We've got a bear up here. Quiet.'

The leader turned from addressing the edge of the cliff, beneath which the breathless and tired second was now resting and wondering what in hell was happening up above him. Turning ever so slowly the leader looked towards the bear. Thankfully he saw that the bear had stopped and he was industriously pulling up blueberry bushes and filling his face. Once done he moved to the next bush, which was closer. The leader quickly took in whatever slack he could find and urged his second to move it.

A hand appeared, followed by a head and another hand.

'Christ, that was........'

'Shush. Zip it. Look.'

The breathless but relieved second looked as indicated and thought seriously about retreating quickly back down the cliff again. He even thought of just falling off! All three animals froze in a still life tableau. Needless to say it was the bear that made the decision and he sniffed one last time and turned to amble contentedly back down the cliff-top path. He had made his point. He didn't think those new interlopers would try and eat his berries again. Honour was satisfied. A week later I was reading the Hut log book and came upon this entry from the previous week written in a somewhat irregular and spidery hand. It described the route and complimented the first ascent leader on a fine line. The final moves are dramatic it added, and quite unique, although there are barely (bearly) any safe belays on the top.

Helmut Microys was one of the leading lights in our Club at this time and he had put up the first ascent of a climb he called "The Entertainer". Soon after he had done this Helmut offered to lead me up this demanding route. It rose straight from the lake in four long pitches to the highest point of the cliff. You have to understand, or perhaps picture Helmut standing tall. He is six feet six. At a personal modest five feet seven at full stretch I found climbing with Helmut was always entertaining, irrespective of what route we were doing. I had to climb bits of the route Helmut never saw or could miss out. The first pitch started delicately out of the rocking boat and climbed steeply but straightforwardly up for seventy feet to a convenient ledge stuck on this steep face. Safely anchored to a well-placed nut I held Helmut on belay as he led the second pitch which traversed left and then went straight up a vertical wall.

I step aside for a moment here, figuratively speaking, and explain a little bit about climbing to those of you not too familiar with this pastime. Normally we climb using fingers and toes, crammed into boots of course, the toes that is, balancing up on ledges, cracks, and nubbins. Occasionally we have to wedge knees, thighs, bums, shoulders and arms into cracks, and on the odd occasion climbers have confessed to gripping whatever was to hand with their teeth but that is unusual! In doing all this pushing and pulling we use whatever is there naturally on the cliff. Suddenly, just as Helmut has found, we find a part of the cliff which is all smooth. There are no ledges, bumps, wrinkles, spikes and all we can see is a smooth fifteen foot wall. Above that it is still steep but we can see footholds and handholds so the question is how to get up this wall? In modern day rock climbing you don't see too many ladders being carried around and so you look again. Tilt the wall backwards and it would make a slab and you could friction up it. In fact there are several friction slab climbs here at Bon Echo but this was not the case right here on the Entertainer. It was a steep wall but providentially split with a vertical thin crack. The crack was too narrow to slot fingers or toes in but it would take some artificial aid. When climbers run out of natural holds, like with this steep smooth wall, there are three options. Number one is retreat and this is very real in climbing. Knowing when to say no is important and life-preserving. Option two is drill a hole and insert an expansion bolt but this is slow, laborious and deemed unethical on such short routes. Helmut had first climbed this route using option three and that is to hammer a piton, a metal spike, into the crack. Now this is a lot more technical than it sounds. First of all, and somewhat obviously you need a piton and a hammer. In fact you probably need several pitons because cracks come in a variety of shapes, sizes and orientations. Cracks and pitons do not come together in a "one size fits all" combination. Moreover, if the wall is long you will need more than one piton to make any upward progress.

I won't elaborate on the techniques involved in artificial climbing as it is called, with a skilled use of pitons, karabiners, etriers, slings and careful rope work but I watched Helmut successfully ascend with four well-placed pitons in this vertical crack and then continue free climbing another eighty feet to a lofty perch under a beetling overhang.

'On belay, climb when ready,' the Austrian voice tumbled down the cliff. Well, ready or not here I come I muttered under my breath and I untied my anchor.

'Climbing' I shouted positively back up the cliff and I traversed left off the ledge. Soon I was at the foot of our vertical wall looking up at the line of pitons silhouetted against the clear blue sky. Metal flowers I thought. Mark you, if you did the climb today you probably would be using nuts or chockstones instead of pitons but that was then and two "Lost Arrows", one "Leeper" and one "channel" peg lined up above me. I mentioned before Helmut stands tall and with long arms his reach extends further than mine. As a result his pitons are further apart than my usual extension and the first one was out of reach to even start with.

With a little ingenuity I slowly mounted this artificial ladder collecting quite an array of slings and karabiners in the process. Above the wall I climbed slowly but steadily and the space below my feet grew bigger and bigger as the drop was sheer. Entertaining I thought, well it certainly was that. I joined Helmut in a cramped niche wedged under an overlapping roof and for five minutes we wriggled around like two bugs on a smooth boulder trying to change places and stay safe all at the same time. Fortunately Helmut spoke good English because my German was limited to "Achtung".

My tall leader explained that the route didn't try and go up over the overlap above our heads for which I was eternally grateful but went left out onto the face with a rope move and I looked again at the overhanging roof to see which I preferred! After some twenty feet in tension Helmut said there are holds and you can climb upwards. The next pitch is about one hundred feet but you probably won't be able to see or even hear me when I belay he told me. Just charming I thought. Then it struck me. If Helmut was going to lead on a tension rope move I was going to have fun following this. Having got ourselves safely organised and holding Helmut on belay I watched him climb upwards for fifteen feet and clip into a piton right up under the roof. He descended back down to me and then leant left on the tight rope. Doing a tension rope traverse requires skill in knowing how far to lean and how much to trust your feet stay smeared to the rock by friction alone. There really aren't any holds to talk about and so you lean and slowly walk left as your attentive second gradually eases the rope. Lean too far or slip with the feet and you swing violently back under the overhang and crash uncomfortably into your rope-holding life-saving belayer.

I watched intently and tried to work with Helmut as he gradually inched his way to the left out onto the smooth wall towards the suggested line of holds. It would have been a bold lead the first time he ever tried this I thought. The rope ran more quickly now and after another five minutes my leader had disappeared. After a while sitting in this little niche tucked on a steep wall one developed a sense of loneliness. Suddenly the rope movement stopped and I assumed he was finding an anchor. A climbing rope often demands a lot of assumptions. You have to interpret the messages that bounce up and down this thin little cord. The rope ran quickly now and soon was tight on my belay. Time to move I thought. Climbing second on a rope tension traverse offers two choices. Think about it. I had to climb up the fifteen feet to the piton under the roof and unclip. Once I had done that there was very little to stop me swinging wildly across the face until the rope was vertically above me. There were no holds and Helmut had done this leaning against the tension in the rope behind and above him. I didn't have that option. If I didn't want to swing I could fix some loop back through the piton behind me and brace myself between the rope pulling left and the loop holding me back to the right. Gradually I could move left and then pull the loop free from the piton behind me. I didn't have a long enough loop!

Okay I thought, time for a little ride. I shouted up the cliff what I intended to do but Helmut was out of sight and probably out of hearing too. Trust I thought. Trust in my partner and trust in my equipment. Swinging across a cliff two hundred feet above a sheer drop down to the lake is not a common climbing move. Most climbers try very hard not to let go of the rock. We are always taught to have three points of contact at all times. Now I was about to have one, peripherally as my feet scrabble across the face at speed. Well here goes nothing and I edged my way sideways using the tension in the rope as much as possible until the elasticity in the rope upset the balance and I found myself looking at a rope stretched tightly vertically above me. Trying not to be too frantic I found footholds and handholds for balance and considered my location: dramatic to say the least. I climbed upwards away from the glittering water. The last pitch was conventional, steep but conventional, and I congratulated Helmut on a fine climb. I thought the name was most appropriate. Two or three times later I led this climb and found it more enjoyable on the sharp end of the rope. Although the steep artificial wall still needed some techniques Helmut could bypass when he did it, I found the rope tension pitch was easier to lead than second, but overall it was a memorable and entertaining climb.

Equally memorable but a lot easier was the first climb ever done on this cliff: well ever done and officially recorded in some climbing journal. David Fisher climbed this route with three other members of the Toronto Section and seeing as one of the first-ascendeurs was his wife Marnie and it was her birthday they decided to call the route Birthday Ridge. The strata of the rock at Bon Echo is decidedly sloping bottom right up to left and over time the rock movement and erosion has created several steeply sloping slabs cut into the cliff. These all face south and are pleasantly warm for most of the day. The lakeside edge of these slabs provide easy but exposed ridges and Birthday Ridge was such a route. Three pitches of good clean rock set at a moderate angle made for a popular and easy climb. Large, safe, level ledges at the end of each pitch made for a route well suited for beginners. The location was dramatic on the cliff edge of the slab with an exposed drop down one side straight to the water but the route was well supplied with footholds and handholds and not difficult. You could take your mother up there with no problem. Better still, take the mother-in-law up there and grin a lot, menacingly!

Teaching people to climb on multi-pitch routes needs to be done carefully, especially if there are five of you all together. If you don't pay attention wandering feet stand on the rope, which can cut it with the little stones underfoot, and four ropes tangle themselves together far better than one does. In addition you need to watch carefully that everyone is safely anchored, and although it is tempting to wander sideways a little for a better photograph, 'Don't step over that edge Veronica!'

When you climb with a trusted partner the dialogue often disappears. No words are needed and you both know what to do and what your partner is doing. It is quiet, peaceful, even serene up there on the cliff doing what you enjoy doing. Teaching a group on the other hand tends to be a little noisier.

'Step up carefully there Stefan, up with the left foot. Good. Deidre, don't fool around up here love. Just sit and look at the view. Good Stefan.

Now up with the right foot onto that sloping crack. It will stay there. Don, keep that knot done up son. We don't need to practice rescue just yet. Look at Stefan and tell him what you did there. It wasn't too hard was it? Fine Stefan, you just hold it there while I make you safe. Okay, you can sit down now and have a drink. So group, that's pitch two and we have one more to the summit. We just climb directly up this rib above me. Think this is good? Better than Rattlesnake?'

The group nod and they're right. It is better than Rattlesnake Point as a place to climb with Bon Echo being a big cliff. There is more exposure here, more a feeling of really climbing as opposed to the short one-pitch routes on the Niagara Escarpment at Rattlesnake Point. Making sure everyone is still safely tied in and that the ropes are not too entangled I have Deidre put me on belay. Don and Veronica are sitting looking at the boats below and waving while Stefan is still getting his head back together.

'Stefan, you will be the last here again son. Feel safe up here do you? Know how to undo the anchor and bring up this jammed chockstone? That's good. You did well on that last pitch. There are a couple of tricky moves. Watch where I go and try to follow my line. Right Deidre. Am I on belay?'

'On belay, climb when ready.'

'Climbing' and off I went up the last pitch. On the top I brought Deidre up and then had her belay Don up. In turn he arranged the belay to bring up Veronica. Still checking everyone was still safely anchored because anyone could trip off this top ledge I let Veronica get herself organised to hold the rope for Stefan. Turning to the assembled group on the top I asked them what they expected me to do next.

'Have a rest and a drink,' Don said. 'This is a little different from Rattlesnake. It's not as strenuous but the climbing is very different.'

'How about climbing down?' I asked.

'No way.'

'Then how do we get down?' I asked.

'It's too far to lower us like on the Escarpment,' observed Veronica.

'Right, so how do we get back to the foot of the cliff?'

The four of them sat and thought about that.

'Like on the Escarpment you taught us about the "Easy way down", although you said it was a misnomer and that it wasn't always easy.'

'Right Stefan and this cliff has several "Easy ways down" and most of them aren't easy. Still, how else could we get down?'

Again the group thought about the question.

'As you suggested we could climb down, or couldn't we…how do they describe it? Rappel, yes that's it, rappel down. I've seen them doing that on television. They slide down the rope.'

'Yes, we could do that and you need to learn how to do that too. Also you need to climb down but today we will rappel down as Deidre suggested. Next week at Rattlesnake I will teach you to climb down.'

I had enough ropes to organise the necessary two rappels down to the foot of the climb and use a safety rope on each student. I explained the need to be extra careful doing this because so many things can go wrong. At the foot of the cliff they pulled down the ropes, untied the fisherman's knot and coiled them up. Good kids. Learn well. Well done.

'Why do we need to learn to climb down if we can rappel?'

I told them the story of Arnold and his friend Harry while we waited for the boat.

Arnold was a bright lad who attended one of the climbing courses at Rattlesnake Point and he was keen and ambitious. Unfortunately Arnold was over-confident and eager to show off his newly acquired skills to his good trusting friend Harry. Having successfully completed his beginners climbing course and been told he had potential Arnold thought he was a climber. Eagerly he went to the local climbing store and purchased a helmet, a rope, a harness, several slings, karabiners, nuts and of course a brand new pair of climbing slippers. Now he was a climber Arnold didn't want to be seen climbing in sneakers. Before the week was out Arnold had persuaded his good friend Harry that they just had to go climbing.

'So I can show you how it's done Harry. Now I'm qualified I can lead you up the cliff. You'll love it. It's a real blast. I'll teach you and that way you won't have to go through all the time and effort I had to and so you can become a climber too.'

Harry was a trusting soul and he liked Arnold a lot. Two days later Arnold was confidently walking along the foot of the cliff at Rattlesnake carrying his rope and gear over his shoulder, wearing his new helmet and swinging his new climbing slippers in his hand. Harry followed, looking apprehensively upwards every now and again at the vertical faces of limestone cutting across the clear blue sky.

'Here,' cried Arnold, 'Here's where I climbed. Right up here above us. Easy it was. We did five or six other climbs too but this was the best. The Instructor said I did best on this climb so we'll start here. He went up first and then I followed but now I've graduated I'll lead and you can follow. If you get stuck I'll shout down instructions, just like my leader did.'

Arnold was smart and he remembered how to uncoil the rope, tie into his harness with the right knots and arrange his slings and nuts just so. He quickly took off his sneakers and donned his new climbing slippers.

'Look just like a climber now don't I Harry? And I've got the game to go with it too,' he added assertively. 'Now, you hold the rope and make sure it doesn't snag or pull me off. Come here. I'll show you how to hold it. Around your back and over this arm. Wrap the rope over the arm and don't ever let go with that hand. The other hand pays out the rope as I climb upwards. Understand all that? It's easy once you've got the hang of it. You'll soon learn.'

Looking up Arnold remembered he had climbed well at climb number 14. To make it easier at Rattlesnake Point, and because the cliff was used by so many groups teaching with routes very close together, the guidebook committee had decided to mark the start of every climb on the cliff and identify them with numbers. The corresponding number in the guidebook gave a name, a grade and a brief description.

'You say on belay. Climb when ready and I say climbing,' said Arnold. He paused but Harry didn't say anything.

'Harry, I said you say on belay and I say climbing. Got that?'

'Sure Arnold. Off you go then and I pay out this rope. Is that right?'

'Yes,' said Arnold in exasperation. 'Climbing' and he put his foot clad in his new and professional-looking climbing slippers on the cliff. Now the first ten feet or so is straightforward and Arnold moved competently up the route. The next ten feet got a little harder and Arnold was a little more hesitant. It was different without the rope in front of his face. Easier in some ways. At twenty feet he remembered his Instructor putting a nut in the crack. Oh yes he thought, some protection. Standing in balance he looked down at the nuts he had slung over his shoulder with the slings. After the third attempt Arnold found a nut that kind of fitted in the crack. He pulled hard to make sure it would stay in the crack. The nut slipped down a little and then jammed solid. Good thought Arnold. Remembered that bit about making sure it was safe. Now a karabiner and a sling with another karabiner and clip in the rope he thought. Oh yes, make sure the gate is facing upwards and can't open under stress. He pulled at the climbing rope to lift it up and clip it through the gate. He pulled. Nothing happened. The rope was stuck. It was tight. Arnold looked down. Harry was standing on the rope.

'Harry, don't stand on the rope mate. You'll cut it. Never stand on the rope Harry. Now I need some slack. Slack. Slack! More rope. I need to lift the rope up and clip it through this karabiner.'

Harry knelt down and letting go of the rope he tried to untangle the mess that the rope had created. It took a while but eventually there was enough rope for Arnold to clip in to the karabiner.

'Runner on,' called Arnold remembering the correct expression.

'Eh?' called Harry. 'What runner? I thought this was mountaineering not baseball. Is it a trick question Arnold to see whether I'm paying attention? You know, the story about "Who" is on first and "I'm" on second? So "Who" is not on first he's the runner?'

Arnold was getting a little hot under the collar as he quietly listened to Harry's monologue. When Harry slowed down and stopped Arnold called down very politely with his teeth clenched. 'Harry, pick up the rope and hold it like I showed you. With this runner you've now got my life in your hands so pay attention. This is serious my friend. I'm climbing on.'

Satisfied that Harry now fully understood the seriousness of the situation Arnold reviewed the face in front of him. Really he thought, Harry can be such a dolt at times. Ten feet higher up and still fuming about Harry's lack of understanding Arnold suddenly realised he was stuck. He had found the past ten feet difficult but now there was no way up. There must be he thought. We climbed here before. Yes it was hard and I had a tight rope a couple of times when my foot slipped off but it was only for a moment. Arnold tried moving his right hand up but he couldn't find a hold. At full stretch he tried with his left hand. His right knee started to shake. What was it his Instructor called it? Yes, "sewing machine knees". After a few minutes he heard Harry shout. 'The rope isn't moving any more Arnold. Are you stuck?'

'No, just resting Harry.' Stuck, was he stuck? Arnold took stock. Yes dammit he was stuck. His hands started to get sweaty and the shakes came back in his right knee again. The left foot felt uncomfortable and as he glanced down he felt his right hand slip a little on the small ledge he was gripping. It was a long way down.

'Arnold I need a piss man. You okay up there for a minute 'cos I've got to go.'

Standing thirty feet up the climb with a runner at twenty feet the runner will stop me before I reach the ground thought Arnold. That's the whole point of the runner, to protect me.

'Arnold! I've got to go.'

'Harry, hold the rope tight. I've got to come down.'

'And I've got to go man. You hang on there. I won't be a tick.'

Arnold tentatively lowered his left hand and glancing past his chest he frantically searched for something to grab on. His body obscured his vision but he daren't lean out any more on that right hand. Thankfully his fingers wrapped over a good ledge and bending his knees he could bring his right hand down beside his left. In doing this his right foot eventually slipped straight off its hold and banged down the cliff. He felt his knee scrape against the rough limestone and knew he had removed skin. Taking a quick look down Arnold could see another possible hold for his uncomfortable left foot and as fast as he dared he gripped very tight with his hands on the ledge and lowered the foot. When he put some weight on the left foot his slipper promptly slipped straight off again and he found himself hanging with his full weight on his fingers and arms. This proved to be too much and Arnold found his fingers involuntarily unfolding and felt himself falling. Three feet lower both his feet landed on a flat ledge where he had stood to place his runner. Arnold was conscious enough to grab the sling and his feet suddenly stopped descending. He clung on for dear life.

'That's better' called Harry. 'God I needed that Arnold. Now, hold the rope you said. Fine, I've got it. You okay? You're lower than you were before. I thought you told me in the car you never had to climb down. Got lowered you said. The Instructor thought it was too hard to climb down so you never did it. Well, seems you learnt without him. You coming all the way down? Don't you need to get that runner thing you talked about? You're going to leave it? I thought you'd just bought it. Not like you to throw money away Arnold. No, I'm not standing on your precious rope mate. Look, why don't we pack this clobber away and go and have a beer somewhere? After that piss I'm dry again.'

Sitting with the four youngsters at the foot of Birthday Ridge I repeated, 'learning to climb down is important. In the old days, before equipment really improved, we learnt not to climb up anything we couldn't climb down. Nowadays it's not so serious to fall off as climbers have better equipment and safer rope-handling techniques. Still, you should learn a couple of lessons from my little tale. One is to realise that climbing second up something doesn't necessarily mean you can lead it, and that admitting you can't is not a disgrace. It is prudent. Even if you have led it before it doesn't automatically mean you can do it again. You might not feel so good or the conditions may not be as ideal as last time. So, turning back and down-climbing can be life-saving. Secondly, there are times when you have to down-climb. It may not be possible to rappel for a variety of reasons and you have to climb down. This is often much more difficult than climbing up. The body obscures your vision and it is hard to hold on and still see where you are placing your feet. Some kinds of climbing moves are very hard to reverse, for example a mantelshelf or a layback. So, practising down-climbing is important if you want to be a mountaineer or an all round rock climber.'

'But don't cliffs like this and even mountains have an "Easy way down"? You said there were several off this cliff. Couldn't we have done that?' asked Stefan.

'Yes, when we were on the top we could. If we had been stuck half-way up the climb we couldn't. But, let's talk about Easy ways down and the one just along from here is a good example. Usually they are dirty, dusty and messy gullies so there is a good risk of people scrambling down kicking all sorts of loose stuff down on the folks below. Secondly, you've just come up a serious climb and successfully and safely reached the top. You're excited and after the stress of the climb you relax a little. On the Easy way down it's so easy that you don't need the rope and you relax too much. A slip turns into a slide, and because it is steep, a fall. If you don't knock over someone else you might fall a long way. Even a short fall can injure and sometimes kill. So, you still have to stay very vigilant on this Easy way down. Lastly, and this applies here too, you climbed a pure clean rock climb in smooth-soled climbing slippers. For this purpose they are excellent. It's only a short walk across the tops to the way off and you didn't want to drag a pair of sneakers dangling behind you all the way up the route so you walk off in your smooth-soled slippers. On grass, especially damp or wet grass in the early morning dew smooth-soled climbing slippers can become short skis very quickly. Dusty, sweaty gullies can be smooth and there too you have to be extra cautious descending this so-called Easy way down. Until we are safely back to the foot of the cliff or well away from the edge at the top you have to be vigilant at all times. It's a grand game, and can really get the adrenaline going, but it is also potentially life-threatening. So climb carefully people.'

That teaching weekend was good and everyone had an enjoyable time. We all learnt something. Perhaps I should have learnt to practice what I preach because a couple of weekends later I needed a lesson in humility. One can get too complacent. I suppose I have always found this particular climb easier when I am drunk. You know the feeling, when you've had a good day and a couple of celebratory beers. Your friend and partner suggests 'How about an evening doddle up Baby's Bottom?' You're feeling mellow and Baby's Bottom is a great little climb. It is a steep smooth face, or bottom if you like, that rises straight out of the lake for one hundred and thirty feet. Technically it is a slab climb and it demands balance and good feet. Still feeling good from the four or five beers you shout 'I'll grab my gear. Take two ropes and then we can rap straight down again into the boat. Should be a gas.'

You race the Club boat down the lake past most of the towering cliff which beams happily in the early evening sunshine. Steep smooth rock looks warm and appealing, and the lake is calm as the afternoon breezes have fallen away. Cutting the motor you nose into the little bay that embraces Baby's Bottom on one side and the steep brutal face and overhangs of Womb at the Top on the other side. Two very different types of short climbs sit side by side in this part of the cliff. Just over one hundred yards away are the Narrows which nearly nip the lake in half. Evening strollers from the Provincial Park on the west side of the lake stop and watch as you moor the boat and set about roping up.

'This should be a bit of a giggle' you say as you tie onto the sharp end of the rope with a figure of eight knot. Slinging the rack of nuts and karabiners over your shoulder you do one last check that you've got enough slings and boldly look at the smooth slab of rock bumping against the side of the boat.

Laying crossways along the length of the centre thwart your partner lazily calls 'On belay, climb when you're ready and all that rot' and you suddenly realise what you are doing. A swirl of alcoholic chemicals race around your brain but any concerns are submerged again as you step off the side of the boat and firmly onto the smooth baby's bottom. 'Climbing' you state rather obviously as the boat rocks violently behind you and your partner falls off the thwart and lands heavily in the bottom of the boat. Fortunately he wasn't holding your rope too tight or he would have pulled you off straightaway into the lake. Blissfully unaware of the chaos behind you you look for wrinkles. Now I realise there shouldn't be any wrinkles on a baby's bottom but fortunately there are or you would never get up this climb. The route is steep. Standing vertically with both feet boldly smeared on supposed holds your hands reach horizontally forwards and just keep you in balance. There is little or no pulling here. You step smoothly from smear to smear using most of the soles of your climbing slippers and trust to friction. There are very few sharp edges and horizontal ledges. Well you wouldn't expect them on a baby's bottom now would you?

After twenty feet of upwards balance demonstrating man challenging gravity you look for a runner. A baby's bottom has a crack in it doesn't it and so there should be a crack somewhere about? A small number three stopper slides gratefully into a vertical rough-sided crack and you give it a gentle tug, just to make sure it is sitting snug. Don't pull too hard or you'll overbalance and join your partner in a hurry. On with the karabiner, clip in the rope, breathe again.

'Runner on,' you shout confidently. 'Climbing.'

Now you should realise that the first comment told your partner that the rope might go suddenly and quickly upwards followed by a hard jerk should you have fallen off, and come tight on the rope and runner. The second comment however, told him that the rope might go smoothly and slowly upwards as you progressed further up the slab. Looking for bulges and wrinkles for my feet I journeyed upwards, smoothly and slowly. I was just lifting my right foot up quite high for a very welcome ledge when my left foot decided it wasn't comfortable where it was and wanted to go lower. As my hands were just resting against this smooth wall my entire body started to move downwards without much constraint. I remembered my trusty runner and as I was only ten feet above it I anticipated an abrupt stop ten to twelve feet below it. I hadn't taken into account my partner, and after my mind registering the twelve foot marker going past and I was still descending at an ever-increasing speed, I realised my partner had fallen asleep. 'Falling' I communicated, somewhat pointedly. The net result was an abrupt stop with my feet inches above the water and my partner looking embarrassed. I turned away from my partner's red face and scanned my flayed fingertips. A little blood dripped forlornly onto the foot of the baby's bottom.

'Found a tricky bit,' I offered.

'No problem,' my partner replied. 'Go and finish it off. You'd done the really tricky bit at the bottom.'

My partner's reassurance overcame any feeling I might have had about his incompetence, and once again the five beers subsumed any doubts I might have had about my own abilities.

'Climbing' and once again we ascended from smear to smear in balance. First the right foot and hands just feeling with the tender fingertips. Then move up the left foot and on again. I passed the runner, which was now more firmly settled in its crack. Bombproof I muttered to myself and continued my upward sortie. The old mantra of "look, think, see it and do it" spun in an endless loop through my mind, and I balanced up another twenty feet before seriously looking for another break in the smoothness.

'How's it going?' floated up the cliff. I realised that my partner was reassuring me that he was now wide awake and suitably prepared for any more rapid descents on my part. I in turn was quite determined not to give him that satisfaction. The horizontal crack presented an opportunity and a challenge. Any normal nut or stopper would just slide out but if we partnered together two tapered stoppers we could make the top one jam the bottom one like a cam. After a quick inspection of the hardware on my rack I selected two likely nuts and engineered a neat and safe running belay. Another karabiner on the innermost nut's wire and clip the rope through and 'Runner on' drifted down the cliff.

Looking up I took stock. The evening shadows slowly lengthened and the descending sun turned a deeper red as its light penetrated the dust-laden atmosphere closer to earth. Pretty I thought: peaceful and quiet. In front of me the baby's bottom was also peaceful, quiet but a lot less pretty. All of a sudden it had gone smooth. There was a little overlap, which may not be anatomically correct for such a young person but a distinct challenge for yours truly. A couple of vertical ribs offered some variety in climbing technique. I could use them for pinch holds I reasoned, and quickly walk my feet up higher, or I could semi lean or layback on them and brace my feet sideways. It would depend on what was ten feet higher. In semi-automatic mode I found myself up another twenty feet and here I had to make a decision. I established a really good runner and looked about me. The original first ascent leader had been so freaked out by what he had done so far he had climbed diagonally left to the rib and easier ground. That was the Baby's Bottom route as described in the first guidebook. Over the years, as techniques improved and leaders became bolder, someone had waltzed up to where I was and decided the route would be better as a "diretissima".

'Looks a little hairy' I explained to my now attentive second. 'Goes straight up?' I asked but we both knew that it went straight up, and we both knew that I was playing for time. My partner didn't ask how a baby's bottom could be hairy as he knew this was just another delaying comment. I remembered a book I had read where climbers explain why they can't climb on this particular day or this particular route. There were all sorts of excuses but as I stood on my little ledge by my bombproof runner I couldn't remember any excuses that fitted my present situation.

Concentration, technique, fear-quenching alcohol and a little luck enabled me to stand thirty feet higher in the next two minutes. I mean to say, if you've got it you may as well flaunt it. The rope dropped straight between my legs and snaked its way down through the three runners to my attentive partner. Strange thing the climbing rope you know. When you tie on you have to realise you are taking on a serious responsibility. At times you may have your partner's life in your hands, quite literally. There is a lot of trust embedded in that climbing rope. You should only climb with a partner you trust. Climb with a friend, and be careful if you climb with a friend who has a wife you especially covert. There is a very sensible warning in the front of all climbing guidebooks. After advising you of the dangers of the sport, and shunning any responsibility for your safety after reading this guidebook, the author usually has a short sharp sentence advising you never to climb with a psychopath. Well, just imagine it! There you are climbing up a steep wall at the top of a climb that is harder than you thought, and needing a tight rope from your leader on the summit. As you come up over that last overhanging piece, and you're pleading through a very dry throat that you need a tight rope, you see your leader's smiling face encouraging you and holding you tight with his right hand. You make the last desperate move and his smile turns to an evil grin and he slashes at the tight rope with the sharp knife in his left hand. That's the stuff nightmares are made of: dreams to bother the troubled mind. No, trust me, climb with a friend.

The last thirty feet to the top were consistent. Here the Baby's Bottom Direct was smooth, steep and kept your attention to the last. I mantleshelved up onto the final ledge and arranged a perfect hexagonal chock in a convenient cracked boulder. Quickly I fixed my anchor and took in the little amount of slack down to my partner. I threaded the rope through my belay plate and onto the gated karabiner on my harness. Confidently leaning out over the drop I shouted 'On belay. Climb when ready.'

I tightened the rope down to my partner and just as he was about to step from the boat onto the foot of the climb I gently reminded him 'Have you made the boat fast?' I could have added because we don't want to rappel down again in the dark and find the boat has drifted away. He in turn probably muttered that he wasn't such a daft berk and of course he had made the boat fast. I in turn probably muttered he normally was such a daft berk and that is just the thing he would have done if I hadn't reminded him. Neither of us heard each others mutterings and all I heard was a positive 'Climbing.' I took in the slack.

Sitting at the top of the climb I let my mind drift and I looked across at the next door climb. Womb at the Top is a brutal little climb. As the name suggests the last twenty feet or so are a tight thrutch up an overhanging cleft in the cliff. You try and wedge yourself in as you lean backwards over space but you can't wedge too tight or you'll never climb upwards. There is a delicate but strenuous balance between in too tight and not being in far enough. Before you even reach that last twenty feet there is some seriously steep face climbing which traverses from the apparent safety of a gully out onto an ever-exposed face dropping sheer to the lake below. The further you go right to reach the final womb the more you're over the edge of nothing. Quite different. Hard to take in.

'Take in!! You asleep up there? I'm falling all over the coils down here. Take in!'

Yes I thought, take in and I dutifully remembered my partner and took in the slack.

'That's me' and peering downwards he was right. It was him and now the rope between us was tight and offering safety. As I said there is a lot of trust running up and down this climbing rope.

I looked around again and the sun sunk lower to the tree tops in the park opposite. In automatic mode I pulled in the slack.

'You're pulling me off. This is tricky. Slack!'

Its all go you know this climbing game. You have to pay more attention as a belayer than when you are actually doing the climbing bit. The climbing bit comes somewhat naturally, automatically on occasions, especially after a few beers. Yes I thought, I could just do with a beer right now. Perfect it would be.

'Take in!!'

Peering down again I pulled in the few feet of slack and made sure the rope didn't tangle beside me. 'Bit hairy the next bit,' I offered as encouragement. 'Straight up though' and this was just to remind my second that I wouldn't accept any sideways bail out. Think about it. If I could lead it he should second it now surely? 'Twas only fit and proper I thought.

'Good lead that partner. Fun route. We going to rap off?'

'It'll be easier a bit lower down off that tree on the edge. That way we won't have to leave any gear behind. We can just wrap the ropes around the tree.'

We scrambled down the ten feet to the tree and knotted the two ropes together. That way we could make just one rappel right into the boat. The boat? Yes, it was still there in the gathering gloom. It's a neat and easy rappel down Baby's Bottom: just lean back and walk down slowly. There's none of this dramatic bouncing off overhangs which puts an enormous strain on both the rope and the anchor. It may look good on television but no climber in their right mind rappels that way. More people get killed rappelling than in any other part of climbing and mountaineering. There are too many things that can go wrong.

Dusk fell as we slowly motored back to the Hut and the necessary beer.

'It'll go down smooth,' I suggested.

'Just like a baby's bottom,' agreed my partner.

Thinking back I suppose the climbers based in Toronto were

lucky. True enough we were a long way from the mountains but we had an assortment of areas to rock climb quite close to home. Niagara Escarpment and its steep limestone was just down the road and there were several locations there with many routes. Bon Echo was a favourite spot and it offered swimming, boating, and lazing around in the sun for those not inclined to climb. A little further away we climbed in the Gatineau, in the Adirondacks and the Shawangunks in New York State. These all offered something different in both the climbing and the surrounding pubs but Bon Echo was probably a favourite. It really was a special kind of place.

BRIDGE OVER THE RIVER LA SURE

AT SCHOOL YOU HAVE TO make choices, choices about which subjects to take. As a young lad of fourteen, at a school in suburban London England, I just knew that I would end up retiring to Kelowna BC, spend all my winters down in Mexico, and therefore need to speak Spanish. So, when the choice came to take Latin or German, I obviously chose Latin, because that was the basis of Spanish. It really was a no-brainer. However, at the time of this story I was nowhere near retirement, nowhere near Mexico, and definitely in need of some German. It was obvious when you thought about it. I should have paid attention at school, at least in French classes. Thinking back though to my school days, how could anyone be expected to learn French from a Welshman, especially one who insisted on singing? Our teacher was a small rugby player called Taffy Evans and he believed in singing. He also insisted any one of his pupils should sing too – typically standing on their desk so all the class could see you as well as hear you as you mangled the French imperfect. Not content with just singing Taffy kept us in this classical and artistic theme by having us learn some of the poems of La Fontaine by heart. To ensure our understanding of this sophisticated language we had to learn the translation by heart too of course, although sometimes it was a bit of a puzzle which French word actually tied into the right English word. Still, the parables of La Fontaine weren't going to help me much in the present circumstances I thought, neither was Latin for that matter. Lying on my back in the upper berth of our Volkswagen Camper I gazed at the ceiling and mused over our present status. Officially we were under "house arrest" and our four-wheeled house was not to leave the campsite. At this time I was camping with my wife near Echternach in the Grand Duchy of Luxembourg, but unfortunately I was not on speaking terms with the Duke. Had I been I've no doubt we could have cleared up this little mess quite quickly.

What mess you ask? Well, I'll set the scene. Having explored the fascinating ramparts and "Bock-Casemates" of the fortress at Luxembourg City we were en route for the Rhine valley and the alcoholic delights of Rudesheim. In a very slow and circuitous fashion we were driving to the Alps for some mountaineering, but it was too early in the season for that and so I decided to see the rock climbing in Luxembourg. Ha, bet you didn't know they had rock climbing in Luxembourg now did you? Well, just on the edge of the neat little village of Berdorf at a challenging altitude of three hundred metres, above sea level that is, there is a whole series of weird, contorted and steep cliff faces. The area even boasts an Alpine Club campsite and a Climbing School that is concentrated in an area of climbs called the Seven Gorges.

We had driven easily down from the capital and found a comfortable and shaded campsite near Echternach. That afternoon we had wandered over to Berdorf to walk around and sample the area. Quiet woodland paths twisted and turned through this rocky sandstone wonderland and soon we found a band of youngsters being introduced to the mysteries of rock climbing. We stood there quietly and watched. Back in Ontario Canada I had spent several years teaching rock climbing on the Niagara escarpment, educating both youngsters and adults. It is always interesting being in a new climbing area and especially educational watching other people teach. Even though the youngsters were from Holland I was intrigued to hear the commands in German. There were two Dutch adult instructors with twelve kids. We watched as they learnt to tie the right knots, hold the rope safely, and finally understand the procedures for belaying. The instructors didn't rig top ropes but led the climbs and allowed a procession of pupils to follow. It was a slow process. During a break in the action one of the instructors came over to my wife and I and asked whether we were climbers? Well, soon enough I had become enrolled as a spare instructor and promised I would be there tomorrow with some equipment to help. My wife and I wandered on through the maze of paths around the woodland before going back to the campsite in a refreshing drizzle.

So for the next two days I learnt the requisite thirty words of German needed to communicate climbing commands. If the pupil had any problems outside climbing I was completely at a loss as I didn't speak Dutch and the kids didn't speak English. However, it's amazing what one can do with hand actions, and kids climb naturally so the instruction was more about making sure they did things safely. The last day of this interlude was a National holiday in Luxembourg and the cliff was very crowded. All around there was a babble of voices and helpful suggestions in French, German, Dutch and probably Flemish. I also learnt that the Dutch have this very friendly custom of kissing the leader when you reach the top and finish the climb. Well, they do say that travel broadens the mind. This rather pleasant and unexpected activity ended on a Friday evening. My wife and I shopped for food items for the next day and successfully exhausted our supply of Luxembourg francs as they didn't do much for anyone outside the Duchy. Saturday we were all set to leave Luxembourg and drive down to Trier, through Hunsruck to the Rhine valley and Rudesheim.

It was a bright and cheerful Saturday morning and we breakfasted happily before lowering the hinged Volkswagen camper roof and locking it into place. Gently gently I thought as this particular year Volkswagen had changed the design of the roof. This year they had moved the hinges to the rear of the roof and this had resulted in a bigger and heavier roof. Unfortunately the brackets and bolts were a little frail for the weight and size of this extended roof and several owners had discovered things coming apart. This led to our excursion to Wolfsburg later on and a trip to the factory and some roof repairs but at this point in time all was well, as long as you were gentle.

With a right-hand drive vehicle it was an interesting experience driving in Europe. The activity became a team effort quite quickly with my wife deciding whether over-taking was a life threatening event or not. There was always the question of trust? Mark you, we got some funny looks sometimes when people overtook us. We watched drivers and passengers do a double take when the supposed driver of our camper had her feet on the dashboard and was reading a map, or a book!

Having made sure we had left nothing at our campsite and had left the area quite tidy I drove slowly out into the narrow and twisty streets of Echternach. We went through the Place de Marche and by the large Basilica of the old Abbey here. The main road curved around towards the bridge spanning the river La Sure and the frontier. Now to fully understand the story you have to picture this slow moving twisting river that separates Germany from Luxembourg. Essentially the frontier runs down the middle of the river and so the two countries have custom posts at each end of the bridge in Echternach. Cheerfully we drove past the Luxembourg authorities and onto the cobbled bridge. There are three small arches and one large one spanning the navigable centre of the river.

I slowed as I approached the German frontier. Recognise this was

1974 Europe and the European Union had resulted in non-existent frontier hold-ups. We had already moved from Belgium to Holland, back to Belgium and on into Luxembourg without any problems. My wife in fact was rather frustrated with not getting passport stamps to show her friends back home in Canada. So it was somewhat surprising when a German Customs Officer stepped purposefully out of his station and held up his hand. Dutifully I stopped. The following conversation was conducted in a mixture of German, French and English but as I only speak English and very limited French I have translated it. It went something like this,

'Papers?'

'Papers?'

'Yes, papers?'

There followed a rummaging around looking amongst the array of maps, guidebooks, grocery lists and other paraphernalia that tended to clutter up the front of the camper. Eventually we dug out our passports and flourished these spectacularly. I was travelling on a British passport, which at the time tended to get me almost anywhere, well in the civilised world that is. My wife, being a Canadian, was understandably travelling on a Canadian passport. With beaming faces my wife offered these to the officer.

'Car Papers?'

Obviously our friend, well we thought he was our friend at this time wasn't too interested in us but in the magic bus with its four wheels and proud Volkswagen insignia. Another search revealed the vital triptyque, the car's registration papers and a very comprehensive English insurance document. As we were planning on driving all the way out to India the insurance papers had taken a while to sort out you know. This car insurance took us all the way through Turkey, which it later did very successfully, but we had been told that the world was a different place beyond there. Later we found out that this was true but let's get back to our German friend, the one requesting car papers. I watched as the officer looked briefly at the insurance papers, then at the triptyque, and finally he came to the registration papers. He read these very carefully and then turned to the back page. His eyes lit up and he looked up at us.

'No good. Verboten, and other German words, many other German words.'

'Ich no verstehen,' or something like that I uttered.

There followed a further outburst in German followed by some rather Italian hand actions that I did understand. With difficulty I did a three-point turn on the bridge. Back to Luxembourg. There seemed no point in asking why if the officer didn't speak English and his hand actions were quite definite. Maybe I can ask back in Echternach where my French might rise to the task. We'd had no problems before so maybe this was because we had a German-made vehicle trying to get back into Germany. That must be it I thought. There has got to be a way to overcome this as we wanted to see several places in Germany. I'll sort it somehow in Luxembourg. I asked my wife to see whether she could find the police station on the map of Echternach. Now it turned out later, minutes later in fact, that this request was redundant. I drove slowly back over the bridge to Luxembourg.

'We got rid of all our francs. It's Saturday and the banks will be closed. What will we do for money?'

People in authority however preceded this problem. At the Luxembourg end of the bridge a Customs Officer appeared and solemnly held up his hand. Again, I dutifully stopped.

'Papers?' although this time in French.

We went through the same shuffling routine and passports were offered to the officer.

'Car papers?' again in French.

Once more the insurance, the triptyque and the registration papers moved from hand to hand. Once more there was a slow perusal.

'This car can not be driven in Luxembourg.'

'Pourquoi?'

Now I felt I could ask why in French but I wasn't prepared for the explanation that the German authorities had telephoned over the bridge and stated that my vehicle did not have valid registration papers. My wife and I looked at each other and I flippantly asked whether she would like to spend the rest of her life in no-man's land driving to and fro on the bridge over the La Sure River? I didn't like the response any more than I did the one I got from the Luxembourg Customs Officer.

My French managed to convey a need to see the police and get an explanation and within ten minutes an Inspector arrived looking very neat and professional in a smart uniform. More importantly, much more importantly than his attire was his capability to speak English. Following him I drove to the police station, which my wife hadn't yet found on the map, and we all ended up in his office to sit in a very civilised fashion in chairs ready to converse.

In a mixture of English and French I explained to the Inspector who we were, where we were going, where we had been and that I didn't speak or read German. He in turn explained to us, in very eloquent English, that the car registration papers we had needed to be authorised in Germany. As they were he said the car was not properly registered anywhere. He tapped the back page of my German registration papers and showed me the words, not that it did me any good. He also explained that the registration papers had expired some time earlier in April. He thought I must have paid for one month as the amount shown was a small amount of only eighteen deutschmarks. I should have renewed the registration when I completed the insurance in England. Volkswagen authorities in England had made a mistake but the history of who had done what when was of little importance at the moment.

'So impasse?'

'No, not at all. It is simple. On Monday you go over the bridge and get a bus to Bitburg and in that town there is a registration office. Get the papers stamped and authorised and return here. All will be well and you can go. Enjoy the weekend in Echternach.'

Under police escort we drove back to the campsite we had left so cheerfully that morning and the neighbours looked at us rather suspiciously as the police car drove away. House arrest. No viable currency. Bus travel on Monday. I looked up at the ceiling of the camper some three feet or so above my face and slowly went over my story for the umpteenth time in French. The dictionary beside me didn't really help and neither did the phrase book. The question to the hotelier that there is a mouse in my bath wasn't really relevant in this situation.

Saturday passed without too much sleep and Sunday was just a day of waiting and waiting and waiting. I had this concern whether the new registration papers would have different numbers and these would be different from those on the insurance papers and the precious triptyque. I suppose I could see too many problems but then came Monday morning and I decided that doing it might be a lot better than just thinking about it. I left my wife in the camper, in Luxembourg, without car papers, and not having much confidence in being able to drive a stick shift vehicle. Pensively I walked through the town to the infamous bridge. My wife wondered whether she would ever see me again and she wasn't on speaking terms with the Duke either. Full of confidence and empty of German words I strode the few metres separating Luxembourg from Germany and entered the unknown. The German Customs Officer on the bridge spoke no English but was very helpful and explained where I could catch the bus. With my limited vocabulary, except for rock climbing, this took a while but was helpful. Two busses later, and the odd hour or so I found the government offices and the afore-mentioned car registration focal point. Before entering the official government building I had been thoughtful enough to find a bank where I sensibly exchanged traveller's cheques for deutschmarks. Back at the government office I found that my old British cultural pastime was being played out in full in Germany. What you ask? Easy I say. Get any three Brits together and they will form a queue, and so I joined the queue. I stood in line still mentally chasing my story round and round in my head, in French of course. I reached the clerk and managed to say good morning, in German. Then I politely asked in my best accent whether the clerk spoke English. He smiled and politely replied 'Nein'. I thought what to say next and with a flash of intelligence I asked whether he spoke French. Again he smiled politely and said 'Nein.'

Another impasse. Now some people go out of their way to be helpful and a middle-aged man three places back in the queue spoke up and said in French that he spoke German and French and could he help? So there we stood the three of us. The people behind in the queue were exceptionally patient as words in English, French, and German flowed to and fro complete with the exchange and scrutiny of car papers, passports, triptyques and whatever else came under discussion. The clerk was very interested in our trip and where we were going? He explained that he had a relative who had done something similar and were we going to see this and that, wherever? Fascinating. Isn't communication wonderful?

The queue behind me became longer and I could hear conversations up and down the line and no doubt the locals explained to each other that the dumbcluck Englishman couldn't speak the language and was en route to find the Abdominal Snowman. After some time the clerk read the back of my registration papers and became quite excited, laughed and started waving his hands about. Words followed. A mistake, an oversight, all was in order. No sir, there is no problem. The expiry date only applied within Germany and the papers were valid for one year anywhere outside Germany. I'll give you an extension until the end of June. Just needs this stamp and there is no charge. Thump, thump. Fixed. Enjoy your stay in Germany. Auf wiedersehn.

Relief flooded through me. No more arrest. No more car hold-up. We can go. I thanked the clerk, through my interpreter of course. I thanked my voluntary interpreter. I thanked the patient queue behind me. Everyone wished me well. I left the office clutching my precious papers and set off to find the bus. Now you have to remember that my thirty words of German get a little stretched finding a bus, especially the right bus. However, I found that pleading words, a worried face, thoughtful hand actions and finding English-speaking Germans helped me get back to the magic bridge in Echternach. Feeling somewhat light-hearted for a Monday morning I tripped over the bridge looking for Billie goat gruff but the Customs Officers on both side of the bridge were completely unconcerned with a foreign-looking pedestrian.

In the police station I found my friendly Inspector and sat down with him to explain the whole set of circumstances. In our mixture of English and French he found the whole incident very funny. It appeared that the Luxembourg police don't understand German any better than I did as they had misunderstood my registration papers. However, an adventure to remember he added. Well that was true I thought. My wife greeted me as if I had returned from a three month expedition up some climber-killing mountain and I dutifully explained that we were free to go. Our neighbours in the campsite still looked a little suspiciously at us.

Once again I lowered the roof very gently and locked it into position. Once again I carefully checked we had left nothing behind in the campsite. Once again I slowly drove through the streets of Echternach and down to the bridge over riviere La Sure. I waved to the Luxembourg authorities at their end of the bridge. Midstream I turned to my wife and offered her one more chance to live on the bridge. She demurred. We drove up to the German authorities and I dutifully stopped and offered my array of papers. Without any concern the Customs Officer waved us on and our Volkswagen returned to its native soil for a very enjoyable and just as memorable series of adventures and stories in Germany. We left the bridge over La Sure behind with its gentle reminder that paying attention in school can be useful later in life.

12 CLUNKERS

'You know those clubs they advertise on TV which show the usual Saturday foursome standing there, and the one player with the new clubs pounds it past the other three and smilingly turns to the other blokes and just shows them the name on the club?'

'Yes,' I said, not knowing what was going to come next from Sebastian, one of my usual Saturday opponents.

'Well, I think that's all baloney. I mean it is okay for the pros to play with such clubs. Maybe for them it does make a difference, but for most of us it's not a ping we hear when we hit the ball, it's a clunk. I'm seriously thinking of trying to produce a set of clubs called Clunkers. I reckon they'd sell much better.'

'Oh come on,' I said. 'Who'd want to play with a club called a clunker? We all know we're not pros, and sorely lacking in talent, and so we try and make up some advantage over our competitors with better clubs. It stands to reason that the quality club will help any of us. Just look at the success of the bloke in the ad.'

'But that's my point,' he said. 'Just think of the ego points if you win, if you beat those other slobs we play with using a club called a Clunker. Man, could you grin then eh? There they are, standing there with those

251

elite clubs which are supposed to go ping but rarely do when they hit the ball, and you've just won with a Clunker. I think they'd sell like hot cakes. It stands to reason that a win with a set of Clunkers would be worth three or four wins with any other clubs, just in bragging rites alone. I'm going to see a friend of mine and make up a set of Clunkers. You'll see.'

Well, I didn't think any more about it I suppose. We finished our round and I won one up at the last hole. Sitting over a pint in the clubhouse I thought about the suggestion Sebastian had made. Clunkers eh? I suppose the name says it all really. When most of us hit the ball, and we usually manage to do that you know, the noise we hear is much more of a clunk than any TV ping. Perhaps this would work? With a friend who is a bit of a blacksmith, and also a dedicated but hopeless golfer, we managed to cobble together a set of clubs that we could call Clunkers. My blacksmith friend had taken a course on golf club component fitting so he claimed he knew what he was doing. Mark you, gluing together a fabricated head onto a purchased shaft and fitting a grip over the shaft doesn't actually constitute golf club construction so I was a little dubious about the merits of these Clunkers. I knew they would be within the official specifications for golf clubs but the actual characteristics of the clubs would be a hit and miss affair I thought. Then I rethought and hoped it would be a hit and cheer affair. So, I had relatively low expectations when I took the set out onto the driving range very early one morning. I had to be out there early as I didn't want any of my other club members to see what a disaster this new set of clubs might be. There I was, just after dawn with all those birds doing their noisy breakfast thing and I was peering through the mist trying to see the fifty yard marker. I could just see it.

Now our driving range prides itself on being managed in a very neat and tidy way. At the end of each day a small boy is charged with collecting any of the balls that the ball-picker machine has missed. The old man driving the ball-picker is nearly ninety, age that is not handicap and he doesn't see too well. He's not at his best much after six o'clock either so on a long summer's evening there are a large number of balls strewn about the range. Obviously last night the small boy wasn't too diligent either for there were several small white spheres adorning the dew-laden grass. I tramped about for fifteen minutes and collected two handfuls, cursing that the small boy had been diligent enough to pick up all the baskets. In the fifteen minutes I managed to drop as many as I collected even when I folded them into a self-made pocket using the bottom of my sweater. I walked back to the teeing area with soaking feet, a dripping nose and two dozen red-striped range balls. As I dumped them at my feet I noticed one that didn't have any stripes on it. I pounced on this ball immediately and having picked it up I looked around to see who saw me retrieve this nearly brand-new Titleist. As there was no-one else there my find wasn't noticed and reported to the Ethics Committee and so I slipped the found ball into my golf bag.

I took out a four iron and a five iron. Well, that's what the stamping on the club heads said but I wasn't too sure the lofts were that precise. Holding the two clubs together I started to slowly swing the weight in a horizontal arc to loosen up the shoulders. That's the theory but my hands were still wet from collecting the scattered range balls and the clubs slipped out of my hands at the end of a particularly aggressive arc and sailed in a perfect parabola out into the mist. My oath was gobbled up in the still white air and I set off to retrieve my warm-up tools. I came back and dried my hands on a towel. My wet feet were past drying.

Back on the tee-box I rolled one of the balls with my foot onto a helpful fluffed lie on the ground. I don't usually apply this technique out on the course, except under dire circumstances, but it seemed easier than bending over and getting my hands wet again. For starters I selected a seven iron. In my usual set of clubs this is the one club that I can rely on no matter where I am on the course. When the pressure is really on I know that with my seven iron I can chip that delicate ten feet on to the green, and, just as easily, I can hit it one hundred and thirty yards closer to the hole when I am two hundred and ten yards out. I am reliable with my seven iron.

So there I was that misty morning with my set of Clunkers and I took my regular couple of practice swings. The usual and essential forty seven swing thoughts went through my head as I practised. You know most of them. In fact you may even have the same thoughts, or even a few more if you're really a fanatic. Finally we reached the moment of truth. Knees flexed, hands softly on the grip, eyes on the ball. It's amazing how it can sit there and grin at you. Range balls particularly seem able to bend the stripe into a nasty grin as if to say I dare you to hit me. Of course, on a really bad day, you can visualise the grin as belonging to the mother-in-law and then the shot becomes much easier. Not necessarily better or even accurate but you sure can hit it. But, back to the range and ready to take the club head away, slowly brushing the grass and extending the arms. Up to the top and a slight pause, well in theory, but on the first swing there's usually a bit of a snatch at the change of direction and then smoothly down and through. The hips open out of the way quite naturally and the right arm comes through on the inside. No flying elbow please and there is a pleasant clunk. The club head continues forward taking a neat divot along the line of flight and then arcs finally up to the left. I did mention that I was a right-hander? You stand there in balance with the shoulders now square down the driving range but what happened to the ball? It felt good. It sounded good. If you could have smelt it it smelled good too, no doubt about it. But where?

It took off looking good, well I thought so but then I still had my head down and my eyes on the divot. Bringing my head up I thought I saw it launch forth in the right direction, even at the right flight height like a rocket into the embracing mist. Good stuff eh?

For the next ten minutes I continued to swing easily and strike this trusty seven iron. The set of divots were neat and I noticed they were all straight down the line of the range. I knew this was unusual for me but impressive I thought. The mist continued to swallow up my shots. I tried peeping; looking at the ball flight a little early but that resulted in the expected mis-hit and two rather thin shots that scuttled through the dew.

Suddenly, just like that, without any warning, the mist lifted. It rose about forty feet above the ground and then just sat there like a white dome. I could see the fifty yard marker, the hundred and even the blue two hundred yard marker. Now I was excited. I looked around for a ball to hit but of course I had exhausted my pitiful two handed collection so it was off back down the range again for another round up. The grass was still dew-laden and once again I dried my hands on my souvenir from St. Andrews towel. I had never been to St. Andrews. In fact I had only been over the border into Scotland once and as it was pouring with rain I decided that once was enough and so the towel was bought at the local Sunday flea market. However, I thought it looked good and suggestive on my golf bag. It added a little class to my otherwise mundane set of clubs.

Yes, set of clubs. Now we can see whether the actual results are as good as they sound and feel. I plunked my collection of balls back on the ground and tapped one into position. I watched with amazement. The ball sailed out in a lovely arc and landed softly but with authority just in front of the one hundred and fifty yard marker. I quickly checked to see that I had indeed hit a seven iron. That's what the club head said, seven. No way I told myself. I've never hit a seven iron that well. A Clunker too. Wow!

Well we had to repeat it didn't we? Could have been a fluke. We all get that occasional shot once or twice a round, no maybe once or twice a year is more likely when everything goes right or at least the result is wonderful. You know the feeling, the sight, the sound and once again I suppose the smell and taste too when the ball sails exactly where you wanted it to go. Your other three players lean on their clubs in awe and can't believe their eyes. Immediately there is a whole plethora of comments about, 'Where did that come from? Why didn't you do that before? Have you been having lessons? Did you really do that? Bet you can't do that again?' They're all true of course and you wonder yourself where that shot came from. But, here on the range, with no pressure and a smooth seven iron you just hit the ball one hundred and fifty yards, well almost.

Now because of the mist still sitting at forty feet above the ground you didn't actually see the ball go from your position to where it landed because it disappeared pretty early on into the whiteness and then suddenly appeared hurtling down to earth near the marker. You suppose it actually was your ball? You quickly scan up and down the line of the tee-box. No-one else here, no-one obvious anyway so it must have been your ball. Well fancy that.

Five more seven iron shots convinced me it was no fluke. I hit those five shots smoothly and they all landed within ten yards of the first one. Magic. Okay then, let's try one of the other clubs? Perhaps my blacksmith friend has a thing about seven irons like I do. To cut a long story short I went though the set of irons and couldn't believe what I saw. After another thirty minutes, including three more sorties out down the length of the range to retrieve balls, the mist lifted and I could see the entire parabola of the shot. Wonderful, absolutely wonderful. Clunkers I thought. I lifted the club I was holding up to my lips and kissed it. You wonderful things; I can't wait to get on the course with these. Then I suddenly realised that I had gone through the set of irons but hadn't even looked at the woods, well fairway metals I suppose they are called these days. Weird name really but you can't call a metal club a wood when it isn't. Changes the game of course. Another noise has disappeared. There is no soft thwack or clip that there used to be when you caught your spoon right on the screws. All gone now. So we were back to a metal Clunker. Rather dubiously I selected a five fairway metal. It even sounded strange just to say it. I swung and it whistled in the morning air. Flex felt good. Weight felt good and the grip fitted nicely in the fingers or rather the fingers fitted nicely on the grip. You know what I mean?

Good balanced stance, knees flexed and all the rest of the pre-shot routine and then whoosh, wow, out of sight, well not quite but a long way down the range. Now on a good day with the wind behind me, and my shoes fitting well after a satisfying non-fat breakfast, I can hit a five metal about one hundred and eighty yards, or one hundred and ninety yards with a positive roll. My first Clunker shot sailed, actually sailed nearly to the two hundred yard marker and fetched up just past it. Way to go I shouted. I turned round quickly because I had embarrassed myself but there was no-one else out that early and so I needn't have bothered. I picked myself up off the ground. In my quick turn I had fallen over two of the range balls and described a three point landing but fortunately there was no-one there to award points for posture or entry splash so I didn't feel too bad. My ankle felt a little squiffy though. I ran my hand over my ankle and managed to smear some mud on my smart clean that morning Argyll socks. Dam. I hate to look untidy on the golf course.

The other fairway metal Clunkers performed like the five metal and I sat down with a feeling of overwhelming wonder. Now I was unbeatable. I couldn't wait for the weekend. After carefully gathering up the clubs and rather reverently sliding them gently back into the golf bag I rushed back to my car and drove home.

'You look cheerful,' my wife said. 'You usually come home from the range and offer me your clubs to put out with the dustbin. Fortunately I never listen to you and carefully place them in their proper corner of the garage. Otherwise you'd never find them come Saturday when you run around the house wondering where you last put them and I have to gently point out they are where they are supposed to be, in their normal place in the garage. Anyway dearest, why the grin?'

'I've got to phone Ronnie. I've just got to.'

'Darling it's seven thirty on a Thursday morning and Ronnie will still be lying in bed. You know he doesn't have to be in his office until ten and Dolores hasn't shouted for him up the stairs yet. I can picture her now with that false blond hair of hers all caught up in those awful curlers she uses holding onto the banisters and leaning up the staircase and bawling in that dreadful northern accent of hers. What does she say now? That's it: "Time to get up pet!" And Ronnie is up there lying in bed probably thinking about that new secretary he has just hired. You know, the girl with the blouses that are at least two sizes too small and show that she's a well built girl if you know what I mean. And he's lying up there imagining I don't know what. Well I probably do know what but I'm not repeating it in this kitchen. Henry! Are you listening to me at all love? Oh, you're on the phone. Who? I've just told you he won't be up yet. You'll want the usual I suppose? Two eggs easy over with two rashers and a piece of fried bread? Tomatoes too? Not listening I see. Well then you'll get what I give you and like it mate.'

"Ronnie, Ronnie is that you? Oh Dolores it's you. Ronnie's not up yet? Well get him for me will you love? It's important, absolutely life threatening. Yes Dolores. It is important. When have I ever lied to you? At the New Year's Party? I never promised to do that did I? But I don't know that I could even do that if I tried. We did try? But I was too drunk to make it work. So I lied. No never Dolores. No I don't think it would be good to have a foursome, well not that kind of foursome. Where's Ronnie? He's coming? You don't think he has come for the past twelve months, well not with you. Dolores I must speak with Ronnie. Ah, there you are Ronnie. Yes good morning to you too. Ronnie, now listen. Listen will you and stop fighting with Dolores. She was doing what? Never, well maybe not never now I come to think about it. Ronnie, what are you doing this morning? Going to work. What did I think you were going to do? Yes of course. Yes I know it's Thursday, but this is really important. So, what are you doing today? Yes, well can't you have a sickie or something? Dolores isn't well. She has to go to Hospital. No I don't know whether Dolores is really well or not that was just a suggestion. No Ronnie, I don't know anything about Dolores's condition, especially not with her waterworks. Ronnie take the day off. Take the whole day off and we'll go and play golf. Why? Well why not? We've put the years in at work haven't we? How often do we take days off? Every month? Ronnie I've never taken a day off in my whole working life and you're telling me you take at least one day off a month. But that's cheating, cheating on the Company. No wonder it costs me so much to do my banking. If all your staff did that the bank costs would be sky high, and it's me the customer who's paying. All I'm doing is paying you to look after my money, my money that's what pisses me off you know. I actually have to pay you to let me put my money in and take my money out of your poxy bank and all the time you're taking days off. I suppose you take days off with that new secretary of yours, the one with the blouses two sizes too small who really makes Carol here grind her teeth? No I didn't tell Dolores but Carol might have done. No Ronnie I don't know anything about blouse sizes, too big or too small. I'm just repeating what Carol said.'

'Carol says breakfast is on the table. You can have it now, hot, which I would really appreciate seeing as I have been standing here sweating over a hot stove for the past fifteen minutes while you have been rabbiting on about Ronnie's sweet young thing, or you can have it cold, which I don't give a toss about as it's your breakfast and you wouldn't catch me eating all that cholesterol, not if you paid me. Your call.'

'Yes. Thanks Carol dear. I'll be right there. Now Ronnie, you still there? Right, I'm booking a ten o'clock tee time for the pair of us this morning. It's really absolutely without a doubt essential you be there. Got it? So see you just before ten on the practice green. Got to go, breakfast's on the table.'

I slammed down the telephone and sat down to my breakfast. 'This looks extra specially good this morning my love, cooked to perfection. You are my little charmer.' I smiled sweetly at my wife who stood with her hands on her hips as she looked closely at my face. 'You been smoking something?' She sniffed loudly. 'Who did you see this morning? We don't have no new girl on the paper route? Where did you really go? I know you brought back your golf clubs but they look like new so where did you go? The golf shop's not open yet so you couldn't have gone down to any golf sale or anything like that.'

I sat and smirked. I dipped part of my fried bread in the egg's yolk. Scrumptious. The yolk sort of dripped onto the table cloth and I smeared it up with my finger tips and tasted part of the driving range. 'I've been practising and now I think I've got it. I think I've got it.'

'Who do you think you are, Eliza Doolittle? Every time you come home from the driving range you think you've got it, well except those times when you want me to throw the clubs away and you swear you're never going to play that silly game again. What is it you say? Who wants to pay, and I mean really pay, to go and get disillusioned, demeaned, demolished and downright desperate? Trouble is you seem to say that most Saturday and Sunday afternoons when you stagger home breathing beer fumes everywhere. But now, on this bright and sunny Thursday morning, you actually think you've got it? Well my love I really hope so.

After what Dolores told me about your efforts at the Golf Club's New Year's party I didn't think you would ever get it again.' Carol giggled. 'You should have heard that blond hussy describe what you tried to do? It was priceless. She said it was your idea too which I thought was even funnier. I never knew you could even try and do it that way. Anyway sweetest, I'm so glad to hear that you've finally got it. I'll look forward to you proving it some time soon eh?'

Carol swept out of the kitchen and went upstairs to dress. I sat and looked at the scattered remains of my breakfast on the plate. Now if this is the ball and this is a sand trap you could blast out and oh shit, egg all over Carol's nice tea pot. Quick wipe and lick the fingers again and that's fine. Must get the greenskeeper to change the taste of that herbicide he uses. Herbicide!! Slurp the tea and wash it out of my mouth. I wolfed down the breakfast and wanted to keep the energy levels high for the big game this morning. Lots of sugar in the tea and another cup? No, I'll be wanting to find trees all over the course to fertilise and that's not down the middle of the fairway so we'll limit the fluids but build up the carbohydrates. Do this scientifically I think with those Clunkers. They certainly deserve respect from their player. I telephoned the Club House and booked a ten o'clock tee-time.

'Yes, just a twosome, important competition you know, rather special event. What is it? Well it's the Clunker Open, really well established competition. I used to play it in the last Club I was at. Never won but came second twice.'

Didn't tell the old fool that there were never more than two people in the competition but who's to know. I went upstairs to change into some nice new slacks. Bright pink they are and very fetching on the course. Lots of the Lady members were really interested in knowing where I got them and whether I knew what size I was. I had been absolutely smitten with them when I saw them in the golf shop and just had to have them. I knew they'd be a sensation and today was just the right day to wear them. I had a little difficulty with the zipper being on the side but the zipper didn't interfere with the pockets to hold the necessary tees, ball-mark fixer tool, ball marker, spare ball, new glove, cleat cleaning brush and the very necessary spare pencil with a rubber on the blunt end. Of course there was the back pocket for the fresh score card and its attendant pencil and necessary rubber.

The bottom of the slacks didn't have the usual turned up cuff and were flared a little which I thought looked really naval. Sort of "Here comes the Fleet" kind of swish noise when I walked. To go with the pink slacks I had this incredible top of the line golf shirt from the best store in town. Carol had bought it for me one Christmas. Last Christmas if I remember correctly and she thought it would be good for special occasions. Well Carol, how right you were I thought and I carefully peeled the wrapper away from the shirt and stuck two of the pins holding it together into my little finger. I dropped the shirt and energetically danced around a little and sucked the blood dripping from my fingers and tasted the range again. The blood didn't reach my new pink slacks and so I felt that was a good sign. After that I managed to remove the other pins without further blood-letting and Carol asked why I was dancing around the bedroom sucking my fingers? I explained in my low soft bedroom voice that I was experiencing the delights of her Christmas present, and reliving the moments when she gave it to me that past Christmas morning with her fluffy mules, big smile and not much else. She said, 'Forget it. I've got to go shopping,' and swayed out of the bedroom leaving me somewhat limp and bloody-minded.

The shirt fitted like a glove. It was two sizes too small and I had difficulty lifting my arms above shoulder height. I tried a full swing and succeeded in constricting my chest such that breathing became a challenge. Lowering my arms I decided that the new and love-donated shirt really wasn't going to do the business. The colours of vertical fine stripes of chartreuse and lemon green with an odd diagonal slash of vivid red didn't quite go with the pink slacks anyway. Looking through my wardrobe I noticed someone had been meddling with my little shelf where I kept cuff-links, tie-pins and condoms. I counted them. Sure enough there was one missing. I counted again. One of the cuff links was missing. Now this was rather surprising as I only had one pair of cuff-links so who would take just one cuff-link and not its partner? Rather sadly I noticed that the number of condoms was the same as it had been that past Christmas. Still sex isn't everything I thought when you've got Clunkers, and what Clunkers.

Having found another really impressive shirt to go with the flared pink slacks, suitable for this historic occasion, I went downstairs and found that Carol really had gone shopping. Now this wasn't surprising as she said that's what she was going to do. Unfortunately she took the car to go shopping. Two years ago we had had a real heart to heart about finances, and whether her allowance was really adequate as it had not been adjusted for the past ten years and some things have become more expensive my love she complained. Personally, I thought she was trying too hard. But, we did agree to compromise on the expenses and try and cut back a little so I sold her car. Carol didn't think this was exactly the result she was looking for out of our discussion. Nevertheless, I told her she was right, and I agreed with her one hundred percent that we did need to cut down a little on our expenses, and that having two cars really didn't make sense as she could easily get to her job on the bus. Of course she had to make one change but the connection was usually pretty efficient and the wait at the junction rarely exceeded thirty minutes so I sold her car. I mean, I needed mine for the job but now my car was sitting idle somewhere in a shopping mall parking lot while Carol was supping a latté in one of those new-fangled coffee bars. You know where

I mean? The places that tend to be the congregation spot for many of those young twenty-year old lotharios that hang around shopping malls looking for bored but flatterable housewives with too much time on their hands. I'd seen them ogle my wife. My emotions boiled up inside me and I thought about Clunkers as weapons. Clunkers! Yes Clunkers as clubs, but what about golf? My brain suddenly lurched down the list of deadly sins from jealousy to pride and the need to show off my Clunkers. In a flash of inspiration I phoned my office and coughing loudly down the line I explained that I had woken up this morning very early and nearly had the fright of my life. The early morning mist had really got to my throat and I had ended up with very wet feet, like sweat almost and found myself quite overcome with emotion. As I thought this was contagious I had thoughtfully decided against bringing this dangerous body of mine in to the office today and hoped I would feel better tomorrow. In fact I said I can almost guarantee I will feel better by late this afternoon and should be bursting to come to work by tomorrow morning. Felt I would be positively leaping to work.

Having settled that little problem there was still the issue of transport. Now it is true the golf course was only one hundred yards down the road from our front door but one could hardly arrive on foot on such a momentous occasion. It just wasn't on. From the end of my back garden I could gently throw golf balls onto the sixteenth green but again walking over the course in from the sixteenth wasn't really kosher either. So I needed wheels. Ronnie, I could phone Ronnie. But, let's think. After the event Ronnie will want to drown his sorrows and he'll be too drunk to drive so that would be unwise. And could I really sit in Ronnie's car, him the loser after my dramatic victory? That wouldn't be very sporting either, unless of course we put his car up as part of the prize money, then it would be mine and that wouldn't be so bad. But how would I get to Ronnie's car if I did phone him and suggest he take us both to the course?

I could walk to his house. It wasn't far seeing as he lived next door but that wouldn't look like a winner either now would it?

In the end I telephoned for a taxi to come at nine thirty and take me to the course. That would give me plenty of time to practice my putting and loosen up a little after this morning's energetic work-out. I knew the clubs were fine. Clubs. Clubs!!! Where were the clubs? Did I take them out of the boot of the car? Carol has them. No no no, Carol has them in my car stuck in some stupid parking lot slowly roasting in the boot alongside the half a leg of lamb and best mince. I rushed out to the garage. It was empty of course, well of the car anyway. But, there in the corner stood my golf bag looking a little bashful at having to hold such a precious cargo of Clunkers. Ah those Clunkers. I let my breath slowly dribble out of my lungs and as I had been holding it for fully five minutes there was rather a lot of it and it took a long time to dribble out. When it was all out I had to think quickly and breathe in again or I would have died on the spot, right next to my Clunkers. A suitable resting place surely but a little premature. Today was the day.

When the taxi blasted on his horn, 'That's the third time sir and I was just about to give up on you', I jumped and nearly wet my new pink slacks but managed just in time to squeeze hard. Quick as a flash I sprinted for the washroom but nothing happened and so I just nonchalantly washed my hands as if there was no crisis and sauntered back into the garage to pick up the golf bag and my Clunkers. The heads rang together nicely, almost in harmony, as I walked purposefully down my driveway to the waiting taxi. I looked about me as I strode down the driveway taking notice of the crowd watching me and hoped they'd remember this point in their otherwise drab and unremarkable lives as the vital moment when their lives changed. The day the Clunkers ruled the world. I reverently laid my golf bag on the back seat of the taxi and gently closed the door. The taxi started to drive away and I had to beat on the door a couple of times to get the driver to stop so that I could open the front door and slip in beside him. In so doing I managed to squash several pieces of paper he had scattered there including the latest edition of the Racing Times, a tattered copy of Lady Chatterley's Lover and the remains of yesterday's chapattis and curry paste. Luckily my pink slacks didn't get too close to the curry paste but they did brush against the most thumbed pages of Lady Chatterley's Lover and I think that may have been the reason I didn't play so well on some of those kinky holes.

I paid the taxi driver at the end of the hundred yard trip and gave him the appropriate tip: Lady Chatterley in the three thirty at Litchfield on the nose. He gave me a rude sign and drove away. I screamed loudly and started to chase after him at great speed. I had just caught him when he reached my house and by banging furiously I managed to get him to stop. Opening the back door I retrieved my golf bag and the precious Clunkers. Slowly I counted them to make sure the taxi driver hadn't stolen any in my absence. When I was satisfied I walked slowly back to the Golf Club carefully carrying the golf bag and making sure none of the heads had been banged about too much.

Ronnie was standing in the entrance way to the Golf Club and he rather obtusely asked why I had come in a taxi, and then run back to my house after the taxi when it had safely dropped me at the Golf Club in the first place?

'I thought that would be obvious even to a dense chump like you,' I said rather abruptly. 'The rather overpaid and under-taxed simpleton of a taxi driver managed to get his fare to the right destination but failed dismally to unload all of the accessories. He tried to abscond with my golf clubs. Really, I don't know what this country is coming to when a fellow's golf clubs aren't safe in sight of his own Clubhouse.'

I turned to look at Ronnie and my mouth fell open. 'Why did you come in fancy dress?' I asked.

Ronnie was wearing brown plus fours, vivid patterned Argyll socks where red was the predominant colour, and a pair of multi-tasselled brown golf brogues. Above the plus fours Ronnie sported a very business-like white shirt partly hidden under a brown Harris Tweed jacket whose style had gone out of fashion after the war, the First World War, and a rather non-descript thin brown tie. He had topped it all off with a very working-class flat cap. How appropriate I thought, playing with a comedian on this historic day.

'I suppose you are playing with wooden-shafted clubs, gutta percha balls and using a pinch of sand on the tee boxes?' I asked. 'Is there a reason for this return to the swinging twenties? I suppose next you'll expect us to hire caddies to carry the bags rather than use our golf carts? Really Ronnie, this is just a normal Saturday game except Toby and Sebastian won't be here. Just you and me. Usual rules: match play, even handicaps, you know the score. We play it every weekend for the past I don't know how many years. Are you up for it old man or is the fancy dress a rather sporting way of saying you're not quite in top form and looking for an advantage of some sort? Sorry old chap. Even-Stevens, that's what we've always played.'

'Actually Henry, I'm still trying to shield my eyes from those rather flamboyant pair of ladies slacks you're sporting. I can see why the fair sex were so interested last time you wore them. Mark you, last time it was pouring with rain and the grey skies sort of muted the gaudiness, but my, aren't they flash? Actually, how do you manage it in those pants, you know, when you have to go? Must be rather awkward, unless you're better endowed than I thought. Sort of ability to go round corners. Dolores did mention something about that last New Years. Can't remember exactly what she said but it was something to do with size. So how can you sensibly squirt it with that zipper on the side?'

I looked. I had never noticed. I suppose there had never been a need.

I have always been a sort of camel when it comes to that so the question had never arisen.

'Nonsense Ronnie, you're just trying to put me off my game, and before we've even reached the course. You must be desperate this morning to try such tactics this early in the competition. No problems there old man. Jump over tall buildings if we have to. We've got time for a quick competition on the practice green before our tee time. Are you up for it?'

'With those pants you'd better not be old man,' Ronnie chuckled and we walked over to the putting green. After firmly rolling putts into the cup from one foot I realised I was on form and as Ronnie hadn't managed to find his putter yet I decided it was time for our tee-off. We tossed my two-headed coin for honours on the first tee and I called heads. I reached over quickly to pick up the coin before Ronnie could and slipped it back into the special pocket on my golf bag.

'Well old man, let the best man win eh?'

I put down a long tee for my driver and found a reasonably new ball for the first shot. Our opening hole is a dog leg left with a veritable forest of embracing bushes on the right-side corner. Needless to say this is an oft-frequented spot for most right-handers who tend to slice the ball on their hurried first-tee nerves shot. And needless to think about as I had my Clunkers. I carefully pulled my driver out of my bag.

'New clubs eh? Look a bit weird but then it's hard to see with the glare off those pants. Didn't you say you found a really good deal at a car boot sale last weekend? Are they them? Look a little suspect to me but then I play with the top of the line clubs as you know. Perhaps that explains why I tend to win most of our games. You've seen the advert? You know, where our usual Saturday foursome watches with awe as I strike the ball so perfectly and land it softly close to the pin. Seem to remember that I do that fairly regularly now. Can't remember we ever got beyond the sixteenth hole in the game. It's usually two or three up by that time and you've typically threatened to throw your clubs in the pond and walk off the sixteenth green into your back garden vowing never to play again. Now, if I remember right, we get you to play on and we win the bye just to add salt to the wound. Anyway, are you ever going to hit it old man? I think the starter's getting a little anxious that we're going to be here all day and the foursome behind are already stamping their feet. If it's too hard with the new clubs I might think of some sort of handicap system, just to make it a game. Play away.'

My drive sailed out from the tee box in that familiar arc, familiar from this morning that is, and landed over two hundred yards in the middle of the fairway perfectly placed for the dog leg. I wasn't blocked by the trees on the inside corner and I would have a clear view to the green from there. Ronnie didn't say anything. The foursome behind us applauded. 'Great shot sir.' 'Straight as an arrow.' 'Right on the money.'

Ronnie's drive faded a little and found the right rough about one hundred and eighty yards down the course. 'Slightly too quick,' he muttered. 'Coming in a little from over the top.' He went on muttering as we walked down the first fairway and by the time we had reached his ball he had muttered seventy four different things that had gone wrong with his first shot.

After three hours we stood on the eighteenth tee-box all square. As I had won the seventeenth hole it was my honour. Ronnie was a little bit flustered by this time and kept twirling his expensive clubs. I wasn't sure whether he was trying to psyche himself up or intimidate me with his flashy clubs. I just reached over my golf bag and kissed my Clunkers. Just to add to the tension of the moment you should know that our eighteenth hole is a straightaway par four and the hardest hole on the course. It is a little over four hundred yards long and starts with a one hundred and fifty yard carry over a pond. Trees line both sides of the fairway and close along the left hand side is out of bounds with Granny Fetchup's cottage situated about two hundred and twenty yards from the tee-box. It is a pretty hole, pretty narrow, pretty threatening and pretty dammed hard. However, as Ronnie had mentioned on the first tee, our game is usually over by the time our foursome stands here so we are pretty relaxed by this time. Inevitably one of us will recount the infamous golf pond joke. You haven't heard it? Surely? Well okay, but it is pretty corny. Let me think for a moment. Fine.

This golfer, who was a singleton and rather timid too, was out on the rather empty course playing with his dog. Now the dog was a wonder. He was short, short-legged, short-haired and could be short-tempered but he was brilliant as a line finder on greens. The dog would stand behind the ball and look towards the hole. When the golfer lined up his putt the dog would wag his tail one side or the other to get the line straight. When he thought his master had got the right line he would wag his tail up and down vertically. Then the dog had to move aside quickly because it is against the rules to have someone stand behind your line on the green. However, with the right acceleration the putt would follow the line and drop neatly into the cup. Bingo. As I say, the dog was terrific on the greens, but that isn't the real part of the story because we had this pond. I mentioned before that this golfer was rather a timid chap and so when he came to a par three which was all carry over water to the green he looked in his golf bag and pulled out an old rather scruffy ball obviously reserved for water holes. Just as he was teeing up a clap of thunder rolled around the heavens and the lightening flashed. God spoke. 'You little wimp! Be a man and play a real ball.' The timid man looked about him but there was no-one there but his tail alignment dog and so he thought about the voice. Well okay, perhaps this once, and he looked again into his golf bag and found a real golf ball, used but not so scruffy. He replaced his water ball in the bag and carefully and rather fearfully put this better ball on the tee. He looked over the pond at the green again and it still looked a long way away. Selecting a club he walked up to his ball and took his stance. All went quiet. Then he did something unexpected. He stepped back a pace and took a practice swing. Immediately there was another crash of thunder and the lightening was absolutely dazzling this time. 'Put back the water ball. Oh, and pray a lot.'

Not funny? No, I suppose not, not when you've heard it I don't know how many times. I reached in my pocket and found a tee and carefully placed it by the left-hand tee-box marker. I remember my teacher telling me to hit away from trouble and although I usually hit the ball from left to right I didn't want to come over the top and duck hook it left out of bounds. So I placed my ball on the tee at the left-hand side. I took a couple of smooth practice swings. I felt relieved because silence followed – there was no thunder and lightning. Ronnie broke the silence.

'You remember the joke about the timid golfer and the water hole? You sure you've got the right ball there old man? Wasn't that a new ball starting on the seventeenth you've got? Bold I must say.'

I let Ronnie prattle on trying to do my mind in and stood there quietly gazing down the fairway. Eventually he resignedly quietened down and just stood there jumbling loose change in his pocket.

I stood up and addressed the ball. Slow and smooth I thought and I made my little press, slowly drew the club back and completed the backswing with a smooth transition leading to a ever-faster downswing through the ball and a satisfactory clunk. I let the club head follow its own inertia into a full turn and finished in balance with my hips open and shoulders square to the flight of the ball. Marvellous. I watched the ball take off and move outlined against the clear blue sky in a lovely arc to land and bounce a yard forward right in the middle of the fairway clearly two hundred and thirty yards out. Pretty. Pretty to watch. Pretty good.

There was a grunt as Ronnie stopped jingling his loose change. 'Pretty impressive for flea market cast offs,' he said. 'Now let's see what real clubs can do. Move aside there sport and we'll show you some top quality magic. Just remember the smile in that advertisement.'

Ronnie took out his driver, which cost more than my whole set of clubs, and casually tossed the head cover over by the tee-box marker. He forcefully swished the club in his hands and it sounded really impressive, really professional. After he tee-ed up his ball he took another couple of practice swings as he walked up and down rather nervously I thought on the tee-box. He seemed to be having difficulties getting to the ball and I could hear the foursome behind just finishing on the seventeenth green. Eventually Ronnie took his stance and within a moment he had slashed at the ball with his utmost ferocity as if he was trying to send it into orbit. The swing was so powerful he pitched forward and stumbled over his feet with the momentum. 'Did you see that? Did you see that?' he exclaimed. 'Out of sight.'

'Well, no Ronnie, not quite. Impressive though. You hit that over two hundred and forty yards.'

'You sure? I didn't see it but it felt terrific. I told you these clubs were top of the line didn't I?'

'Yes Ronnie you did. You have, many many times and they are impressive. But yes, I did see it, and it must have gone two hundred and forty yards because it bounced off the roof of Granny Fetchup's cottage.'

'And bounced back into play?' asked Ronnie. 'And so it must be over two hundred and sixty yards out. That's only what, a flick with an eight iron in to the green? Piece of cake really. Ready to concede old man?'

I paused. I counted to ten like I had been taught in witness training courses when asked a confrontational question. Looking at Ronnie I decided to answer truthfully. Clunkers do that to folk. 'Well Ronnie, hold your horses a moment because when it bounced off the cottage roof it pitched forwards and is somewhere in Granny's vegetable patch, probably around where she has her tomatoes, or maybe the beans. I'm not sure. I haven't been in there lately.'

'Tomatoes, beans, what are you talking about? It must have bounced back into bounds and be down the fairway somewhere. You just didn't see it.'

'No sir, your fellow player is quite right. It hit the roof and carried on over into the vegetable patch as your friend here says. I agree with his first suggestion though.'

'His first suggestion?' asked Ronnie, rather red in the face at this stage of the discussion.

'Yes sir, I too think it went into the tomatoes.'

Ronnie thumped the ground with his driver and the tee-box sort of shook. 'So that's three off the tee,' I said rather quietly.

This time Ronnie took a little more care with his preparation. Well you know, he had a bigger audience this time and he needed to show that his top of the line clubs were really the cats meow. The swing certainly was a little slower and the weight transfer a little more controlled but somewhere in the middle of the backswing Ronnie had moved his weight forward to hit this ball very hard. In a flash he realised he might miss it altogether if he was not careful and so he came down very steeply on the backswing and hit a good inch behind the ball digging an unwanted divot in the tee-box. The club almost went under the ball at point of impact and as a result the ball went skywards exceptionally quickly and shot upwards like a rocket. Fortunately there was enough forward momentum to also move the ball down the fairway and after a phenomenally long hang time the ball landed with a loud thump a good one hundred and fifty one yards down the fairway, having safely carried the water hazard by a good yard. It was right in the middle of the short grass. Excellent.

The foursome behind us was silent and Ronnie and I picked up our clubs, stuffed them back in our bags and trundled our golf carts off down the path that skirts the pond.

'What's the name of that set of clubs?' he asked.

'Clunkers,' I said. He grunted.

'Expensive?'

'No Ronnie, not these. We just sort of cobbled them together really. Sort of hit and miss.'

'But you don't do you? You don't hit and miss? You have hit the ball today better than I've ever seen you hit the ball.'

'Sure Ronnie, but it's not the clubs. It's me. Today I feel good. The swing's working. I've got it. I told Carol this morning that I've got it but she just made some sexist remark that I haven't had it for a long time. She even made some remark about something she heard from Dolores, something about last New Year's Eve party, but I couldn't remember anything about that.'

'That's not what I heard Dolores say. She didn't say you couldn't remember she just said you couldn't. Still, wearing those pants it doesn't surprise me. Well here we are then. Good lie don't you think? A smooth shot should put me on the green. It's what, just under two hundred and fifty you think?'

I stood back and rubbed my eyes. It wasn't the sun shining on my slacks that was dazzling me it was Ronnie's audacity to think he could hit the ball two hundred and fifty yards off the fairway, even with his clubs. I watched him take a rescue hybrid club out of his bag and swing smoothly a couple of times. The foursome behind us was wandering about on the tee-box and I saw that another foursome had joined them. I wondered where the course marshall was? I must have been reflecting on this question when I caught Ronnie's swing out of the corner of my eye. The ball took off like a rocket, straight and pure, and flew some two hundred yards through the air; a really good shot. As luck would have it, and that's golf isn't it, the ball landed fair and square on a sprinkler head and bounced with fully-loaded springs a further forty yards to land two feet in on the edge of the green. It trickled three feet further up the green and caught the slope in the front and stopped, started to roll backwards, and eventually came to rest some six inches on the green.

'Too much backspin,' muttered Ronnie. 'I should have kept my right arm more outside and pronated the wrists more don't you think? Would have been right up there close to the pin. Great clubs these are. Absolutely first class.'

I watched Ronnie slide the rescue hybrid back into his bag. I didn't say anything but I knew that that particular club was not part of the top of the line set but a club he had picked out of a barrel of rejects in the second hand shop at the end of our village and had cost less than a pound. It had been a good shot and had nothing to do with the clubs but I didn't say anything. The eight people on the tee applauded Ronnie's shot and then started to tee up, sort of hinting that we should get a move on as we still had to reach my drive and play my second shot.

'Oh tough luck. That's golf though. Rub of the green I think is the expression.'

My drive had been first class, long and perfectly in the middle of the straightaway fairway, but it had landed in the middle of a horrendous divot that was fully a foot long. Someone had stood here and tried to redesign the course, plant potatoes or just practise trench digging for the next invasion. My little white ball sat grinning at the bottom of this divot and the top of the ball might have been level with the surface of the fairway. I grinned back at the ball. Well what else was I going to do?

Ronnie stood a little to one side and rested his weight against his golf cart. He glanced back at the eighteenth tee-box. 'Those fellows are getting a little restless you know. Think we can pick up the pace do you? I'm on the green and out of the way so it's up to you old man.'

One hundred and seventy yards out, well to the flag that is: perhaps only one hundred and fifty to the green. What had I found out that morning on the driving range, apart from how wet the dew was? These Clunkers were good and suited my swing perfectly. So, sitting in this divot the ball will come out low and fast, especially if I hit down hard on the back of the ball with the ball further back in my stance. What was the expression, "Hit the little ball before you hit the big ball"? It is like a knock-down shot, a trap shot, so how about a smooth three iron and make the ball run? Sounds good our kid so do it. I took my three iron out of the bag and assessed the situation one last time. The sun shone as I took a couple of practice swings and pictured the shot in my mind. Clearly I saw the ball fly all the way to the green and faithfully run up the slope to the shelf at the back where the flag was. Sweet. I made sure I was going to hit down on the ball. I felt relaxed. I was in a really good position and set to win this hole and the match. Hurray for Clunkers. All set to make par. In the middle of my downswing a loud shout of "fore" caused me to half start and I closed the face of my club and trapped the ball. As a result it scampered along about three feet above the fairway like a projectile. I watched as it bounced through the sand trap guarding the front left of the green and continued at speed off the lip to land some five yards over the back left corner of the green in the long lush grass.

'Tough luck. Great shot considering. Wonder why those chaps hit? I didn't wave them on did I? Didn't think I did. Shout came just at the wrong time. I'll have to talk to the Ethics Chairman about that group. Do you know any of them? Perhaps they are guests and don't know enough about etiquette? Don't worry old man. I'll talk with them when we've finished. I'll just putt out and wait for them on the green.'

I put my three iron back into the bag and quietly pulled my golf cart up the slight slope that leads to the perched eighteenth green with its false front. Ronnie's ball sat still on the front of the green. He quickly marked it before it decided to roll off the false front and down the slope. He could have been forty yards short of the green if it had rolled backwards off the green completely. Well you needed luck in this game.

At the back left corner of the green I found my ball sitting in some lush grass about five yards off the surface of the green itself. The flag was on the far side of the top shelf so I did have some green to work with. Perfectly placed for a full swing flop shot I thought. High up into the air, land softly and trickle over to the flag. Easy. Well it would be if I was Phil Mickelson and I could execute a flop shot. That shot terrifies me. You really have to hit it but if you miss hit you could be through the green and into that enormous sand trap on the right hand side of the green, or even worse be down the steep slope towards the trees. No sir, that was just too high a risk. How about using a fairway metal and sort of pinching it out up in the air to clear the long fringe and then release like a putt across the green? Sure, and I'm not Tiger Woods either, so let's be practical for a moment.

All the time I was thinking through my options Ronnie was standing quietly at the foot of the green. He had trundled his golf cart up to the back of the green out of the way and was standing there holding his putter watching me. Every now and then he would turn round and look at the approaching foursome getting closer and closer down the fairway behind us. When it looked like I was ready Ronnie walked up the green and stood by the flag. 'In or out?' he asked.

'Oh leave it in Ronnie. It helps me judge how far the hole really is from the edge of the green. Thanks.'

Ronnie continued to stand by the hole. He grinned at me, pointedly daring me to hit it somewhere close.

I picked out my sand wedge. This had a pronounced bounce on the flange and was real dynamite for blasting out of sand traps. Never failed. What I had in mind was to try the same sand trap blast shot. Well nothing to lose I thought and after a couple of practice brushes through the long grass to get a feel of the lie I swung smoothly and let the club slide firmly under the ball. Unfortunately there was a hard bump of dirt right behind my ball that I hadn't noticed and the club caught that and bounced halfway up the ball so it didn't flop out high and gently but came out low and hot. Fortunately I had terrified myself on the downswing and slowed the shot down to almost nothing by the time it reached the ball. I had been so worried I was going to overswing and end up across the green that I had severely decelerated to almost nothing by the time the club head hit the equator of the ball. The ball came out low but not as quick as it might have and bounced onto the green and rolled fast. It rolled and rolled and I started to get excited. It ran straight at the hole and just as it got close Ronnie started to lift the flagstick out of the cup. Fortunately he was too slow and the ball hit the flag stick and dropped into the hole. He almost threw the flagstick like a spear into the green but thought better of it.

'Well that's an interesting shot I must say. You kind of half flubbed that old man and had a couple of lucky bounces there on the green. Hit a spike mark you know that jerked it back on line. Still, shame as it was an illegal shot, well an out of turn shot really. You were closer to the hole than I was and so I was away.'

He picked my ball out of the hole and tossed it back to me.

'You'll have to drop and wait your turn. Don't think there's any penalty for playing out of turn in match play but that might cost you if we had been playing stroke play. Now, if you don't mind I'll make my putt.'

He thrust the flagstick back into the cup and walked nonchalantly down the slope of the green a good sixty feet to his ball. I looked back down the fairway and the foursome behind us was glaring daggers by this stage and taking some very aggressive practice swings. I walked back to where I had been in the rough off the green and looked where I would drop my ball as legally as I could. I hadn't marked the spot and so it would be approximate but I went through the proper drop process and the ball nestled down in the long grass. I was really startled when I heard Ronnie shout, 'Did you see that? My Lord did you see that? Absolutely out of sight. That was some championship putt if I do say so myself. It must have been all of sixty, no seventy feet, maybe more. What do you think? Seventy feet probably? Well how's that for a birdie partner? Drive, approach and a monster birdie putt. My hole I think?'

I walked over to the hole and there nestling at the bottom of the cup and wedged in tight next to the flagstick was Ronnie's ball. I thought about how Ronnie had played the hole. He seemed to have conveniently forgotten about three off the tee but I kept quiet. I filed that thought into my back pocket, my ace in the hole so to speak.

'What? You checking that it's my ball? You didn't see it did you? Think I ran up and rolled it in there do you? Well ask the group behind. They would have seen it. Hey, be a good sport man. Fair and square putted legally right up the green and straight into the cup. Absolutely beautiful. You should really get some good clubs old man.'

'You putted on the green Ronnie right?'

'Sure. I was a good couple of feet on the green. You saw my fabulous second shot. Can't beat that.'

'And you putted with the flagstick in the cup?'

'Of course. I couldn't see the hole if the flagstick wasn't in there.'

'So the ball hit the flagstick and dropped into the hole?'

'Sure.'

'And I think that that's a two stroke penalty. Hitting the flagstick with your ball while your ball was on the green.'

'No way. That's in stroke play surely?'

'Actually, in match play, that's the loss of the hole old man.'

'But you did the same with your shot. You hit the flagstick. Doesn't that count? Same thing surely?'

'Ronnie, read the rule book occasionally. Counting strokes you have a two stroke penalty and your birdie is really a bogey. You write down five on your scorecard not three or you would be disqualified if you signed it for a three.' I still kept quiet about the three off the tee.

'This is just a friendly game mate.'

'Ronnie, we've always agreed to play our friendly games by the rules. You made me play again because you were further from the hole.'

'And you haven't played yet have you? You're lying two there and okay I made five so it's likely to be my hole from that lie you have. There's no way you'll get so lucky a second time from that lie.'

'This time, do me a favour and leave the flagstick alone as I asked. In fact just back off the green can you?'

I could hear the muttering down the fairway and one of the foursome behind started to walk towards us as if to ask whether we were ever going to get off the bloody golf course? I chose the same club. I swung the same way although this time I was bolder and did get under the ball and it did float out of the long grass and loop up into the air as it was supposed to. However, I wasn't bold enough, and the ball landed and stopped some ten feet from the hole. I was lying three and had a ten foot putt to win the hole.

Now my putter wasn't a Clunker. I had had my putter since I was a kid. It had a wooden shaft that was slightly warped with age. The grip had been leather but I had built it up so it was nearly one inch thick. The shaft was quite short for it had been a kid's putter.

Over the years putting has always been a challenge. It is for most golfers. I had tried everything. Left hand low, hands together, hands apart, reverse overlap, claw grip, thin grips, thick grips, with my feet together, close together, really far apart, left foot forward. Any one who has played knows the list could go on and on. For a while I tried to play with the butt of the club pivoting off my chest but with a short shaft I was bent over so much I couldn't straighten out on the next tee-box after leaving the green and so I stopped doing that pretty quickly. After all my years playing the game I had come to use left hand low on the short putts and pull the putter through the ball and almost steer it to the hole. Also, I had really shortened the back stroke so it was a very small pull through the ball as I let the putter head track through and end up pointing at the hole.

I stood over my ten foot putt. Don't lift the head until you hear the ball bounce in the bottom of the cup. I think it was Gary Player who said that. Putt with your eyes closed. That was probably Sam Snead but then he played as a country lad in bare feet and he could feel things us city folk never could. Actually I had tried that, putting with my eyes closed. Hell, if people can play golf who are blind then they must have to putt that way. Trouble was you never really learnt what happened to the roll of the ball if you kept your eyes closed and you could learn some valuable things for the return putt when you missed the hole. So eyes open, head still, breath normally, well breathe at least. Left hand firmly back and through the ball and end up pointing at the hole and yes by Jiminy it's in, it's in the cup. Par. My hole!

I put the flagstick back in the hole and walked off the green. There was some sarcastic applause from the twelve players, three foursomes now grouped down the fairway.

'Well old man, that was close. I'll have to check whether you incurred a penalty playing out of turn back there. If you did then I won the hole and you buy the beer. What do you say? We split it?'

I thought about the three off the tee but kept my mouth shut.

'Whatever Ronnie, but that was good. My old Clunkers did well today don't you think? Sort of put your top of the line clubs in their place, or perhaps my swing really does do well under that sort of pressure. Did you remember which club you used for that pretty second shot you had back on the eighteenth? One of your special clubs wasn't it? The one you picked up in the village?'

Ronnie had the good grace to blush, which rather clashed with his brown jacket but did complement the red in his socks.

'Great game old man, even for old Clunkers like ourselves. Let's have another one?'

HUNGRY LIONS DON'T ROAR

ORIGINALLY, WE ALL THOUGHT THIS would be a good career move. Later, we weren't so sure, but it was exciting at the time. The four of us worked for the World Bank in one capacity or another, and we had all decided that an off-shore project in a Third World country would enhance our qualifications and look good on the resume. Before the project was put together we had known each other a little, and in various combinations we had done things together, but this was all a little different. As I said, there were four of us, and it was a somewhat eclectic mix.

Lee Raymond came from a small town in western Colorado and had previously worked for his State Tourism agency in marketing wildlife hunting/photography safaris and other outdoor activities. As an outdoor person I don't think Lee owned a tie, let alone a suit, and he probably rented those for his job interview in New York. In contrast, Roly Davidson was probably born in a three-piece suit in his parent's New York apartment, and he had grown up in the world of finance, money movement, audits and innovative accounting practices. He only had to go next door for his job interview. I knew Harry best of all. Harry LeClair came from a southern gentleman's world of plantation life, the Club and knowing the right people. However, despite coming from the flat south he was an avid mountaineer. Professionally he wrote advertising and marketing literature for agro-tourism in the southern USA, but as often as possible he joined me for adventures in the Pacific Northwest. Officially, I had just finished post-graduate work at Washington State University, having come from five years working for the New South Wales Tourism Board in Australia. During vacations I had worked on short-term assignments for the World Bank. I also preferred living in the outdoors.

As fate would have it the four of us ended up as a project team for the World Bank in Zimbabwe in the mid nineties. To help you understand why this rather motley crew was en route to Zimbabwe let me give you a fingertip history lesson and you can decide whether we went there to work or to have fun. I mean to say, we were all in our thirties, and that's not too old to have fun now is it?

Over one hundred or so years ago a peaceful array of peoples lived in the hills and dales south of the great Zambezi river and north of the often dry but marked-on-the-map Limpopo river. These were Shona people of various tribes and factions and had been in this part of Africa for centuries. However, all was not quite so peaceful because sometime earlier, in the 1830s, there had been an invasion in the southern end of this area. From deep down south the Zulu peoples had increased their war-like activities and there was a great Exodus-style *mfecane* from around Natal of peoples who were the Ndebele, and these people mass-migrated into an area around Bulawayo in southern Zimbabwe. Although these two groups of peoples were traditional enemies they had joined together for a common cause in a Chimurenga, a War for Liberation in 1896 to oust the British. Although this failed, and the leaders were hung, they prophesised a second uprising, a second Chimurenga. Later, much later, this prophecy came true and culminated in independence in 1980. The war of independence from 1965 through to 1980 came about because the political factions of ZAPU (Zimbabwe African People's

Union) and ZANU (Zimbabwe African National Union) joined forces and started the second Chimurenga on April 28, 1966. This loose amalgamation went through several splits and reunions. During this Rhodesian Bush War (according to the whites), or a Second Chimurenga (according to the blacks), Ian Douglas Smith ruled a white minority unilaterally-declared independent Rhodesia. After ten or more years of war, economic sanctions and international pressure Smith negotiated the Internal Settlement with biracial rule and a coalition government led by Abel Muzorewa. However, behind Smith's back, Robert Mugabe negotiated the Lancaster House Agreement with the British in 1980 and this superseded the Internal Settlement of 1979. The Agreement and the subsequent election of Robert Mugabe resulted in the emergence of the country of Zimbabwe. Essentially the blacks kicked out the whites and achieved freedom from British rule. Robert Mugabe came to power as the Prime Minister with a majority of ZANU seats in parliament. However, with a new country that was seventy five percent Shona and about twenty percent Ndebele, the democratic process led to Shona rule. Historically, the Ndebele had been warriors, aggressive, war-like and rulers over the Shona. Democracy changed that. In 1983, soon after independence, Mugabe sent his North Korean-trained Fifth Brigade to quell any imaginary disturbances of the Ndebele in Matabeleland and many thousands died. As our group were mostly environmentalists we were quite interested that several hundreds of the Ndebele ended up endangering the water supply as their dead bodies filled up the rural wells!

Many of the guerrilla fighters that served the ZANU party had been trained in Red China. Together with Mugabe's apparent liking for one-man one-party one rule the new country developed close political and trade ties with China. The neat and tidy concept of communism, and the practice of dictated Five-Year Plans with defined objectives, appealed to school-teacher Mugabe. My children will do as they are told and we will progress he said. My one-party Marxist State will show the world. Somewhat as an anomaly Mugabe kept several whites with their farms, their technical expertise and their wealth to help run this brave new world. With tobacco and gold as valuable commodities on the world market the economy flourished in the early years, mostly from enterprises run by whites.

Two five-year plans came and went and progress happened. Come the nineties and the nation started a downward spiral. Our little World Bank project was supposedly to help reduce this downward spiral and perhaps stop it. Sure, dream on. Unfortunately come the nineties came the drought. For the twelve months of 1990 it was hot and dry and for the following twelve months it was hotter and drier. Crops withered. Animals died. People died. Even though the British Queen Elizabeth brought rain to Bulawayo when she visited and gave her opening speech in the early nineties the country still suffered. To try and offset some of these disasters the Zimbabwean government launched ESAP (Economic Structural Adjustment Programme) which was really formulated by the IMF and World Bank. The two international agencies put money into the country and most prices immediately went up leading to even greater hardship for the masses. To try and offset the increased muttering the government approved the Land Acquisition Act. When the people rose up to fight against the British in the seventies they were promised land and so far they hadn't seen any.

It was into this struggling geo-political mix of twelve million people that we came. The World Bank wanted to see that the money they had put into the country was "doing the right thing", whatever that might be. The Zimbabwean government argued that once the money was in Zimbabwe it was up to them to decide where it should go and what it should do. The World Bank said there were strings attached to the money.

The Zimbabweans said so what. We had come to see whether the strings still existed and report back. Officially, our project had its own separate funding. Primarily we had the task of transferring technology, which in our case was expertise, skills and procedures for the effective promotion of tourism. The Zimbabwean economy was partially dependant on the export earnings of tobacco and gold, and as these dwindled in the nineties there was a move to promote tourism. The country offered dramatic scenery with Victoria Falls, the ruins at Greater Zimbabwe, the aura of Matobo Hills and the lush greenery of the Eastern Highlands. The first two are World Heritage Sites. Over and above that were the numerous National Parks which covered twelve percent of the land and contained a vast array of wildlife, including the big five of elephant, lion, leopard, buffalo and rhino. It was the wildlife that particularly interested three of us and Roly didn't know any better. I doubt whether he had ever seen animals, except those in the Bronx Zoo.

'Why did we come here the long way?' asked Roly. 'I bet we could have flown direct from Atlanta you know. Did Head Office think it diplomatic to come here on a British Airways flight? I thought England wasn't on Mugabe's Christmas card list?'

'Hell Roly, I don't know. I'm just some country boy,' joshed Lee. 'At least this way we get two night's sleep on the plane.'

'The flight from the US goes into Johannesburg Roly I think,' I added. 'We would have had to come up from South Africa and that would have meant more visas or something. Don't fret about the details man. Enjoy the jellied eels for breakfast.'

Roly shuddered, curled up and looked out of the window as we flew south over what looked like uninterrupted and empty forest. The area has been called the Belgian Congo, Zaire, the Democratic Republic of the Congo and many other things. We flew on to greet the early morning in Zimbabwe. After landing in Harare an official of the US Embassy helped get us and our gear through Customs and Immigration without too many hassles.

'You'll have to go down to the Immigration Office later in the week and get your temporary visas. It's easier for you to walk in today as visitors and sort out the working relationships later. Trust me.'

So we did and what a pain that proved to be. The Immigration Office was on Baker Avenue and tended to open when the boss man said so, or when he came in, if he came in. First, you had to sign the book down in the entrance hall with name, address and somesuch under the watchful eye of a uniformed clerk. We later realised we could have signed in as Mickey Mouse because no-one ever did anything with the book but it gave one more person a job. You had to sign out too when you left!! This was an early example of the Zimbabwean way of life. If in doubt employ someone to do something, preferably a relative. Government jobs were the best because you couldn't get fired from them and with fifty percent unemployment in the country this was an important benefit. Of course the wages were no hell but then living without a job was even more desperate.

Through the embassy we found a house to share in the northern suburb of Harare called Mount Pleasant, near the University. What we didn't know was the house came with a live-in maid, gardener, pool boy and night guard. The property included accommodation for these staff within the high garden walls and secure gate. These "defences" weren't a leftover condition from the times when this was an exclusive white suburb and every Englishmen's home is a "castle", but a result of the droughts and mass migration to the cities. With people dying in the rural areas many had flocked to town and when you are starving you beg and steal to stay alive. Walls, locked gates and guards had resulted. Some residents had dogs. You had two to chase an intruder; two to tree an intruder; and two to bite an intruder. As I said, if in doubt employ someone, preferably two someones, or should that be sometwos?

'Seen my purple shirt Terry?'

'Didn't Alice put it in the laundry and wash it?'

'Probably.'

'And hang it on the line?'

'Probably.'

'Then it may well have gone walkabout Harry. I know it's a drag but everything has to be under lock and key here mate. I'd never seen a telephone with a key before I came here. When I asked what the key was for, Gerry at the office laughed and told me to look closely at the next telephone bill. Seems the hired help phone their relatives when we're not at home, hence the key. Some of their relatives live in the next country, like Zambia or Malawi.'

'Hell fire Terry, I liked that shirt.'

'Pay little Robert a few Zim dollars to do laundry guard duty,' I laughed. 'Hey Roly, did you fix up a booking at that game farm we got told about? You know, the one north of Harare, up near Bindura somewhere Michael said. He told me he'd been there with his family and they'd all had a good time. Said they went swimming, riding, climbing up some mountain as well as watching the animals. He also reckoned it might be a good place to go for a small conference to discuss plans and activities with our Zimbabwean counterparts.'

'Terry it's booked for next weekend, starting on the Friday. We'll go up Thursday evening and come back late Sunday. Think it'll be casual dress or should I take a suit for dinner?'

'Roly if you don't take it you'll feel uncomfortable and under-dressed but I doubt whether you'll wear it. Ask Michael this morning. He'll explain the custom. I'd take some form of boots though if you're thinking of walking anywhere. Like back home in Australia it's the little critters that kill you. You know - spiders and snakes.'

'Terry you're a cheerful sod in the mornings mate. I'll walk in front of you Roly as the guide and make sure you're safe. Just like you'd do for me if we were in New York City. Terry you got the car keys 'cos it's time we went to work. At least you know how to drive in this crazy place. With all this noisy traffic driving a gear-shift van down the wrong side of the street blows my mind. You ready to go Harry?' asked Lee.

Now our project team was based in the capital Harare, and ostensibly the objective was to persuade the Zimbabwe government to spend World Bank monies wisely. After working in the country for a while we all realised that this noble objective was somewhat unrealistic. True, we all reported back to Head Office in the States that things were going according to plan and there were several very worthwhile projects going ahead. This reporting took place once a month over a very intermittent and fragile telephone system. Well, the system was fragile at the Zimbabwe end and had tendencies to only work about fifty percent of the time. Come to think about it though that was in tune with the rest of the country. Much of the rest of the place only worked about fifty percent of the time.

According to some National approximations the capital city of Harare, which had been called Salisbury under white rule, included 1.6 million souls with another one million some forty kilometres away in the high-density suburb of Chitungwiza. Our office was in the downtown business core of Harare on Samora Machel Avenue, and fortunately we had official parking. Coming from Sydney driving for me wasn't an issue but parking could be a nightmare in the city. The office hours schedule demonstrated another local custom that made all of us re-think our life style. Everyone was at work sharp on seven-thirty and morning tea was the only interruption until lunch at one o'clock. We worked in this period because after lunch you could forget it. I never did learn the Shona equivalent of siesta but it was a local tradition. So, after lunch on Thursday the four of us left the office and went home to collect our gear for our first safari.

Several of the white folk in our office had waxed eloquent about this game farm safari area called Dombawera. As a kind of dry run, and so we didn't frighten our city-dweller Roly, the four of us had visited a "Lion and Cheetah Park" about half an hour outside Harare on the Bulawayo road. We had done this the previous weekend. In this park we could walk around as well as drive. Most of the animals here were the offspring of the original orphan animals when the park started. Although we had a guidebook it helped to read the signs to identify the various animals. Harry of course was fascinated with the Nile crocodiles and made comparisons with his home native alligators.

'Ever swim with any 'gators Harry?' Lee asked.

'Not knowingly,' said Harry. 'Even being out in a boat fishing can be hazardous.'

'What about sharks Terry?' Lee said.

'Not my favourite ocean companion thanks Lee. Actually any water activity in this country is hazardous. Crocodiles and hippos like to re-arrange boats.'

'And swimmers too?' asked Roly.

'Sure Roly, and if the larger animals don't get you then there is bilharzia which will invade your body and take over.'

'Terry is anywhere safe in this country?' asked Roly looking anxiously around.

'Here Roly, just look in that basket and stroke the fur.'

We had come to the refreshment kiosk near the centre of the park and there was a sign welcoming us to carefully pet the lions. That's right:

Pet the lions. Inside a deep basket were four very small lion cubs with their spotted fur, mewing mouths and ever-flexing claws.

'See Roly, let me take a picture. Now you can send that to the folks back home by Central Park and tell them their big white hunter son walked with the lions.'

'Just don't try that if they get any bigger though.'

The drive north to Dombawera followed the Mazowe valley for much of the way and this was fertile citrus-producing country. At Bindura we branched north driving around the tailings ponds and mounds from the gold-mining activities here and through mixed farming country up a narrow twisty surfaced road.

'We going the right way Terry?' asked Roly.

'You've got the map Lee. I just follow instructions,' I replied.

'Looks good to me mate. We're supposed to pass some posh country club in a few kilometres. Perhaps we should drop Harry there. He's part of that set.'

'Not me Lee. I want to ride those elephants. Hey, but those are pretty jacaranda trees. See, around the farm house down there. They're not native. I think they are from South America but they sure are a lovely colour. Sign coming up Lee.'

'I see it. That's for the club. Should be another twenty kilometres or so. How's the gas Terry?'

'Now you ask me. If the gauge is honest Lee we're fine. Another twenty k you say?'

'Brahmin cattle everywhere.'

'Actually, I think they're the local *mashona* cattle with those humps. *Mombe* on the hoof so to speak.'

'Did you see that jump? Lee, did you see that jump man? Right over the fence.'

'Sure Harry. Wonder if you could jump that high when a lion is chasing you.'

'There are no lions at Dombawera?'

'Who said?'

'The owner. He re-assured me we could walk anywhere on the safari area. There are lots of animals he said but they are all safe. They are all herbivores.'

'Sure,' I said, 'Cape buffalo, one of the most dangerous of the big five, and the ostriches which kick. Doesn't the owner have elephants on site too? He was offering elephant rides. Now there's a herbivore you don't want to upset Harry.'

Dombawera called itself a game park but in reality it was much more than that. The prime industry on the property was a tobacco farm, complete with the housing, school and clinic for the two hundred or more workers and their families. In addition there was an ostrich farm, with breeding pens, incubator sheds and open paddocks. Almost as an afterthought there was a water-hole where several large thatched-roof buildings and seven rondavels provided shelter for housing and entertaining tourists. There was a fence around the property, a ten foot high fence but we weren't sure why.

That long weekend at Dombawera proved to be very useful. The facilities were excellent for the size of group we had expected. The meals were good and being in a place away from the office would help everyone concentrate on the task at hand. After work one could relax and either wander about the safari area or just watch the animals come to the water-hole. Scattered throughout the property were herds of zebra with their constant wildebeest companions. Small groups of giraffes stood out as they grazed high on the bushland vegetation. Families of impala ran everywhere and occasionally one would see eland or kudu. These were all "safe" herbivores but the farm also had a few Cape buffalo and of course their five semi-domesticated elephants. We'll talk about the elephants later.

'You know this place is quite fantastic. Being a farmer back home you build a farmhouse, one or more barns, maybe stables and just occasionally some living space for any hands you might have. Here it's a whole different story.'

'Yes Lee, but that's because you come from some forgotten backwater in the Middle West. Way out in Wyoming or somewhere isn't it? Well I come from the south and there we built farms that included all of the above and lots and lots of houses for our workers on the cotton fields.'

'Weren't they called slave quarters Harry?' I joshed. 'In some ways the tobacco farm here must resemble some of your cotton plantations down south, only here they pay the workers.' And this was the way it was as the whole "farm" was one large comprehensive community. Later in our stay, during the riots to oust white farmers and re-possess their land, these entire communities were broken up; people displaced, employment lost and the economy disrupted. During our stay at Dombawera the four of us decided to try out most of the facilities on the site. We all went on a very informative tour of both the tobacco farm and its drying sheds plus a quick visit through the ostrich farm buildings. We learnt it had been a trying experience to determine the correct cycle to incubate ostrich eggs.

'But haven't they been doing that in South Africa for years? Surely they would know?'

The owner laughed as he regarded the four of us. 'Just because I originally came up here from South Africa doesn't mean my fellow countrymen will offer me trade secrets. Don't forget I am competing with them to raise and sell birds. A mature ostrich fetches about three thousand dollars U.S. on the international market. Farmers south of the border aren't going to help me take away their trade. No lads, we had to figure it out for ourselves.'

'So there's quite an art to getting it right then?'

'Yes Harry, and it's not just one constant temperature from start to finish for the best results. Still, let's move on. Hi Anna, how are you this morning?'

'I'm fine boss, just fine.'

'What's her job then?'

'When baby ostriches break out of their shells they identify as "mother" the first animal they see. They see Anna here and she becomes their mother and they will follow her anywhere. It helps keep the youngsters in check. Now, you wanted to go riding I heard?'

'Yes, if possible. Two of us come from riding backgrounds and we thought we'd like to go out on the horses. We heard that is a really good way to get close to the animals.'

'That's true. The zebras, gnus and even the giraffes sometimes will accept the horses as natural and you're just a funny lump on the horse. You can get close on horseback. What about your companions?'

'They've never ridden horses so we thought Roly and Harry would sample elephant rides,' I said. 'At least they have their own drivers we heard.'

'Right. Tomorrow morning then and we'll fix up some bush activity for you. You need to be out early for the elephants, around six-thirty, and back in an hour or so for breakfast. After that we let them roam free through the property. That okay?'

'Sure. Fine. Thanks, we'll be there.'

The blokes back in our office had mentioned Dombawera has a swimming pool and recommended we book the two rondavels down close to this pool. Now it's true that being in the rondavel close to the pool was convenient. However, the pool was a concrete lined basin between three enormous rocks and must have been thirty feet across at the widest with a length of maybe thirty five feet – some pool! Yes, one could safely cool down after a hot day but the pool came with a price. When we first arrived the other lads were delighted at this rural setting close to this wet basin but later we all agreed the price was high. Darkness fell that first evening and we retired to bed fairly early. We were probably all asleep under our mosquito nets when the cacophony started. The volume of croaking gradually increased until I couldn't hear Harry in the bed just across the room.

'Terry, go and tell them to turn down the volume mate. You picked this spot so sort out your noisy friends.'

I stepped outside and gazed up at the brilliant twinkling sky. It was full of stars – absolutely amazing.

'Terry, you there? Muffle the folk in the cheap seats.'

I turned on my torch and shone it over the pool. There was an immediate silence. I could hear the excitement in my breathing as I gazed once more at the night sky. Nothing moved. Nobody spoke.

'You're a regular charmer you are Terry. Speak to the animals you can mate.'

I turned off the torch and the bedlam returned. I moved forward carefully to try and see the origin of this blasphemy in the silent night. A movement caught my eye and I saw a small green frog. Then I saw another one. They were both small and I mean small: about half the size of my thumb. Again I doused the torch and immediately the fortissimo croak rent the velvet silence.

I sat down on one of the boulders beside the pool and laughed.

'If you think that's funny mate you're really one warped Aussie. You just sit out there with that flashlight on and let us normal human beings get some sleep. Good night!'

Watching carefully I let the torch beam wander around the edges of the pool and gradually saw more and more of these small frogs. The volume of sound was clearly disproportionate to the size of the source. Another mystery of nature I thought and I turned off the light and went back to my bed listening to the curses from the humans.

'The roan or the more palomino-coloured horse Lee?' I asked.

'Don't matter Terry. As long as it's got four legs, head and a saddle I'll manage. Even the saddle's a luxury as I grew up on horses back home.'

I too had ridden for a long time in my life but I was more interested in watching Roly and Harry with the elephants. The five elephants had come here as orphans from poaching activities and they were all less than ten years old. Over the past two years several of the employees, with guidance from the owner, had gradually "trained" the elephants to accept people on their backs. Now you have to remember these are African elephants with no long time tradition of working with humans. If anything, African elephants have every reason to avoid mankind wherever possible. Typically we meant trouble.

Soon after we had arrived in Harare, Lee and I had gone to see one of the local wildlife experts. We had wanted to find out from a non-government person about the various species and the opportunities for tourism. Before we had flown out Lee had read a book about the CAMPFIRE programme. This programme helped local communities develop communal natural resources including the management of wildlife. Of particular concern was the management of elephants. With pressure from the outside world, and through an organisation called CITES, elephants had been declared a threatened species and the ivory trade had been stopped. Now this might be all very well for the conservationist sitting in London, Paris, or even Chicago, but for some rural Zimbabwean communities it meant trampled crops or even trampled bodies. It was difficult persuading these villagers that world experts knew that elephants were rare, threatened and endangered. As the villagers pointed out elephants eat a lot and they don't know tended crops from wild fodder. It was the big grey beasties doing the threatening. Any reduction in the hunt for ivory and culling of herds led to serious habitat destruction. Within Zimbabwe we learnt there were three times as many elephants as the habitat could sustain. In order to maintain positive relationships with local communities the country needed to manage the elephant population. We could understand all of that. What was unknown to Lee and I, and what was unpalatable to the press and the general public was the biology of the elephant and the necessary method of culling. Elephants move around in herds led by dominant matriarchs and all of the knowledge of the herd is in the heads of the oldest females. They know when to move, where is the best grazing, where are the water holes, and where best to breed and look after the young ones. Our expert explained that it took a few years of human study to understand the importance of this herd knowledge. Let me explain why. With many animals when you want to cull you kill off the oldest, the biggest, and those closest to natural death. This is true for many natural things. We cut down the oldest trees for example. The trouble was that didn't work for elephants. If you killed the largest oldest animals in the herd you annihilated all of the knowledge of the herd. The young ones would all die anyway. They had no leadership, no knowledge of how to survive. So, said our expert, the best way to manage the overall population of elephants in Zimbabwe is to eliminate completely some herds and that means shooting little young ones. Photographs of baby elephants being slaughtered doesn't go down well with breakfast croissants and coffee in a Paris boulevard. The biology might be right but the PR stinks.

'But hunting of old males is okay?' I asked.

'Yes, the hunting experience is good and it is a marketable product.

The ivory gets stored in the warehouse of the Department of National Parks in Harare.'

'But that doesn't get the population down fast enough?'

'Unfortunately true, and it's often the herds that do the damage to local communities.'

'So culling a complete herd is the best solution?'

'Yes Terry, but within the population numbers for the region within the country. It is a difficult and controversial decision, even in this country where the over-population damage is obvious and in the papers most weeks. AIDS might be the big killer in this country but over thirty people a year get trampled to death. Not a pretty way to die.'

Lee and I took this lesson on elephant biology back to the rest of the team and we had a different attitude about the species when we went to Dombawera.

I said the elephants had got used to carrying humans on their backs and that was partly true. The "driver", who had some mutual bond with his elephant, carried an iron tool bar and a bag of feed-nuts. To get into the "driving seat" he pulled on the elephant's ear, stood on his knee and swung himself up onto the elephant's neck. The driver was in his seat along with his "steering wheel". We watched the driver steer his elephant with a random mixture of thumps on the head with the tool bar and feed-nuts placed on the end of the curled back elephant's trunk. It was a living example of the stick and the carrot. However, looking closely at the elephant's eye I was never really sure whether it was all a big joke to the elephant and he or she was really in control at all times. The owner told us a story about one guest who had shouted at the elephant and kicked with his feet. Apparently the elephant then loped off with the guest on his back and somewhat deliberately brushed under several low hanging branches. Need I say more?

'Roly, the driver wants you to climb up on that wooden tower-thing. Up another level.'

At this point Roly was balanced on a spindly arrangement of poles with a slanting platform at the top. Running from this platform was a pole across to another similar platform about ten feet away.

'Now hold the pole above your head and swing your leg over the back of the elephant.'

The driver had manoeuvred the large elephant between these platforms and under the joining pole. Across the back of the elephant was a rough piece of canvas with two by fours nailed on each low side. Nailed to the canvas and not to the elephant dear reader just in case you were confused and concerned about animal cruelty, especially after the bit about the tool bar.

'No Roly. Hold the middle of the pole man and just swing a leg over, over the canvas thing. Right, now you can let go of the pole.'

'Where are the stirrups or whatever you put your feet in?' asked Roly. 'Where are the reins or steering wheel?'

'Feet down against those two by fours and it's automatic drive for you. If in doubt hold your driver but let go of that pole Roly or you'll be swinging in space man.'

Roly let go of the pole just as the elephant engaged first gear and ambled away from the towers. Fortunately the driver turned sharp right or Roly would have been brushed off by the branches of the neighbouring tree.

Harry had watched this little drama with growing concern.

'Your turn Harry,' Lee said with a laugh in his voice.

'Okay for you mate. You don't have so far to fall off that pitiful nag.'

'Come on Harry. Roly's off down the track and your mount wants to join her. Let's get this circus on the road.'

Being a climber Harry athletically jumped up onto the platform which swayed alarmingly.

'Bring the beast here Charlie,' Harry shouted to his driver. 'Don't stop and I'll swing on board like Tarzan. Off after my mate now and we'll leave these two horsemen in the dust.'

Harry's enthusiasm was almost too energetic and as he swung onto the lumbering grey back he nearly overshot. Fortunately he managed to regain his balance and off we all went. The other three elephants came with us with their drivers as elephants are very much an animal of habit and herd. Similarly, Harry's mount had to move at speed as she was the leader and always went first. Eventually the drivers got the five elephants into a hierarchical line and we rode alongside on our horses. When we were out on the ride we talked to Geoffrey, the Dombawera animal guide about the different animals and their characteristics. As Geoffrey had suggested we could infiltrate the various herds of zebras, gnus, and impalas without too much interest from the wildlife. Both Lee and I rode mares so there was no challenge to the alpha male zebra who did give us the eye. Giraffes ignored us.

'No lions Geoffrey?'

'No boss, not usually.'

'But sometimes?'

'Yes boss, sometimes.'

Now I thought, is Geoffrey trying to please me with his saying yes or do they really get lions here sometimes? I started to pay more attention to my surroundings.

'Leopards,' I asked, 'up in those hills for instance?'

'Yes boss.'

I was at a loss again because I had asked two questions and had Geoffrey said yes to leopards here or yes to leopards up in the kopjes across the valley?

'What do the elephants do after the ride Geoffrey?'

'They walk through the forest boss.'

'Could we see them?'

'Sure boss, after breakfast. We can follow them. We can walk after them.'

'What about the lions?'

'No lions boss.'

I shook my head. I wasn't sure I was any the wiser.

During breakfast Lee and I felt fine after our rather funeral ride. No matter how hard I had tried my horse didn't know how to find second gear and we ambled along behind the rolling gait of the elephants. I noticed that Harry and Roly did a lot of wriggling at breakfast.

'Saddle sores Roly?'

'I'll have you know Terry elephants have very bony and pronounced backbones. That piece of canvas had no padding like your comfy saddle. After an hour trying to get in tune with my elephant's rhythm I decided our two backbones don't fit comfortably together. As a result I think I'll walk later this morning.'

'But we're all walking this morning Roly. We're going elephant tracking. Should be good practice for that trip we've planned to Mana Pools. You can walk around there you know, and there are lots of elephants at Mana Pools.'

'What about the lions?' asked Harry.

'You heard Geoffrey Harry. There are no lions at Dombawera.'

'I thought he said yes when you asked him the second time.'

'Well that will be good practice for Mana Pools too. The guidebook says there are lions as well as elephants at Mana Pools. Anyway, Geoffrey will come with us and show us where the elephants are and he'll bring a gun or something.'

'Jesus Terry, being out with you in the bush is one drama after another. We've had some climbing adventures together but this is more of an adrenaline rush. Me, walking through the bush trying not to get trampled by bum-shattering elephants and keeping a lookout for tawny man-eaters who think I might be lunch. I used to think a hard climb and chasing off marmots was a thrill.'

'Harry you're full of it mate. Just finish your coffee and let's go and see the lumbering beasties.'

'See them boss? Down by the grey rock. Slowly now.'

'Geoffrey I can't see bugger all mate. Which rock? Hey, that rock moved. Jesus, now I see one. Lee you see that?'

'There's another,' said Harry, and he grabbed my arm and pointed down through another dip in the bush.

Silently, slowly, five large grey pachyderms tip-toed through the forest. For animals of that weight and bulk they were amazingly quiet. The only sound was the occasional ripping of branches as they plucked the occasional snack.

'Amazing,' said Harry, 'absolutely amazing. I would have stumbled into them if Geoffrey here hadn't stopped us. They just blend in.'

'Like everything else around us Harry,' Lee added. 'With the light and the shade casting dappled shadows everywhere it's hard to see what is real and what is imagination.'

Trying to be quiet ourselves the five of us slowly followed the elephants for another kilometre. Very occasionally one or more of them would stop and look around waving their trunks.

'Just sniffing to make sure we are following them,' said Roly.

'With your aftershave mate anything could check you were following. It's like walking in a scent factory.'

'Do lions smell you Geoffrey?'

'Yes boss.'

'How do we make sure we are safe from lions then? How do we know when they aren't hungry? You know, when they are fat and full and not keen on chasing two-legged snacks?'

'Well-fed lions roar boss. They happy.'

'And the hungry ones? The unhappy ones?'

'They quiet boss.'

'Like our elephants?'

'Yes boss.'

With this valuable piece of bush lore we walked ourselves back to the rondavels and the water hole. Each of us appeared to be more aware of our surroundings. Just like bear country back home I thought, where Lee and I walked around sharp blind corners much more cautiously.

I looked back and caught Geoffrey smiling. When I raised my eyebrows in a half question he just said, 'Good boss. You learn.'

It's amazing what things you learn. Some rather inconsequential items suddenly become really important and you have to be aware of the local culture. I'll give you an example we learnt at Dombawera. After we had watched the elephants range silently through the forest we were walking back to the water hole and our rondavels for lunch. We were along the edge of the fence line and came across one of the gated roads into the property. Sitting at the gate was a very old and grizzled black worker.

'He's the gateman?' I asked in innocence.

'Yes boss,' agreed Geoffrey as usual.

'And the cage he has beside him is to keep unwanted guests out?' I said jokingly.

'Yes boss,' said Geoffrey again.

'Geoffrey old son, how is that ancient man going to stop unwanted guests and then put them into that small cage? It doesn't make sense.'

'When people visit the Big Boss they bring a gift. People come and see their friends, their relatives. We all one big happy family Boss.'

'But some guests are not so friendly?' I asked, still somewhat at a loss as to what this old man really did.

'The gift here is usually a rooster Boss. People bring a rooster. Bring good luck.'

'I can understand that Geoffrey, but what does the old man do, and why the cage?'

'We have chicken flu' in the district Boss, Newcastle disease. The Big Boss he don't want no new roosters coming in. Bring flu' and his big birds, his ostriches die real quick. Lose money that way Boss. Friends usually bring old rooster, sick rooster. Old Moses here he stop friends and put old rooster in cage. Friends he let go on.'

Obviously running an ostrich farm, and ostriches are really large chickens when you come to think about it, you sure don't need old sick roosters running around crowing their heads off. We also learnt another piece of ostrich bureaucracy while we were at Dombawera. The real profit in raising ostriches is export of the birds themselves. Yes you could sell the eggs and the meat but the real money came from export of live birds. But the Government in its wisdom, and its strong Natural Resources Department, had labelled wild ostriches as a rare and threatened species. As a result there was a ban on the export of endangered species. Ostrich farmers repeatedly pointed out that their ostriches were fifth, sixth or even seventh generation and were not wild, were not endangered and were really large chickens. Shouldn't ostrich farming be in the Department of Agriculture and not Natural Resources? No no said the DNR. We need to keep ostriches in our domain, our budget, our workload, our employees need jobs and so no export. We learnt the same was true for commercial crocodile farmers although we didn't investigate that so closely. Still, we did observe that ostriches are rather silly birds. When in their prime, you could only put two females in the same paddock as a single male. Otherwise there was marital misunderstanding apparently. Now what male in their right mind with options wants to be confined with just two females?

After another week in the office wrestling with the pace of life in Zimbabwe the four of us sat down in the local bar to debrief. It was Friday lunchtime and we had to bring Roly up to date on our progress so far. Officially Roly was the project leader, which means he had to report back to the States over the jungle drums.

'Terry, I'm getting more and more confused with the English here. I was working with Ambrose and Godfrey this morning and asked directions to the British Embassy.'

'So,' I said. 'What was so confusing?'

'I got directed to one robot where I was supposed to turn left and then pass a second robot and carry straight on.'

'Daleks?' Lee asked.

I laughed. 'Yes, that word confused me for a while too. I think it comes from South Africa as it's not English or Australian. So, you were directed from one robot to the next? Did someone eventually explain what robots are?'

'Yes Terry, they are traffic lights.'

'The word I find most confusing is "now". You guys come across this?' I asked.

Roly and Harry looked blank and it was Lee who answered. 'That word seems to come in a graded series. There is "now" and then there is "now now" and finally there is "now now now".'

'Translation please?' asked Harry.

Lee looked at the three of us. 'No joking, but I would translate the three phrases in reverse order as "now within the next hour" to "now in the next day" to "now in the next week maybe". That about right Terry?'

'Just be thankful chaps they speak English at all. This job would be even more confusing and definitely slower if we had to go through translators. Still, enough of this, what about the long weekend in seven days time? We on for that camping trip at Mana Pools? This is a World Heritage Site chaps and the area is only open to vehicles during the dry season, like now you know. Everyone coming?'

'Terry, let me read the guidebook during the next week. Sometimes your enthusiasm is contagious and sometimes it's downright dangerous. You and Harry must have had some wild escapades mountaineering.'

'No Roly,' Harry said. 'Our Terry here is quite level-headed, well for an Aussie that is. It's our outback western cowboy Lee here we need to watch. He's the dark horse. He'll probably want to go out at night-time with a flashlight and watch the hunt.'

'Harry we're trying to convince Roly this is like a stroll in Central Park or something. You know, something civilised and under control.'

'Sure Terry, but your example of Central Park isn't all that civilised at night-time I've heard.'

'Rest easy Terry. I'm on for the weekend,' added Roly. 'I mean to say, we all learnt a lot at Dombawera and this can't be much different.'

Mana Pools National Park is bounded on the north by the Zambezi River and it is fifty kilometres or so downstream from the massive Kariba dam. I drove a fully-loaded Toyota Landcruiser out on the Chinhoyi road towards Kariba. The scenery was typical rolling uplands of open savannah until we dropped off the edge of the escarpment and down into the Zambezi valley.

'Looks like a road-block up ahead Terry. That the army? Certainly guys carrying guns. We going to stop?'

'I don't have much choice,' I said. 'Let's hope we've got all the right papers or whatever they're looking for. Seat belts on?'

We stopped and the guard came over to the driver's side window.

'All out,' he said, and then added something I didn't quite catch. Seemed we were a little slow in understanding because a second 'out' was a little sharper. We unbuckled and clambered out of the Toyota. Immediately four guards materialised from somewhere and poured into the car. There was a rushing noise of spraying as the guards doused everything inside. I looked at the first guard questioningly.

'Tsetse fly.'

I was about to mention that the tsetse fly lived in the lowlands and the risk was carrying it out back into the high veld and so wouldn't this make more sense if we were leaving when I caught Harry's eye. I zipped my lips. Jobs for the boys obviously. Perhaps we would get resprayed when we left. The guards hung about as if looking for some hand-out but we just piled back into the rather smelly car and drove on.

'Seemed best Terry not to state the obvious guy. You were going to tell them about the fly living in the lowlands weren't you?'

I laughed as I thumped the steering wheel. 'You're right Harry. There are times in this country when it is better to listen and stay quiet.'

We turned off the Kariba road at Makuti and on to the Parks Entrance where we had to show our permits and explain how long we were there for. The checking was slow and laborious and it was this kind of process we were trying to make more user-friendly. Part of our overall project was to try and gently persuade the Zimbabweans that they would get more and happier tourists if the processes were simple and speedy. Unfortunately this was a hard sell as efficiency measures usually led to fewer employees and the unemployment was already over forty percent. Staff reductions were not really an acceptable option. Within the culture we needed to be innovative and perhaps have the parks staff offer a wider variety of services. For the most part the Park's policy was policing and anti-poaching. It was as if they tried to keep people out of the parks. We had all spent some time explaining and providing examples of visitor programmes and opportunities to employ parks staff expertise to enhance the visitor's experience. It was a tough sell.

Soon after leaving the Park's entrance the road dropped away steeply as it fell down into the low veld of the Zambezi valley. Here the vegetation changed and we saw baobab trees for the first time. Not long after the drop-off we were actually within the park boundary and so we stopped again at Nyakasikana Gate. As I said, it was like trying to break into a fortress as we went through a second inspection and showing of Park permits. Another forty kilometres of dirt road brought us to the river and the Ranger Station for a third check.

For our first night we were camping at Vundu camp some twelve kilometres upstream and so I slowly and carefully traversed the dirt roads through the bush. We had already seen a few elephants wandering up the several dry riverbeds and I wasn't sure what would be round the next corner. The campsite was in an open clearing with a clear view down to the river. I stopped and turned off the engine.

'Man it's humid,' exclaimed Harry as he stepped out of the air-conditioned car.

'Welcome to thirty plus degrees Harry and one hundred and ten percent humidity. This is the dry season mate. Just imagine what it's like in the wet.'

'Sticky,' said Roly as he unwound himself from the back seat. 'Just like New York on a summer's day.'

'Don't knock it,' said Lee. 'It's clear, and look we can see right across the river into Zambia. Fabulous mate. How about a bite and then let's check out the neighbourhood?'

'Lee, can we unload and set up the tents first? Let's get organised before we wander off into the bush.'

Harry got back into the car to start bringing things out but he changed his mind and immersed himself in a book.

'Out Harry. This is our tent sport. Just come and help.'

'Hey Terry, this guidebook says that hungry lions don't roar, just like Geoffrey said. So if you hear lions when we're in the tent tonight we're safe mate. Of course, the hungry ones are just creeping silently around outside waiting for you to go for a leak. That's if the yelping hyena, the grunting hippo or the trumpeting elephant doesn't get you first. Just think about it. You could be ground up, rolled on or neatly squashed. Take your pick.'

'You read too much Harry. All those words are doing your head in. Just pull your side of the tent square and let's get it pegged out properly. Still, I suppose it's a bit different from our usual campsites with bears and marmots.'

'Terry you going to go on yapping all day? We've grub to fix and then Lee wanted to go on some walking safari. He was all excited about this being one of the few National Parks where you can actually get out of the vehicle.'

'You sure we're safe in this tent then Harry? The walls are pretty thin and the locals will smell the goodies if you insist on bringing your late night snacks into the tent like you usually do when we go camping. This isn't Colorado you know. Even there we upend the foodstuffs away from the bears. Here it's us as well as the food bag that is dinner pal.'

'Jesus you're a whingeing Aussie. I thought you told us that it was the pommies who did all the whingeing in Australia. You're just as bad Terry.'

'It's a bit of a giggle though Harry. Just look at our campsite. Usually the humans go and visit the animals in cages. Well, just look where we have camped. Our nice comfy tent is neatly hidden under a concrete shelter which has wire mesh walls. Looks like we're in the cage mate.'

'You two ready?' called Roly. 'Lee is straining at the leash. He thinks this is just a big version of Dombawera. I keep trying to tell him that some of the animals here are dangerous but he thinks that's just the guide book trying to keep the tourists in check.'

'Roly, Dombawara was a safe haven compared to this place. Dombawera was a little self-contained game farm where the animals were all docile. This is the wilds mate.'

The weekend ended up as a series of highs and lows. We saw and managed to track elephants and ended up with some good photographs – well good enough to impress folks back home that this was in the wild and we were that close! Down by the river we saw lots of hippos and numerous crocodiles. Herds of impala appeared every time we turned a corner and although these were supposed to be instant breakfasts for lions we never did manage to see those tawny cats. There was a disturbing array of noises at night-time but we never found any footprints through the camp the following morning. The biggest scare came one evening when something provoked a hyena to charge out of the darkness and through the light of our campfire. He virtually stumbled through the blazing wood before leaping off into the dark again.

I suppose in retrospect it must have looked rather funny if you were observing us from up on high. Three of the four of us had adventured out in the wilds for most of our lives but here we were cautious. From up above you could see the four of us carefully inching our way through the bush and peering to look in all directions, starting at every noise and making sure we knew where the car was if we had to beat a prudent retreat. When we got tired of tracking this one particular elephant we got back in the Toyota and found an enormous herd of Cape buffalo. These we discreetly observed from afar.

'No lions Terry?'

'None we saw Harry. Next time though I think I'll share a tent with Lee. You sniff and grunt in your sleep mate.'

'No way. Sleep like a lamb I do Terry. That probably was a lion looking for you mate. You should have gone out and shone that magic flashlight of yours. It sure kept them frogs quiet. Probably would have done the same for the lion.'

IF YOU GO DOWN IN THE WOODS TODAY

'THE SIGN IS QUITE CLEAR. Do not pass Go. Fine of more dollars than we've got and probably banned from hiking in National Parks for all time. As the song says, "If you go down in the woods today you'd better go in disguise".'

'Lou, you're full of it you know. Grizzly bears don't like gnarly males like you, and Laurie and I haven't washed for a week. No bear in his right mind is going to bother us. You just read the guide book and we'll outpace any bear in the Park.'

'Hold on there Vince. Lou's got a point you know. I'm not mad keen on challenging any warden. Bears I can deal with but wardens are a different kind of animal.'

'You guys wanting to go to Sentinel Pass? Three's one short you know,' said a new voice. We three turned to the hiker standing there in the parking lot looking at us.

'We're just debating the pros and cons of talking nicely to wardens,' Vince replied.

'Look, I don't know whether it's any help but down at the hostel someone had posted a notice asking for partners for Sentinel Pass today. There were at least six names on the list. I heard this morning that several people were thinking of going up there. Why don't you wait a while and team up with them?'

The rules and regulations in Banff National Park were quite clear. The policy with regards to bears explicitly stated groups of four or more. Furthermore, you had to walk no more than five metres apart and not be out of sight of each other, which could prove embarrassing when stopping for calls of nature. Perhaps National Parks weren't worried about the ethics or morals of humans but more concerned with looking after the wildlife. As the team of Lou, Laurie and Vince made three there was a problem, even if they walked no more than five metres apart.

'Suppose we could wait but it seems a bloody shame as it's a brilliant day and we should be up in the hills. Still, it's a grand view just standing here. Valley of the ten peaks they say and it's dramatic.'

The three were standing in the parking lot by Moraine Lake in Banff National Park. The sky was a clear blue with a few puffy cumulus clouds pottering about and last night's rain in the campsite had fallen as sparkling snow on the upper parts of the mountains. Today's plan for the three had been a short climb to Sentinel Pass, which is the highest maintained trail in the Rockies.

'What are any alternatives?' asked Vince, eager to be off.

'Scrambling up the Tower of Babel,' offered Lou. 'Up some loose crappy gully to stand on that insignificant lump over there. It's the easy way down for climbers, but it sounds like a mess going up.'

'Hey, how about that lot? They look like serious hikers. Excuse me. Are you planning to go up to Sentinel Pass?' Vince asked.

'Mais oui. Il y a sept persons, non neuf. Sorry, we are nine people. You come?'

'Sure, yes sure,' said Vince to the petite French lass. 'Come on guys. We've got us a convoy. All aboard for the heights. So, who is in this ménage of folk?'

We stood in a rough circle and exchanged names and nationalities. The sun beamed down on two French Canadian girls, two French guys and a girl, a young couple of Czechs, a fit looking Japanese guy and a lone Canadian male. Seeing as our threesome was Australian, German and English we made a rather cosmopolitan caravan. Fortunately everyone spoke some version of English so communication about being five metres apart and not out of sight of each other was easy. Well, so we thought.

The Czech couple were probably in their early twenties and built like racehorses. It turned out they were on their honeymoon and it was soon obvious that young love didn't slow them down. The girl loped off up the track and it looked as if she floated up. The trail starts steeply here, and climbs over one thousand feet in just over a mile or so in a series of sharp zigzags. Within the first five minutes conversation dwindled and eventually disappeared as the other ten of us struggled to keep up with our floating loping love-bound Czechs. We guessed they wanted to be home early to carry on with the other aspects of honey-mooning. At the junction where the Sentinel Pass trail turns right and leaves the path to Eiffel Lake we had a gasping discussion.

It was a grand spot to rest a moment. The surrounding trees were the rather rare Lyall's larch which only grows in three valleys around this part of the Rockies. Their golden bark and bright green tassels of leaves glowed in the bright sunlight. Across the valley we could now look over Moraine Lake and see more of the grandeur of the ten Wenkchemna peaks with Deltaform Mountain dominating the group. After a breather, an energy snack and a quick pull on the water bottle we decided that having the two French Canadian girls lead might make life more manageable for the rest of us. That way we might keep no more than five metres apart. They were quite pretty French Canadian girls and walking behind them was a delight. Keeping only five metres from the little French lass had its rewards too.

'Is this your first time in the Rockies?'

'No, we came two years ago but were further north, up around Jasper.'

'Why come to the Rockies with the Alps on your doorstep? Our group has all hiked in the Alps, and they are more dramatic in places. The mountains are steeper, more rugged.'

'Maybe, but here there is more open space, more nothing so to speak. Here you can go for many kilometres and not see any roads, any houses, and almost any people. Here you have wildlife, even bears according to the warning at the trailhead.'

'I suppose that's true, especially here in the Parks.'

Other worldwide discussions included, 'Do you have hiking like this in Japan my friend?'

'Oh yes. We have several areas where there is hiking and mountaineering.'

'Do you climb?'

'No, that is something I have never done.'

'The pass we are climbing leads to one of the easiest big peaks in this area. The trade route up Mount Temple goes up the west face and ridge from Sentinel Pass.'

'What is this "trade route"?'

'The easiest way to the top,' Lou laughed. 'It's the way most people climb the peak but it's still a serious undertaking. Just think - we left the lake at what, 1800 metres and the pass above us is 2600 metres. The summit of Temple is just over 3500 metres. That's over five thousand feet in my book. It's true, you probably don't need ropes, but it's still quite a scramble up the final ridge.'

'Not for me thank you,' joked the Japanese. 'Even climbing in snow in the middle of summer is a little different from back home.'

After leaving the junction of the trails the path to Sentinel

Pass climbed gently up through Larch Valley and passed the three Minnestimma lakes. According to First Nation's language this means sleeping waters and they certainly were today. Each lake was a dark still pool and all the surrounding ground was covered in a foot of new snow. The long rising ridge of Pinnacle Mountain embraced one side of the cirque containing the lakes and as the ridge reared up to the summit the rocks appeared more and more shattered. From a rock climbing point of view the whole area looked violently dangerous. It was as if some giant had shaken the mountains and they had cracked and split but stayed precariously upright. We all hoped that the glistening snow would keep the unstable mass from crashing down while we were there.

'Aren't you cold in those shorts?'

'Non, c'est bon. It 'elps the tan.'

'With sneakers on your feet I would have thought you would find it slippery.'

'It's a beautiful day. You should enjoy the scenery, the experience.'

'Yes,' Laurie muttered, 'and I just hope we don't have the experience of having to carry you out anywhere,' he said under his breath.

'What do you think Lou?' Vince asked quietly.

'I suppose okay for any more usual summer's day out here, but conditions this morning are a little different, a little more severe. Climbing down over the other side of this pass might be more dangerous. It'll be in the shade and that much colder. Just keep your eyes open Vince.'

The headwall of the cirque leading to the pass was sufficiently steep that we made four or five traverses in wide zigzags. A group had been up here before us and the path had been beaten down in the soft snow. There was no avalanche danger but there was a risk of wet feet as the snow turned a little sloppy in the sunshine. At the top of the pass we all took a welcome breather and there was a great opportunity to take photographs.

'Hold still there, just a moment. Thanks. Great.'

'You too Vince. Just smile mate.'

'How high Lou?'

'I don't know Laurie. The map's in my sack. Somewhere up over twenty-six hundred metres or so. High enough to have to gasp.'

'See those guys up on Temple? No higher, up below that cliff. Wonder which way they go to bypass the cliff.'

'According to the magic book of words there is a gully they go up.'

'Thanks Lou. They've still got a ways to go.'

'We off then? Air's so clear up here, and those clouds drifting up the valley over Moraine Lake look neat. Time for one more photo.'

'You seen the view the other way, down into Paradise valley?'

'What's that tower, or perhaps I should say spire?'

'That's Grand Sentinel. About one hundred and twenty metres high. Neat eh?'

'Looks like a pile of totty blocks.'

'Laurie we aren't climbing it mate so just photograph it in awe and grab your sack. It looks like our Czech gazelles are anxious to be off.'

'Where's the trail?'

All of the previous groups who had climbed up through the snow to Sentinel Pass that morning had either continued up Mount Temple or retreated back down to Moraine Lake. The north-facing descent to Paradise valley was a virgin snow slope with a large number of rough boulders making it obvious that this was a scree slope underneath. Looking further down the descent cirque you could see the outline of the trail and visually tracking back upwards we could all estimate a likely line to take. Our intrepid Czechs ploughed downwards diagonally. The snow was now over a metre deep. This was August Vince told himself. Summer! Still, summer in the mountains can bring all sorts of weather. The scree slope was rough underfoot and every so often one of us would break through the soft snow into a jumble of boulders underneath. Great place for sneakers Laurie thought. Wonder how those girls will make out here with deep snow and rough underfoot. Just the place for shorts and sneakers.

'You muttering to yourself down there old man?'

'No Lou, I'm just thinking about those two girls with sneakers. Here's me with pants, gaiters, boots and poles and I'm watching a couple of girls with shorts, sneakers and lots of giggles. I'm just hoping that we don't have to carry anyone out over this lot. It's not the bears we will be worrying about. No self-respecting bear would be up here anyway.'

'You need a rest mate with all that whingeing. Just enjoy the view and chase after those Czechs before they end up five hundred metres away from us.'

'Hold up you two while I take one last photo of that tottering pile of rock.'

'Vince you must have filled your camera twice over by now mate. You have a new hiking rhythm of five steps and one click of the shutter.'

'En avant mes enfants.'

'Okay Pierre, we're off and away.'

The caravan of twelve slowly snow-ploughed its way down through the upper part of the cirque and soon they reached the outline of the path and a few cairns. Half an hour later the group reached a trail junction.

'How about lunch at Giant's Steps?'

'That's back over the other side of the valley.'

'Yes, but according to the map it's only two kilometres and the view down the valley will be good, as well as being able to see the north face of Temple. That's an impressive face.'

'Okay. The group looks together. Trail's straightforward now and we'll make good time.'

For a bunch of people who had only met this morning it was amazing how easily we all fell into the plan and as forecast the multi-national team splashed across the wet Horseshoe meadows leading to Giant's Steps.

'Now that's sensational.'

'Vince, it's a pile of rocks. It's a set of ledges with water splashing down. It's a stream-bed.'

'Laurie you're a philistine. You don't see beauty mate. You don't see form and setting. You don't see juxtaposition of colours, of water movement, of sunlight glistening on water drops on the bushes.'

'Vince, here, have a power bar and expand your vocabulary. You need to be more poetic mate. Laurie here's just a wally from the outback. He comes from the great grey green dusty wagga wagga outback full of faded colours and dryness. He don't know green.'

'Lou's right there Vince, but you're right too mate because it is different and it is spectacular. Trouble is there are no bears. This is supposed to be a regular caravan route for the little buggers and I haven't seen any sign of bears all day. No bears, no fur, no scratched trees, no scat! So why the big commotion at the trailhead with the signs and the warning?'

'According to the good book of words Laurie we are on a regular migratory route for the furry creatures in their traverses from Lake O'Hara through here. It's not called Paradise Valley for nothing Laurie.'

Slowly we all finished lunch and Vince eventually satisfied himself that he had photographed everything in sight, including the two French Canadian girls in shorts and sneakers. Everyone looked around to ensure we had left the site clean and tidy before shouldering rucksacks and contemplating the path down the valley.

'The trail down the north side of the valley is closed for maintenance according to a notice we read in the hostel this morning.'

'So we've got to retreat back to the junction of earlier this morning?'

'Yes, back the way we came and then down the south side trail. The one that passes under the north face of Temple.'

'And passes by Lake Annette?'

'That's right. According to the map we climb back to our first junction and then it's all downhill back to the road.'

'Far?'

'About twelve kilometres or so.'

'That'll make for a good day. Until we met you we had only planned on going to Sentinel Pass but this makes for a far better day. Glad we all met up.'

'That's true. We arranged for cars at both trailheads so we can take one of you back to Moraine Lake when we come out to pick up your car.'

'Thanks. That'll save a long and boring road walk.'

'Okay, back up to the trail junction and then down the valley.'

The skies had clouded over a little as the group left the sunny slopes under Mount Lefroy but everyone was pleasantly warm by the time they pulled up to the trail junction. Vince took one last photograph up the valley leading to Sentinel Pass before plunging into an evergreen forest embracing the trail. Every so often the forest would open out onto scree slopes with long avalanche chutes leading up the slopes above us to the foot of the immense north wall of Mount Temple. People had climbed it but it was a very serious undertaking. Vince and Lou discussed various options as there were several possible starting points but it really was a massive face.

The group stopped and took a break on reaching Lake Annette. The view from here up the face of Mount Temple offered another set of options and a realisation that the face had several problems. It was quite broken up, and after climbing or bypassing the initial massive buttress there was another serious set of gullies before the final face. The clouds continued to darken and coming up from the south they appeared to pour over the lip of the face and flood down.

'Goats,' shouted Vince. 'Look, up there on the ledge; two of them.'

'Where Vince?'

'Other way Laurie, other way you clown. Up towards Sheol Mountain. No. Look higher.'

Laurie tried to follow Vince's agitated finger but he was so excited with his camera that the hand jumped all over the place.

'I see them Vince. Looks like a mother and kid. Got a telephoto? They're too far away for my camera.'

'Of course I've got a telephoto you dink. Hold still my beauties.'

The rest of the group had gathered around and soon the air was full of the sound of 'click, click, click'.

'Well if we can't have bears we'll make do with goats,' exclaimed Lou.

'Looking at their matted coats it's a good job they are that far away,' muttered Vince. 'I'll bet they smell as bad as gnarly Lou here.'

'Perhaps it's a good job your pics don't have sounds and smells tracks then,' added Lou.

'Any others?' asked Laurie.

'No, I just see those two. They can climb though can't they?'

The trail continued to descend and soon reached the junction that led up beside Sheol Mountain to the Saddle, which was a short steep hike above Lake Louise.

'So we were up there yesterday?' asked Lou.

'Yes, and if you remember we couldn't come down here because of that other great bear sign.'

'Where we stopped for a snack?'

'Where we stopped for a breather before that final flog up Fairview.'

'Glad we did that though. Fantastic views from the top.'

'You've done Fairview?' asked one of the French guys. 'We were thinking of doing that but the guidebook says it is a scramble after reaching the Saddle. We were not sure Marie here could do that.'

'After today mate she'll have no problem. It's really only a steep path. Gets a bit exposed on the final ridge but you don't need your hands and the trail is clearly marked. It's a lot easier than coming over the pass today. Highly recommended, and as we said the views are dramatic.'

Soon after the junction with Sheol Mountain the path descended further into the wooded bottom of Paradise valley. Tree sizes increased and there were some large spruces as well as subalpine fir but still no signs of bears. An hour and a half brought the group to the trailhead and a parking lot. One of the French guys drove Laurie, the Czech man and one of the French Canadian girls up to Moraine Lake to collect the other cars.

'So our simple day of running up and down Sentinel Pass turned into a longer adventure,' Laurie proclaimed.

'In all we did twenty odd kilometres,' said Lou, 'not to mention eight or nine hundred metres of up.'

'Which for old farts like us is not bad,' added Vince. 'Hey, some of these photographs have come out really well. See this one Laurie. It's just what you wanted to see all day.'

'Where did you see that? Don't tell me you saw that when I went to get the car? I suppose it was walking up the road when I was up at Moraine Lake?'

'What is it Vince? What's the picture? A bear! I never saw a bear Vince. We never saw a bear Vince. All through the woods to grandma's house and we never saw any bears. Where did you see a bear?'

Vince curled up in the back of the car laughing. 'You should see your faces. They're incredible.'

'So where mate?'

'Didn't you see the sign?'

'What sign?'

'At the trailhead there was a sign warning about bears. It was just like the one at Moraine Lake.'

'So, we all saw that sign. I can remember reading it out loud to all of us earlier this morning,' said Lou.

'Well, when we came out from Paradise valley there is also a big and realistic poster of a grizzly bear. I took a photo of the poster. Here's our only bear of the day.'

Lou and Laurie both threw things at Vince.

'With or without the bears it's still a great day's hike,' said Vince.

'A multi-national walk in the woods,' added Lou.

'Just need that Czech couple to walk at a normal pace,' concluded Laurie. 'They went so fast the poor bears didn't have a chance to catch up.'

COACHING THE TEAM

'So TED, HOW DOES IT feel to have won the UEFA Cup? Actually, come to think about it, you've won them all this year haven't you? Been a good year? I set this little session up with no real time limit to hear you recount your successes. As long as you can spare me the time I'm prepared to sit here and just listen mate. You're the talk of the sports world at the moment Ted, and everyone wants to hear how you feel. So my friend, why don't you sit back and relax and just talk with no pressure? I'll throw in the occasional question and you ramble away. How's that for an easy media interview? Let's start with this year's success and you tell the folks what happened this year.'

I stretched back into the comfortable sofa and looked across the coffee table at Don Gasper. He was a top reporter for one of London's largest dailies. Although he now wrote as the sports reporter Don had covered most things in his career, including real national news. Like me, Don was into his third or fourth career and we were both about the same age. I felt comfortable with Don and he knew that this could be a very easy and relaxed chat between friends.

Charlie and Rose Mason had created a baby, who they christened Edward at St. Andrews Church. I was the eldest and Harry and Helen followed soon afterwards. Our family lived in number thirty seven Mafeking Road, which was a three minute walk from the Farmyard. The Farmyard you ask? In the depths of the East End of London? The Farmyard was the home ground of Markton United, one of the top football teams in the Premier League of English soccer. Markton was a wonderful word combination of the Roman's Marcus living on a farm. Marcus became "Mark" and "ton" came from the Anglo Saxon word for farm. As the name Markton was someone's farm it was logical that the home field became the Farmyard. Whoever decided to call the club United also had this thought of binding together different peoples into a team, and this became a concept dear to my heart.

Around the Farmyard were ten streets all named after famous battles in the Boer War and all the houses were built at the start of the twentieth century. I grew up like most of the kids in our neighbourhood playing footie in the street and getting in to watch United on match days. We all lived and died football but I was the lucky one. I had been born a southpaw, although as a kid I just thought I was cack-handed! Anyway, at school with pens and real ink, the authorities decided we must all write with our right hands. Writing left-handed smudges real ink and copper-plate hand-writing was an essential part of learning in those days. Today I am ever grateful. I must have reasoned at an early age that if I had to write with both hands why not learn to do everything with both sides of the body, and so I learnt to kick with both feet. Now that may not sound very astute but as a football player that is a useful attribute. Look at some of the top players who are essentially one-footed. Sure they are brilliant with that one foot using the inside, the outside, the toe and all sorts but you can guess which way they will turn to use their best foot. Having two equally good feet is better. Along with my two feet came a real feel and skill for football. Through some luck, perseverance and my dedication to Markton I joined the club early in my life.

I had become a professional player for the club at fifteen, long before the days when we had an Academy. From there I was playing for the first team by age sixteen and never really looked back. Life was easy in many ways. I was living my dream. Work was pleasure and it was only a five minute walk down the road. It also started me on my long campaign to show how we were all alike, all the same. No matter where you came from, no matter what colour, creed, class or even gender, we were all the same underneath. We might have different values: we might look at things from different angles: we might even have different beliefs in some things but we were all people of this earth. I suppose I have spent a lifetime expounding this belief of mine and I have tried to put it into practice.

My first exposure to this came in two ways and about the same time. I joined Markton United and found myself playing with people who weren't English, weren't English-speaking, weren't even English-thinking but they all played football together as a team. It was a revelation, mind-blowing and it worked. Our coach in those early years thought ahead of his time and he could bring us all together. We were all the same he would say. We were all football team players and he stressed the word team. This came as a shock to a teenager from the East End until within a week it came to hit me another way. We still played football in the streets and a new family moved into thirty two Mafeking Road, just opposite us. They were a refugee family from Kenya and I suppose they spoke Swahili or their own native language amongst themselves and the kids had no English. There were two boys in the family, who I later learnt were Maasai, and they were fifteen and sixteen. Both were tall lads and they both could run which was just as well as the street bully with his gang of toadies was trying to intimidate the pair of them. Unfortunately the two black lads had run themselves into a dead-end as Devlin O'Connor and his gang caught up with them. By this time in my life I had built up some street cred with playing for the local professional team and I happened upon this confrontation on my way home from a practice at the Farmyard.

'Hold off there Devlin,' I shouted. 'The two lads don't understand English, not that you speak English anyway you Celtic peasant.'

'Got to teach them respect Ted. Got to let them know who's the chief here.'

'Devlin you're not the chief. You're just a bully with an army of other losers.'

'Stay out of this Ted. This isn't about footie. This is about Mafeking Road and making sure we all band together. We've a battle coming up with the lads from Bloemfontein and we need to make sure we're all together.'

'And beating up these two lads is going to help Devlin?' I asked.

'Got to see whether they are fighters Ted.'

'Know how the Maasai boys become men Devlin? They fight a lion to death mate, solo. These lads are close to coming of age. Think you're any match for a lion, one on one? Why don't we try and learn how to get them to fit in, or do you really want to go and fight them solo?'

Devlin hesitated.

'Get a ball Devlin and we'll team up and see whether we can work together,' I suggested.

Five minutes later I was watching a fast-moving couple of black lads neatly moving a football up and down our street. They could fit into any team and seemed to enjoy the opportunity to do something with other people. We may not have understood each other's language but we could work together. Devlin was no slouch as a football player and he too realised there was more than one way to bond people together. All the same underneath I thought and took the message home. Later on that year, Tommy, the eldest Kenyan, told me he and his brother remembered that incident and thanked me.

I played on the team of Markton United for nearly twenty years. As a kid I had played inside left, just behind Marcus Starski who was centre-forward. Marcus, or the Mighty M as he was called, was a large man and a tower of strength. He usually played with his back to the opposition's goal and would head, chest or tap the long balls that came up the middle to me just behind him. Close to the goal I could shoot around the right side or the left side of Marcus with the goalkeeper unsighted. We played really well together and even developed a shot where I kicked it straight and Marcus just did the splits over the ball. With two feet again this was very effective. Now Marcus himself was no weak player when it came to shooting either. Occasionally we would reverse roles and I would dribble forwards and back heel or flick the ball backwards to a waiting Marcus for one of his pile drivers. Markton United was permanently in the top six in the League in those years. Twice we won the League and I got a winner's medal for the F.A. Cup when I was eighteen.

When I was twenty-one I started to ask management about the chance to build a Football Academy. I had helped out locally with providing our neighbouring streets with a League playing on a renovated park but I wanted to offer the opportunity to help kids from all over who had potential. What I had in mind was an Academy for thirteen- to fourteen-year olds. I envisioned something that would take potential talent and really improve it while still providing schooling and supervision. Even back in those days I was thinking world-wide. Why not bring kids here and let them develop their dreams? I was back into my long-held passion for equality – give all of us a chance no matter where we're from. True I wanted to bring in and develop the best. I wanted our Club to be the best.

The concept of the Academy was fairly easy to sell but the practice of making it a reality was a lot more difficult and time-consuming. I had come from a family which believed you should be rewarded for work well done. There were no free hand-outs. As a result I had not become involved in any sponsorship funding and even worked as a professional without an agent. So I had to persuade the Club that this was their chance to show the world what football was all about.

Success came eventually when I turned twenty-three and much of that came from the dedication of Joyce. Old Mr. Thompson, the owner of Markton United, must have had his ears hammered by my Joyce but she won in the end. Joyce Harris lived at number thirty six Kimberley Road and we shared a common back garden wall. Like mine, Joyce's family had lived in the neighbourhood for two generations and we shared common backgrounds as well as back garden walls. I married Joyce and we held the wedding with most of the neighbourhood present at the local St. Andrews Church. We both decided that we were part of the neighbourhood and wanted to stay that way and so I bought number fifty nine Mafeking Road and we have lived there ever since. It was a simple house with three up and two down in a terrace of similar houses. True, I had some renovations done. We improved the plumbing and put in better heating but otherwise it was the same house as both our parents, and the rest of the neighbourhood for that matter. Joyce had worked in a Public Relations office up in the City and she was full of drive and saleable ideas. After we married she didn't stop work until the kids arrived but she applied her talents to getting the Football Academy a reality. However, she didn't stop there because she took on the arrangements for getting the attendees housed and looked after. This proved to be more complicated than we ever realised because we had to find people who spoke a variety of languages not to mention some food that none of us had ever heard of. Overall it was a fascinating time. I had been made captain of the team and moved into a centre-half position.

We continued to play top-level football and virtually every year we played in the UEFA Cup competition. As a professional football player I got to see other parts of the world, especially Europe. As much as possible Joyce came with me and we both enjoyed seeing and meeting other people from different backgrounds. At many of these trips Joyce would be off explaining and promoting the Football Academy. She and I shared the same beliefs that we were all the same.

As much as I could I was around in our neighbourhood. We had started up a local football league and I helped with the promotion of this to include teenagers, then juniors and finally seniors. With Joyce we got a girl's league started. We both pestered the local authorities to improve and maintain any parks around us. This all fostered a strong community spirit and Joyce and I tried to gently bring the community to support the Club. I had the management work out some special rates for locals so that the Club really was a strong focus for the community. In turn the Club offered its facilities for any special local match as well as hosting other community events.

As you might know, professional football is virtually a twelve month activity but I managed to practice two other pastimes as I grew up. These were golf and rock climbing. Now you might wonder how anyone from the East End of London could possibly get involved in these two sports. Rock climbing was the easiest one because I had grown up in the war and all around me had been a climbing playground. First of all it had been broken buildings to clamber over and after that we had scaffolding on new buildings. You learnt to climb on all sorts of things and keep your footing on a variety of surfaces; wet and dry, stable and loose. Quite by chance I had gone on a couple of outdoor weekends with scouts and the leader had taken us down to Harrison Rocks in Kent. From football I had good balance and from chasing around building sites I could climb up anything. The scout leader had been a rock climber and once I had visited Harrison Rocks a couple of times I was hooked. Somehow, through all my years growing up as football player, I managed to find people and places to climb. As I grew older I even managed three or four years when I got to the European Alps. I found climbing a fantastic step out of football – it was a very different scene and I found I could leave any football worries completely behind when I set foot on the rock.

Now golf came a different way but it too provided another method or activity to move my head from one place to another. Golf offered a completely different set of challenges and opportunities. As I grew older I found that I really enjoyed all three sports in both similar and dissimilar ways. The mental challenges were different and so were the reasons why I did them.

When I turned thirty five I reckoned it was time to hang up my boots as a Premier team player. I had had several good seasons and it was time for youth to take over. I had been captain for the past twelve years. Right from the start I had told the manager who first hired me that I wouldn't play for any other club. If they ever traded me I told him I would quit. Playing football might be important but I only wanted to play for Markton United. As a naive but skilful teenage youth this had been a big decision and a lot for the manager to swallow. However, I bargained that I would sign for only a small salary – just enough to live on, and that I would contribute one hundred and ten percent to Markton. This continued over the years and the club honoured my conditions. I never played for anyone else. In turn I never demanded outlandish salaries. Joyce and I lived in the house on Mafeking Road. We didn't have a car let alone a boat or a plane. We could both walk to work as Joyce soon left her job in the city to become a full-time worker for the Academy. We didn't need any of the trappings that some professionals seem to want around them. We turned much of our money into things for the community plus some extras for the Academy that Joyce had failed to get from the Club.

Our two kids went to the local school and our holidays were no more exotic than most of the neighbours. Whenever possible we were down at number thirty seven or number thirty six and both kids learnt a lot from their grandparents.

However, there came the time when it was the last game, the last kick and the final whistle. It was time to change horses and so I worked full time for the Academy. We expanded to try and interest people from new countries. We started a section just for girls but that was much more difficult. It proved harder trying to convince parents and countries that their children would be well cared for and protected from the ravages of the English world, but we tried to open doors and enable one or two talented people to see a different environment and maybe a better future. The Club benefited too in that several graduates from the Academy played for Markton United and then we traded them to other clubs as they further developed their talents and their value. Overall the Club saw the Academy as a worthwhile investment and it made money in the process. Joyce and I were far more interested in helping people meet and play with other people, people from other parts of the world.

As I moved into my forties I talked to Joyce about other opportunities I might have and we both agreed that perhaps we could find a new form of enjoyment and gainful employment in professional golf. After retiring from the first team I had gradually increased the amount of time playing and practicing on the links. We seriously contemplated competing to play on the European Senior Tour. The two children had grown up and both were now away at College. So, when I was approaching fifty years old, the Tour became our next objective. If I made the Tour Joyce planned to come with me and visit as many parts of the world as possible. We had been frugal with our money and thought we could survive on my talent without any sponsorship handouts. I entered the initial tournaments to see whether I could qualify for the Tour when I turned fifty.

'Well Don, you're right. It has been a good year but I was just thinking back over my life and overall I think it has been a productive life. Like you I have managed to come through two or three careers and overall it's been a positive journey.'

'Ted, our readers know all about your early life as a player, and then your development work with the Academy, but what really happened when you played golf? That was a bit different and a new adventure for you?'

'Yes and no Don. You have to realise that I had played golf almost as long as I had played professional soccer but it was always a relaxation thing for me. Let me explain the differences and similarities between the two sports, especially if we compare at the professional level. This may take a while so sit back, take a pull on your pint and think on my words.' Don eased himself back in his chair and when he looked comfortable I continued.

'When I started to play golf I found I could fade away from any other concerns or worries. I found I could get my head concentrated one hundred percent on just propelling that little ball from the first tee-box to the eighteenth hole. Everything else fell away and the joy was in the art of moving that white ball. If you've never played this might be hard to understand, but there can be a complete involvement in the four major steps of the game. From anywhere on the course it is the same four steps and it doesn't matter to me whether I'm playing a fun round or a professional tour event. I'll explain that in a moment but think on these four steps. You walk up to the ball and you look. Where am I in relation to the next target? What is the lie like, the wind, the terrain in front, the position of the flag and so on? Next you think, and this action improves over time because it relates to how. You know in football I used to delight in being able to play with both feet, shoot with both feet and move the ball either way? Well the same applies in golf. There is often an array of options of how best to move that ball from A to B and the thinking part is important. Well it is to me. During this step you use all the information from looking and decide which shot you're going to play.'

'That's all very well Ted but how many golfers actually do that?'

'Don I have always wanted to do the best I can, whatever the sport, and in golf that became even more important to me. I'll elaborate on that in a minute but let me finish my four steps so you can get a more complete picture. Having decided the next shot I stand there and picture it. If you like I see the shot and the result in my mind. I visualise the stance, the address, the swing, the contact, the flight and the ultimate landing and roll. I literally imprint on my mind what I want, expect to happen. Step four is just the simple act of doing it, which may or may not exactly mimic step three.'

Here Don laughed. 'You know Ted, there are not many of us who go through such a procedure, but even for those of us who perform steps three and four there are even fewer of us who do step four anything like step three.'

I laughed too because Don's statement was right on. 'True Don, too true. Even as a professional I couldn't always do what I had envisioned. Few of us can, but for me that was a key element to enjoyment and success. In fact for me that was the ultimate in enjoyment and success. Look, when I played, and it didn't matter whether it was professionally or otherwise, my ultimate goal was to do just that.'

'What Ted, do just what?'

'To perform the four steps resulting in the ball in the right final position. I wanted to be able to look, think, see it and do it such that the ball ended up in the right target position. It's true enough that some of the time the ball did end up in the right spot but only by chance or luck. That was okay if you cared about the score or match result, and for me that was acceptable but not what I was aiming for. I needed all four parts to be right. Now if you think about that you will start to realise that the score doesn't really matter and neither does anything any other golfer does either. What I am trying to say is that when I played golf I didn't play against my fellow golfers. I didn't try and win anything playing against other people. I played against myself, my own supposed capabilities. Now I stress this because it was so different from football.'

'True Ted because there you always played to win. I know you Ted. I've seen your career from being a young player right through now to being a coach and you've always played to win.'

'Yes Don. In football the team is everything and success of the team is paramount. And here you have to remember what I've often said before when interviewed, that the team is not just those eleven blokes out on the pitch. When I was a kid, and when I was the captain, I have always explained that we play as a team and that includes the subs on the bench, the other blokes not on today's roster, the coach, the trainer and all the people in the Club. I suppose I should have said the Club is everything because that is who I played for.'

'What about the fans though Ted? Didn't you play for the fans? Same on the golf course, don't you play to please the crowd as well as yourself?'

Here I sat back into my settee and reflected. This was always an awkward and controversial question and answer for me. I looked across at Don and thought how best to say this.

'Don, I have hinted at this before in interviews, and I suppose with golf it is even easier than with football, but my answer is not what you might expect. It's also not what most of your readers will expect either. In fact it will probably piss off a few of them if truth be told but I will be honest with you. I hope I can make it sound sensible.'

Don sat forward and looked attentive. Up until now he had heard nothing particularly new as he had followed my career as he said.

'I inferred a moment ago that when I play golf the overall objective is to play as well as I can. Now we're all human, and the mind and the body tend to vary a little from day to day, so the best we can do may vary from day to day but on any particular day we each have a best. My objective on the golf course was to strive for that best on any day. Notice there is no mention of competitors and certainly no mention of fans. Let me be clear about the fans, the spectators, the paying spectators who I know come out faithfully in all weathers to watch. I realise that they get enjoyment, perhaps entertainment in coming out and walking around watching us play. I hope they feel they get their monies worth but for me they are not there.'

'What do you mean not there?'

'Don I don't see them. Not only do I not see them but I don't hear them, feel them or smell them. It wouldn't matter to me whether they were there or not. They are not a part of my game, my enjoyment and I do not play golf to provide them with entertainment explicitly. I enjoy golf with absolutely no reference or awareness of the crowd. Actually the same applies to my fellow golfers too. I don't really see them, hear them, touch them or smell them either. True I will shake hands and murmur hello at the start and shake hands afterwards but it is all outside the actual game. For me personally they needn't be there either.'

'So scoreboard watching doesn't come into your game? You don't change what you're going to do according to what your score is relative to the other players?'

'Don let me give you an example. I was playing in a tournament in Germany in my second year on the tour. Now I had won one tournament in my rookie year and so there wasn't any media or fan pressure to win my first tournament or anything. I was tied for first place and the co-leader had finished his round as I stood on the eighteenth fairway. The hole was a long par five and after a good drive I was two hundred and fifty yards to the hole. I needed a birdie to win in your world. Before the green was a lake. If you know golf imagine the fifteenth hole at the Masters in Augusta. Any title-chasing golfer would lay up in front of the lake and then chip and putt for a birdie and the win. Now remember that isn't why I play. I don't play to beat other people I play to perform as well as I can. It's me I'm playing against. Going through the four steps the shot that was the right shot was a high fading three wood to curl around the lesser part of the lake and drop softly on the green. The flag was over to the right-hand side and there was an upper tier to the green so there was a rise which acts a little like a backstop. My lie on the fairway was excellent. There was a wind from right to left which will hold the ball up a little. The distance was just close to the limit for my three wood. However, as I had to hit it high and make it fade I knew that I would lose a little distance on my normal shot so I needed to be extra firm on the execution. So Don we do the looking and the thinking.'

'But no thinking about the score? No going for birdie with a lay-up?'

'Right Don because that was not the shot to play from here. I visualised the shot and saw the ball land softly on the green left of the flag and roll down to the right to end up as a tap-in eagle. I saw the ball actually go past the hole and come backwards off the rise in the green. That was what the designer envisaged and what the hole selection committee saw that day when they placed the cup where they did. Execution was close to perfect and I rightly felt very pleased with the entire four steps. The previous parts of my final round had been good and I was truly delighted when the ball landed to roll up the rise on the green and then stop before slowly curving right and down to actually drop into the cup. I had scored an albatross. In a way this was better than I had envisaged. A bonus if you like but it was the right shot for the time and place. Now that example is perhaps somewhat dramatic but I have attempted shots like that before when it was the right time and place. Several times the execution has not been that perfect and sometimes downright ugly. But, just as right for me that is, there have been times when I felt the right shot was to lay up and then chip. All the time remember this has nothing to do with the score, the competition, or the crowd. As a result some of the press write-ups have often been vitriolic or dismissive. He's a has-been football player and should never think he is a golfer.'

Don chuckled as he took a pull on his pint. 'You're right Ted. I don't imagine any of my crowd would understand you and we can be quite sharp when an opportunity arises. Still, controversy sells newspapers my friend and your last comment could certainly be construed as controversial. But then you've always had several bees in your bonnet haven't you Ted? Before we leave that though what about the fans at the Farmyard? Did you play for them? Did you hear them?'

This time I laughed as it would have been hard to completely ignore the noise at the Farmyard. You would have had to be stone deaf.

'Okay, you're right, one couldn't dismiss the fans at the Farmyard in just the same way as the more refined crowd out on the links but it was similar in a way you know. I told you earlier I played for the team, the Club if you like. My entire playing career I personally played for the team. If pleasing the crowd helped the Club then well and good but essentially my whole career was for the team.'

'But the fans were there Ted. The fans were always there. In fact you and Joyce did things in the neighbourhood to promote fan attendance. Didn't you arrange for reduced prices for locals or something? That was for the fans surely?'

'Yes Don, Joyce and I did try and be part of our community and do things to help the neighbourhood at large. Again, in that respect we both thought helping others was something we all should do but when it came to playing I suppose there were two objectives. The first was play as well as I could with the other ten blokes on the pitch to do our best. Football is very much a team effort or so I have always believed. I have never been one for superstars and ego trips on the pitch. In the Academy we explain the difference and we let the pupils decide who they are but we will stress our own beliefs in team effort. We try and foster team play but still allow certain individuals their chance to perform. When I played though, and certainly when I was captain, the emphasis was upon the team.'

'You just said there were two objectives when you played football. If the team was the first what was the second Ted?'

'The same as in golf Don. In a match, or even when practising I tried to do as well as I could. In a way, although in a very different time window there was the same look, think, see it, do it routine. I suppose I was lucky Don as I was born with some God-given talent whereby I did the right thing somewhat instinctively, but when I got to teach or coach I started to realise there were those four steps. It's just when I was young they all happened very very quickly. It's funny you know because it is the same routine I go through when I am climbing.'

'Whoa, whoa Ted, before we get to that let's finish with the fans at the Farmyard. So you played for the team and you played for yourself but didn't the crowd come into the picture? What about the score in a football match? You might have ignored the score on the golf course but what about the score on the pitch?'

'Okay, you've asked several things there. Let's answer your question on the fans at the Farmyard. I told you with golf that I realise there are people who love to come and watch. People like to see other people do something, whatever it is. I suppose that is the whole rationale for entertainment, being part of the audience whether it is looking, listening, maybe feeling or even smelling in some cases. Taken to the limit it might even include closing your eyes and imagining. I don't know about all that Don and I'm no psychologist but I do accept people like to watch football. People really enjoy getting wound up and excited about the plays, the tackles, the shots and the saves. Accepted, but I suppose it all became a white noise to me. My head, my mind, my whole self was on the ball and the other twenty one blokes. Twenty two if you include the referee. Any shouts, roars, boos, jeers, catcalls or whatever passed me by. Concentration was paramount and my little brain could only absorb the position of the ball, the players and the goal. You know Don there is more to football than just watching the players with the ball. Particularly as captain you have to see where everyone is and move accordingly. The whole back four in defence has to move forward as a unit to execute the offside trap. The defenders on the posts for a corner kick have to watch their goal-keeper and the attacking forwards. When I played up front we found it was vital for Marcus and I to always know where each other was plus the defenders. And of course it is all dynamic. Nothing is standing still and in English football it all moves very quickly. We play the game at a frenetic pace most of the time, quite unlike South American football for instance.'

'So the crowd isn't there?'

'Needn't have been Don as far as I was concerned. It wouldn't have changed what I did or felt whether the stands were bare or full. Remember those Italian clubs who got penalised for game-fixing and had to play with empty stands? The Club lost revenues, that's for sure, but had I played there I wouldn't have played any differently. The team and my own personal efforts were all that counted.'

'Yes, in a way I can understand that, although as you say it is unusual. Some players just play for the crowd, sometimes more than they played for the team.'

'Never me Don. In fact I went further you know and that really turned a lot of fans off. My coach and my manager gave me a good tongue lashing but I sat and explained much as I have told you and eventually they accepted.'

'Accepted what Ted? I'm not sure I know what you're alluding to.'

'Autographs Don. I never sign autographs. The only place I put my signature is on cheques and legal documents. I don't know what it is but I have this hang-up that signatures of sports players are not worth the paper they are written on and I don't want any part of perpetuating that stupid practice. Same thing happened in golf and once again the authorities were not impressed. They kept trying to tell me that the fans expected it and it was the fans that pleased the sponsors who put up the money. They couldn't understand why I laughed.'

'Laughed?'

'Yes Don, I laughed, because that argument has no effect on me at all. Remember I don't play for money. I couldn't care less whether there are no crowds, no sponsors, no money Don. I play golf to compete against myself, not for money. Hell, Joyce and I gave virtually all of my winnings away. We did the same with trophies. In football all my trophies are with the Club. Joyce and I don't have any fancy trophy cabinet or room. For one there's no room in the house and secondly we don't need all that. What's done is done and we both know how well we did. In golf I gave any trophies I won back to the host club. I don't play for trophies Ted. With the financial winnings we took out money for fares, accommodation and meals, after looking after the caddie of course, and either put the rest into the Academy or found a local charity. Did you ever know how we travelled or where we stayed?'

'No Ted I suppose I didn't. I assumed you stayed with the rest of the competitors and travelled first class.'

At this stage in the conversation I stood up because my bum was getting tired of resting on the settee. I walked up and down in the room and thought about those days. It really didn't matter what Joyce and I did people would always assume.

'Okay Don, let me tell this just once. For Markton we travelled with the team and stayed with the team. That was all organised through the Club. When we worked for the Academy we travelled coach and stayed at three star hotels. On the golf tour Joyce and I did much the same thing. I told you earlier we've never had a car, a boat and certainly not a plane. We regarded ourselves as normal working people, business people. Sure we promoted the Academy and we always got involved in any Club event promoting local charities but it was all low-key. So no autographs.'

'What did you do when fans asked?'

'For football it rarely happened because you were with the team. In golf I would hand out balls, tees, gloves but nothing was ever signed. At press conferences I would explain my attitude but it never really showed up in print. You know that was one of the pleasures of climbing I suppose. You were a nobody and when you got back from a climb there was no waiting fan club.'

'It's part of the baggage that comes with being a star, a celebrity Ted.'

'Maybe Don but I wasn't going to react and not be myself. Right or wrong Joyce and I have never pretended we are someone else. We have always tried to be true to ourselves. I certainly feel more in tune with myself like that and I think I know who I am.'

'Changing the subject for a moment what about the score?' Don asked.

'Different from golf Don because for the team the score was important. On a personal basis, playing golf, where the opposition was myself, the score wasn't the right measure of success. It might be a proxy measure but it didn't really reflect what I was trying to do. In the team sport of football though the measure of success is goals scored and goals stopped. Now it's true that team play other than goals is also just as important, but it's much harder to measure than in a single person game. As a coach you try and assess how well the team is playing together, and you also try and pass that information back to the team. When I was captain I would always talk with the coach, or coaches really about how well we all played together. Did we gel as a team? What could we do to improve the quality and effectiveness of the team play? However, for the Club and for myself, the score was important, and we would change tactics depending on the score. You've seen what I have done in the last three years as coach, and much of that revolves around the psychology of scoring. I'll explain a little later.'

'So, I hear you say that football was different from golf Ted? There was no team in golf. What about your caddie and your sponsor? What about your trainer and mental guru that all players seem to have nowadays?'

'Personally Don I was a little different. In fact I may have been a lot different. Some of the other players were a little surprised and some a little resentful or discerning about my approach to golf. Yes I had a caddie, but if you remember I didn't have one fixed caddie and very often just employed someone local at the host golf course. Right or wrong I used them to carry my clubs because I did all the reading of greens, finding out about hazards and any other relevant local topographical feature. If I couldn't get to play the course before an event I at least walked the course to see the layout. Remember, I played against myself and the course, and I always found it useful to know my adversary. So my caddie was never really part of any team. I have never had a sponsor and when I think I have a problem with my swing I find a reputable teaching pro to see what I am doing. We talk and I try and fix my problem. Perhaps from playing professional football, and perhaps from climbing, I found I never needed any sports psychologist or mental coach. When you climb you learn very quickly that the hardest parts, the most challenging parts are mental. Your body will quickly teach you what you can and can not do in climbing and so the major learning comes from that little six inch space between your ears. Many climbers reckon the hardest part of any climb is that six inches. Does that explanation answer your question about any "team" in golf? If you like the team was a team of one – me, myself and interestingly enough the opposition or challenger was me too. I played against my best and the course, nothing else.'

'That's certainly a very different perspective from most golfers Ted. Some of them are quite outspoken about playing against top quality name players and the psychological impact of them being in the field. They also talk of the benefits of playing in front of the home crowd. Virtually all of them seem fixated on the scoreboard and where they stand at any point in time. Perhaps I can understand now why some of them thought your ideas weird.'

'Don, golf is a really funny game in many ways and offers up challenges to all sorts of people for different reasons. Just ask any number of amateurs why they play and you will get a multitude of answers. Some play for the competition, some for the hustle, some for bragging rights, some for the camaraderie, and some for the social aspects of wearing smart clothes with the right people. Professional golfers are similar although the reasons may concentrate more on the money and the prestige as for them it is a profession that brings in the daily bread. It's a job like any other job. Joyce and I approached it very differently. I played for the reasons I gave you above and Joyce came to enjoy the locations, the people we met, promote the Academy and be with me. If there ever was any "team" in my golf activities it was Joyce and I, and in that context my objectives were wider than just playing eighteen holes. For us it was partly a means to an end and the end was the Academy and the promotion of bringing youngsters together from different parts of the world. I suppose if I had started life as a golf professional rather than a footballer we might have started a Golf Academy. It would have had the same fundamental objective of promoting youngsters but with a golf framework rather than one of football. There was one other benefit I suppose, a sort of sideline bonus. One reason I go climbing, particularly mountaineering is that you do this in dramatic surroundings. I love mountains. But, as I said before about football, I prefer to be a player and not a watcher. So I am not content to just go and see mountains but I need to be doing something in, on, and around mountains. Hence I climb. Likewise in golf, the bonus I alluded to is that you play that sport in attractive and sometimes dramatic settings. In football one pitch is much like any other although there are sometimes some subtle differences. With climbing or with golf the "playing field" is ever variable and usually outstandingly beautiful or dramatic. That is my bonus. Much as I love my neighbourhood Don there are some things missing in the East End of London and so I go looking for them when playing other games.'

'But then you quit playing golf. Why was that? You were not too old surely?'

'Don, Joyce and I loved it. The game, the locations, the people and the experiences were fabulous. Still, like football, I reached a level when I knew I was not performing up to my potential or my previous potential. I had crested my capability curve and just like the time when I hung up my boots I decided to put away my clubs in a professional sense. I still love the game and I still play. In fact I still have the same objectives but like football I felt it was time to step off the public stage. I said I never played to the crowd and I believe that is true but I do have respect for the fans. I do believe they are entitled to see the best and in comparison with others I was no longer close to the best. Time to go.'

'Ted, you placed a great deal of emphasis on the team in football. How did you handle mistakes and responsibilities? Is it different in the other sports and is it different now you have moved from a player to a coach?'

'Let's take the first question first Don. Responsibilities in football are simple I find. When I was the captain, and now I am the coach, then any mistake by a player on the pitch is the joint responsibility of the team. The player himself already knows and feels bad about his mistake and is mentally working on how not to repeat it or how to prevent it. The rest of the players and the supporting members in the Club have the responsibility to train, coach, mentor and practice to ensure it doesn't happen again or it can be minimised. Fortunately any mistake in football is not life-threatening. It may result in a foul, a penalty, a goal or even a dismissal but rarely is there serious injury or death. So, in football, we are all responsible.'

'That's easy for you to say but how do other players feel about someone repeatedly making the same mistake, whether it is a player or even the coach? Shouldn't an individual be singled out? Isn't it ultimately the responsibility of the coach? When a team plays poorly, irrespective of whether it is one or more players, it is often the coach that gets fired.'

'I never captained that way and I certainly don't coach that way. I tell everyone up front what I have just told you, but I also allow, no, I actively seek comments, discussions, bitching sessions, you name it to ensure we keep an open team spirit and communications. Again, remember I favour a squad of players who want to play as a team and not want to demonstrate individual brilliance to the exclusion of the team. Don't misquote me because I will foster and promote individual talent and skills but on game day all of that ability is channelled to the team effort. We work, play and share the spoils collectively. The catcalls likewise.'

'But that all changes when you played golf if you were the team?'

'Don think about mountaineering first because that was still a team thing but suddenly several things change. The most obvious is that there are no spectators. When I climb, or perhaps better put where I climb there is nobody else. No-one is watching and so my partner and I are not "playing" to any audience. The team is often two although four is safer and preferable in serious mountaineering. The mistakes can be a lot more serious. Suddenly a mistake can cost you your life and/or that of your partner. Now the responsibility has come down to fewer players and the mistakes can be much more painful than giving away a free-kick or receiving a yellow card. Believe me, when you are climbing as a pair, that rope binding you together is very very important. At some time in the game you may be literally holding someone's life in your hands. You and you alone are responsible for your team player's safety. In many ways it is an awesome responsibility and that is why I said earlier that climbing is mostly in the head. As you get older, and you realise you are no longer an indestructible teenager or twenty-year old, that responsibility usually results in one of two things and you can see this in top level climbers. Some people, like Walter Bonatti, the famous Italian mountaineer, climbed solo as he got older. He felt he was safer being alone. Other climbers will lower their challenges, attempt easier climbs where the risks are supposedly lower. As in most things in life there is a cliché about "there are bold climbers and there are old climbers but there are no bold old climbers". There is one other thing you should note with climbing that is not really relevant in football and that is the terrain and the weather. A football pitch is a football pitch is a football pitch and even the weather doesn't make an enormous difference. In climbing the terrain is rarely consistent and the weather conditions can change a simple route into something much more serious or even impossible. In football the referee can blow his whistle and the game is called off. In the mountains you don't necessarily have that option, especially when you're halfway up some serious cliff face.'

'And golf has got to be different again because the mistakes aren't life-threatening but the team is now down to one. You and you alone are responsible for mistakes and success. This is like climbing solo surely?'

I laughed and I thought about the question. 'You should ask Joyce whether she thinks my playing golf is like my climbing solo. She will tell you they are poles apart. She enjoys watching me play golf whereas she is on edge if I talk about climbing solo. Primarily, the results of mistakes are perceived to be serious in climbing. Now that is true but there is the reverse which most people do not realise. In golf you are apt to make mistakes quite frequently. Very few of us ever play a round where we play perfectly. There are usually one or more errors where we could have done better. The result is one or more dropped shots. Big deal. Climbing solo one very very rarely makes a mistake and you may not have the opportunity to make a mistake twice. Very often when climbing solo you deliberately carry some form of backup equipment, plan, or time horizon to minimise any mistake you might make. We're back to head games Don.'

'Ted I started about an hour ago asking about this year. We've been all around the houses mate and I appreciate the insights but you left playing football. You left the Academy. You left the Tour. This past year is year three of coaching and this has been the best season yet for Markton. How do you feel about that and what have you done to help this happen?'

'Good Don, I feel good. I suppose I think that some of my contributions as a team player have been successful, have proved positive. I have tried to have my coaching style be real live actions that put my philosophies into practice. To use a hackneyed cliché I like to think that I practice what I preach. For one we have a team with players from all over and I like to think we have twenty or more players who are nearly all capable of playing wherever on the team. I have always wanted players with two feet and our practice sessions emphasise such ability. We also practice as individuals, as groups of two or three, and as a team. You will have noticed that when the team plays a game individuals will swap sides, spend five or ten minutes all forcing the play up the right or left side. We try and have all ten field players dictate the time, pace and place of the game. When he has the opportunity our goalie too varies the tactics.'

'You usually play a different game in each half though. You have an overall game strategy that breaks the ninety minutes in different tactical periods. For the first year this approach was fundamentally different from everyone else and gradually over the next two years other coaches have caught on and so you have changed tactics.'

'At first Don I had a simple strategy of dominate the first half and be in the lead going into the dressing room at half time. In the second half close the game down. To facilitate this idea I would play in a 4 – 1 – 5 arrangement to start with and flood the opposition's half of the pitch with five attacking forwards covering the wings and three in the middle. We kept a traditional four in defence but they would play up to the half-way line as much as possible and frustrate the opposition with the off-side trap as often as they could. I wanted to play in their half of the pitch and score goals as fast as possible. It was a blitzkrieg approach. It meant one other thing. All five forwards, or at least four of them had to do a lot of running and be exceptionally fit. Typically I would make two substitutes at the start of the second half and that would be two of the forwards. Usually this was the choice of the captain who was either a mid field player or in defence and could see the five in front. In the second half we would revert to 4 – 4 – 2 and defend with again two forwards running hard. I have always been a strong believer in fore checking. I don't like to let the opposition have a lot of time to move the ball out of their half so I play a fast attacking game. In addition I am not a believer in our team holding the ball and just passing it in the backfield. Wherever possible I want our players moving the ball forwards. You rarely score from within your own half.'

'But other coaches recognised your approach and tried to upset your tactics. How did you change in years two and three?'

'First of all the arrangement was always fluid and although we never changed the basic strategy I wanted the captain to call the changes. My prime role as coach was helping the players in practice sessions. Once the referee blew the whistle for the game the primary guidance came from the captain. He was the on-the-ground leader. Basically we kept the same tactics but changed the timing. We might start for the first five minutes conventionally and then the captain would signal a period of intense 4 – 1 – 5 to see whether we could force a quick goal. Similarly the captain would read the opposition's defence and adjust our concentration up the right side only. If you've ever watched American football Don you will have seen something similar. Both teams run plays and both offence and defence adjust the play according to the other team's reaction. Now football here is much less stop and start than American football but the role of the captain was similar. So, what was a very simple strategy in year one evolved to be more flexible in subsequent years. Nevertheless, with virtually every team we ever played one of the primary objectives was to score one or more goals in the first ten minutes. Very occasionally, and you may have seen this in the final game of the UEFA Cup this year, we switched to 4 – 1 – 5 in the last ten minutes of the game. In fact Gordie went one better just to show how versatile we are by playing 2 – 3 – 5 which is a very old-fashioned layout and very forceful. For those last ten minutes we had everyone in their end except our goal-keeper. It forced a goal as you know. The goal wasn't needed at that time but Gordie wanted to show everyone how we could really play as a team because we could also handle any breakaway as we did. Pressure soccer my friend with one touch passing.'

'So where do you go next Ted? Will it be more of the same or have you some undiscovered new ideas up your sleeve? Talking of new challenges what about coaching a National team? Have you ever been approached?'

'Don, you must have remembered my position on National teams? I'm not a fan. Nothing to do with football or any other sport for that matter but I have gone on record several times about my attitude to national teams. I'm not interested. I think it is a nineteenth century concept and I won't elaborate here because it is all on record elsewhere. Yes, I was asked to play nationally and I said thank you but no thank you. Some people have come back recently and asked me whether I have changed my mind and I said no. I believe in teams of people who come from all over the world playing similar teams of mixed players. This is why I particularly like UEFA and not the World Cup. Where will I go next? My contract covers next year and that is as far as I am thinking. Joyce and I tend to live from day to day and maybe week to week. Now that I am over sixty I don't believe in looking much further ahead. We'll refine the players next season. We'll keep a diverse mix with everyone versatile, fast and team oriented. We'll play exciting and skilful football. The Farmyard will continue to be an arena where you can see positive and entertaining team football. What is it you say in your profession? "Watch this space".'

16 TRIBUTE TO A FRIEND

THIS IS A TRUE STORY. Well, it is as true as most mountaineering stories go. You've probably heard lots of fishing stories and mountaineering stories are similar. You tell me you don't know anything about mountaineering. No matter. This is really a tale about people and we all know about people, don't we?

It was February and here we were stuck in North Wales. Barry and I were both undergraduate students at the University College of North Wales, which is at Bangor in what was Caernarvon-shire before they went all patriotic and the area became Dylli. Winter in North Wales is usually the pits because there isn't enough snow for serious winter mountaineering in the hills. In addition it is not cold enough for any large ice accretions whereas it is cold enough to freeze your fingers off trying to rock climb on the glazed cliffs. Yes, I know, life can be tough some times. As Barry and I were both in our final years with graduation examinations looming up in June we were supposed to be cramming our heads. However, the University authorities thoughtfully arranged for one week in February to be free of lectures so that students could get their heads around the material of the previous four months, or in our cases

353

the previous three years and four months. Officially it was swot week. We decided to go climbing instead.

You have to realise that Barry and I came from the flat riverside meadows around London. He came from the flood plain of Battersea and I came from the suburb of Ilford. Despite this flatland start to life we both climbed. So, it was not very surprising that each of us independently found our way to the University of Wales, especially the College in North Wales which is just on the edge of the mountains of Snowdonia. Moreover, we were not content with being ten miles away and so we were living in digs in the quiet village of Bethesda, which was five miles closer to heaven. The reason Bethesda was quiet was not very surprising as close to forty percent of the locals were unemployed. Above the village the massive world-renowned slate quarries were silent. Gone was the work for the village men. People didn't want slates any more. Builders put those funny tiles on their roofs now. Less labour intensive they say, and we have lost the skill of splitting slates and shaping them with all their fancy names for the sizes. Gone were the Empress, the Princess, the Duchess and the Countess. Gone were the less flattering Broad lady and Wide lady. Sure they could use it locally for flagstones down the path and defining the side of the roads but not on the top of houses anymore. The quarry loomed as a giant's staircase carved out of the hillside but the giant wasn't home. All was quiet and with no quarry there was no more railway. The village went to sleep.

While living in Bethesda our landlord was Idwal Roberts, and Idwal had worked on the railway all of his life. True, you have to say worked with a slight smile on your face because at the height of the industrial era there were only four trains a day. Now they were all gone and so Idwal had joined the unhappy band of locals collecting the dole. This sad state of affairs however, did not diminish the smile and cheery voice of his wife Kitty. Kathleen Roberts was a wild and bustling woman with three children under her feet and three lodgers to feed. As a young girl Kathleen hailed from Liverpool and so she was obviously half Irish at least.

The three lodgers included Barry, my wife and I. In order to honour the traditions at my Forestry School it was important that I was living with my wife. Apparently it was a custom that someone in the graduating class had a child. You have to realise that there were no women in my graduating class and I was the only member married. As a result there was a lot of pressure this final year, over and above school work that is.

Barry and I had done our homework before swot week arrived. In fact it was around Christmas time that we hatched our plan. I was working for the Post Office up in the Bethesda that holiday and wild that was to be sure. In the wet sloppy snow I had trudged for miles from farm to farm with cards, parcels, packages and other paraphernalia. I got fit from walking and developed an ability to drink innumerable cups of strong tea in farm kitchens. Somewhere in between I managed to post a letter to the Scottish Mountaineering Club and book their hut under the Ben for swot week.

The Ben, well a particular Ben in this case: Ben Nevis to be precise, and that is the highest point in Great Britain. In addition, Ben Nevis is famous for the ruins of an old observatory on the summit, although, as I have only been there in winter and everything was buried in snow you'll have to take someone else's word that it exists. More importantly, much more importantly as far as Barry and I were concerned, the north face of Ben Nevis contains the largest cliff in the U.K., some two thousand feet of rock. Winter-time this becomes two thousand feet of rock, snow and ice and a winter mountaineer's paradise. Some say this cliff offers the best snow and ice climbing in the U.K. although several other Scots will no doubt argue this point over their amber-filled glasses. The Scottish Mountaineering Club had thoughtfully built the Charles Inglis Clark

Memorial Hut under this stupendous face and a wonderful situation it was too. We had booked four spots for swot week. As students it was important to get the priorities right.

February arrived and we got organized. There were boots to prepare, as well as ropes, slings, karabiners, ice screws, ice axes and crampons. Clothes to organise with stockings, gaiters, gloves, helmets and windproofs. Food to plan, although that was easy in Scotland as everyone eats porridge all the time. Dump it all on the floor in the living room, complete with the tent and puzzle out how to fit the mess into two rucksacks. What about torches, bog paper, and so it went on?

We left. We left the books, the swotting, and a pregnant wife. I didn't mention that before? That she was pregnant I mean? We left and began our adventurous trip by bus down from Bethesda to the coast road and started facing east towards Liverpool. As students we were flat broke, and between us we possessed a bicycle and so going to Scotland meant hitch-hiking. At this time in English history, the start of the swinging sixties, hitch-hiking was a fine art. You had to know where to stand, how to dress, how to appear and look in need. You must place yourself just after the road junction or the roundabout, which translates as traffic circle for North American readers and not any fairground contraption. This is where the driver is relaxing after successfully navigating the seven possible exit roads. He hasn't yet had time to accelerate away from that flashing blue light on the car behind him which has now turned off on another exit. Suddenly, in his moment of relief, he sees you standing there hopefully twisting your thumb. And it is a hopeful gesture. A couple of years previously another climbing friend and I had hitch-hiked from North Wales to the Lake District. Peter had come back from this trip and immediately wrote up a sad little piece for our University Climbing magazine. He described the process and results for calculating the thumb raising/door opening ratio. The number was large and disheartening. Barry and I stood hopefully on the coast road exercising our thumbs.

Knowing what to wear can influence this thumb raising/door opening ratio. A University scarf definitely helps. At that time you had to wear a bright-coloured distinctive University scarf. This immediately told the driver that you were a student and therefore poor and in need. It also told him that you had made the personal sacrifice for higher education and you were semi-literate, maybe even intelligent. Another useful prop was the rucksack. Carrying a large rucksack signified you were going on a serious trip somewhere and not just popping down to the off licence for a crate of beer. However, you had to be thoughtful about the rucksack. It mustn't look too big or it wouldn't fit in the boot. Similarly, carrying the ice axe and crampons on the outside was a real no-no.

In the day-time the facial expression was important too. At night-time you just looked like a white-faced blur and whether you were grinning or not really didn't matter. You needed to look attentive and able to offer conversation to keep the long-distance driver awake but not bore them to tears. As I said, it was a fine art.

Now Barry was a perfect hitch-hiking companion. He stands thin, poor-looking, wearing National Health wire-rimmed glasses and half-heartedly he raises his arm and wiggles his thumb. You can't help yourself. You have to stop for him.

'Going to Manchester are you? Fantastic. That'll be a great help. Thanks a lot. We'll just fit the sacks into the boot. No, I can clamber over into the back seat. Lots of room. Come far?' and away we went. A few hours later we stumble out where our helpful driver has crossed the A6 and we need to go north.

If you look at a map of Great Britain you get some idea of how awkward it is to hitch-hike from North Wales to Scotland. You have to go sideways a long way before you can go north, and then you have to go a long way north. Inevitably, going up to Ben Nevis, which is just outside of Fort William, you have to bump into Glasgow. Looking at the map it is obvious that all roads in that area go to Glasgow. It sucks them in like a black hole. The trouble is getting out again. First of all you can't understand a word the locals are saying so asking for directions is a challenge in itself.

We had arrived in Glasgow in late afternoon in the gathering gloom. Everyone was rushing somewhere; for the bus, for home, to the pub, somewhere. Eventually we found someone who spoke a dialect of English and we heard about buses to Balloch. Looking at the map we found this is at the foot of Loch Lomond, and somewhere north of Glasgow. Effusive thanks and let's get out of here Barry. After a useful bus ride, where the conductor wasn't too sure about accepting money that wasn't issued by the Bank of Scotland, we found ourselves out of Glasgow. The sides of Loch Lomond were peaceful that February evening. I've been there since and it is a beautiful part of the world but that evening, long after the gloaming, it was deserted. Nothing moved. We certainly didn't.

'Barry, let's crash mate. We've been on the go all day and there's no-one thinking of going north tonight. I'll put the tent up and we can catch some sleep. I'm knackered mate. We'll have some of those butties and kip for the night.'

Barry took off his glasses and rubbed his eyes.

'Fine,' he said. Man of few words was Barry.

We clambered over the stone wall into the adjacent field. I did a quick check that there were no obvious white woollies wandering around. Camping in Wales you would get invaded around two in the morning when some of the local four-legged inhabitants decide that your tent would be a great place to sleep rather than the wet grass. As there was nothing obvious in sight I put up the tent. Now that tent was my pride and joy. It had been a birthday present from the wife. Remember the wife left behind, pregnant that is? But the tent - well just look at it. A Meade mountain tent was the height of luxury for two people. I laughed when I remembered sleeping six in it at a Mountain Hut in the Swiss Alps but tonight there was just Barry and I. The tent was made of sturdy green cotton with a sewn-in groundsheet, sleeve entrance and pockets for personal effects. It weighed thirty five pounds but it could stand up to any gale. Two years previously it was one of the six tents still standing on the beach at Glen Brittle in the Isle of Skye after a gale had scattered the other one hundred and sixty tents. This was just as well as the tent had been home for the necessary three weeks residency for my fiancée and I while the banns were being read for our forthcoming marriage. We had the first marriage on the Isle of Skye for years as all the locals went to the mainland. We even hitch-hiked to the wedding but that is another story.

It was a peaceful night. Snow lay quietly blanketing the hills and we slept well. Morning found us waving our arms about to keep warm and attract the attention of any north-bound motorists. Up through Crianlarich, over Rannoch Moor, and then down through the wonders of Glen Coe. Here there were tempting faces and ridges but we had arranged to meet our friends on the Ben. Slowly the lorry took us over the ferry at Ballachulish and on into the cold wind-swept streets of Fort William.

Lucky for us the shops were still open and we had the chance to get a quick meal and a strong cuppa before facing the snow-covered climb to the hut in Allt a'Mhuilinn glen. This path usually takes two to three hours when you can see the path and you know where you are going. That particular evening it was snowing, neither of us had been there before and I managed to fall into the burn twice in the dark. Now you have to realise that falling into the burn was easy and as the water was frozen solid I didn't get soaked. However, the steep banks were buried under drifted snow and the climbing back out again with my overweight rucksack was another story. Had we known it we should have followed the bed of the burn as that would probably have been easier but resolutely we had to follow the path. After two hours of flailing around in the deepening snow I was exhausted. Looking back on it I didn't realise how shattered I was. I can remember collapsing for the umpteenth time and then Barry realised that reaching the hut that night wasn't going to be an option. He put up the tent around me. Actually he must have put up the tent and then dragged, rolled or threw me inside because I woke up next morning relatively warm, less weary and looking at the green canvas flapping above my face. Rolling over I found I was looking at Barry's sleeping face.

It had briefly stopped snowing and it didn't take us long to stagger up the rest of the track to the hut and the comparative civilisation of other bodies. Our two friends from Bangor had been lucky in their hitches and had reached the hut yesterday afternoon before dark. Shame they hadn't left the track a little clearer. We revelled in tales of missed rides, terrifying drivers, luck at being at the right place at the right time and cups of tea. Lots of tea. We stoked up the pot-bellied stove, collected ice for water, unpacked and dried out our gear and prepared for a week's climbing.

Barry made sure I had recovered from my collapse and we talked of things to do. We all went to bed that night feeling optimistic and ready to do battle with the Ben. Unfortunately Mother Nature decided to thwart us and the wind howled, the snow fell and the temperature dropped. For three days we listened to the elements play with each other outside while we all felt the three-foot walls bind tighter together to keep us warm and safe. I decided not to test my mountain tent in such a storm. We all decided not to venture outside. In fact for those three days none of us ventured outside except for those absolutely, can't help it, inevitable non-public trysts with bodily functions. There are times when it pays to stuff the alimentary canal with eggs and cheese. On day four we woke to a weak light and a hazy hint of a golden orb floating somewhere in the heavens, although obviously hidden from us tucked under this northern cliff. At least it had stopped snowing and we could see where we were. Barry was out of the door in a flash and ready to go in a minute.

Now you have to realise that climbing with a strong leader is both good news and bad news. We'll start positively with the good news aspect. I had a leader who was bold, courageous, safe, and perfectly prepared to tie into the sharp end of the rope. That meant he went first. Barry dealt with all of the worries about where did the route start, where did it go, and how could it possibly go up there? I dutifully followed and retrieved equipment. Well, that leads into the bad news part. I followed when I could. Barry being that good he wanted to do hard climbs, very hard climbs, in fact never-before done climbs. Following was a challenge. There were times when I was in deep water, in over my head so to speak. No, that's not good using a water metaphor in a climbing environment. Let's just say I occasionally got stuck, not able to go up or down. At least that happened on the routes that I didn't fall off.

Fortunately that first morning, when the storm had abated, Barry decided that all four of us should at least reach the top of this hill before us. I mean to say, it is the highest point of land in the U.K. Having cleared away the breakfast things, which meant licking out the porridge bowls and emptying the tea leaves, we geared up to storm the ramparts. Three continuous days of snow had been contorted by the wind into drifts, heaps, ridges and bare icy patches. Experience told us to try something simple and safe or we would find ourselves riding down avalanche waves.

We floundered up Number Three gully, which is normally used as an easy descent route. The slope is not too steep and we could climb straight up rather than having to zigzag. That way we didn't cut across the gully floor and start any uncalled-for avalanches. The day was peaceful and the wind had dropped away to nothing. The only noise was the grunting and gasping of three unfit climbers clambering slowly up behind leader Barry. The summit of Ben Nevis was still below the bottom of the clouds and we could look south-westwards out towards Loch Linnhe, the Firth of Lorne and the sea. Elsewhere, wherever we looked there were rolling snow-covered mountains. The observatory ruins were buried deep under the summit's snows.

Barry decided the next morning we should really try something worthwhile; something like Zero Gully. I tried to point out that it had only been climbed once before and all Barry said was 'shame'. This particular route was vertical, more than vertical in places and usually made up of hard, flaky ice. Supportively I said we could go and have a look. I was always prepared to look. Standing at the foot of Zero gully it was difficult to look. First you were standing on a very sloping surface that was hard snow bounded by vertical rock. To look up you had to crane your head backwards, no, more than that, and try and avoid the little rushes of snow that continually fell down the gully. These obscured the view temporarily before they found their way under your collar and melted disgustingly inside your underclothes. We belayed. Any fall from this gully would result in an exciting and probably uncontrollable glissade down to the bed of the corrie. The climbing rope was stiff with the damp and cold but we managed to untangle the coils and let the loose part slide down the icy slope. I managed to find a rock piton as well as a dubious ice screw to provide an anchor. I adjusted my helmet, wriggled my feet in my boots and prepared for an icy wait.

'Climb when you're ready.'

'Climbing.'

Well maybe. Barry balanced carefully on the front two points of his twelve-point crampons and scrutinised the next few feet. A larger avalanche hurtled down and scoured the bed of the gully. Barry stood there and new snow flakes floated down out of the heavens. Placing an ice screw up above his head Barry fixed a runner and moved up another few feet.

'Tough.'

'Looks it,' I endorsed. I wasn't sure whether Barry meant the ice which he was flaking all over me, or the next few feet, or the whole bloody route. Another much larger mass of snow embracing chunks of ice came hurtling down.

'Too tough.'

'Bloody lethal I reckon. Wait until it's safer. There's too much loose stuff coming down Barry.'

I didn't realise at the time how prophetic were my words. We did retreat and find something less lethal that week on the Ben. We did some worthwhile but less sensational climbs. At the end of the week we all shuffled down the glen to the grey stone cold of Fort William and the challenge of getting home. As usual when hitch-hiking long distances this did prove to be a challenge, but finally I slowly and painfully hobbled along from Bangor railway station down to the bus station below the Castle Hotel. I was wearing narrow, too-tight Italian Frendo climbing boots and they were killing my feet. Barry and I had given up hitch-hiking somewhere near Chester and caught the train back to Bangor. Now there was just a short walk and a bus ride to reach Bethesda and some home comforts. Well not quite. As I walked in the door looking for a cup of tea and sympathy for the state of my feet I got a bollocking instead.

'How could you go off climbing somewhere that mad with your wife in her state? You could have been killed. She's stuck here working all hours and you and Barry have gone gallivanting. I hear he had to rescue you. Pick you out of the stream.'

I held up my hands in surrender.

'Peace Mrs. Roberts, peace. Let me get my boots off at least. My feet are killing me.'

'I'll kill you you thoughtless boyo. Just look at your wife here. Never a word. Not a peep. And Barry, you're just as bad.' Barry wisely kept silent. Remember, he was a man of few words.

'Hello love. Sounds like it's been a bad week? Weather been okay? Ours was the pits. You're looking good. Come and give us a kiss. Mind the feet, the feet love. Ouch. Barry I need protection mate. Keep these mad women off me.'

'No mate. I'll look after you on the hill but not at home. You're on your own.'

Fortunately I wasn't on my own. I had been lucky. I had climbed with a great leader, a fabulous climber. I was also lucky in having a forgiving wife. Life slowly returned to normal in Bethesda, and to my contorted feet, and all quietened down again. Between bouts of relearning forest management and tidying up my thesis I thought back to that week on Ben Nevis. Bloody lethal that Zero gully Barry.

Those words however came back to haunt me four months later. My wife and I were happily walking around Top College at my graduation ceremony. Following tradition I wore a gown and mortarboard, and clutched a door-opening piece of paper called a degree. My wife carried our newly-born daughter.

'Have you heard? Peter just told me. He heard from an old friend from London who was out there.'

'Heard what?'

'Barry's dead.'

'No, surely not? He's supposed to be here for his graduation. I haven't seen him but he should be around. I know he left our digs a couple of weeks back but I thought that was to do with his parents back in London. He must be up here.'

'No. He's dead. Killed on the Eiger. Climbing the north face. Hit on the head by a stone fall somewhere above the Second Ice Field. Trying to climb straight up to the Spider. Didn't kill him apparently but he broke his back when he fell off. His partner tied him off somewhere on the Second Ice Field and bivouacked nearby for the night. When he went back in the morning Barry was gone. Lethal that face is.'

Lethal, bloody lethal I thought and remembered my words on the Ben.

Many years later I went back to Switzerland. I made the pilgrimage to Grindelwald and stood in the graveyard amongst the tombstones, many of whom were markers for climbers. The inscription was simple and clear.

> 'shattered my glass ere
> half the sands had run –
> I hold the heights,
> I hold the heights I won'

Too true I thought with your life just starting and then cut so short. But in that short time you had won many heights my friend. I won't forget though Barry. I will remember you mate. You saved me up there on the Ben and I thank you. I won't forget you my friend.

ABOUT THE AUTHOR

JOHN OSBORN WAS BORN IN 1939 in Ipswich England but grew up in the East End of London where he learnt to sail. In North Wales he graduated as a professional forester and rock climbed three days a week. After working as a field forester for three years in Australia John went to Vancouver, British Columbia for postgraduate studies and the Flower Power movement of the sixties. While working for thirty years for the Ontario Ministry of Natural Resources, both as a forester and a systems analyst John sailed competitively, climbed mountains and taught survival and winter camping. He finished his professional career with three years consulting in Zimbabwe, walking with the lions. Now retired, although working part-time at the local Golf Club, John lives with his wife in Kelowna, BC where he hikes and x-c skis from his doorstep.